# THE
# OCEANS
## AND THE
# HUMAN HEART

a novel by
Michael Mitton

Also by Michael Mitton
*The Face of the Deep*
*The Fairest of Dreams*
*Beauty Born Anew*
*The Road of Brightness*

He sees into
the oceans and the human heart,
and he knows
the secrets of both.

THE BOOK OF ECCLESIASTICUS 42.18

# 1

The inhabitants of the small fishing village of Tregovenek celebrated the fact that every one of the motley collection of houses, from the grey stone farmhouse on Crantock Hill to the whitewashed fishermen's cottages by the harbour, was owned by their Cornish occupants. This was in marked contrast to the neighbouring village of Pedrogwen, where the buy-to-let brigade had arrived in force. Pedrogwen not only had the misfortune of looking like a tourist's idea of a Cornish village, but it was also easily accessible by both road and sea. Tregovenek boasted few buildings that could be called beautiful, and was not easy to find by either motorist or yachtsman. Those who did turn off the main road and take the winding and narrow lane to the village would be hard pressed to know where it actually began. The signboard that welcomed people to the village went in the storm of '87, and was never replaced.

For centuries, there had existed two parts to the village: the upper village, at the centre of which was the church; and the harbour, whose centre was the Pilchard Inn. Nowadays, it would be fair to say that the beating heart of the upper village was no longer the parish church, but the Spa shop, which, though small, seemed always to have the very thing you needed. Down at the harbour, the beating heart was most definitely the Pilchard Inn, where you could enjoy your cider either on the salted seats of the breezy garden, or on the tar-black benches in the gloomy saloon lounge, whose walls still carried the stain of stale orange from the days when the air was thick with tobacco smoke.

The lack of tourists ensured that the locals enjoyed a sense of undisturbed peace. Some of the villagers found work in the nearby towns, and they were the ones who came back to tell tales of queues, congestions, inebriations, litter and lurid language, that made the others even more delighted that somehow or other they had managed to find a habitation on earth that was spared the vulgarities of sightseers and holidaymakers. The reclusive nature of their village suited them well and it was very rare for this peace to be disturbed. In fact, it was almost unheard of.

But then came that damp Friday the thirteenth of April that the villagers would never forget.

Someone went missing.

And it was a very surprising someone, because it was the old retired priest, Father Solomon Ogilvy, who was renowned for being someone to whom absolutely nothing sensational had ever happened, nor was ever likely to happen. Over eighteen years had passed since the day that he retired to this his birth village after a long and undistinguished ministry in the diocese. He had volunteered to take pastoral charge for this parish, allowing the official Rector to concentrate his energies on his other eleven churches. When it was discovered that this retired priest's father was a former Rector of this parish, he was welcomed with open arms.

The arms of the villagers had never been open to Solomon's predecessor. 'Rev Bev' (as she liked to be called) had finally been persuaded to give up her ambition of hauling the village church into the twenty-first century, and had moved on to another parish that was more receptive to her modernist ways. The day after her rather awkward farewell party, the wardens moved in and delivered the church of its garish banners, projector with unsightly screen, and the contentious *Trego Kids for Jesus* corner in the lady chapel. Into this haven of now restored, respectable Anglicanism walked the newly retired Father Solomon. On his first Sunday he emerged from the vestry brandishing a new cassock that eloquently declared that he was in for the long haul, called by God to do his bit to maintain the ecclesiastical order to which the village had previously been accustomed. The Bishop assured the village that she was more than happy for Father Solomon to continue to shepherd the flock of Tregovenek for as long as he felt able, which was proving a considerable time. Only recently had the old man celebrated his eighty-fifth birthday.

Father Solomon was popular with the handful of regulars at the church, who were now assured that proper Anglican worship would 'see them out', as Margaret (the head of the three-strong choir) put it. And this priest was also popular with the villagers, who seldom darkened the creaking oak door of the church, yet were keen that this eight hundred

5

year-old place of worship should show some gasps of life, as it was needed for weddings and funerals, as well as important annual events such as harvest and Remembrance Sunday.

This parish priest could not have looked more the part: tall, gaunt, pale, hollow-checked, lavish eyebrows above steel-rimmed spectacles, and what hair he still had was neatly oiled and combed back over his sunned and freckled dome. His voice was rich, deep, quavering and melancholic. It was near impossible to stay awake during his sermons, for the timbre and cadence of his voice would lull into blissful sleep even the most hardened insomniacs. And if any did manage to stay awake, the strongly academic style of his sermons meant that only those with a theological degree stood a chance of following his train of thought. He was celibate and high church and knew exactly how to do a proper liturgy in the language of Cranmer. No, Father Solomon, was exactly what the village needed, and there was every expectation that the old man would still be clambering into the ancient oak pulpit well into his nineties.

This was most definitely a resident of the village that you could count on. So when, on that fateful Friday 13th April he went missing, there was not so much concern at his fate, nor sorrow at his absence, but rather dismay that the village had been robbed of one of the bastions of its state of peace. If the Father went missing, who knows what other disturbances might be set off?

It was Ethel Cairns who discovered it. She always kept her Spa store open until 7pm, a late hour due to her preference for a generous three-hour lunch and siesta break. On this particular Friday evening, she locked up as usual and made her way home in the gloom of a coastal drizzle. She was not a churchgoer, but whenever she passed the lichgate of the church, she would make it her custom to curtsey, just to keep on the right side of the Almighty, whom she referred to as 'Your Honour.' On this particular evening, having acknowledged her Honour, she raised her head, and then realised that something was not right. The church door was ajar, and the nave light was on. Now, on a Thursday, this would be normal. The three elderly choir members practiced on a Thursday night. But this was a Friday. She looked left and right, suspecting danger.

This was most untoward and presented a real quandary for Ethel. She would have much preferred to ignore this irregularity and get on her way home before it got too dark. But could she just walk away from this most unnatural and intriguing occurrence? Admittedly, the most likely explanation was that the Rector was in there, and there was nothing to worry about. But he was a man of extreme predictability. He was never in the church at this time of night on a Friday. Ethel considered possible explanations, and dark imaginings started to chill her as she sheltered in the shade of the lichgate's leaky arch. Maybe there was an intruder in the church, who might not take kindly to the arrival of the local shopkeeper?

And if that threat was not enough, there was the no small matter of God, whose house this was. She nursed a strong and certain conviction that it was necessary to keep God at a safe distance. She was in no doubt that if she were to get too close to the Almighty, almost certainly he would sniff out some grave offence in her life and express his divine disapproval in any number of terrifying ways. Venturing beyond the lichgate and entering that building of his, when not on official business such as a funeral, felt extremely risky. So, by her reckoning, there were very good reasons for turning away from the lichgate and making straight for the safety of her home. But there was one internal driver that was stronger than even her fears: it was her irrepressible nosiness, which was the reason for her being a valuable receptacle of local information for the villagers when they visited her shop. Yes, it was clear. Ethel Cairnes had to be the one to discover the cause of this most disturbing irregularity and to enlighten the villagers accordingly. So, breathing in the cold Atlantic ozone for courage, she clutched her bag close to her chest, and strode across the uneven flagstones of the pathway to the open door of the church, doing her best to subdue the gnawing fears regarding aggressive assailants and disapproving divinities.

On reaching the ancient oak door, she knocked on it and called out, 'Is there anyone there?' There was no reply, so she called again, 'Are you in there, your Reverence? Don't want to disturb you if you are saying your prayers. Beg pardon, but just thought I should check. The door's not usually open at this time of night, you see.' She hoped that chattering like this would draw the priest to the door. But no. The cavernous building was ominously silent. It was clear that solving this puzzling mystery was going to necessitate her stepping inside, and with impressive bravery, she entered the building. Only a couple of the ceiling lights were turned on, providing a ghostly glow in the main body of the ancient building. The choir stalls and altar were only just visible in the unlit chancel. There was no sign of the priest. She supposed he might be in the vestry, a small room that was entered through a door in the east end of the church, just beyond the organ. She called out again in the direction of the vestry, but the only reply was the echo of her own voice, sounding off the dark stone walls.

Although the church was feeling undoubtedly spooky, so far there was no obvious sign of the Almighty being offended by her presence in his church. But she still felt profoundly anxious as she made her way down the aisle, scanning the building, searching for a reassuring explanation for the open door and the lights. 'Are you there, Father Solomon?' she called out again, more to embolden herself than in expectation of an answer. Then, just as she was feeling a little more at ease in the building, she saw something that caused such a bolt of fear to shudder through her body, that she nearly tumbled backwards. For there, on the foot-worn marble tiles of the nave floor, she saw the unmistakable sight of a pool of crimson blood. Not a great quantity, but enough to cause her own blood to rapidly drop in temperature. She attempted to swallow, but there was no saliva, and her dry mouth hung open. Very slowly, she turned around and walked cautiously out of the church, her heart thumping so hard she feared it would leap from her chest. Her only desire now was to get out of the building alive. Somewhere, hiding among the pews, an assailant could be hiding, waiting to launch another attack. Great was her relief when she reached the door, and once out, she hurried past the threatening tombstones to the lichgate, where she met the welcome figure of a fellow human, whom she knew well.

'Oh, Lisa,' she said, grasping the woman's hand. 'Am I pleased to see you!' Lisa Micklefield was the niece of the priest. She and her husband, Matt, had taken him into their spacious home when he retired to the village.

'What is it, Ethel?' said Lisa. For a few moments Ethel said nothing, simply holding Lisa's hand, and looking back to the doorway of the church. 'Did you see Father Solomon in there?' asked Lisa. 'It's just that he's been gone for a long time now and his supper's getting cold. I thought all he was doing was locking up the church, but he must be sorting something out in there and has forgotten the time.'

The saliva in Ethel's mouth had still not returned and she was now fearing that she would vomit. Lisa could see she was not well. 'What's the matter, Ethel?'

'In there,' said Ethel huskily, pointing to the door.

Lisa was more curious than anxious. She knew that Ethel was one who could muster up dramas from the most mundane of life situations. She hooked her arm through Ethel's, and confidently walked her up the path and led her into the building. She could feel Ethel shaking as they moved to the central aisle of the church. Ethel paused. Holding out her arm, she pointed down the long, tiled aisle and managed to utter the word, 'There.'

Lisa spied a dark liquid spread over the marble paving stones of the aisle between the ends of the front pews. She released Ethel's arm and walked quickly towards it to investigate. Half way down the aisle it became all too clear that the liquid was unmistakably a fresh pool of blood. 'Oh, God, no,' she said, her face reddening. She hurried to the spot and bent down to gain a closer look at the clear evidence of human injury. She noticed there was blood also on the pew end. Ethel had followed her, and Lisa looked up to her asking, 'Whatever happened, Ethel?'

'I don't know, Lisa,' said Ethel, still clutching her bag hard, and shaking her head. 'I just came in here because the light was on and I found... Well, I found that.'

Lisa stood up slowly and, as Ethel had done before, she became concerned that the assailant might be still in the building. 'Are you in here still?' she called out boldly. 'Because if you are, we need to know what you have done with Father Solomon. We wish you no harm, but we just need to know if he is all right.' Her voice echoed around the stone walls, but no reply came.

'We must check the vestry,' said Lisa, and with a boldness that impressed Ethel, Lisa stepped over the puddle of blood and walked into the dark of the sanctuary and tried the handle of the vestry door, but it was locked. 'Are you in there, Uncle Sol?' she called, but there was no answer. She returned to Ethel. She placed one hand on her hip, and with her other she brushed her russet hair back behind her ear and took one more look around the church. 'Where is he?' she said.

'There ain't nobody in here, Lisa,' replied Ethel. 'I'm sure of that.'

'I agree,' said Lisa. Then, looking at Ethel, asked, 'Have you got your phone, Ethel? I've left mine in the house. We must phone the police.'

'It's here,' said Ethel, fishing in her coat pocket and pulling out her phone. 'Here, you do it,' she said, handing the phone to Lisa. They walked back up the aisle, and by the time the two women reached the church door, Lisa was reporting the situation to the local constabulary.

And that is how the once safe and somnolent village of Tregovenek became more troubled than it had been for as long as anyone could remember.

# 2

It was not long before two police cars had pulled up and parked by the lichgate, their flashing lights dazzling the many villagers who were now gathering there. A young constable stood at the gate ensuring no-one entered the grounds. Inside the church, Sergeant Jim Wickham was sitting on a pew in the middle of the church talking with Lisa and Ethel. Another police officer was cordoning off the area of the apparent attack, and yet another was searching the building.

'SOCO will be here soon, ma'am,' said the Sergeant. 'And they will test the... You know, they will take samples and check it. Just to see if it is...You know... Your uncle's...'

Lisa nodded slowly. 'You can talk frankly with me, Sergeant,' she said. 'I'm a professional counsellor and there's not a great deal that shocks me nowadays.'

'Oh, of course, ma'am,' said the Sergeant. He caught the fragrance of her perfume and, glancing up at the attractive face of the early middle-aged woman, he imagined that she was exactly the kind of person *he* would confide in, should he ever have to meet with a counsellor. But he also recognised that spending time with those hazel eyes might be distracting. So, he looked back at his notebook and said, 'Now, may I just check one thing, ma'am. In the area of the...er... blood, there is a fair bit of moisture on the floor. Has someone been cleaning in here today?'

Lisa thought for a moment. 'I'm sorry, I'm not a church-goer, Sergeant, so I'm not too sure...'

'She comes in on a Friday,' said Ethel. 'Always here on a Friday. That will be her doing - that damp on the floor.'

'Thank you, ma'am,' said the Sergeant to Ethel, making a note in his book. 'I take it you are referring to the church cleaner?'

Ethel nodded. He was about to say something else when a police officer called to him from the back of the church, saying 'Sarge.'

'What is it, Corey?' called the Sergeant.

'This box,' said Corey, lifting the remains of a large wooden box. 'Found it on the floor. It's been smashed to pieces.'

'Oh my God,' said Lisa. 'That's the poor box - or whatever it's called.'

'So, there would have been money in it?' enquired the Sergeant, as Corey came down the aisle holding the damaged box with his gloved hand.

'Not a lot, I imagine,' said Lisa.

'Well, I think we have our motive,' said the Sergeant, studying the important piece of evidence nursed by Corey.

'Oh, to attack an old man for just a few bob,' said Ethel. 'What is the world coming to?'

'You'd be surprised, ma'am,' replied the Sergeant in a tired voice. He had long passed the stage of wondering what the world was coming to. He felt a keen sense of disappointment that the dark aspects of humanity that he all too frequently had to encounter, had now extended to this sheltered village. 'Now we don't want to be worrying ourselves too much at this stage.'

'I appreciate, Sergeant, that there may be a perfectly innocent explanation for this,' said Lisa. 'But the fact is we have two clear pieces of evidence of violence taking place here: blood on the floor, and a smashed money box. I think that actually does provide plenty of cause for worry.'

'Of course, ma'am,' said the Sergeant. 'I can assure you we will do all we can to find your uncle. I shall be reporting to the Inspector right away, and I would expect she will be coming in to see you first thing in the morning.'

'That's reassuring, Sergeant,' said Lisa. 'But I very much hope you will start searching for my uncle right away. It's getting cold out there, and he is a vulnerable old man.'

'Of course, ma'am,' reassured the Sergeant. 'Our team's already working on it.' He smiled a nervous smile at Lisa, inhaling once again the beguiling fragrance.

12

The two women made their way out of the church, and walked carefully over the unlit flagstones to the lichgate. 'Come in for a drink, Ethel,' said Lisa.

'No, if you don't mind, Lisa,' said Ethel. 'I'd rather be getting home.' She glanced at her watch. 'And it'll be Monty Don soon. He'll calm me down, he will.'

Lisa stretched out a hand and placed it on Ethel's arm. 'I'm so sorry you had to witness this,' she said.

'Oh, don't you worry about me, Lisa. I'm a tough old girl, I am,' she said, not quite convincingly. But then with some force she said, 'Just as long as they catch the bas… The man who did this terrible thing.' She felt obliged to adjust her language as she was still close enough to the church for any deity lodging there to overhear her. Then looking at Lisa, she said, 'Let's hope the Father is not too hurt. I'm sure they will find him soon, poor love.'

'Yes,' nodded Lisa. 'Yes, I'm sure they will. Good night, Ethel. And I hope you get some good tips from Monty for that lovely garden of yours.'

The two women parted, and Lisa made her way back to her home, which was only a short distance from the church. When Lisa entered the kitchen, Ella was sitting at the table fiddling with her phone, her ash brown hair falling around her lightly-freckled cheeks. Still studying her phone, she said, 'Why did you take so long? Dad and I have finished supper. Uncle Sol's will have gone cold by now.' She glanced accusingly at her mother and added, 'And where is he, anyway?'

Lisa sat on the chair next to her daughter. 'Something really odd has happened, Ella.'

'Like?' said Ella. With an effort of will she pulled her gaze from her phone and looked at her mother.

'Uncle Sol's not there,' said Lisa, pulling up the sleeves of her blouse.

'Thought he was just shutting up the church like he usually does?'

'I know. That's what we all thought. But something happened while he was there.' Lisa was frowning, studying the empty unused plate in front of her. She pulled in her bottom lip.

'What happened, Mum?' asked Ella. She leaned towards her mother and bent her head enquiringly, fixing her with her Nordic blue eyes.

'There's... Well, there's blood on the floor near the front of the church.'

'Blood?' said Ella, frowning and turning down her mouth in disgust. 'God, no!'

'Yes, blood,' replied her mother calmly. 'Not a lot, but enough. I'm not sure what to make of it, if I'm honest. But I'm afraid it looks like he may have been attacked. That's assuming it's his blood, which it may not be, I suppose. Let's hope not, anyway. But the poor box has been broken into. I...' She was unable to hold her calm exterior any longer. She clutched the plate in front of her and, turning to her daughter, said 'Oh, Ella, I do hope nothing has happened to him. He's far too old and frail to be attacked like that. I mean... I can't see him surviving something like that, can you? Not at his age. And he could be wandering out there injured and confused.'

Ella blinked several times, her eyelashes flicking her fringe. 'I'm sure he's all right,' she said, more trying to comfort herself than her mother. Neither were comforted.

At that moment, Matt came into the room. He saw the concern on the faces of his wife and daughter and said, 'What's up? Someone died?' Both his wife and daughter frowned at him, then Lisa explained.

'Christ,' said Matt, opening the fridge door and pulling out a beer. 'Poor old sod. I'm sure there's a reasonable explanation. I expect he slipped over and knocked his head and one of his old biddies is now giving him a cup of tea in her home and looking after him. He'll be back soon, I'm sure.'

This was one explanation Lisa had not considered, and it seemed a most reasonable one, and this did comfort her. Matt signalled that the match had already started, so, clutching his beer, he made his way to the lounge. Ella, whose pale face had reddened during the course of the conversation, was studying the flurry of texts on her phone. With her thumbs rapidly scripting messages, she got up and made her way out of the kitchen to her room.

14

Lisa put a very small amount of the lasagne on her plate and heated it in the microwave. She went to the fridge and pulled out an opened bottle of Pinot Grigio and poured it into a glass. She took several swigs from the glass, then refilled it before returning the bottle to the fridge.

She sat down at the table. The empty place next to her looked so disturbing that she quickly swept the cutlery, mat and plate to one side and continued poking at her meal. Where could her uncle be? Though he was such a quiet presence in the house, his sudden absence felt deafening. He had been part of the household for a long time. Ella wasn't even born when he arrived. At first, he came simply to lodge for a few weeks, while the Church Pensions Board searched for a suitable property. But it proved very difficult to find a property in the village, and so a few weeks became a few months, and the months then became a year. Then Ella was born, and after a while, he became an established part of the household. This did not please Lisa's mother, who felt that if her brother was to settle with family, then it should have been with her and Ted in Pedrogwen. But Solomon was adamant that he did not want to live with his sister. It was one of the very few things that he felt strongly about. Moreover, he was determined to live in Tregovenek and to offer his services to the church that had once been served by his father.

It would not be true to say that Lisa had a strong affection for her uncle, but she did respect him. So quiet was he, that there were many days when she hardly noticed his presence in the house. She could say in all honesty that he was no trouble. Matt had bought Altarnun House a few years before Solomon retired to the village. It was he who suggested taking in Lisa's uncle, assuming it would only be for a short time. They put him in the spacious spare room with ensuite and two windows, one overlooking the front garden and gravel drive, and the other commanding a glorious view of the sea. This room provided enough space for his many books, his quaint old Victorian desk and chair inherited from his father, and a somewhat threadbare yet comfortable armchair, where he could sit and gaze out at the sea. He would often spend all day in his room, only emerging for meals and his daily walks: up the road in the morning to unlock the church and say morning prayer, and then in the evening, to return and lock up the church.

15

Though Matt respected Lisa's uncle, he more tolerated than enjoyed the old man's presence in the house. When it was clear that Solomon would be staying longer than just a few weeks, Matt set up a legal agreement and, against Lisa's wishes, ensured that Solomon paid a monthly allowance to be reviewed annually. Matt was a businessman to the core. But while Matt found Solomon's presence in the house a little irritating, he nonetheless enjoyed the kudos it gave to his household, to be the home that accommodated the much-loved cleric of the village.

Ella was the only member of the household who actually enjoyed the old man's company. She never knew a time when he wasn't part of her home. She had fond memories of the evenings when, as a young child, she would knock on his bedroom door and wait patiently for him to open it. For a few moments he would stand awkwardly by the door studying her through his misty spectacles. Then his face would crease into its endearing smile, and he would usher her in. There she would study the rather lean collection of children's books that only filled half a shelf of his extensive library, while he settled himself in his armchair by the window. Then, having made her choice, she would clamber onto his bony knees, fold her arms, and then, gazing out of the window at the ever-changing ocean, she would listen to the story, which was usually one she had heard many times before. Yet none of the stories ever lost their magic through familiarity. Every now and again the old man would point to an illustration with his thin, waxen finger. After the story, they would chat together for a short time discussing the story, and Ella would tell him about her day. During these conversations, he never spoke about himself, so she knew very little about him. But that never bothered her. She just liked being in his presence. What she loved more than anything else was his serenity - a quality that was noticeably absent in her parents. This salubrious serenity was mostly conveyed through the rich timbre of his kindly, reassuring voice. Other voices in her home were easily raised, but never her great uncle's.

Uncle Sol had become a particularly safe and welcome harbour in recent years when the family seas had become rough. When he was present for one of the marital rows, she observed how her great uncle would emotionally withdraw even further than usual, remaining completely silent, retreating to some inner, storm-proof cellar. These

16

rows would often gain strength at supper time, when everyone was tired and tetchy from the stresses of work. And Ella could not deny that she could also contribute to the storm with her own fiery brand of teenage intolerance. As these storms stirred, she would observe the old man rise silently from the table, and slip quietly away to the hall, and, despite the clamour in the kitchen, she could hear the creaking boards of the old staircase, as he made his slippered way to his room. At such times she would leave her parents to fight it out on their own, and tread her own path to his room.

He had given up reading to her when she reached adolescence, but he would always welcome her to his room, and he would choose a book from his collection, dust it lightly with his sleeve, and hand it to her with a smile. His was a smile she cherished. She loved the way that, when he smiled, the wrinkles in his cheeks dimpled into great semi circles of kindness and his dove grey eyes gleamed through the spectacles with warmth and humour. Seldom did his shyness allow him to turn those eyes to meet hers, but when they did, she felt they imparted something so tender that she wanted to weep. She would sit in his armchair with its threadbare arms. With her legs curled up under her, she would skim read the book he offered her. The content of the theological book seldom interested her, but what she did cherish was the feel of it, the smell of aged paper, and the knowledge that it was a book loved by Uncle Sol. She would flick through the pages of the book until the storm had abated, and it was safe to return. Once or twice, when the storm seemed particularly wild, Uncle Sol would rise from his desk and, with the lightest touch, would place his fingertips on her shoulder, resting them there for a few moments. In turn, she would reach up and place her hand over the slender fingers. He would gaze through the window at the sea, and she would study her book, but their minds and hearts were set on the strength that each was giving to the other. Ella drew such courage from the delicate touch of those fingertips.

She recalled all this as she sat on the edge of her bed, leaning so far forward that her hair was brushing her bare knees that broke through the carefully designed holes of her jeans. She was sniffing hard and reached for a handful of tissues from her bedside table. She surprised herself at the strength of emotion that she was experiencing. After

17

blowing her nose several times, she rose slowly from her bed and then crept across the landing to the old man's room. She heard the frantic sound of the football commentary coming from the lounge below. She discretely turned the handle of Solomon's door and entered. It was the only time that she had entered the room without him being present, which made his absence feel all the more acute. A waxing moon was shining its gentle and comforting light on the familiar armchair. She sat in it, and there she wept and sniffed until the beam of the moon left her. 'They must find him soon,' she whispered. Then looking out to the silken surface of the moonlit sea, she said, 'Please keep him safe,' daring for a moment to offer a fragile prayer to the deity whom her great uncle served with such faithfulness.

Lisa was not sure what to do with herself. Matt was in the lounge with his beer and football. His current addiction was his work, which was preferable to the drugs, but it still meant he had little emotional space for his wife or daughter. And he certainly displayed no concern for Lisa's uncle. Ella was no longer the sweet-natured girl of her childhood, as the swings and moods of adolescence had done untold damage to the relationship with her mother that had once been so strong. So, Lisa was on her own.

Well, almost.

There was… him. Troy Faversham, the Canadian divorcee, recently recruited to the partnership. She had planned to meet him this very evening. He was due to text soon. He was going to pretend there was a client in crisis, who needed urgent attention. It was planned that she would gladly respond to this cry for help. This would be another of their clandestine meetings. But she knew she couldn't go out to see him now. Not with her uncle worryingly missing like this. But she felt desperate to see Troy. It was the early stage of this dangerous liaison. It was heady. It was exciting. She had never known anything so thrilling. *And* he was a man who would actually *listen* to her, a quality markedly absent in her household. So far, they had not slept together, so technically she could plead she had not committed adultery. But she knew that very soon the force of desire would become stronger than the fears and principles that were restraining her.

18

Her phone flashed a text. It was from him. 'Hi Lisa. There's a client at the centre requesting urgent help. You able to go?'

She grasped her phone and sat at the table. She looked around, checking that both her husband and daughter were well out of range. She texted, 'So sorry. A real problem here. Can't come.'

'The client's desperate,' came the reply.

'So am I,' texted Lisa, forgetting the roles they were supposed to be playing.

His next text flashed on her screen, 'I'll be parked near the bus shelter. Be there in 15.'

'We mustn't be seen,' she texted.

'No street lights there. Will be fine. Leaving now. xxx'

Lisa was breathing fast. This felt so risky. Yes, he had chosen a dark and secluded spot, but someone may still see them. How would she explain it? It was a daft plan, but she needed him. So, with a shaking hand, she texted the thumbs up symbol. She used up the fifteen minutes clearing and tidying in the kitchen, then grabbing her coat, she crossed the hall to the lounge where she opened the door and, calling to Matt, said, 'I'm just popping out to check the church again.'

'Cool,' replied Matt, keeping his eyes fixed on the animated screen in front of him.

'Text me if he turns up while I'm out,' she called to the back of her husband's head.

'Oh, pass it, pass it, for Christ's sake,' shouted Matt, responding to a matter he viewed as being of far more importance. Then, with just the slightest turn of his head to his wife, he added, 'I'm sure the old boy's fine. He'll be in soon, you'll see.' Then, turning back to the TV screen, he called out, 'What the hell are you playing at? Christ, what a bloody shambles!'

She glanced upstairs as she crossed the hall. The usual music was throbbing from behind the closed door of Ella's room. She left the house and hastened across the gravel, and made her way down the lane to the bus shelter. She spied his car parked nearby. He was right, it was so dark, the car itself was barely visible, let alone its occupant.

An hour later she was walking back over the gravel drive to the front door. As she had guessed, his listening and thoughtful presence had been deeply reassuring. Furthermore, no beam of headlight interrupted their time together. But she had never felt so aroused by his presence, and her desire for him almost overwhelmed her. But despite her passion, her mind kept returning to her uncle, whose life could well be in danger, and this was enough to hold her back from surrendering to her intense longing. When she reached the front door, she paused before opening it. She did her best to tidy her dishevelled hair, and redid her scarf. She could smell the aftershave strong on her, and she knew she must keep her distance from Matt and Ella, and make straight for the shower. She entered the house, and made her way to the lounge. Matt was watching the match post-mortem as she opened the door and asked, 'Any news?'

'Three nil. We were sodding useless,' he replied, keeping his eyes fixed on the screen, much to her relief. She did not point out that the news she was enquiring about was to do with her uncle, not the football. She was just glad she did not have to enter the room, so she said, 'Just having a shower.'

'Sure,' he said. 'I'll be up soon.'

Lisa felt a profound sense of relief as the water of the shower flowed over her, rinsing her clean of the tell-tale fragrance. But when her tears joined the flow of water washing over her, she was far from sure whether they were tears of guilt for her illicit meeting, or tears of anxiety for her uncle. Either way, life was feeling very precarious.

*

At eight o'clock the following morning there was a ring of the doorbell. 'Who the hell can that be on a Saturday morning?' grumbled Matt, as he reached for his phone to check the time. Lisa reluctantly pulled herself out of the bed and left the bedroom to peer through the landing window.

20

She hurried back to the bedroom and, grabbing her dressing gown, said, 'It's the police.'

'I expect they've found the old man wandering around the village somewhere,' said Matt, and lay back in bed. As far as he was concerned, Solomon was Lisa's department, and he was going to keep well out of it.

Lisa hurried down the stairs, doing her best to tidy her hair. She reached the door just as the bell was being rung for a second time. Awaiting her on the doorstep was a tall and sturdily built uniformed woman of a similar age to Lisa. She was holding out to Lisa an identity card. 'Inspector Littlegown' she barked.

'Littlegown?' said Lisa with the hint of a smile.

'That's the name,' said the Inspector, rising to her full height and jutting forward her chin. 'May I come in?'

'Well, yes...' stuttered Lisa. 'But, as you can see, we are not exactly at our best. Late night, you see...' The guilt returned briefly and flustered her. 'But do come in.'

Lisa led the Inspector into the kitchen, who surveyed the scene as she approached the table, instinctively on the search for clues. She removed her cap and pulled out a chair from the table, and sat down. She still seemed tall to Lisa even when she was sitting. Lisa filled the kettle and placed it on the Aga.

'Right,' said the Inspector, stretching the word out to its fullest extent. 'I've got no news to report, I'm afraid. But I can assure you my team are on it. Tea, with one sugar. Not too milky.'

'Certainly,' said Lisa, gathering some mugs from the dishwasher.

'But I discovered one new bit of evidence when I searched the church this morning,' said the Inspector, as she dug into her pocket and pulled out a plastic bag. She gripped it between her thumb and forefinger and presenting it to Lisa, said, 'Recognise this? I rather think you will.'

Lisa came over and inspected it. Frowning, she said, 'Well, that's his dog collar, isn't it? Where did you find that?'

'And might it be the one he was wearing yesterday evening when he entered the church?' asked the Inspector, raising her chin a little further.

21

'Yes, I think so.'

'Right,' said the Inspector, again extending the word.

'Where did you find it?' enquired Lisa.

'Good question, madam,' came the reply. Lisa frowned. She knew she was quickly going to find this Inspector irritating. 'Right, I'll tell you where I found it,' continued the Inspector, holding out the plastic bag in front of her. 'My Sergeant said he thoroughly searched the church last night.' She shook her head and inhaled hard through her nose. 'He's from the Midlands, you see.' She shook her head again and pouted her mouth. 'They don't train them properly there. We're working on him, though.'

Lisa returned to the kitchen top and brought the mugs of tea and sugar bowl to the table. She sat down opposite the Inspector and said, 'Yes, but could you tell me, where did you find the collar?'

'Right,' said the Inspector in the way that Lisa was finding particularly aggravating. 'I found it, would you believe, under a pew.' She pinched her lips closed, and nodded her head again. She put in a generous spoonful of sugar, stirred it briefly, then took a slurp of her tea. Her mouth seemed quite impervious to the heat of the steaming liquid. 'I went on a search first thing this morning, and there it was as plain as day. Not near the pew where the blood was, mind you. Oh, no. Five pews from the back, it was. Five. Seems to have been ripped off and thrown down. Strange, don't you think?' She took another large slurp of her tea and was already half way through it.

'Very,' said Lisa, taking a tiny sip of her tea.

'Right,' drawled the Inspector. 'Tells you something doesn't it?'

'Does it?' said Lisa.

'It does,' said the Inspector, and drained her mug. 'It seems that someone didn't want him recognised. Makes me think he was alive when they took him out of the building. No point taking a collar off a corpse, is there?'

'Inspector Little…' started Lisa.

'Gown,' completed the Inspector, tipping back her head. 'Littlegown. Good Cornish name.'

22

'Is it?' said Lisa, far from sure. 'Anyway, Inspector Littlegown. My uncle is much loved in this village, and we are very distressed at his disappearance. I want every assurance that you are doing all you can to find him. If he is alive, he is almost certainly seriously injured.'

'We've got to check if it's his blood, of course,' interjected the Inspector. 'Could be the assailant's blood. There might have been an altercation.'

'My uncle is 85 years old, for God's sake,' protested Lisa. 'I hardly think that at his age he'd be launching himself at church thieves and attacking them with a candlestick.'

'Right,' said the Inspector again. 'Now, can you tell me if there was anything suspicious about the Reverend's behaviour yesterday. Did he say anything about meeting anyone? A homeless person, for example? Anyone come to the door asking for money? Anything like that?'

'No, no,' replied Lisa. 'No. Yesterday was a perfectly normal day.'

'Right,' came the inevitable response. 'Did he always go out at that time to lock up the church, may I ask?'

'Yes,' replied Lisa. 'Except Thursdays, when there's choir practice. He goes at nine on Thursdays. Most days it's usually sometime around seven-thirty.'

'Right,' said the Inspector. Lisa pursed her lips to stifle her irritation. 'We shall be doing a house-to-house search today to see if anyone has seen the gentleman. Might I take a photograph of your uncle, please?'

Lisa blinked a few times, for she had no idea where she could find a photograph of her uncle. He never seemed to be around when photos were taken. She felt somewhat ashamed that she couldn't quickly lay a hand on one.

'On your phone perhaps, madam?' suggested the Inspector, looking at the phone on the kitchen table.

'Of course,' said Lisa. She opened her phone and scanned some pictures for a while, but she knew there was no chance of finding a photo of the old man. 'Perhaps I could email you a picture when I have found one?' she offered.

'Well, the sooner the better, madam,' said the Inspector. 'In the meantime, could you give me a description of the gentleman.' Lisa then gave a description of her uncle to Inspector Littlegown, who carefully wrote down all the details that Lisa had provided. She then folded up her notebook, gave her card to Lisa, and stood up, saying, 'I'm sure it won't be long before we find him. Are we going out today?'

'Er, I haven't decided yet,' replied Lisa.

'Well, jot down your phone number here, if you please,' said the Inspector, thrusting the notepad and pencil in front of Lisa. 'If you hear anything, please let me know straight away.' She took the notepad back from Lisa and added, 'Thank you for the tea. I'll be getting along now.'

'Right,' said Lisa in response, deliberately using a briefly-articulated version of the word. She watched the Inspector insert her tall frame into her vehicle and drive the short distance back up to the church.

'Any news?' called Matt from the top of the stairs.

'No,' called back Lisa, and she returned to the kitchen. 'Where are you, old man?' she said, as she sat back at the table and wrapped her hands around her warm mug of tea. For a few moments she almost felt like saying a prayer, but then decided against it. It felt too risky to draw the attention of God to herself after the way she had been behaving these past few weeks.

'You told your Mum yet?' said Matt, as he came into the kitchen.

'Oh, God,' said Lisa. 'Yes, I'd better let her know.' She sighed a very long sigh, then said, 'Let me finish my tea first.'

# 3

Friday 13th April this year had been lucky for some in the village. Sid had enjoyed a spectacularly good catch of haddock; for his eighth birthday, Jamie had been given the Lego model that he had been praying for; and Ella's friend, Phoebe, had finally been invited out on her first date. Father Solomon Ogilvy had absolutely no time for the concept of luck, and had never entertained the thought that one day a Friday 13th might turn out to be a very unlucky day for him. Well, this particular Friday 13th *was* unlucky.

At least, it was at first.

He had spent most of the day at his desk. In the morning he finished off his sermon, and after his post-lunch nap, he spent some time writing in the notebook that served as his journal. It was in this book that he recorded his secret thoughts - musings that he had neither the desire nor the courage to share with others. As the light faded, he drew his jottings to a close and moved to his armchair, where he watched a darkening mist gather on the undulant waters of the Atlantic. Even under dark cloud this view seldom failed to comfort him. It was one of the many joys of living in this home. But this was a day when the sight of these familiar waters failed to ease his mind.

Solomon was troubled. Long ago now, Lisa, the only child of his difficult younger sister, had taken him into her home. He wished he had the emotional language somewhere in his soul with which to express his affection for his niece. He also wished that he had been able to establish the kind of relationship with her which would allow her to share her problems with him. He could see she had problems. It was clear to him that the marriage had been in trouble for some time now. The family had made an awkward recovery from Matt's drug problems that had caused such disruption a few years back. Solomon was concerned for all three of the family, but his main concern now was for Lisa. He was pretty sure that she was having an affair. Oh yes, he noticed far more than anyone in the family imagined. He may have said very little, but Solomon Ogilvy was an observer and a listener, and he was as skilled at listening to the non-verbal communication as he was to the verbal. He heard between the lines, and he heard things that others were too busy to hear. And what he heard concerned him.

And there was Ella. He so cherished the memory of the days when she was little and would come into his room. How he loved it when she would choose a book and, grasping his hand, would draw him to the armchair, and then sit on his knee insisting on his reading her a story. As far as he could remember, this was the only time in his adult life when he really knew physical closeness with another human. At one level, he was scared stiff. If people saw a little girl on the knee of an unmarried priest, surely, they would think the worst? Such a thought appalled him. There was no way he could ever hurt this dear child. He'd sooner have the proverbial millstone around his neck and be cast into the sea than harm any child. And Ella was far more than any child - she was everything to him.

He had never learned the vocabulary and grammar of the heart, so felt totally ill-equipped to verbally convey his feelings of affection. Once or twice he had tried to find words to express his love for his great niece, but such a wealth of emotion would rise up in him that it blocked any words that attempted to come to mind. Nevertheless, these two, the old man and the young girl, found their ways of connecting their hearts without the use of words. He could read her temperament well, and had no difficulty in understanding and accepting the variation of moods as she made her troubled way through her adolescent years. He knew when she was sad. He knew she always suffered when her parents had their rows. And he knew that she suffered much more than she let on when she had her rows with them. Nearly always in these conflicts, he found his sympathies lay with her, despite his affection for Lisa and Matt. To him, Ella always seemed the most sensitive of the three. He loved that his room had become a sanctuary for her, and he loved that she trusted him. It was one of the few things he did in life that he felt might actually be of some value. But he wished - so wished - that he could have done more for her. Not only done more, but *said* more. But all those words were tightly locked up inside of him, and at this stage of his life, he was certain that they were so far buried that they would never find their release.

26

The evenings were starting to draw out, but on this particular evening, the sea mist was thickening and the village was shrouded in heavy cloud. As Solomon looked out from his window, the waters of the Atlantic faded into the drizzling mist. He glanced at his watch. It was time to go and lock up the church, so he exchanged his slippers for his shoes, and made his way down the stairs. He could hear Lisa in the kitchen getting the dinner ready. He grasped the huge church key from its hook in the hall, and went out the front door. The evening air felt damp and chilly, so he pulled his jacket collar up around his neck as he crunched his way across the deep gravel of the driveway. It was a short and familiar walk down the lane, past the trickling water of the holy well, through the ivy-covered lichgate, over the unsteady flagstones, into the porch, where swallows would return to nest in the summer, and then through the creaking oak door into the dark peace of the medieval building, and the familiar smell of damp sandstone and wood polish.

The heavy evening cloud and the tall graveyard yew trees meant it was gloomy in the church, so he turned on a couple of the lights just to check all was well before locking up. He looked down the aisle and saw that the tiled floor was wet, the pink stone glinting under the lights. Mrs Hadfield had clearly not long left after doing her weekly mop of the floor. That reminded him: the previous Sunday, he had carelessly spilt some of the *Vino Sacro* Communion wine on the carpet in the vestry. It was a threadbare carpet, but nonetheless the wine stain was an embarrassment and disturbing evidence of a growing weakness in his hands. Mrs Hadfield reassured him that it would be no problem to clean it off when she was next in. He was keen to see if she had succeeded in removing the tell-tale signs of his clumsiness. Checking his watch, he decided that if he was quick, he could check the vestry before locking up, and then be back in time for dinner.

Thus it was that, with a little more haste than usual, Father Solomon made his way down the centre aisle of the nave that evening of Friday 13th April. As he reached the front pews and was about to take a step to ascend to the chancel, his foot landed on a particularly wet part of the floor and shot from under him. Falling backwards, he hurled his arm out to catch hold of something - anything to prevent his fall. But his hand found nothing but thin air. He heard the crack of his skull as it

27

struck the cold wet tiles, but only for a few moments did he feel the piercing pain in his head. He never felt the warm blood ooze from his cranium, and he never heard the strange gurgling noise coming from his throat as he entered the world of unconsciousness. In fact, from that moment onwards, for quite some time, he remembered very little.

He never knew how long he lay unconscious on the nave floor between the ends of the two front pews, but at some point, he returned to his waking world. But the world he re-entered felt strange and unfamiliar. Though he was lying in the church he had known all his life, it now seemed completely foreign to him. With some difficulty he pulled himself up and sat on the damp tiles, leaning against the end of a pew for a few moments. He became aware of a pain in his head, and when he touched the location of the pain, he felt moisture. He looked at his hand and noticed the blood. How had he hurt his head? And what was he doing lying on a church floor? He knew the building was a church, but it was not one he recognised. He grasped the sturdy pew, staining it with his blood, then with some difficulty he stood up. He felt giddy, and for a few moments he simply swayed awkwardly, grasping hold of the pew end to steady himself. He spied the altar and somehow sensed it would help him if he made it there. But his legs would not carry him and, after ascending the few chancel steps, he slumped into one of the choir stalls.

There he sat for a while, his eyes closed and brow furrowed. The where and how questions were now being replaced by a far more disturbing question: it was the *who* question. Who exactly was he? Panic rose up in him as he became aware that not only did he not know his own name, but he had very little clue about anything at all to do with his life. He was an old man, wearing a dark suit. But there was a tight collar around his neck. He undid the stud and pulled away a clerical collar. He looked hard at it. Why on earth was he wearing a clerical collar? But that brought at least one memory to him: he remembered his father. Yes, a long, long time ago, he had a father who did wear a collar like this. But why would he be wearing his father's collar? His father was a priest. But he was…. What exactly was he?

His train of thought was interrupted by a sound of sandaled footsteps entering the church. He looked towards the west end of the building and saw a woman making her way down the side aisle. As she approached him, he observed she was a middle-aged woman of small stature, bright-eyed and ruddy complexion. Her long greying hair was gathered behind her head with a simple cloth. She was wearing a corn coloured hessian robe and a leather satchel was slung over her shoulder. She walked purposefully, with a slight limp, supporting herself with a rough-hewn stick that tapped loudly on the stone floor. 'There you are, my friend,' she called, as she saw Solomon. 'I've been so looking forward to meeting you.'

'You have?' said Solomon, staring at the approaching woman. The only explanation for this bizarre situation was that he was in a dream. Soon he would wake up and then he would re-enter a world of blessed normality. He thought of trying to wake himself up, but there was something intriguing about this lady approaching him, so he decided to stick with it for a time.

'How do you do,' said the woman, as she settled herself next to him on the pew. 'Oh, my. It's good to take the weight off my feet for a few moments, that it is,' she continued. She kicked off a sandal, and reached down, rubbing her tanned and rough-skinned foot.

'May I...? Have me met?' asked Solomon.

'Oh, forgive me,' said the woman, sitting back up. 'My name's Monnine. Pleased to meet you,' and she held out a sun-tanned hand to Solomon.

With some uncertainty Solomon reached out his pale hand, which was clasped warmly by his new companion. He knew that in his normal waking world he would have introduced himself, but even if his life depended on it now, he could not do so, for he had no idea who he was. So instead, he said 'And I'm pleased to meet you, madam,' though he was far from sure that he was. He was in such a state of bewilderment, he would have preferred to have been on his own.

'Here. Let me take that from you,' said the woman, holding out her hand. 'You won't be needing that for a time.' Solomon detected an Irish accent. He looked down at his hand and he discovered he was still clutching the clerical collar. He obediently handed it over to the woman.

Monnine noticed the wound on the back of Solomon's head, and said, 'Now, you've had a nasty knock to the back of your head. So, let's see what we can do for it.' She opened her satchel. 'Where are you, you blessed thing?' she muttered as she rummaged through the contents. 'Ah, there you are,' she said, pulling out something like a large cloth handkerchief. With this she dabbed the wound on Solomon's head, and wiped the trail of blood that had been making its way down to his neck. She then fished in her bag again, and brought out a wad of something that carried a strong, herbal fragrance. She applied it to the wound. After dabbing it for a while, she pulled her hand away, admired her handiwork and then, giving the compress to Solomon, said, 'Just hold it there for a wee while, would you? The bleeding's stopped, and you should soon be feeling some relief.'

Solomon dutifully reached up and took the wad of material and held it over the injured part of his head. Sure enough, the pain did start to ease. 'So, where are you from?' he asked.

'Oh, from Eire,' she replied. Solomon nodded. So, he was right about the Irish accent.

'And you'll be impressed when I tell you this,' said Monnine, leaning forward and patting his knee. 'I was converted by none other than Patrick.' She leaned back and nodded hard.

'Patrick?' said Solomon, still holding the swab to his wound. 'Have I met him?' He could think of no one that he knew by that name.

'Oh no, bless you! You won't have met him,' replied Monnine. 'No, no. I knew him when I was a young girl.' She beamed a confident smile. 'And not just Patrick, but I also spent a bit of time with Brigid in Cill-Dare.' Her smile broadened as she said, 'Well, aren't you impressed? You don't get better credentials than that, surely?' She chuckled and raised her eyebrows. Then she added, 'Seriously, all that stuff counts for nothing! But the fact is they were both mighty inspiring people, they were, and I have a lot to thank them for. My, my.... Mind you, Brigid had a temper on her. Not the goody-goody some say she was. Oh, dear me, no!' She chuckled again.

Solomon's confusion deepened even further. His mind had emptied itself of crucial information such as who he was and where he lived. But

30

it could recall quite clearly that the two people that this woman was now referring to as contemporaries, lived many centuries ago. Yes, he knew Patrick and Brigid all right, but only as names of saints from ancient history.

He was about to protest about the implausibility of this claim, when Monnine continued, 'I saw Patrick not long before he left us.' She shook her head, and looked up to the rafters. 'There was still fire in those piercing eyes of his, mind you. Such fire. He was a man of fire and wounds. You could always see the wounds in the man, inflicted in his early years of suffering. He never minded folks seeing the wounds. But when I last saw him, there was a frailty in the man. Still the fire, of course. But he was an old man, he was.' She turned her gaze from the rafters back to Solomon and, after studying him for a moment, said, 'But I don't think he was as old as you. You have journeyed through a good many winters, I would say. God has certainly blessed you with a long life, has He not? And you've had your wounds. But I wonder about the fire?'

Solomon still wanted to protest about the implausibility of this personal acquaintance with the great St. Patrick of old, but he felt so tired, he had not the energy to argue. He lowered the swab from his head and studied the creased, anaemic hand that was gripping it. Monnine had observed that he had journeyed through a good many years and the witness of his hand certainly confirmed this. 'Yes, I do appear to be very old,' he said. Although it was clear he was an old man, he felt like a lost child, pining for home. Tears were threatening, so to stall them, he said to Monnine, 'Madam, forgive me. But I believe I find myself in a very strange dream, and I would really much prefer to be awake. So, I'm now going to do my best to wake myself up.'

'Ah,' said Monnine, pursing her lips. 'I think you're going to find that very hard to do.' She grasped his cold hand again, saying, 'Take my word for it. You are not inhabiting the world of sleep. Oh, no, you *are* awake, old man. And I think for the first time in your long life, you are going to become fully awake in a way that you have never been before. It will feel a bit strange at first, that it will for sure.' She bent down again, and pulled her sandal back on to her foot. 'Ah, that old foot's had a nice rest. Should serve me well again for a while.'

31

Solomon felt cold with dread. If he was not dreaming, and this was reality, then he was inhabiting a very frightening world. Furthermore, he was in the company of a woman who seemed perfectly nice, yet was either highly deluded, or was a spiritualist claiming to be in contact with the spirits of the dead. He felt panic rising in him, and after blinking a few times, he said in a feeble voice. 'It's been very nice meeting you, Mrs Monnine, but I think I need to be on my way now. I'd like to get myself to a hospital just to get this wound checked.' He squeezed the swab tight in his hand and started to rise.

Monnine grasped his sleeve, saying, 'Well now, I don't think that would help you just at the moment. I have a much better idea.'

'You do?' he asked, almost in a whisper. He sat back in the stall.

'I do,' said Monnine confidently. 'You see, I was sent here to collect you. It's all meant to be. Don't worry about the confusion that's bothering you at the moment. You've had a mighty big bang on your head, you have, and it will take a little while to feel right again. So, would you trust me to help you?' She reached out her hand to his.

Solomon had absolutely no intention of letting this woman take him anywhere. All he wanted to do was to get out of the church and hope that something outside would trigger his memory so that he could return to whatever normal life was before he found himself in this appalling situation. But he then looked at Monnine and saw a face that was in its own way utterly beautiful. He recognised it as the beauty that resides not so much in the body as in the soul. Yes, she was certainly pleasant looking: a sun-tanned face in which was set her two forest green eyes, greying hair that showed signs of its original redness, and a mouth that seemed to be always on the verge of a smile. She was comfortable but not overweight. Solomon sensed a clarity and strength in her spirit. And, perhaps more than anything, there was an endearing warmth in her. For just a few moments, she reminded him of his mother. His mother, that is, as she was before she married his step-father. The anxiety drained from him as he felt himself to be the five-year-old boy again, placing his slender hand in the warm hand of his tender, bereaved mother. The days when it was just the two of them, drawn together to survive heartache. Yes, those memories were perfectly clear. He grasped Monnine's hand

and felt its strength and warmth. It was the most obvious thing for a lost child to do. He looked into her eyes that evoked a sense of shelter, and said, almost in a whisper, 'Yes, I trust you. If you think you could help me, I would very much like to come with you.'

'Very well,' said Monnine. 'So, could you try standing up?'

Solomon stood up very carefully and was pleased to discover no obvious sign of concussion. 'Yes, I think I can walk all right,' he said.

'Well now. Let's be going,' said Monnine, gathering her stick in one hand, and grasping the clerical collar in the other. 'We'll go up the side aisle, I think. There's a bit of mess in the middle aisle. We'll leave that for someone else to clear up in the morning. Here, take hold of my arm.' Solomon held firmly to Monnine's arm as they made their careful journey up the side aisle. She was still clutching the clerical collar, but said, 'I think we'll leave this here'. She threw it to one side and it skidded under one of the pews. As they approached the door, Solomon felt quite woozy and nauseous, and to steady himself, he reached out his hand. In so doing, he knocked the rickety old collection box from the shelf that was attached to the back pew. It went crashing to the floor, and he could see he had damaged it.

'Oh dear,' he said, attempting to bend down to it.

'Och, be leaving that alone,' said Monnine. 'There's nothing in it.'

'Very well,' said Solomon, renewing his grasp of Monnine's arm.

'Are you all right to carry on?' she asked.

Solomon inhaled deeply, and said, 'Yes. Quite all right now, thank you.'

'Then let's be going,' said Monnine, and together they left the church and went out into the misty, dark night.

# 4

'Mum?' said Lisa, as her mother answered the phone. She could hear the usual Christian music playing in the background.

A voice on the phone responded, 'Ted, turn it down, could you?'

Lisa heard her father's response, 'Well it's your bally music. Why do you have it on so loud in the first place?'

'Look, I'm on the phone to Lisa,' said her mother's distinctive Cornish voice a little way from the phone. 'Just turn it down... The remote's right next to you... Sorry, love. Good morning.'

'Morning, Mum,' said Lisa.

Again, Lisa heard her mother, 'It's that button there. Yes... that's it. Sorry, Lisa, love. Great praise album, mind you. New one from *Revelation Lights.*'

'Yes, Mum. Sounds lovely,' said Lisa without conviction. 'But I'm phoning to let you know that your brother's gone missing.

'Gone missing?'

'Yes, last night.'

'How can he just go missing?' exclaimed her mother.

Lisa knew this would not be easy for her mother. For all the time she had known them, Lisa had witnessed a coldness between these siblings. Solomon was the only child of David and Freda Ogilvy. Soon after his marriage, David arrived as the parish priest of Tregovenek, a couple of years before the outbreak of war. Not long after their arrival, Solomon was born. He adored his father, but just after his fifth birthday, David felt the call to go as a Chaplain to the British forces, and he was sent to Singapore. But only months after he arrived there, Singapore fell to the Japanese, and he was taken to Changi jail. He did not survive his time at Changi. Witnesses who did survive said that David died trying to protect one of the men who was being subjected to a severe beating.

Both Solomon and his mother were left distraught. They had been close before, but their bond was even tighter in their grief. They had to move out of the Tregovenek Rectory, and rented a small cottage in the next-door village of Pedrogwen. However, in time, Freda married again. She married Trevor, a local man from the village, who took an instant dislike to Solomon, jealous of the affection Freda had for him. Freda's way of maintaining peace in the home was to put emotional distance between her and her son. When Solomon was ten years old, Freda gave birth to Jean, and both parents doted on her. Solomon felt a stranger in his own home and became semi-reclusive. His most precious possessions were a photograph of his father, and a simple wooden crucifix that had belonged to him.

While Solomon followed his father in espousing an Anglo-Catholic faith, Jean followed her parents' faith. They blazed up with a new-found zeal that they discovered in an American Pentecostal church plant in the nearby town of Porthann. For Solomon, the services he endured there were purgatory; for Jean, they were paradise. Solomon and Jean had always known that there was a great emotional and spiritual chasm between them and they managed this, not through hostility, but through emotional distance and avoidance.

Lisa was aware of this history, and knew that her mother was more likely to be irritated than distressed at her brother's sudden disappearance. She gave her mother the details of how her brother had gone missing, and it was no surprise to her that her mother responded to the crisis without any sign of emotion. If there was any emotion, it was irritation. 'He is getting on, you know, Lisa. You need to be keeping a closer eye on him,' she said.

'Yes, mother,' responded Lisa. 'Actually, we do keep a close eye on him, but we don't keep guard over his every move. He's not exactly taking his life into his hands every time he goes over to the church. He does it every day.'

'Even so...'

'Well, it's no use going over what we should have done,' interrupted Lisa. 'I'm just telling you, so you are aware. The police are on to it, and are hopeful of finding him soon.'

'Well I hope they do, Lisa,' replied her mother. 'But you say there's blood on the floor of the church and he's nowhere to be found? It doesn't sound good, does it?' She paused for a few moments, and when she spoke again, Lisa noticed an unusual hint of affection in her mother's tone. 'I mean, I know we've not been close and that. But he is my brother, and I do have feelings.'

'Yes, Mum,' said Lisa.

But in Lisa's view, her mother then lowered the tone by adding, 'Anyhow, the Lord will be looking after him. He doesn't know the Lord personally, but he'll still get the protection. I'll get the prayer group on to it.'

'I'll keep you in touch, Mum,' said Lisa sighing. She had learned long ago that there was no point in discussing religious faith with her mother as it would only lead to an argument. She put down the phone. She wished her mother was the kind of mother who would be of comfort in situations like this. Lisa was a trained counsellor and supported dozens of people through their times of crisis. She was an expert on helping people manage anxiety. And yet, she had to confess, she was as much a victim of anxiety as were her clients. In that regard, she often judged herself as a fraud. Her mother's reference to her religion didn't help. Her rampant and pushy faith was far more likely to create anxiety in Lisa than calm her, so at times like these, she needed to keep off the subject. Given the choice, she preferred her uncle's quiet faith. But then she cared little for what she regarded as his starchy churchiness. And she saw no evidence of it having any real effect in his life. Maybe it was doing so now? If he was alive, that is.

She sat at the kitchen table. Her coffee had gone cold. Her phone was lying near the mug. There was someone who could comfort her, and she could phone him now. He had been very understanding last night. Maybe she could just have a quick chat with him. He would be so reassuring. Matt was out, and Ella was upstairs with her music blaring. Lisa had made a personal rule never to phone him from home. But this was an emergency and she needed him now. She got up and attempted to close the kitchen door. For a long time now, it had been warped and never fully closed. She returned to the table, picked up the phone and paused for a few minutes. Then, taking a deep intake of breath she dialled the number. After all, he was a colleague. There was nothing odd about phoning a colleague.

'Hello, you,' said the voice.

'Troy, are you at the centre?'

'No, I'm at home this morning.'

'You alone?'

'I'm very sorry to say I am. Far too alone, and much in need of company. You free?'

'No, I can't come. I just needed to hear your voice. I don't know why, but this situation with my uncle is really getting to me.' Hearing Troy's voice immediately calmed Lisa, and she felt more emboldened as the conversation progressed. She ceased lowering her voice and started wandering around the room as she spoke to him. Unbeknown to her, Ella had come out of her room and down the stairs just as Troy had answered the phone. She paused at the bottom of the stairs as she heard her mother talking suspiciously quietly. She crept a little nearer the slightly open door, and heard her mother's words very clearly. She even heard the unfamiliar voice of the man at the other end. She heard words from her mother that she never imagined she would hear. Her mother was saying things like 'I need you so much,' and 'I will try and get over soon.' Worst of all for Ella, was the several times that she heard her mother calling the man 'darling'.

Ella started to shake. Hers was not a happy home, but there were at least some fixed pieces to it, and one was her mother's steadiness. Her father's behaviour had been very erratic when he had his problems with cocaine, and he was still unreliable now. Her mother was the strong one. The responsible one. The one who held things together. But now Ella was listening to a conversation that most clearly revealed that her mother was behaving in a far from responsible way. She was deliberately engaging in an act of deceit and betrayal. Ella knew her unstable father would never tolerate news of an affair. It would send him straight back to the cocaine. There was no doubt in her mind: what she was hearing was going to lead to the end of the marriage, and therefore the end of

37

the relatively safe foundations of her life. It was bad enough to be without her Uncle Sol, who had mysteriously vanished. But now she was facing the break-up of her home.

She had now made her way close to the kitchen door, with her ear to the narrow opening. Her mother was not speaking, but she heard the sound of the man's voice at the other end of the phone. This terrible sense of a fragmenting world was making her feel faint. She was biting her thumb nail hard. Fear was quickly being replaced by anger. Anger, that at a time like this, when Uncle Sol was missing, her mother should throw the family into even greater chaos by consorting with this man, whoever he was. Her face reddened, and when she heard her mother saying the words, 'I do love you, darling,' she had had enough. She threw open the kitchen door and called out, 'Who the hell are you speaking to?'

Lisa glanced at her daughter, then said to the phone, 'Sorry, I'll have to speak later, Mr Smith. Thanks very much for calling,' and rang off. 'Just a colleague,' she said putting the phone under some papers on the sideboard, then rubbing her hands hard together as she looked rapidly around the kitchen.

'Stop it, Mum,' scolded Ella. 'I was listening at the door. That's not how you speak to colleagues. You don't call them *darling.* You don't tell them how much you bloody love them!' She tried to say more, but the force of her anger was stifling her words, and tears were threatening to break out in her already reddened eyes. 'Dad's going to go apeshit. He'll be back to those sodding drugs, you know he will! You will tear our family apart. How could you? How *could* you? At a time like this!'

Lisa felt trepidation in her soul. She knew she couldn't deceive her daughter. Clearly Ella had been listening at the door. She grasped the back of one of the kitchen seats, inhaling deeply. 'Ella, let me explain. It's really not as bad as it sounds.'

'Oh, I think it is,' said Ella, her normally pale face now flushing crimson. She was standing on the opposite side of the kitchen table from her mother and was wringing one hand with the other. 'What do you think it's been like for me these past months listening to your bloody rows? You've both become so selfish, never thinking about what this

38

home is like for me and Uncle Sol with your moods and fights. I'm not surprised Uncle Sol's gone. I expect he's had enough. More than enough, poor man. And now with your affair, there will be more fights. Well, I don't want to be around when that happens. I've had enough!' She thumped her fist into the palm of her hand. She turned to the door, calling out, 'And don't follow me upstairs. I don't want to talk about it.'

'But we've not done anything, honest,' pleaded her mother, following her into the hall. 'Darling, it's just…'

'Oh no. Don't "darling" me,' snarled Ella from the staircase. 'Someone else is your darling now, apparently. And as I told you - don't follow me. I want to be on my own.' Lisa watched her daughter stamp her way up the remaining stairs, and slam her bedroom door firmly shut. After a few moments, the sounds of Taylor Swift blasted from the girl's room, and Lisa stood limply in the hallway as a grim and dark tide of shame threatened to overwhelm her. She felt a sense of utter exhaustion as she nervously rearranged some fading flowers in the hall table vase. She slowly returned to the kitchen and sat back down at the kitchen table. For the first time in a long time, she buried her face in her hands and sobbed like a child.

Upstairs Ella was also sobbing. Both her parents had let her down badly. Neither could now be trusted. Her grandparents were not much better. They weren't off having wild affairs, but they had become Jesus freaks, and every time she went to them for any kind of comfort, all they did was 'pray for her' which meant her grandmother laying her hands on Ella's head and saying the kind of prayers which were thinly disguised judgements. The last time she went to them for help, they tried to exorcise her. No, her immediate family was a great disappointment. All except Uncle Sol. The one dependable relative. She would be in his room now, if he had been at home. She would be sitting in that chair by the window. He would be scribbling away at his notepad. And if he saw tears in her eyes, he would come over every now and again and tap her shoulder. How she longed for that tap now. She put her hand on her shoulder and imagined the aged, sleek fingers giving their reassuring message of kindness.

And it was while she was holding her hand to her shoulder that she got the idea: why shouldn't she be the one to find him? Yes, it would be the right thing. She was the only one who loved him, so she should be the one to find him. She knew him better than anyone, and once she started putting her mind to it, she would discover where he was. She had that sixth sense and it worked well at times like this. She was sure he wasn't dead. She would feel it, if he was. No, he was alive, of that she was sure. She was far more likely to find him than the police, who were far too busy with other things. But she must leave *now*. Oh, the bliss of getting out of this wretched house. Leave now and she would mercifully miss the trauma of her father finding out about her mother's affair and the inevitable tongue-lashing that would follow. Yes, she'd need to be gone for a few days to get well clear of this domestic storm. Rapidly, plans formed in her mind as she gathered some belongings into her bag.

She went to her very overcrowded desk and searched for a sheet of paper. She got a pen and paused for a few moments, before writing:

Mum and Dad

I've gone out to look for Uncle Sol. I may be gone for a few days. I think I can find him. <u>DON'T</u> come looking for me. I'm 18 soon, so pretty much an adult and can look after myself. I'm not taking my phone as you'll only use it to track me down. I'll be quite safe, so don't worry.

See you soon

Ella x

She was thinking about saying something like, 'Mum, you must tell Dad', but thought better of it. Her mother might never show the note to her father if she did that, and she wanted him to see it. She turned off her music, put on her coat, grabbed her bag and made her way downstairs. The house was completely silent. The kitchen door was ajar and she could see the back of her mother, who was sitting at the kitchen table with her head resting on her arms. For a moment, she felt just a little compassion for her. But her anger was the stronger emotion, and her resolve to find her Uncle Sol was firm.

'Just going out to see friends,' she called to the kitchen.

'Mm,' replied a tired voice.

Ella was relieved her mother asked no questions of her, and she carefully placed her note on the hall table. Then she opened the front door, and slipped out into the fresh air of the April morning.

In the kitchen, Lisa hardly noticed her daughter's departure. Her head remained buried in her arms, and the only sounds she could hear was the thudding din of her sorrow, her shame and her awful loneliness.

# 5

When Solomon awoke the next morning, he was in a state of profound confusion. Absolutely nothing was familiar to him. A primal fear gripped him, which caused him to shake uncontrollably for a few moments. He had slept fitfully and, in his dreams, he saw faces that he knew were familiar, and yet he had no idea who they were. He saw places he recognised, yet had no idea where they were. He remembered being in that large building the previous evening and meeting an Irish woman called Monnine. Yes, that was certainly a fact of which he could be certain. But how did they get from there to here? He remembered leaving the building, but nothing more than that. And where exactly was *here* ?

He was lying on a very simple bed, and seemed to be in some kind of outbuilding. Morning light was seeping in through the considerable gap between the rough wooden door and the frame. He sat up in bed and was arrested by the pain in his head. He leaned back again on a pillow which, by its fragrance, was clearly stuffed with straw. Though he was haunted by this terrible sense of confusion and disorientation, he could not deny that there was something homely, even comforting about this very modest room. He rested back on the pillow and decided to... pray. Yes, he remembered. He used to pray to God. He had not forgotten God. *I believe in one God, the Father Almighty, maker of heaven and earth and of all things visible and invisible....* Yes, these were words he could access. They felt wonderfully familiar. *All things visible and invisible...* He had a curious sense that whatever world he was now inhabiting, it was something more to do with the *invisible* than the *visible.* Had he died? Maybe he had entered the shady world of Sheol. Was this purgatory? Would someone come in soon and lead him to a place of judgement? Would he have to meet his Maker any minute now? Maybe this really was it. The 'it' that he had been dreading all his life. Yes, he could remember that dread, all right.

His hands were grasping the fulsome sheepskin that had kept him warm in the night. More words came to him. *I acknowledge one Baptism for the remission of sins; and I look for the resurrection of the dead, and the life of the world to come. Sins...* yes, he knew what those were, all right. But quite what his sins were, he had forgotten. *Resurrection... life of the world to come.* Was this the life of the world to come? Was he now resurrected. Perhaps purgatory was behind him? Was his loss of memory a gift so he did not have to remember the purging? But the pain in his head and the weariness in his bones told him all too clearly that he was still very mortal.

*Let us pray.* He heard his own voice say the words. Words he knew he had said countless times in the past. In ancient, cavernous buildings like the one he left last evening. But what exactly did he pray? At first, he couldn't remember a single prayer. He laid back on the straw pillow and closed his eyes.

*Almighty God...* Yes, there was the beginning of a prayer. It was coming back to him. *Almighty God, unto whom all hearts be open, all desires known, and from whom no secrets are hid...* He hauled himself up again, this time more slowly. His head was throbbing, but it was manageable. He pulled his feet from the bed to the floor, and wrapped the sheepskin around his shoulders. His bare feet were resting not on a carpet, nor wood, but on hardened earth. He played his toes over the dusty surface.

*From whom no secrets are hid.* These words intrigued him. They were loaded words that had work to do somewhere in his being. 'But I am now a secret even to myself,' he said quietly. He looked up to the ceiling above him that was made of a tangle of twigs and straw. 'But my secrets are not hid from Thee,' he said. 'What dost Thou make of them?' And something about saying this drew moisture from his eyes. He wiped his eye with his hand and looked at the damp residue on his fingers. Though he remembered so little, he had a strong sense that such moisture had not been allowed release for many, many years.

At this point the door opened slightly, and he recognised Monnine's voice who, from behind the door asked quietly, 'Are you awake?'

'Yes,' replied Solomon. 'Yes, I think I am. Do come in.' He pulled the sheepskin tighter around his shoulders as the open door let in a cool draught.

'So, how's the head doing?' enquired Monnine, as she entered the room. She was clutching a bowl of water. She placed the water on a large, sawn log that served as a table, then sat on the bed next to him. 'You had a nasty crack on your head last night, and it will be awful hurting for a time yet. I'll get another compress for you soon. Now, those pieces of glass you like to use for helping your eyes are just next to the water on the wood there. You can use the water for your washing. And there's a pot in the corner, which I see you've already discovered. I'll take that off to empty it. And I've gathered some meat and ale for you when you're ready.'

'Please,' said Solomon, holding out his hand. Monnine took hold of it. 'Please,' he continued. 'I really don't know where I am or what is happening. Can you help me?'

'Oh, I'm such a fool, I am,' said Monnine. 'Of course, this must be very puzzling to you. Look, can I suggest that you get yourself up and washed, and then come out when you're ready. Then I'll do my best to explain to you. But you really don't need to worry yourself. It will all be clear soon enough.' With that she departed the room with the chamber pot. Solomon reached for his spectacles and somehow the world felt a little safer now that he could see more clearly.

It was not long before he had washed and was ready to leave his chamber and venture outside. He saw his suit jacket hanging from a hook on the wall and put it on. He opened his door and saw he was in some kind of compound. There were quite a number of people dressed similarly to Monnine. There were men, women and children, who all seemed to be busy about their business. The sky above was clear blue, and he could hear, and even see, a couple of ebullient skylarks above him.

'Och, you're out now, are you?' called Monnine, as she came over to him, wiping her hands on an apron. Dara is bringing you some food and ale in a moment. Sit yourself down here. Solomon dutifully sat down on a wooden bench next to a rustic table.

'So, where am I?' asked Solomon, with raised eyebrows and hands outstretched.

'Hmm... Yes, well this is the difficult bit,' said Monnine. 'I'd sooner you'd had some ale in you first before discussing this, but I can see you are longing to know. So, let's give it a try. What do you know about time?'

'Time?' asked Solomon with eyebrows still raised.

'Aye, time,' said Monnine. 'I mean, do you have a very fixed view of time, or do you see time as having a bit of movement in it? A little bit of flexibility, shall we say.'

Solomon felt very confused, but replied, 'I think I've always had a rather fixed view of it.'

'Yes, I guessed as much,' said Monnine, and pursed her lips for a moment. She then looked towards a young man making his way towards them with a tray of refreshments, and said, 'Ah, here comes Dara with your meal. Oh, and he's brought a fresh compress for your head, he has. Good lad, Dara,' she called, as the man arrived.

Dara placed the tray on the table, and said, 'Good day to you, Seanchara'

'Thank you,' said Solomon, as he received a plate of cooked meat and a mug of warm ale. As the lad left, Solomon looked at Monnine and said, 'He called me something like "Shenhara". Is that my name? Am I Mr Shenhara?'

'Ah, well now,' replied Monnine. 'You get going on that food before it cools, then I'll explain.' Solomon was feeling hungry and thirsty, so he gratefully received the meal. Monnine explained, 'When we arrived last night, you were half conscious. Several of the folks were asking you your name, but it seems you have forgotten it.'

'I can't deny that,' said the old man. 'I dearly wish I could remember it.'

'Well, we realised the knock on your head had delivered you of that important piece of information. So, the folks here have given you a temporary name, which is Seanchara. It's a name used in my homeland for someone who is a good friend.'

'Well,' said Solomon. 'It's kind of you to think of me as a friend.' Although he still felt very vulnerable, he was nonetheless feeling more comfortable in this strange world in which he found himself. He took another piece of meat, and then said, 'But Monnine, you were trying to say something about time.'

'So I was,' replied Monnine. 'Now, don't forget to be dabbing your head with that compress, will you?' She pushed the strong-smelling compress towards Solomon, who dabbed his head with it for a time. He winced as it stung him a little. She then continued, 'Well, you say you have a fixed view of time, and that's all well and good. But in our experience, that's not always the case with our old friend, time. She can shift to and fro a bit, if you get my meaning. She's not really one for being pinned down. Like now, for instance.'

'Now?' Solomon was mystified.

Aye,' replied Monnine. 'You are here with us now. But there is another "now" going on, which is where you normally are, if you get my meaning.'

Solomon was frowning. Neither "now"s made much sense to him. 'Well, let's start with this "now",' he said, continuing to frown. 'What is the time and month and year... now?'

'Oh, the time?' said Monnine. She looked up at the sky. Oh, I guess it's still morning. The month? I am not sure about the month, but as you can see by the larks and the height of the sun, we are well into the season of Imbolc now. It will be Beltane soon. As to the year. Well I'm really not an expert in these things, but our Lord's rising was about five hundred years ago, so we understand.'

Solomon paused his eating and said, 'So... We are about 530AD?' A few things were still clear in his mind and memory.

'AD?' said Monnine with a frown. 'I'm not quite with you there, but I have heard something like 530 years, yes,' replied Monnine. 'I'm never one for putting figures on things.'

'I rather think I belong to a very different time,' said Solomon, now dabbing his wound again. His eyes were blinking hard as he was trying to understand the impossible. His rational self was protesting the sheer implausibility of his situation. He felt panic rising in him. A dizzying sense of severe disorientation. And yet his intuitive self felt remarkably at ease, and this was in no part due to Monnine, whose company was proving so reassuring. It was the intuitive self that was the stronger presence in his soul today and quietly subdued the panic.

'You do belong to a different time,' said Monnine. 'So, what has happened is that you've simply slipped to our end of things for a wee while. You've fallen back a few centuries, I would say. We've seen it before. Not often. But be assured, it's always good news. You'll see. How's the lamb?'

'Very nice,' said Solomon. He was coming to accept the fact that, for reasons he would never understand, he was now living in a different time, far, far away from where he belonged. Wherever that was.

'And *where* is this?' he asked.

'Ah, this is our community,' answered Monnine. 'We've been going for about six years now.'

'So how did it get started?' asked Solomon, as he took another grateful swig of his ale.

'Well, I could make this a long story,' said Monnine. 'But I'll spare you the lengthy version. You see, I was with Brigid for a few years. I had a great time there. Though, the truth be told, she and I didn't always see eye to eye. Anyhow, you couldn't settle long in those communities in Eire. The wings of the Spirit of God were always unfurling, you see. Most of us, sooner or later, got the call. In my case, it was probably best that it was sooner rather than later, else Brigid and I might have got to fighting. But it was the call of God, I have no doubt.'

'The call?' asked Solomon.

'Aye,' said Monnine. She leaned back on her bench and turned her face to the sky. 'Just look at the beauty of those clouds, will you?' she said. 'The wind takes them speeding on to do their work of bringing refreshing rain where it's needed. Well, Seanchara,' she said, returning to look at her visitor. 'It is the same with us. We are like the clouds of God, being blown by the Spirit, ready to take his refreshing streams to wherever his humans are thirsty. And over a period of... oh, two winters,

I'd say, I got an ever-strengthening conviction that I was being called to travel. And sure enough, the day arrived when we all knew it was time to get going, and a few of us journeyed to the coast and got in our little boats.' She smiled a wounded smile for a few moments and then added. 'It wasn't easy to leave our homeland. We loved it so much. And our family and friends, of course.' She then chuckled and added, 'And the coracle looked none too strong either! Only God knows how we survived those waves. But we did. We had no idea where we were heading, but we just knew we had to trust and keep going until we landed somewhere.'

'So, where did you land?' asked Solomon.

Nodding to her left, Monnine said, 'We landed on the beach just over the sand dunes there. We discovered we had come to Kernow, which pleased us, as we'd heard a bit about this land. The day we arrived, a hermit who was living nearby spied us. Corman is his name, and he welcomed us. So good it was, to have his kindly welcome. He'd already consecrated a piece of land in readiness for our coming.'

'Someone told him you were coming here?'

'Och, no. Corman was a listener. Had been since his earliest years, so he said. He listened to the thrumming of the land, the sighing of the sea, and the moods of the sky. But more than anything he listened to the sweet and mighty voice of the Spirit. That was why he heard we were coming. So, it was good to be welcomed by him, and I and my sisters settled here. We built some little houses, and then went off to do good to the people who live locally and told them about the God in heaven who loved this world so much that He became one of us. Oh, they were sure pleased to hear the good news, they were. Why, in our first year, we must have baptised about five hundred of them. All ages. Many of them have become part of our community here.' She smiled at the memory. 'Och, the faith of some of the people in these parts is quite wonderful. Of course, some of them had lived in terrible fear under the dark powers that had held them. But they got free, and wonderful was their freedom. Oh, I love them so much, I do.'

'So, who is the leader here?' asked Solomon.

'Well, at the moment, it's the woman you're speaking with right now,' answered Monnine. 'But I think it will be time to pass it on to one of the others soon. It's not good for a person to lead a community for too long.'

Solomon found himself enthralled in Monnine's story. Whether it was the effects of her story, or the lamb or the ale, but one way or another, his soul started to feel far less troubled. He was less concerned about his loss of memory, and was becoming more interested in this surprising new world in which he found himself.

'Now, look, you've finished your meal. Can I show you around?' said Monnine.

'Please,' said Solomon, rising from the table.

And so Monnine ushered Solomon back out into the main compound. He was quite a striking figure in this community - taller than any of the others, and generally older. He was also still wearing his dark suit and black shirt, albeit without the clerical collar. Many of the children were fascinated by these curious clothes and the strange framed glass that was perched before his eyes. Had any of his family or the villagers of Tregovenek witnessed this, they would have been astonished, for the quiet and retiring Father Solomon, was not being quiet and retiring at all. He was chatting away with all and sundry, and could even be found laughing - something very seldom witnessed in the world from which he had so recently departed. But that was a world that was now almost completely lost from the mind of the elderly priest.

# 6

When Matt Micklefield entered his home that evening, he was engrossed in a phone conversation with a colleague. Therefore, when he dumped a pile of papers on the hall table, he was so absorbed in his call that he did not notice the neatly folded note that had been placed there earlier by his daughter. A note that had also failed to catch the attention of Lisa, who noticed very little that day beyond her own torturous thoughts.

Matt finished his call, then loosened his tie, and undid his top button. 'Hi' he called from the hall. There was no reply. There were signs of supper on the Aga. Then, hearing the sound of the TV in the lounge, he made his way across the hall and poked his head round the door and said again, 'Hi'. Lisa was involved in *Pointless* and waved an acknowledgement in his direction.

'The old man been found?' asked Matt.

'No,' replied Lisa. 'Police have been and are on to it.'

'Ah good. Ella in?'

'She went out earlier. Think she said she was seeing friends.'

'Ok,' responded Matt, retreating back to the hall. 'Just going to change, then will be down,' he called. He made his way up the stairs, and as he entered his and Lisa's bedroom, he was apprehended by a deep sense of tiredness and, throwing his tie in the direction of the wardrobe, he slumped on to the bed. Work had been so hard lately. He had been a house agent for all his career, now owning and managing his own business. Matthew Micklefield was a good and trusted brand in Porthann and surrounding area. It was his diversification into property development that made him a millionaire (hence their blissfully mortgage-free home), and he had acquired a taste for wealth. But just lately the properties had not worked for him. He was discovering that in this business, it was hard work making a million, but it was painfully easy to lose one. And he was on his way to doing just that - and more.

And there was the bank. Why were they being so difficult? If this loan did not come through, then he would be in real trouble. He would almost certainly face bankruptcy, and would be forced to sell this house to raise sufficient capital to get him out of trouble. And he would have to sell it quick. Apart from the utter humiliation of it all, how could he bear to tell Lisa and Ella that they would have to move out of this house that they loved? Despite his many failings of recent years, he had always managed to keep his business going, and keep this roof over the heads of his family.

He got up from the bed and picked up his tie from the floor and, as he slotted it in the rack with a host of other ties, his mind turned to Lisa's mother. He could see the 'I told you so' look on Jean's face as she heard the news of his demise. Their pagan son-in-law getting his comeuppance for his wayward life that manifestly offended the ways of her holy God.

Well, Matt could not deny that his life had, at times, been very wayward and no doubt very offensive to God. Twice he had been embarrassed by the very public discovery of his drug problems. It was surprising that Jean still spoke to him after those episodes. But even more surprising was the fact that Lisa and Ella still spoke to him. However, he doubted that they had ever really forgiven him. He had behaved erratically during that dreadful time. He had assured them that he had now kicked the habit once and for all, but he was all too aware of the times when they looked at him with suspicion. Any display of erratic behaviour, and they were exchanging anxious glances. And they were right to be concerned. Times like he was going through now were very provoking. He still knew where to get the cocaine. It was only a phone call away. He knew it would ease this tension in him that so often resulted in fights with Lisa.

He knew that his marriage had been in trouble for some time. He greatly missed the closeness and affection they had once enjoyed. And recently there had been a couple of very attractive and distracting women who had caught his eye. Women who *wanted* to catch his eye. There would be no shortage of closeness and affection with either of them. But so far, he had kept himself well clear of them. But for how long could he hold out? He sighed a long sigh as he slowly unbuttoned his shirt. The unpalatable truth was emerging that Matt Micklefield, the man who once showed such promise, was a failure at his marriage, failure at being a father, and now it was becoming horribly possible that he would also be a failure as a businessman.

He pulled off his white shirt and then stood in front of the mirror. He studied his 45 year-old torso. Despite all the work he put into it, there was no doubting that he did not have the physique that used to more than impress the girls. That stomach seemed to be growing by the day. He quickly donned a loose-fitting sweatshirt to hide the offensive contour.

As he continued to change, his thoughts turned to Uncle Solomon, this curious man who lived his hermit life mostly in his bedroom, and was now causing something of a sensation by suddenly disappearing. Matt only ever saw him at mealtimes, and the elderly man seldom joined in conversations at the table. He was quite simply an enigma. But Matt had come to regard him as an amiable enigma. And now this enigma was missing. Though others in the family presumed the priest had been abducted or was concussed and had got lost, Matt felt the most likely explanation was that the old man had been attacked and killed. For obvious reasons, he kept this theory to himself. He was aware of just a little sadness at the thought of Solomon's departure from this life. But the old boy was 85 years old and, in Matt's view, his death now would be timely, even though murder would hardly have been the route out of this world that he would have chosen for him.

Once changed, he went downstairs and, on reaching the hall, he grasped the pile of papers that he had earlier flung on the hall table. As he did so, he noticed a note flutter to the floor. He picked it up and recognised his daughter's handwriting. He frowned and shook his head for a few moments, then raced through to the lounge calling, 'Lisa, have you seen this?'

Lisa noticed the urgency in his voice and turned off the tv. She took hold of the note, read it, and looked up in horror at Matt. 'When did she leave this?' she said.

'I don't know,' said Matt. 'It was… Well, it was just sitting on the hall table. Must have been there when I came in.'

'But she...' started Lisa, as she rose from the sofa. Her head was so full that she was struggling to recall the moment that Ella had left the house. 'I think she said she was going to see friends,' she said, looking again at the note. 'She said nothing about going out to look for Uncle Sol.'

'How come you didn't see the note?' asked Matt, taking it from Lisa and reading it again. 'It was on the table, plain for all to see.' He neatly forgot his own oversight of the note when he first arrived home.

'I... I... No...' stuttered Lisa.

'So, come on. When did she go?' said Matt in alarm.

'Er...' Lisa had to work her way through the thick fog of her confusion. She was desperate not to give anything away of the overheard phone call that had precipitated this crisis. 'It was... mid-morning, I think,' she faltered.

'Well, for Christ's sake, she could be miles away by now.' Matt's face contorted into a grimace. 'And she's gone without her phone! Can you believe it? When's she ever done that? She goes nowhere without it. Why didn't she want us to know where she was going? Was she in one of her moods again?'

'No,' said Lisa, shaking her head. 'As I said, she told me that she was off to see a friend. At least, I think that's what she said. I can't quite...'

Just at that moment the doorbell rang. 'That'll be her!' called Lisa, her face lightening. 'She'll have forgotten her key.' She dashed to the front door, and opened it, but it was not Ella. It was the large figure of Inspector Littlegown.

'Just catching up,' said the Inspector, thrusting forward her impressive chin. 'Got a moment?'

'Oh,' said Lisa, trying not to betray her flustered state. 'Yes, come in. Our dinner is ready, but we've got a few moments.'

'Right,' said the Inspector, as she followed Lisa into the kitchen. 'Won't keep you long.'

'Any news?' said Matt, following the two into the kitchen.

'I'm afraid not, sir,' said the Inspector, as she lowered her large frame into a chair by the table.

'So, no progress at all?' said Matt. The shock of Ella's note was making him more anxious than ever. He was still clutching it in his hand.

'We are working with a number of possible scenarios, sir,' said the Inspector.

'Scenarios?' said Matt, settling into the chair opposite her. 'What scenarios?'

'Well, sir,' said the Inspector. 'Firstly, let's assume that the motivation was theft.'

'Yes, the smashed money box would suggest that,' said Matt.

'Indeed, it would, sir,' responded the Inspector. 'So, as I say, if the motivation was theft, then Scenario 1 is that the Reverend gentleman discovered the offender in the church and asked what they were doing. In response, the offender attacked our gentleman and unfortunately killed him. They panicked and decided to remove the body from the church and hide it somewhere.'

'Well, with respect,' said Lisa. 'I can't quite see that happening. I mean, my uncle's thin, I grant you, but he is tall and would still weigh quite a bit. Besides, I doubt if someone could drag him out of the church without being noticed.'

'Right,' said the Inspector, pronouncing the word in her usual extended manner. 'Then we come to Scenario 2: the Reverend gentleman had offended someone. Perhaps someone with mental health issues. A homeless person maybe. Someone with a grudge against the church. Things of that kind. And they decide to attack the gentleman, and take him off somewhere.'

'We still have the problem of someone lugging a body out of the church, or at least taking him by force,' said Matt. 'There's plenty of people passing by the church who might have noticed that. And it doesn't explain the broken money box.'

'No, it doesn't, sir,' replied the Inspector.

'Nor the dog collar, for that matter,' added Lisa.

54

'Nor the dog collar, madam,' said the Inspector. 'I agree. These scenarios beg a few questions, but we have to start somewhere. Right, where are we?'

'Scenario 2,' said Matt.

'Right. So, Scenario 3: The Reverend gentleman has been taken hostage.'

'Taken hostage?' said Matt with a brief, sarcastic laugh. 'Why would anyone take him hostage? I mean, I'm sorry, but who's going to pay any money to have the old bloke back?'

'Matthew!' cried Lisa.

'Well, come on, Lisa,' said Matt, holding out his hands.

'Right,' said the Inspector, alert to the tension between husband and wife. 'We have to consider all possibilities, sir, however unlikely. So that leaves Scenario 4: this being that there was no assailant, but that the gentleman fell on the floor that was wet at the time, and was concussed, and then left the church in some confusion.'

'I have been thinking that myself,' said Lisa. 'I could see that happening. But there are still the questions about the money box and the dog collar. And why wouldn't he make his way back here? I mean, it's been 24 hours now that he's been missing.'

'Good questions. Good questions,' said the Inspector. 'We would have to suppose that he was considerably confused, hence the strange behaviour with the money box and collar. People do very strange things when they are concussed. You see, it's my job. I've seen people concussed more often than I care to say. So, it may well be that our Reverend gentleman leaves the church and is off wandering somewhere. Because he's concussed, he forgets where he lives. Might even have forgotten who he is. This is why we have to search the neighbourhood, which we are doing.'

'Well, there can't be too many places to go to, surely?' said Matt. 'I mean, you can wander around a few gardens near the church, or down to the harbour. Or wander down the coast path, I suppose. If he wandered up to the main road, surely someone would have seen him?'

'I agree, sir,' said the Inspector. 'Plenty of unanswered questions in this case. But rest assured, we will get to the bottom of it.' She then turned to Lisa and said, 'Have we found any photos of the said gentleman, madam?'

'Er, no,' said Lisa. 'I'm sorry, we'll keep searching.'

'Please do, madam,' said the Inspector. 'It would help us a great deal if you could.'

She was about to rise from the table when Matt said, 'And we have another missing person to report.'

'No, Matt,' protested Lisa, firing a fierce stare in his direction.

'Well, we should report it,' said Matt.

'Another missing person you say, sir?' said the inspector, slowly reaching for her notebook.

'Yes, Inspector,' said Matt. 'We have a daughter, Ella. I think you met her last night. Well, she left home today, and we don't know where she's gone.'

'With respect, sir,' said the Inspector, now closing her notebook. 'She seemed like a grown-up girl to me. I would think she's gone to see a friend, wouldn't you? Got a partner, has she?'

'No,' said Lisa. 'But yes, you are right. She does have quite a few friends. We'll get on to them now.'

'I suggest you do, madam,' said the Inspector, scraping the chair noisily on the kitchen floor as she stood. 'If we went searching for every young person the moment they were reported missing, we'd have little time for anything else. They get up to all sorts of mischief, they do. But ninety-nine times out of a hundred, they are fine.'

'That's as maybe,' said Matt. 'Are you a parent?'

'No, sir.'

'Well, take it from me, that when you're the parent, you worry like hell that your child might be the one out of a hundred.'

'Right. Point taken,' said the Inspector.

'We'll keep you in touch,' said Lisa, rising from the table. One more "right" from Inspector Littlegown, and she was worried she'd be charged with assaulting a police officer.

She showed the officer out, and when she returned, she found Matt pacing up and down the kitchen. 'Let's get phoning,' he said.

'Yep,' said Lisa. 'I've got some of the phone numbers of her friends, but not all.' For the next ten minutes they phoned all the friends of Ella for whom they had phone numbers, but none of the friends had seen her.

'Right,' said Matt.

'Oh, don't you start,' said Lisa.

'No, seriously,' said Matt. 'We've got to find her. You know what she's like. She's not got a lot of common sense. She says she's grown up, but she's not. There's no telling what trouble she could get into.'

'She's got more sense than you give her credit for,' said Lisa.

'I know this is a safe village,' said Matt, trying to remain calm. 'But knowing Ella, she's going to search beyond the village. It's clear the old man's not in the village. He'd have been found by now if he was. My guess is that she's gone into Porthann. Probably took the bus. I really don't like the thought of her being in that town late at night on her own. It's ok with friends, but you know what town can be like in the early hours. No, I'm going to go looking for her.'

'I really don't think you need to, Matt,' said Lisa. 'She really can look after herself. She'll be back soon, I'm sure.'

'Lisa, I'm going to at least have a look in town, all right?' said Matt, who was now making his way to the door. So much tension was rising in him. He knew that it was not just his missing daughter that was driving him. As much as anything else, he was looking for an excuse to get out. To do just what Lisa's uncle had done: disappear for a time. Get away from the bank manager, the office, the home. From Lisa. He felt panic rising in him. He paused at the door. 'I'll have my phone with me, obviously. Not like that silly girl.'

'Well, have some supper first. I don't...' Lisa paused and shrugged her shoulders. She could see her husband was determined and nothing she could say could stop him. Matt retired quickly from the kitchen, and she heard him hurrying upstairs.

Lisa sat back at the kitchen table feeling stunned by the pile-up of events that had taken place during the day. Then she heard Matt come back down the stairs and she went into the hall.

'You've got a bag!' she said.

'I may need to be gone overnight,' he said.

'But where will you stay?'

'In the office. I can sleep on the floor.'

Lisa was so emotionally exhausted that she had no energy for stopping him. She stood in the kitchen doorway, leaning against the doorframe. She watched her husband put on his coat, and hasten out of the house. She remained motionless as she listened to the car starting up and then crunch over the gravel. Then it became very quiet.

She slowly returned to the kitchen and sat at the empty table. She reached for her phone and for some moments stroked her finger over its face. She could call him. He could even come here, now that she was in on her own. In on her own all night. But something was preventing her from calling him. What was it? Was it her conscience? Was she finally feeling guilty for betraying her husband in this way? Yes, she couldn't deny that was certainly part of it. She did feel guilty - especially since she saw how it affected Ella. She and Ella may have had their stormy moments, but she never wanted to hurt her daughter. The look of hurt on that sweet face was haunting her.

But there was also another part to this resistance. She did not want to phone her lover, because a voice from an inner chamber of her soul was protesting. It was complaining that the desire for Troy was not coming from her real self, and would simply lead to a painful dead end. And she was becoming aware that something about this crisis of her missing uncle and daughter was opening her eyes just a little to who this real self might actually be.

She was sitting at the kitchen table looking down at the glossy surface of her phone. But it was not the phone that she was seeing: her inner eye was catching a glimpse of this real self. Yes, there she was, and she appeared as a young child. Not the child she was once, but a child version of herself now. It was like this child had been hidden for so long, and the crisis of this past 24 hours had now broken something open that made her visible. Or partially visible, at least. A child's face at a dirty window, calling to her, her voice just audible through the glass. Lisa had done so much of this kind of inner exploration in her counselling training, and yet her defences were so strong she had never seen this in herself. The mix of feelings within her included upset and comfort, fear and excitement. And she knew, without any doubt, that if she were to continue the dalliance with Troy, she could lose sight of this child forever. The child was calling to her, and she knew she had to respond. Quite how to respond was presently a mystery. But though she felt herself to be experiencing a sense of abject desolation, there was also a curious sense that she was on the verge of a discovery.

As the moon rose over the tranquil sea that evening, Lisa sat in the gloaming, weeping tears that felt long overdue. Ella's tears were falling onto the fresh spring grass of the coastal footpath. Matt's tears were making it so difficult for him to drive, that he had pulled in to a lay-by where he sat in the stillness of his parked car. And somewhere, in another time, Father Solomon Ogilvy was the only member of that troubled household who was not weeping.

# 7

Ethel Cairnes had slept very little that Friday night. Monty Don had failed to calm her. Neither had her usual tot of Irish whiskey. For the sight of the blood on the church floor and thoughts of violent intruders kept troubling her normally peaceful mind. She was therefore up early and had opened her shop long before its usual Saturday morning opening time of 9am. However, there was a steady flow of people coming in early, for news had gone around the village that Ethel was the one who had actually been the first to the scene of this disturbing crime. Already there was plenty of misinformation, and people came into the shop expecting to hear reports of the battered body of the old priest draped over the altar and other such garish embellishments. Those hoping for such reports left the shop a little disappointed, for a pool of blood and broken collection box was rather poor fare for those who liked to dine on the kind of stories dished up by the usual tv detective dramas.

Alongside the sense of excitement in the village caused by this drama, there was a genuine concern for the elderly parish priest. What had happened to him after his attack in the church? By lunchtime the police had been round every house and searched every garden and there was still no sign of him. Not even any tell-tale drops of blood or torn bits of clerical shirt. The disappearance of the old cleric was a complete mystery. Speculation was rife, and many more scenarios were added to the ones originally listed by the Inspector. This included schemes by pirates to whisk the old man away, wild animals making their way down from Bodmin Moor and devouring him, and even one extreme theory that Father Solomon was not just a priest, but a spy for MI5 and had been rumbled. Everyone held their own theory, and there was no shortage of conversation in Ethel's shop, as well as in the streets and lanes of the village.

The few members of the church congregation were very concerned, and Marcus Rawlings, as churchwarden, informed the bishop. He was the only person that the police would allow into the building, and it was he who reported to the congregation that it was doubtful that they could hold their Matins service on Sunday. The Rural Dean had sent a message urging them to attend worship at the church in Pedrogwen. All the congregation regarded that as a very unpalatable option, so there was no worship for any of them that Sunday.

By contrast to all the gossip about the priest, nobody knew of Ella's disappearance. She was well known in the village, as were the few other teenagers who resided there. Ella was regarded as one who generally wasn't too offensive. Yes, a few had taken a dislike to her variety of hair colours and styles, and others had commented unflatteringly on her pierced nose and the multitude of adornments that clung to her ears. But she was from the village, and the villagers were therefore loyal to her. She herself had generally enjoyed growing up in Tregovenek. As she grew older, she soon worked out how to sort out buses and lifts to get to Porthann. She also loved walking, and was well acquainted with the several local footpaths. So, when she walked out of home on that Saturday morning, she was stepping into a land she knew well. The question was, where to start?

She had been working on her own theories of what might have happened to her great uncle, and she was favouring the idea that he had fallen and, suffering from concussion, had wandered off somewhere. She walked briskly into the village and noticed the police cars. She spoke to one of the police officers, who informed her that all the houses and gardens had now been searched and there was no sign of the old man. So, he had wandered out of the village. But to where? She made for the coastal path that led to Porthann via the beach. She knew it was the route she must take. It was her instinct. Yes, she was sure this was the path taken by her concussed uncle the previous evening.

As she strolled along the path with her hands in her coat pockets and her lungs inhaling the cool, briny air, her thoughts returned to her great uncle. She found herself remembering a time when she was a child, and it was a warm Spring day like today. She was walking down the lane to the shop to get some sweets with her pocket money, and noticed the door of the church open. She wandered in and spied her great uncle kneeling in his clergy stall. She stood very still and watched him. He was praying. She recalled him being as still as a standing stone apart from a little tremor on his lips. She remembered thinking he looked quite beautiful and imagined it was how the saints looked when they prayed.

Ella had never really been one for praying, but that memory of her great uncle in his stall was stirring her. Perhaps it was time for her to pray? She stopped at a bench that looked out over the heaving Atlantic Ocean. She sat down on the weather-worn wooden slats and closed her eyes, lifting her face to the warmth of the sun that was now beaming on her from a cloudless sky. Every now and again the breeze would draw strands of her soft hair over her face. But this she did not notice, because her mind had returned to the sight of the old man praying. It was time for her to pray. But how to pray? She had no idea how to pray, or quite who to pray to. But in these moments, she desired to encounter whatever it was that her great uncle knew when she saw him praying in church that day.

She then had a curious sense of a hitherto hidden, subterranean part of herself opening up. Something was causing a shifting of the strata of her soul. Something prompted by the disappearance of her great uncle. Something about the shock of her mother's affair. Something about being Ella Jean Micklefield, sitting on this bench at this precise moment in history on the verge of adulthood. All these somethings were activating a part of herself that had long been unfathomed. But what was it? She screwed up her eyes as she strained to identify it. She could not give it a name at first, but she knew it was precious. A treasure long buried, yearning to be discovered. A treasure that was so real and temporal, and yet had about it the quality of eternity. A piece of her earth that was suffused with heaven.

What was this something? The only word that came to mind was the word *faith*. But she recoiled from this word. The word arrived in her mind with her Gran's voice, and when her Gran used the word, it was always loaded. On many an occasion, Gran would upbraid Ella for her marked lack of faith. No, 'faith' would not do. But if it was not faith, then what *could* she call this treasure that she had somehow unwittingly stumbled upon in this deeper chamber of her soul? It had about it a mix of transcendence and intimacy that curiously seemed perfectly natural. Though a little reluctant to admit it, Ella was in no doubt that she was in touch with the Divine. She felt she was connecting with a God who was far beyond her and yet, in these moments with the sun warming her freckled face and the breeze ruffling her unbrushed hair, she knew it was a God who was as close to her as her own breath.

She opened her eyes and scanned the view that lay before her. The gorse flowers burned yellow, the grey cliff fell away to the beach below, and the azure sea sparkled in the morning sun. It was as beautiful as ever, and yet it felt like she was seeing it in a different light, because this time she felt she was in the company of the One who had fashioned all of this. She felt quite taken aback by the power of the experience, and for some time she simply stared out at the distant, shimmering horizon not quite sure if she was terrified or delighted.

She was startled out of her thoughts by a soft, female voice from behind her that said, 'Excuse me, I do not want to alarm you.'

Ella most definitely did not want to be disrupted from her state of tranquillity in which she found herself, yet there was something winsome in the tone of the voice. She turned and saw a girl of about her age, whose dark skin and richly-coloured dress suggested to Ella that she originated from an African country. She looked towards the girl and said, 'Oh, no, cool. Just looking at the view.'

The young woman smiled. 'May I?' she said, pointing to the vacant space on the bench next to Ella.

Ella watched the tall, dignified figure settle on the bench, straight-backed, placing her clasped, long-fingered hands neatly on her lap. Ella noticed her beautifully braided hair decorated with beads of reds and oranges. 'Great beads,' she said.

'Thank you,' said the girl, lifting her hand to her hair.

'You from these parts?' asked Ella.

'Yes and no,' replied the young woman. 'My name is Rahab.' She smiled a beaming smile that revealed a dazzling row of teeth that would impress any dentist. 'May I ask your name?' she asked.

'Ella.'

'Hi, Ella.'

Ella frowned at her new companion and asked, 'What did you mean by *yes and no*?'

63

'Ah, sorry,' answered Rahab. 'Let me explain. *Yes,* because I live near here now.' She nodded her head towards the nearby town. 'But *No,* because originally I come from Eritrea.'

'Eritrea? Cool,' said Ella. Geography had not been her strong subject, and she had little idea as to where Eritrea was in the world, and she rather limply said, 'Eritrea a nice place?'

Rahab, who had been looking at Ella, turned her eyes to the sea, and said, 'Eritrea is my homeland and a most beautiful place. Much of the land is hot and dusty, but my home was near the sea, and where the land meets the sea, there are swaying palm trees that reach up to the sky. And their leaves smile down on the white, white sand. And you can run across that sand with your arms flying high in the air, because next to you is the dancing sea, and you just have to dance with it!' Rahab raised her arms as she said this and looked to the sky. Then lowered them as she continued, 'And when you reach the edge of the water, you hear it sighing with delight because it loves to meet you. And you splash and swim and feel the cool of the water refreshing you. And sometimes you see the dolphins who lift their heads above the waves to greet you.' She turned her gaze from the Atlantic breakers back to Ella. 'For me, Ella, it was Paradise. That's why I thank God so much that I have come to live here. It is also so beautiful, and I never want to be far from the sea.'

'So…what brought you here to Cornwall?' asked Ella. She was over her irritation at having her time of meditation interrupted, and was becoming very curious about this visitor.

Rahab smiled and frowned at the same time. She reached out her hand and took Ella's. Ella looked down at the brown skin of the hand that was holding hers. She felt a strong sense of warmth and delight at being held by this hand. But her feeling of delight swiftly passed when she looked up and saw Rahab's face, for the smile had disappeared and only the frown remained. 'My parents gave me the name, Rahab,' she said. 'Do you know that name, Ella?'

'No, never heard of it,' Ella replied.

'It's in the bible. Rehab was a prostitute.'

Ella winced and said, 'God! So, your parents named you after a prostitute? That's pretty harsh.'

Rahab smiled and just nodded her head slowly for a while. 'Perhaps you don't know my people. You don't know how we listen for names. Do you know the meaning of your name?'

'Er...No,' said Ella, who had never given any thought as to whether her name had a meaning. 'But I don't think it's in the bible. I still think it's a bit harsh that your parents named you after a sex worker.'

'Do you know any?' asked Rahab, drawing some of her long, braided hair behind her shoulder.

'No! Course not,' said Ella.

'Ah, so you judge them like other people do,' said Rahab.

'Well, no,' said Ella, trying to justify her response. 'It's just that...'

'It's just that you wouldn't want to be seen with one?' said Rahab. 'Well, you are mixing with one now. How does it feel?'

'You... You're a sex worker?' Ella felt awkward. She liked this girl, and didn't want to offend her.

Rahab shook her head causing the hair beads to jangle. 'No, not now,' she said. 'But there are some people who think that once you have been a prostitute, you are stained for life.'

'I'm sorry,' said Ella. 'I wouldn't think that.'

'I believe that,' said Rahab, looking at Ella with her chestnut eyes. She looked back out to the sea again and continued, 'You see, when I was born, my parents knew they had brought me into a very troubled world with threats of great darkness. Even when I was a young child they warned me that life would be very hard. But they kept saying that even if the worst were to happen, God would be with me. And the worst did happen. One night, violent men came into our village and my parents were killed. And I was dragged off with those men and sold into prostitution. So, you see. My parents were seers. It must have hurt them to see into my future like that.'

'Oh, my God,' said Ella, bringing her hand to her mouth. 'I'm so sorry. That sounds horrific.'

'Yes, it was horrific,' said Rahab, slowly nodding her head. She looked down for a few moments at her clasped hands, then looked back at Ella, saying, 'I was wounded for sure, and it still hurts. But you see, my sister, God was with me.' Her smile shone again. 'My spirit was strong because my parents had prepared me. They told me about the story of the girl called Rahab in the bible. Yes, she was a sex worker, but she was also commended as a lady of great faith. You should read about her sometime, Ella. I think, like me, Rahab had to work as a prostitute because she was so poor. But God did not turn his face away from her because of her profession. He saw her suffering and her faith, and he rescued her, and he called her to serve him. In the same way with me, God did not judge me, and he heard the cries of my heart. You see, if a woman has to become a prostitute, it does not mean she is a bad woman. She does not lose her soul. Don't you agree?'

'Of course,' said Ella. The breeze blew her hair over her face and she brushed it back behind her bejewelled ears. 'But how long did you have to do that horrible stuff?' she asked.

'About a year,' said Rahab. 'But each day God gave me strength. And one day he opened the door for our escape. Me and the other girls - we ran free. And, well it is a long story, but after a very long and difficult journey we ended up here in this country. We are seeking asylum and it is looking like my case will soon be accepted. For that I am very thankful.'

Ella nodded. Again, her knowledge of such things was very limited. 'So now you live here in Cornwall?'

'I do,' said Rahab. 'Not quite settled yet, but I believe God has a home for me somewhere here. And you, my sister. What are you doing?'

Ella looked down for a moment and scrubbed the heel of her boot against the ground. 'I live in the village just up there.' She nodded up the hill. 'Have done all my life. But today I'm looking for someone.'

"You have lost a friend?' asked Rahab, the frown returning to her face.

'A very dear friend,' said Ella, and looked up at the kindly dark eyes that were studying her. 'My mum's uncle actually. You've not seen an old man walking down by the sea, have you? Or in town, looking a bit lost?'

Rahab frowned deeply and shook her head, and the beads jangled again. 'No, I have seen no old man,' she said. She then reached her other hand forward and clasped Ella's hand with both of hers. 'My sister,' she said, looking searchingly into Ella's eyes. 'Let me tell you this. You are searching for the uncle of your mother. I believe he is safe. You are not to worry. But please bear in mind that as you search for him, you will discover treasures you were not expecting to find. These are the treasures within your own heart. Forgive me. I don't mean to be personal. But it's just... I just see things, that's all. God is with you. I could see you were with Him just now.' Then she released her clasp of Ella's hand.

Ella pulled her head back for a few moments. She felt somehow spied on and it was uncomfortable. She felt suspicious and, frowning, asked, 'Exactly how do you see such things?'

'When you suffer, you have a choice,' replied Rahab. 'You can close or you can open. In their suffering, my parents chose to open, and they saw things. They saw a little of my future. I learned from them, so when it was my turn to go through hard times, I also became open, and I learned to see in a different way. That's all. Now, I must let you get on and continue your search.'

Ella had never had a conversation like this before. Part of her felt Rahab was a weirdo to be avoided, but another part of her felt drawn to her. As Rahab stood up to go, Ella said to her, 'And where are you going today, Rahab?'

Rahab looked up the path. 'I have never been to your village. You say it is this way? I would like to see it and shall therefore go there today.'

'Well,' responded Ella, also standing. 'To be fair, not a lot goes on in the main village, so don't get excited. It's a bit more interesting down by the harbour. Not great, but there's a cool pub down there. Should be open if you want a drink.'

'Thank you, Ella,' said Rahab, pulling her bright cloak around her shoulders. Ella was about to turn to go down the hill, but she was caught by a curiously strong affection for Rahab, and she stepped towards her and hugged her tight to herself.

When she released her new friend, she noticed many tears were falling from Rahab's eyes. 'Oh, I'm sorry,' said Ella.

'Do not be sorry, my sister,' said Rahab, who made no attempt to hide the tears. 'It is just… Well, there are many who do not want to come close to me when they know what I have done in my past. You have been my healing today. Thank you.'

Ella smiled warmly at her and said, 'I'm not sure about that. But I hope we can meet again. Can I give you my number?'

'I have no phone,' said Rahab, opening her empty hands.

'Ah, shame,' said Ella. She smiled at Rahab and brushed more windswept hair behind her ears. 'Well, call in sometime. We live in the big house just near the church. You can't miss it. It's called Altarnun House. Strange name, isn't it? God knows why it's called that.'

'I expect He does,' said Rahab, chuckling. 'God bless you, my sister,' she said, and she turned and walked up towards the village.

Ella watched the tall figure departing. 'And God bless you, too,' she called. She then added quietly, 'My sister.'

She turned, and made her way along the grassy track towards the beach. Yes, she too held in her heart a strong instinct that her great uncle was safe. But nonetheless, she was still determined to find him and lead him home.

# 8

Had Ella been dwelling in the same time zone as her great uncle, she would have bumped into him as she arrived at the beach. However, through the alchemy that was well beyond either of their understandings, Ella and her great uncle were now separated by fifteen centuries. Thus it was that Solomon, who was now known as Seanchara, was walking along this beach on his own. It was a beach that he had walked so often back in his own time. But today he was walking it as if for the first time.

Seagulls squawked and swooped above him in the April sunshine. He was grateful for the strong wooden stick that Monnine had given him, and he made his way slowly along the sand until he came across a rock that was the right height to serve as a seat. He sat on the cold, hard surface, and, despite the discomfort, he was pleased to rest his legs. It was a breezy day, and he was grateful for a warm woollen garment that he had been loaned, that looked to Solomon something like a fisherman's smock. In this world, it was a good deal more practical than his suit jacket. The sense of panic he endured when first being told he had travelled to a different time was now subsiding. He was pretty sure that he had located his 'normal self' to the twenty-first century, and he could picture generalities of that world very well. Brick-built houses, motor cars, computer screens, mobile phones - all these things had come back to him. But try as he might, he could not lock on to any images to do with his own home and family. He was pretty certain that he was a single man without family, but he also felt there were some lives close to him that he cherished. But none of them came to mind. He was feeling very disorientated, but he could not deny that he had been made so welcome by Monnine and her friends, and for the moment, he had no alternative but to view this curious community as a place that he could call home.

The tide was coming in and he watched the frothy water gliding over the sun-warmed sand, creeping towards him. He knew he had watched a scene like this many times, but *where* had he seen it? It was so disconcerting not to have any memory of time and place and people. The worst was not knowing his own name and precious little about the life that he had stepped from when he had suffered this knock on his head. He shifted his position on the cold rock as he endeavoured to pull together whatever strands he could, to ascertain who he was and from whence he had come.

It was evident he was an old man. He looked at the mottled, crepe skin on his hands and guessed they had been serving him for well over eighty years. He had no recollection of where he lived, or anything to do with most of his adult years. But he was starting to form some impression of his earlier years. The people most clear to him were his mother and father. He closed his eyes, and he started to inwardly focus on the face of his father. He felt such warmth and tenderness as he beheld this face. A young man, handsome, tanned with a thin moustache and jet-black hair greased back over a high forehead. His smile lit up his whole face. He was wearing a dark suit and yes… There was that white collar around his neck, the uniform of a priest. So, his father must have been doing some work for God.

For God? There it was again - God. *Almighty God, to whom all hearts are open…* His father used those words, he was sure. But what did this mean? What did it mean to have a God who could somehow prize open the human heart and gaze upon it? He felt anxiety creep into his soul at the thought of this divine inspection taking place into the confines of his own soul. He was fairly sure that any divine face peering into his heart would carry a frown of disapproval.

An image of his mother then appeared clearly in his mind. She was sitting by a closed window, and the rain was splatting against it. He knew that her hair was usually tied up neatly in a bun, but in this image of her, it was untied and falling about her face. When she turned and looked - not at him, but somewhere beyond him - he could see her reddened eyes stark against her pale face. There was a hint of lipstick on her trembling lip. She was clutching a handkerchief in her hand. She sighed a long sigh and looked back out of the window again. Yes, how well he remembered pulling at that soft hand that smelled of coal tar soap, and trying different ways to bring a smile to that wounded face. How often he had buried his face into that white blouse, buttoned to the chin. Now it was damp with tears. He remembered this clearly. He remembered that his father had died in a foreign land. And this meant not only managing his grief, but also the grief of his mother. He and his mother had to cling to one other, adrift on a wretched and turbulent sea of sadness.

Yes, these memories were as clear as the bright Spring sunshine that was beaming on his closed eyelids now. But he was forced to open his eyes when he felt a flow of water over his black leather shoes. The tide had reached his rock. It receded briefly, allowing the old man to rise from his rock and make his way back up the winding path to the settlement where he was currently abiding. The sun was slipping towards the horizon and its heat was fading. 'Can I help you Seanchara?' came a voice from behind him. It belonged to the young lad whom he had met earlier - the one who had brought the welcome meat and ale.

'Thank you,' said Solomon. 'Most kind of you.' He was indeed grateful, as the path felt steep and rugged. The lad helped the old man return to the settlement. 'Why don't you rest in your room,' said the lad. 'And then Monnine will come and get you for the evening meal. We'll be eating it soon after the sun goes down.'

Solomon agreed. Indeed, he did feel weary, and he was glad of a rest and, on reaching his room and simple bed, he soon fell asleep. He was awoken by a knock on the door, and in came Monnine, holding in her hand a blazing torch. 'Will you be joining us for some food, Seanchara?' she asked.

Solomon was ready for a meal, and he was pleased to follow Monnine to a small barn, inside of which was set a long table. He guessed that there were about twenty people gathered around this table - men and women of varying ages, and some small children. Monnine ushered him to a place by her side, and when he had settled himself on the bench next to her, she called for quiet. She then said, 'My sisters and my brothers, here we are at the end of the day. Our beloved sun is now resting from his good labours, and now the moon is beaming upon us her gentle light. Our God has given us the friendship of both day and night. He has also given us our family gathered here. And look what he has provided for us: another feast to warm our hearts and fill our stomachs! So, thank you, beloved Christ, for your sweet mercies to us this day. And more than anything, thank you for giving us a new friend.' Here she laid a hand on Solomon's shoulder. 'Loving Christ, you have brought Seanchara to us. He will be a wonderful gift; may we be a gift to him.' Then looking down at the old man, who had his head bowed and his hands clasped, she said. 'The Lord bless you and keep you and make His face to shine upon you. And more than anything else, may He give you His peace.' And all the company followed with an *Amen.* Her words evoked an instinct in Solomon, and he drew his hand to his forehead and made the sign of the cross over himself.

*

Had this assembly of people been able to transport themselves fifteen hundred years in time, they would have found they were more or less in the location of where Solomon, in the days before his accident, could be found having his supper with his family at Altarnun House. Only on this particular Saturday evening, he was very noticeable by his absence. Indeed, the sense of absence was very strong in this kitchen. Only Lisa sat at the table, where normally would be gathered her husband, daughter and uncle, all of whom were absent for different reasons. And Lisa was worried about each one of them. She was prodding at her half-eaten baked potato when the phone rang.

She pressed the speaker phone and the distinctive Cornish voice of her mother filled the kitchen. 'Lisa? Lisa, is that you, love?'

'Yes, mum, it is.'

'Any news?'

'No,' replied Lisa wearily. 'Mum, this is the fourth time you've called, and I told you I'd let you know if we got news.'

'Well it's all very strange, Lisa,' replied her mother. 'I mean, it's not like my brother to go missing. He's not that sort. We're praying hard for him, we are. We're putting him under the blood.'

72

'Under the blood?' said Lisa. 'In the circumstances, I hardly think that's the right kind of language to be using.'

'Blood of Christ, Lisa,' came the crisp reply. 'Under the blood of Christ. You know very well what I mean.'

'Oh, God,' said Lisa wearily.

'You blaspheming again, Lisa? You know your father is offended when you do. And he's listening to this, aren't you, Ted?'

'No, mother,' interjected Lisa, before her father had a chance to respond. 'Dad's not the one who's offended. It's you. You know as well as I do, that he's used the odd naughty word in his time.'

Her mother hesitated for a moment. She was caught between the need to get her daughter to understand the perils of blasphemy, and the embarrassment of her husband's tendency to use less than edifying language. So, she let go of the problems that the blasphemy was presenting and returned to the subject in hand. 'Well that's by and by. Let's get back to the missing members of the family, which if I'm not mistaken, has now reached three.'

Lisa sighed. 'Look Mum, you don't need to worry about Matt and Ella, they…'

'I do worry about Ella, if you please,' interrupted her mother. 'She's a child, Lisa…'

'She's nearly eighteen, for God's sake…'

'Yes, but that's just the point. She's a child who looks like a young lady now, and you know what that means, don't you? I've told her before about her short skirts. They're offensive to God, they are. And you know where the wearing of those short skirts leads, don't you?'

'Mother, can we stop this,' appealed Lisa. 'I think I know my daughter better than you do, and I'm telling you that I trust her to take good care of herself. She's very fond of your brother, and she wants to find him. And Matt is on the lookout for her. So, stop worrying, will you?'

'Well, I suggest you get praying, Lisa,' said her mother. 'You need to pray for the Lord's protection. I know they are not saved, but God still cares for the unsaved when we pray for them.'

'No mother,' said Lisa, starting to prod afresh at her potato. 'No. You know perfectly well that I don't pray. But can we avoid having an argument about religion? I've got enough to be dealing with.'

'Well,' said Jean, not wanting to let go of her religious convictions just yet. 'I thought you'd like to know that I've phoned round and got our church interceding.' Lisa sighed, which her mother heard but ignored. 'I've spoken to Greg, our pastor, and he says God's told him that there's a spirit of unbelief over your house and that's what's causing all this disturbance. Well, that didn't come as a surprise, Lisa. But he said God told him that it's been there for generations, would you believe? It was there long before you got there. But don't fret too much about that, because we'll be breaking that spirit in church tomorrow.' She then raised her voice and added, 'Isn't that right, Ted? Breaking the spirit of unbelief when we're in church tomorrow?' There was a pause. 'Yes, he's nodding.'

Lisa guessed the look on her father's face - a familiar one of reluctant acceptance. 'Thanks, Mum,' she said in a flat voice. Without conviction, she added, 'I'm sure that will help. Anything else?'

'Yes,' said Jean. 'Ted and I would like to pop in after church. Any chance for a bit of lunch?'

Lisa was too weary to think up an excuse, so she limply agreed and ended the phone call. She pushed the now cold potato to one side and took a sip of her wine. She sighed again. She had been doing a lot of sighing during the day. 'So, there's a spirit of unbelief over the house, is there?' she said to herself. 'Hello, spirit,' she hailed, lifting her glass to the ceiling. 'You having a good time robbing us all of our belief? Not sure you made much headway with old Uncle Sol, though. His belief seems pretty strong. But you've done good a good job on the rest of us. So, cheers. Well done, you!' She lifted her glass again. 'Here's to this unbelieving house and all who sail in her.' She drained her glass and went to the fridge and fished out the bottle of wine.

After refilling her glass, she slowly sat down and, with her brow furrowed, she thought more about this question of faith. Was she really as unbelieving as her mother claimed she was? She had been presented with two versions of Christianity in her life. Her mother, who years ago

74

had managed to catch hold of a stern form of the faith, and felt obliged to bludgeon all who came across her path with it. And there was Uncle Sol, who was so private about his faith that it was hard to know what he believed. But if she had to make a choice, there was something far more endearing in the old man's faith than there was in her mother's. There really was something in him that was... Was what?

She sipped at her wine. *Holy* seemed the best word for it. Something holy in him. But what was the cause of this holiness? It was something in him. A deep well of faith.   And it was a fresh supply. Although he seldom spoke of his faith in the home, Lisa could tell he had access to this inner source of refreshment. It was there in the way that his grey eyes would shine under his dark, bristly eyebrows. It was there in the rich timbre of his voice when he would thank Lisa even for the smallest gestures of kindness. It was there in the slow, methodical way that he would remove the crockery from the dishwasher. And yet he was such a quiet, unobtrusive member of the family, that Lisa far too often failed to pay much attention to him. But now he was missing, she became more aware of him than she had ever done.

The more she thought about him, the more inquisitive she became. She drained her glass and experienced the tell-tale unsteadiness. But she was sober enough to have an interesting idea. 'I wonder if he'd mind?' she said out loud. 'I don't think so,' she answered herself. She only ever entered his room to hoover and dust and change the sheets and towels, but had never spent time there. What would she find if she had a look around? What clues about this quiet old man might she find? She felt sure he wouldn't mind if she just had a brief look. She didn't want to pry. But there was a yearning in her that was reaching out for something. There it was again - the voice from the secret place within her. The child at the window calling her, beckoning her. And there was this sense that something in the soul of her uncle could help free this child within. At that moment her phone flashed a text. She checked and it was from Matt.

In Porthann. suspect she's here somewhere. will stay in my office tonight. will let you know if I find anything. love you x

Lisa replied with the thumbs up emoji. She was glad Matt was keeping in touch. She looked hard at the text. She felt curiously moved by those last two words: *love you.* Yes, the fire of those early years, that had once been so strong, had been all but extinguished. But as she read those simple words at the end of her text, she sensed that the embers from that fire might still have a little warmth. She realised she was missing Matt. She took her phone and texted, *take care.* She then made her way upstairs to commence her exploration of Uncle Solomon's room.

# 9

Matt wrote his text to Lisa while sitting in his Range Rover, which was parked outside his office. A few pre-loaded revellers staggered past. His phone pinged again, and he read the text. *Take care.* He felt the tenderness of the words. He looked at it again, and for a few moments found himself missing Lisa very much. He leaned back in the car seat. He was craving cocaine. Those revellers would almost certainly know where he could get a supply within minutes. And then, all his worries would be gone.

As if.

No, he was determined not to go down that road again. But what road could he go down? His life just seemed such a mess. He looked out of the car window and, rubbing away the steam, he studied the shop window decorated with the latest attractive properties for sale. Above the window was the prominent sign, *Matthew Micklefield - The Estate Agent.* He always liked the catchy alliteration of his name. This was now a well-known and respected name in Porthann. If you wanted a really good property, this was the place to come. The estate agent business had always gone well. And it would still be doing well, had Matthew Micklefield not decided to branch out into property development and bitten off far more than he could chew. How he regretted this now. He knew this wasn't really where his skills lay. And why did he have to buy that huge property on Crescent Hill that everyone advised him against? Now he was landed with a part-developed property that was worth precious little in its present state. Fully developed it would sell very well and all his dreams would come true. He just needed... He shook his head. No, of course the bank couldn't go on pouring more money into this. Why on earth did he imagine they would? How had he become so naive?

He looked through the shop window into the office, and saw the familiar desks. He thought of the three loyal staff in this office. Soon he would have to make one of them redundant. It would have to be Sophie. Gorgeous Sophie. It would perhaps be a good thing if she left the office.

He found himself wanting to spend more time in her company than he should.

Even thoughts of Sophie failed to lift his spirits. He felt so drained of energy that the thought of climbing out of his car and entering his office felt like too much of an effort, and he slumped back in his seat. More revellers passed the misty windows of the car. He watched a group of inebriated, mini-skirted girls making their way down the street and imagined the kind of evening that lay ahead of them.

He was interrupted from his musings by a knock at the side window. He looked and saw a pair of slim, unstockinged legs. He let down his window, and the owner of the legs bent over towards him, revealing an inviting cleavage. 'You want company?' she said.

Matt recoiled. 'What?' he said, and looked around to see if anyone was observing this encounter.

The girl smiled. 'Just wondered if you were a bit lonely, that's all,' she said, adjusting her top suggestively. He detected a Scouse accent.

He felt momentarily intoxicated as he inhaled a waft of seductive perfume. 'Get in,' he said. What on earth was he doing? He knew this was quite crazy. He had never dared involve himself in this kind of dangerous liaison before.

She was soon in the car, settling herself in the passenger seat. She leaned towards him and said, 'Fifty quid for the full works.' Matt felt the heat on his face. He wasn't looking at her, but was staring at the car parked ahead of him. The perfume smelt far less appealing now. 'It's a fair price,' she said, and placed her hand on his knee. He removed her hand immediately, and turned to look at his new companion. He guessed she was in her early twenties. Platinum eyes were looking at him through a frame of straight, long, dyed blonde hair. Her upper lip carried a scar. He observed a touching vulnerability in the young face, and it was the noticing of the vulnerability that released the anxiety he was experiencing.

'Look,' he said, resting his arms on the steering wheel. 'I'm sorry. I'm in a bit of a state, and I don't think I can...'

'It's all right. I'm good,' said the girl. She pulled the hem of her skirt up a little.

'No, no…' said Matt, lifting his hand to shield his eyes from the view. Panic was rising in him. He lowered his hand and looked at her face again. All sense of lust had gone and was being replaced by something that took him completely by surprise. It was compassion. He thought of his Ella, so much stronger than this girl next to him, but also lost, possibly roaming the streets somewhere. This girl next to him here may also have a father somewhere, aching for her.

'You're very lovely,' he said to the girl. 'And I will pay you. I'll give you fifty quid. But not for sex.'

The girl flinched a little and said, 'You kinky or something? You one of those blokes that's just into ogling?'

'No, no,' said Matt. 'No, look. Instead of… you know, doing all that. I'd like to buy you a coffee.'

'You whar?' said the girl, pulling her head back in disgust.

'Or tea?' said Matt.

'Tea?'

'Have you eaten?'

'You being serious with me?' It was now the girl's turn to feel awkward. She pulled the hem of her skirt towards her knees.

'I am,' said Matt. 'Look, just down the road there's a McDonalds, and they have a drive-through. I'd like something to eat. Would you join me?'

The girl turned her mouth down for a few moments and bent her head as she studied Matt. She had never had a client behave like this before, but on balance, she decided that this man was trustworthy. And she had not eaten since a meagre breakfast. So she said, 'All right. Fifty quid and the meal. And no sex.'

'Yep.'

'You're on, son,' she said, still frowning.

'What's your name, then?' asked Matt, as he started the car.

'That'd be telling, wouldn't it?' said the girl. 'There's a name I use for my profession. But seeing as I'm not doing that with you, why don't you give me a name?'

'How about *Angel*?' said Matt. He'd no idea why he decided to choose that. He was aware that the girl had gone very quiet and started sniffing. 'God, sorry,' he said, looking briefly at her. 'I didn't mean to upset you. I'll choose another name.'

She gathered her emotion as she said, 'No, you're all right. Stick to that name.' They arrived at the drive-through, and after Matt bought burgers, fries and cokes, he steered the car to a nearby parking area. He pulled into a parking space, and they opened their substantial burgers.

'Great burger,' garbled Angel, with her mouth full.

They were both quiet for a while as they ate. Then Matt said, 'Sorry about the name. Don't know why I chose *Angel*. But I can't think of another name.'

Angel had just taken a large number of fries and munched them for a while. She swallowed hard and said, 'Sorry.... It's just... Well, look at me. I'm no angel, am I? I suppose you were just being sarky, and I can't blame yer. Any road, what's your name? Blokes never give me their real names, so shall I make one up for yer?'

'No need. I'm Matthew Micklefield,' said Matt. 'And the truth is, I'm in such a mess, that my being seen with a prostitute won't make much difference now.'

'Oh, God, yeah,' she responded. 'I've seen yer name on the shop. You're famous in town, you are. So how come you're in a mess, then? Can't be worse than mine, that's for sure.'

Matt finished off his burger, then turned to the girl and said, 'I think the name *Angel* is right for you, despite what you say. I wasn't being sarcastic. I think you *are* an angel.'

'What? A real bloody angel?' she cried, spitting out a piece of bread roll as she did so. 'Give over.'

'No,' said Matt, smiling. 'I don't mean in a spooky way. But I think angels come in all sorts of guises, don't you? You know - anyone who helps another is an angel really.'

'Guess so,' said Angel, slurping at her coke. 'Not sure I can be of much help to you though. I only really know how to do one thing, and you didn't want to do that. Though, the truth is, I don't do that very well. Least, that's what a load of the blokes say.'

Matt used a tissue to dab off some ketchup from his stubble, then responded, 'I shouldn't listen to them. I expect you're great. But how did you get into this business in the first place?' Angel then told him a little of the eighteen years of her life that had been forged on the cruel anvils of poverty and abuse. Only recently had she escaped to Cornwall, where she hoped for a new start, only to slip once again into the world of addiction and prostitution. Matt listened intently. Something about his own brokenness was releasing this new and unfamiliar feeling of compassion. He reached out for her ketchup-stained hand and squeezed it. 'You poor girl,' he said. 'It's not right, is it?'

She shook her head. 'But I'll get by somehow,' she said. 'From time to time I meet nice blokes like you. That gives me hope, like. And I've got me faith.'

Matt frowned, and with a turned-down mouth, he said, 'Your faith?'

'Yeah,' she said. 'I grew up in Liverpool, I did. Most people were Catholics where we lived. My family were Catholic, but only went to church for funerals. And there were plenty of them. We had Mary stuck up on the mantelpiece and a crucifix in the bog, but that's about as far as religion went in our house. My Dad said he believed in God. That didn't exactly give me a good view of God. Someone told me that God was a father, but I thought if he were anything like me dad was, then he was best avoided. He was not good to me and my mum. Not good at all.' She looked at Matt and, raising her eyebrows, touched the scar on her lip. 'But I changed my view of God when I ended up in the cathedral one day. You been to Liverpool?'

'No, never been,' said Matt.

'Oh, you should go,' said Angel. 'They got two Cathedrals there. Very posh.' She gurgled the last drops of her coke through a straw, then opened her window and chucked the paper cup out of the window. Matt winced. She noticed and said, 'Oh, sorry. You one of them that doesn't like litter, eh? I'll fetch it.' And sure enough, she got straight out of the car, picked up the cup, and returned, chucking the mug into the back seat. 'Where was I?' she said.

'Cathedral,' said Matt.

'Oh yeah. Well, don't go to the Church of England one. Too dark and heavy. Go to the light one. They call it Paddy's Wigwam.' She turned to Matt and smiled a nervous smile. A light from a passing car lit up her face, and Matt could see the tiredness in her undeniably beautiful eyes.

'Great name for a cathedral,' said Matt, smiling.

'You gor' it,' she said, smiling again. She then turned and looked out through the misted front window of the car. 'First time I stepped into the place I were a kid. Never been into any church before. But I was running away from some gang or other, and decided to go into the church. I knew they wouldn't follow me in there, and I was right. It was a sunny day, and when I stepped inside the place it was completely bloody brilliant.' Her eyes were wide open and she raised her hands to the car roof as she said, 'It was massive, and there was light and colour coming from everywhere. Thought I'd walked into Paradise, I did.'

She lowered her hands and continued to stare ahead of her as she recalled the scene. 'And there was this brilliant music playing, with some people singing songs that I'd never heard before. I honestly thought I was hearing angels singing. I kept expecting someone to take hold of me and chuck me out, 'cos I was not exactly in me posh frock. But no-one did. And then this old lady comes up to me and says, "You make yourself at home here, lass." So I did. Well, it didn't feel anything like my home, but it did feel safe. I remember having the strangest feeling - like this was how home was supposed to feel. Know what I mean?'

Matt was looking at her intently, and nodded slowly as she continued. 'I mean, it was bloody massive in there. Far too big for a real home. But... Well, it just felt nice. It was a bloody beautiful place, it was. You never seen anything like it. I used to go back as often as I could. Got to know that old lady well. She was called Beatrice. Great name, don't you think?' Angel grinned broadly, revealing a broken tooth. 'Me and 'er - we'd go to one of the little chapel thingies they have there, and kneel together and say prayers. God, she said such lovely prayers, she did. Beatrice was my best friend in them days. She told me that no matter what happened in my life, God would still be with me. She kept saying, "Just have faith, Jenny...". Oh, sod it, I've just gone and given you my name, haven't I?'

'Sorry, Angel?' said Matt, pretending not to hear. 'Sorry, I didn't catch the name.'

'Yer, you did.' She smiled. 'There really is kindness in you, isn't there?'

'Well, a bit sometimes,' conceded Matt. 'I'm glad you met Beatrice.'

'So am I,' said Angel, whose real name was indeed Jenny. 'You know, I think she could tell where I was heading in life.'

'Why?'

'Well, she used to tell me stories about Jesus, like. You know, the nice ones about how he dished out loads of bread and fish and that, and how he walked on the sea in the wind and rain. But several times she would say, "You know, lass, he had a special love for the people who fell on hard times. Even the prozzies." She talked quite a lot about how he was kind to them. One of his best friends had been one, she said. Course, I knew quite a few prozzies in them days, as loads of them worked near the street where I lived. I used to stop and have a chat, and smoke a ciggie with them, and tell them what Beatrice said, but they usually just laughed at me and told me to piss off. But I tell you this, Matt.' She turned to look at Matt again, and he could see moisture forming in the corner of her eyes. 'When I went on the game myself, I never forgot Beatrice's words. Still think of them, I do. Still hear her voice. Such a nice voice.' She turned away from Matt and gazed out of the side window. 'Hard to believe Jesus would still love me when I'm selling my body like I do, isn't it?' She turned back to look at Matt again and with her lip trembling she said, 'I am ashamed of meself, Matt. Honest to God, I am. I just... I just don't know how to get out of it all now. I'm too far in.' She shrugged her shoulders and turned her damp eyes to the side window again.

Matt struggled to find some words with which to comfort her, but before he could speak, she said, 'You got any stuff?'

'No,' he said. 'No.' He was alarmed that she had supposed that he might be into drugs. He then confessed, 'I did get hooked a few years back. But I'm determined I'm not going back there again.'

'Well, you're a lucky sod,' said Jenny, still gazing out into the dark. 'Don't think I'll ever be able to kick the habit. It's got hold me good and proper, it has.' She then looked over to Matt and said, 'So what's this mess you're in, then?'

Matt folded up the packaging of his burger and said, 'Oh, you know.' He then looked over to Angel and said, 'It's nothing.'

She paused for a few moments, then, holding out an open hand to Matt, she said, 'We had our time now, haven't we?'

'Yeah,' said Matt, and he reached into his pocket and pulled out his wallet. He fished out the three twenty-pound notes that it contained and handed them to the girl.

'Got no change,' she said, looking at the notes.

'I know,' said Matt, and briefly clasped his hand over hers.

'I won't forget this,' she said. 'Never.' She leaned forward and, gently cupping the side of his face with her hand, she kissed his cheek and held her face next to his for a few moments. She then grabbed her bag and was gone.

Matt felt the dampness of her tears on his cheek, and he placed his hand reverently on the moisture, holding it there for a long time. He felt stunned by this encounter with the girl. Never before had he spoken with a sex worker. Never had he taken the trouble to consider the terrible circumstances that might have caused a young woman to sell her body. He had come into town looking for his lost daughter, but instead had found this lost soul. And yet, despite her lostness and brokenness, there was also something so admirable in the girl. Could he honestly say she was more lost and broken than he? He thought about

84

how she spoke about her cathedral. He remembered her words: *Thought I'd walked into Paradise, I did.* He recalled the light in her eyes when she spoke of it. There was a dignity in her soul that he envied.

He placed his hands on the steering wheel, and leaned back in his chair, looking up at the roof of the car. He was unable to control both his trembling jaw, and the streams of warm liquid pouring from his eyes. 'I want to go there,' he said out loud between sniffs. 'I want to go to that Cathedral. I want to meet Beatrice.  Oh, God, I want…' He found a handkerchief in his pocket and wiped his face, and glanced out of the passenger window. 'I want to help her,' he added. 'Poor girl. Oh, sod it. God, please take care of her.' It was the first prayer he had prayed in over thirty years.

Jenny was also weeping as she left the car. She walked fast as the night air was getting chilly. She couldn't face trying to recruit customers tonight, and she'd think of an excuse to tell her pimp in the morning. As she walked back into Fore Street, a girl of her age was walking towards her. The girl stopped her and said, 'Excuse me, do you know if there are any cheap places to stay around here?'

'Yeah,' said Jenny, sniffing. 'You're near it. It's the youth hostel. Just follow the road to the end and turn right. Can't miss it. You new to town, are yer?'

'No,' said the girl. 'I live just a couple of miles up the coast. Tregovenek. Often come into town. What about you?'

'Been here a couple of years,' replied Jenny.

'Cool,' replied the girl. She was about to walk away, when she stalled and asked, 'By the way, you seen a tall, thin old man wandering around town today? It's why I'm here actually. I'm searching for him.'

'Plenty of old blokes here in this town,' replied Angel. 'People retire here. But they'll all be tucked up in bed by now. What's up with him?'

'Oh, I think he's just a bit confused,' said the girl.

'Plenty of those here,' said Jenny. 'Expect he'll turn up soon. What's your name, by the way? If I bump into him, I'll tell him you're looking for him.'

'It's Ella,'

'Ella? Nice name.'

'What's yours?' asked Ella.

'Angel.'

'Cool,' said Ella. Then, smiling, added, 'Can't see your wings, though.'

'Oh, they're there, if you look hard enough,' responded Jenny, winking. 'Ta'ra.' And with that, she was gone.

Ella had guessed the girl's profession and smiled at the irony of her name. She had also noticed her reddened eyes, and assumed that a meeting with a client had not gone well. 'I should have done something to help her,' she said to herself. But she was on another mission and she had to focus. Her first day of searching for her great uncle had been completely fruitless, and she felt exhausted. She followed Angel's directions and, sure enough, there was a youth hostel just where Angel had said it would be. She booked herself in and was told that there was a McDonalds just down the road where she could get food 'til 10pm. So, she zipped up her jacket, and walked swiftly, so that she could get some food before the place closed. McDonalds was warm inside, and she got herself some chicken nuggets and fries, and sat in a window seat. She pondered her chance meeting with two young women who had both been caught up in the sex trade. The two girls had been so different, and she felt a fondness for them both.

Had Matt not reclined his seat and fallen off to sleep, he would have seen his daughter sitting in the window of the diner. And had Ella not been in one of her daydreams as she walked back to her hostel that night, she might well have recognised the Range Rover that was the only vehicle in the car park.

# 10

Lisa climbed the stairs slowly. The wine was undoubtedly having its influence now. She paused for a few moments outside her uncle's room. She steadied herself, then opened the door which made its familiar creak. The room was dark, save for a shaft of moonlight beaming through the sea-view window. She didn't want to turn on the light, for a room lit by the light of the moon looked so appealing. She sat in the aged armchair allowing the light of this celestial neighbour to rest on her. Somewhere, hopefully, this same moon was shining upon Uncle Solomon. She frowned for a few moments as her anxieties surfaced. She imagined shafts of moonlight piercing through the slats of an old barn, alighting on the old man with bound hands, at the mercy of some demented person holding him prisoner. But even if that was happening at this very moment, Lisa sensed that he would somehow still be his same tranquil self. She felt sure he was not suffering and was safe. She would not allow herself to imagine any more frightening scenes. As she sat in his threadbare moonlit armchair, she closed her eyes. The peace of the room enfolded her, and it was not long before she surrendered to a gentle sleep. When discomfort and pressure from her bladder woke her in the early hours, she made her way to her own bed, where she only managed an unsettled sleep.

A particularly loud gull woke her in the morning. The April sun was shining brightly into her room. She showered, dressed and went down to make herself some breakfast. Just the one boiled egg this morning. The house seemed so quiet. No music blaring from Ella's room. No Uncle Sol gathering up his robes and books to make his way to church to lead the service. No Matt trudging out across the gravel to go and collect the Sunday papers. She checked her phone and there was no further message from him. No doubt, he was still sleeping in his office. And she felt confident that Ella had found a friend and was staying with her.

She then remembered that her parents were coming for lunch following their church service, with the pastor strenuously exorcising the great spirit of unbelief that was apparently hovering menacingly over the household. She both frowned and smiled at the thought. She checked the freezer and found some chicken pieces, which she gathered and placed to thaw on the Aga. She had some time before she needed to start cooking, so she refilled her mug with coffee, and found herself being drawn back upstairs to Uncle Solomon's room.

Much of the wall space of his room was given over to bookshelves. All the books looked so formal and ancient. She felt she was surveying a distinguished library rather than a bookshelf in a family home. She ran her fingers over the spines of the covers, and thought about how these books had no doubt inspired this priest as he prepared his sermons over the many years of his ministry. The subject matter of the books looked deadly dull to Lisa, but she knew how much he loved his books, and she was sure that none of them would have been dull to his mind. She noticed on the bottom shelf was a row of children's books. She recalled the times when she had stood on the landing listening to that beautiful lyrical voice reading a story to Ella in her childhood years.

His bed was made with the empty hot water bottle placed neatly at the end of the bed. The armchair in which Lisa had slept for part of the previous night was placed by the window for its commanding view of the sea. The window of the adjacent wall overlooked the gravel driveway, and in front of this window stood his dark oak antiquated desk that had once belonged to his father. Eighty years ago, this very desk would have resided in the study of the large house by the church that once served as the Rectory. The days of such Rectories was long gone. It was a similar size, style and age of house to Altarnun House, and for the first time, Lisa realised that the home they had provided for her uncle had probably felt safely familiar for him.

The surface of the desk was covered by a timeworn green leather, and on this stood an art deco lamp, an orderly tray of pens, a coaster decorated with a faded picture of his previous church, an old-style exercise book with a fountain pen laid upon it, and, to Lisa's surprise, a framed picture of her, Matt and Ella. It was taken about ten years ago. They were all wearing shorts and tee shirts, and were tanned from the summer sun. They were standing on the back lawn, and she and Matt had their arms around each other. Ella was standing just in front of them. She was smiling broadly and had her hand lifted, presumably waving to whoever was taking the photo. Lisa remembered that Uncle Solomon did have an ancient Kodak Instamatic camera that he brought out on rare occasions.

She sat down at the desk and, placing her coffee mug on the coaster, she studied the photo for a while. She remembered the time in her marriage when she and Matt were close. It was before he had become so driven. It was before he got hooked on the coke, when his behaviour became so erratic. Yes, those days when the photo was taken were pretty good days, all things considered. She replaced the picture back on the desk, and then opened the exercise book. She assumed this was the book he used for writing his sermons, but soon realised it was not. On the front page was written in Solomon's neat, spidery handwriting the simple words, *Solomon Ogilvy Journal - Volume 27.* For a moment or two she scanned the bookcases for Volumes 1-26, but could see no sign of them. She turned back to the notebook in her hand. Though she recognised that this had to be a private volume, her curiosity got the better of her, and she turned over the first leaf. It was clear that this was a new journal and there were only a couple of entries.

The first entry was dated *Wednesday 11th April.* She started reading.

I suspect this will be one of my last entries. My days are numbered, I am sure. I'm feeling my age. I'm always tired. It's time for me to leave this world before I become even more of a nuisance to the family here. I am ready. Ready to go to meet my Lord if He will have me. But I can't deny I am anxious. I fear I shall be passing over to a very uncertain habitation. And not just anxious. I'm feeling so many regrets. They keep haunting me.

How does a man deal with regrets? I scold myself for this, but I can't quite stop myself. Last night I dreamed I was a young man again. I can't recall the full content of the dream, but when I awoke, I had such a strong feeling of being young again, I wanted to leap out of bed, but the moment I moved I realised all too clearly that I am an old man, not a youth. But the feeling was strong and there I was in the dream, freshly ordained as that bright young curate that I once was. How full and delightful were those early years of my priesthood. I do think some of the wounds of my childhood were healed in those days, particularly by the kindliness of Father John. And then, of course, there was <u>her</u>. I have tried so hard to put her out of my mind, but have never succeeded. Hardly a day has gone by when I have not thought about her. I've not written about her before in these journals. It's fear, I think. Fear that by writing about her, all those old longings would return. I've done a reasonable job of taming those restless wild beasts. But it is time to write it down. It is something that I need to do before my eyes close their gaze on this lovely world for the last time.

How could I not record something so significant? I never met a soul like hers. I have never met a woman more beautiful than she. She was the only person to challenge my vocation to celibacy. I was so certain about my calling. I had little else of worth to give God. My celibacy seemed to be the one thing I could give him that would be truly valuable. And costly. But now, all these years later, only now, do I wonder whether I was right to give up so much for my priesthood. Was it really the call of God? Or was it simply my pride? Why does it trouble me now? I sit here in my delightful room and have so much to thank God for. And yet, I wonder how life would have been if I had given in to the longings of my heart. Would I have married her? Yes, I think I would have. And would we have been happy? I can't imagine not being happy with her. But then who is to say that the dark in me would not rise up and cause fearful damage. It is very possible that she and I would have fought like Lisa and Matthew have. How I should have hated that.

Here Lisa put down the book for a few moments. For the first time, she was gaining a view of the private world of her uncle. She felt guilty at trespassing in this way, but she was far too inquisitive to stop now. And here she had a sighting of his private world. A sighting of a love for a woman, that he did not pursue because of his calling. And yet there was also an uncomfortable mention of the fighting between her and Matt. She felt so guilty that this warfare should have disturbed the peaceful soul of her uncle. Because his presence in the house had been so much in the background, it never occurred to her that he would be troubled by their arguments. She imagined he would have taken these normal family tiffs in his stride. But clearly, he hadn't, and she felt a deep sense of shame as she continued to read.

I don't understand why they are so unhappy. They have so much. This beautiful home in this blessed part of Cornwall. They have work that they enjoy (though clearly Matt's work has become too stressful). But more than anything they have Ella. Dear, sweet Ella. She has not been in here for a week or so now. I do hope she is all right. And if I had ever married, would I have been granted a child such as she? Surely I wouldn't have been allowed a life so dear?

Ah, you silly old man, stop wallowing in your longings and your regrets. It's time for bed.

Lisa ran her finger over the page. This reported affection and admiration for Ella took her quite by surprise. She knew Ella was fond of the old man, but so quiet and withdrawn was he, that she had supposed that he somehow managed his life without experiencing affection for anyone. She assumed his reading to her daughter was due to a sense of duty rather than affection. But here it was in his beautifully scripted journal: a genuine and strong affection for a fellow human being. She turned the page over and there was just one other entry.

Friday 13 April

It's a most perfect morning. An exquisite sunrise. Calm, calm waters. The cry of the curlews from the estuary. Not difficult this morning to worship my creator. Psalm 40 in the lectionary, "I waited patiently for the Lord." Sometimes I think I have been waiting all my life. I have waited and waited, yet where is He? Some say they feel Him so close. Jean claims this, and yet such closeness has produced such a fierceness in her faith. If her God is the God we must all serve, then I fear I am lost, for I would run and hide from such a god.

I have been reading Augustine yet again. I've just finished his Confession. I've both loved and been haunted by this writing. Let me quote his famous words here:

Late have I loved Thee, O Beauty so ancient and so new; late have I loved Thee! For behold Thou were within me, and I outside; and I sought Thee outside and in my unloveliness fell upon those lovely

91

things that Thou hast made. Thou were with me and I was not with Thee. I was kept from Thee by those things, yet had they not been in Thee, they would not have been at all. Thou didst call and cry to me and break open my deafness: and Thou didst send forth Thy beams and shine upon me and chase away my blindness: Thou didst breathe fragrance upon me, and I drew in my breath and do now pant for Thee: I tasted Thee, and now hunger and thirst for Thee: Thou didst touch me, and I have burned for Thy peace. [Augustine. Confessions, Book X, Ch. XXVII]

It is so late in my life now. And have I loved Thee? There are things deep in my soul that still keep me from Thee. Thou has sent Thy beams, yet my blindness remains. I do hunger and thirst for Thee, but have not found Thee. Oh where, oh where is the God I have tried to serve all my days? I burn with longing for His celestial peace.

But why should the divine look upon this mortal soul with any pleasure? What have I done to impress Him? He called me to serve as a priest, yet I have worked in a hidden corner of the vineyard. My vines are atrophied and poor and surely at the harvest the grapes will be sour. It will be a daunting thing for me to meet the great Owner of the vineyard. My fear is becoming a dread. It feels like a shroud.

Such self-centred thoughts. Why do I write in this way? I am but a tiny part in it all. My destiny is but a grain of sand on the great seashore of eternity. Father taught me to look beyond myself and I must go back to his lessons again. He taught me to look out beyond my tiny world to see such beautiful lives - so many heroic people that live out their lives so nobly on this earth. How will I ever forget Father's final words to me on that day when he left for War. 'Solomon, my son. Three things remain: faith, hope and charity. But the greatest is charity. Be on the watch for these three things, and you will be well and you will do well.'

I have been on the watch for them. I have watched people, whose faith is genuine yet gentle and they have kindled the poor embers of my fire. I have watched people whose hope is strong and tenacious, who have survived such dreadful darkness, and they have been beacons in my gloom. I have watched people who have loved in ways

92

I never dreamed possible, whose kindness has drawn tears even from these arid eyes. Faith, hope and love. That is what changes the world. These dear creatures may be sorely absent in my own timid and sorry soul. But in the world around me, I see them blazing bright. All my days I have caught sight of them. I may have failed. But so many have succeeded. So blessed be God forever.

As Lisa finished reading this the final entry in his journal, she stroked her fingers over the page. This most unexpected window into the soul of her uncle evoked in her both sorrow and wonder: sorrow at the pain that was so evident in this writing; wonder that he was so articulate about the longings of his own soul. Uncle Solomon had always lived on the margins of her life. A quiet, benign soul, who seemed to her always to be living in a half-lit world. She had to confess that she had always treated him as an elderly old man, who said little because he had little to say. Never had there ever been any reason to intrude into his privacy. But here, she *had* invaded his privacy, and she could not deny that she felt guilty at such an intrusion. Nevertheless, she was pleased to discover this hidden part of him. He had far more to say than she had ever imagined.

She closed the book, but continued to stroke the cover, while she gazed out at the empty drive, and felt the quietness of the house. But within her something that had lain dormant for too long was now becoming unquiet. She could not even begin to identify what that something was, but whatever it was, it caused a release of tears that dropped lightly on the cover of the journal. She was weeping - like a child.

# 11

It was the sound of gulls that stirred Solomon from a deep and contented night's sleep. For a few moments in that half-awake world with his eyes still closed, he 'saw' a modern bedroom that looked very familiar. There were two windows, and by one of them stood a sturdy, leather-topped wooden desk, and by the other a comfortable armchair. Shelves of books lined the walls. He could smell the familiar fragrance of books and clean linen. But then the image of that room faded and, as he opened his eyes, he saw dark hardened mud walls and a loosely fitting door fringed by bright light. He felt a strong disappointment, as the first image had felt so familiar and warm. Where was it, that bedroom? He clung hold of the image of it in his mind as he rose from his bed. He washed using the bowl of cold water that Monnine had placed in his room, and he became aware of his unshaven face. He had never grown a beard as far as he knew, but in this place, he would have no choice. As far as he could see, none of the men shaved. He dressed in his suit trousers, black shirt with no collar, and the thick woollen smock that Monnine had provided, and made his way out into the bright sunlit compound.

'Ah, there you are, Seanchara,' came the familiar and welcome voice of Monnine, who rose from a nearby table, where she had been sitting with a group of children. 'I hope you slept well, did you?' she asked as she approached him.

'Yes, a very pleasant night, thank you, Monnine,' replied Solomon.

'Well, you'll be ready for your breakfast, then,' said Monnine, who clasped his arm and led him to the dining hall, where on the previous evening they had enjoyed a generous supper. 'Samuel has just baked the bread and it's so good when it's just out of the oven,' she said, as she led him into the dining chamber. Several people were sitting at the tables and Solomon couldn't deny that the odour of fresh bread was most inviting. Thus, he sat at the table with several of the community, eating chunks of bread smeared with butter, and drinking a mug of warm milk.

Towards the end of the meal, a young man entered the dining hall and was spotted by Monnine. 'Ah, Jowan,' she called. 'Get yourself over here, will you? I want you to meet Seanchara, our new friend.'

The young man made his way over to Solomon, and somewhat to Solomon's surprise, he kissed him on both cheeks, then said 'Peace be with you, my brother.'

'And with thy spirit,' said Solomon, once again yielding to an ancient memory of set responses.

'Will you be joining us for our worship?' enquired Jowan.

'Jowan's our priest,' said Monnine. 'He'd be mighty pleased if you joined us this morning for our Eucharist.'

Solomon was in a confusion of emotions. He knew something was very familiar about words like priest, worship and Eucharist, but he was still struggling to remember exactly what they meant. But he did know it was something to do with God. He simply sat for a few moments, his piece of bread limp in his hands. He looked beyond Jowan to the door of the dining hall, frowning deeply in his attempt to remember. 'Almighty God...' he started, feeling again for the words that were so deeply established in his soul. 'Almighty God,' he repeated, almost as if he were in a dream, 'unto whom all hearts are open and all desires known, and from whom no secrets are hid.' He turned his face away from the door and looked into the young, dark eyes of Jowan, and said in a tremulous voice, 'Is this the One whom you worship?'

Jowan had been standing through this brief conversation, but he now sat down on the bench next to Solomon and said, 'Yes, Seanchara. This is our God. He invites all hearts to open in His presence.'

'And you are the priest?' said Solomon, looking searchingly at Jowan through the lenses of his spectacles.

'I am your brother,' said Jowan, and folded his hand over Solomon's. 'But I also serve you as a priest. Christ is our friend and calls us to gather with Him for his meal. You will be most welcome. Come when you hear the bell toll.'

'I will be there,' said Solomon. He appreciated the warmth of the welcome, but he also felt a sense of caution. He finished his bread and

95

made his way back to his room. He closed the door and sat on his bed. He leaned forward placing his elbows on his knees. He removed his spectacles and then rested his unshaven face in his hands. He was connecting with an indistinct memory. It was that word, *priest.* Had he, like his father, once been a priest? Was that it? The longer he held that possibility in his mind, the more certain he became that once upon a time, once back in his time, he had been a priest. Didn't he find himself wearing that collar when Monnine found him in the church? But how could he have been a priest? What did he know about God? He was afraid of God. How could he have been of use to Him?

Then, still with his eyes pressing into the palms of his hands, the image of his father reappeared. He saw him sitting at an old, oak desk. He was bent over the leather surface, working away at a script. Solomon saw something so tender and gentle in the man, but he also saw a strength of spirit in the determined and definite way he pressed the pen to the paper. He saw his father looking up at him. He reached out and gathered his son to his lap. Solomon was a child again, sitting on the knee of his father, looking down at the neat, firm writing on the notepad in front of him. The memory came to life.

'What are you writing, father?' asked the child.

'I am telling the people about the Good Shepherd,' said the father.

'But he is not good,' said the boy, rubbing a tear away from his eye.

'Why, my son?' asked the father.

'Because a good shepherd would not call a father away from his son and take him off to war.'

'But he is a good Shepherd, Solomon. He will take care of us all. He will take care of me in the Far East when I serve as a chaplain to the men who will be so tired and wounded and frightened. Those men need a touch of kindness. They need to know of the Good Shepherd's care. So, I must be with them. And this same Shepherd will take care of you and your mother.'

Solomon felt a terrible pain of grief. He now felt so keenly an ancient memory of the desperate five-year old boy burying his face in the black shirt of his father, begging him not to leave. And he felt the sobs in the heaving chest of his father. It was the first and last time that he saw his father shed tears. Then, turning his attention now to God, the voice of that child travelled through the length of the old man's eighty-five years, and said, 'But you didn't take care of him, did you?' He felt a long-buried, grief-fuelled accusation surface from a buried part of himself. Sitting up and pointing to the roof of his room, Solomon snarled, 'He suffered in that jail and you did not care for him. He was shot for simply asking to care for a wounded friend. No, you were *not* a Good Shepherd to him. And you were *never* a Good Shepherd to me. No wonder I've kept my distance all these years.'

He could hardly believe the words that he was hearing pouring so angrily from his lips. He was daring to challenge the Divine. He knew this was not how he normally behaved back in his own time. He knew...Yes, somehow, he knew that he never spoke like that to God. How could he? How dare he? And yet, this *is* what he truly felt. He was aware of a curious mix of shock and relief. But rising up, stronger than either of these, was an acute feeling of mourning. He knew he was not imagining this. He had forgotten who he was or where he had come from. But he did know very well that the father he adored, abandoned his mother and son to go as a chaplain to the British forces fighting in the Far East. That memory was painfully clear.

He buried his eyes in the palms of his hands and sobbed out a grief that had waited many years to be found.

*

Ella was also awoken by the gulls and, like her great uncle in his different world, she also felt initially very disorientated. She was in a dormitory of 6 beds, but she was the only resident in this youth hostel. She swept her long blonde hair from her face and pulled herself up. She reached for her phone then realised she did not have it with her. She got out of bed and opened the curtains. Wisps of cloud were drifting lazily across the morning sky. Not much was happening in the street below her window. She then remembered it was Sunday. She sighed. Uncle Sol would be normally getting ready to go off to church now. She used to go with him when she was a child, but as she entered adolescence, church somehow became increasingly boring and irrelevant. Much as she loved her great uncle, she could not bring herself to join him and endure those unsingable songs, sit in the uncomfortable pews, pray irrelevant prayers and feel lost and alienated by the flood of unintelligible words. The sense of awe that she once felt as a child had slipped from her along with all the innocence of her childhood. It was while she was remembering that sense of awe that she heard the sound of church bells starting up. She looked down the road and spied a church building. 'If he hears those bells, he'll go to the church,' she said out loud. 'Yes. That's where he'll be, for sure,' she said confidently, once again putting her trust in her instincts.

She quickly showered and dressed. She decided against doing much to her hair as she cared little about how others thought of her this morning. She threw on her parka coat, and headed out into the street. She picked up a coffee and croissant from the nearby Costa, and headed to the church. She stood outside for a while, inspecting the various worshippers as they arrived for their Sunday devotions. Some of them looked with disapproval at the somewhat damp-haired and dishevelled young lady standing on the church steps supping a coffee and chewing at a croissant. 'Don't leave any litter on the steps,' called out a smartly-dressed man, and shook his head. 'There's a bin over there. Make sure you use it,' said the woman who accompanied him.

'And God bless you, too,' replied Ella, sticking her tongue out at them as they entered the church.

'If it was up to me, I'd suggest we *all* got ourselves a coffee and pastry before heading in there,' said a voice behind her.

Ella turned around and, to her surprise, she saw that the words came from a nun, who was hurrying up the steps towards her. 'Oh, I'm sorry,' she said, feeling an instant need to apologise in the presence of a religious person.

'Honest to God,' said the nun, as she reached Ella. 'I don't know what gets into some people, do you? Fancy barking at you like that. I don't know.' She was of small stature, bright-faced and spoke with a distinct Welsh accent. 'Sister Maria,' she said, holding out her hand. 'I know, I know,' she continued. '*How do you solve a problem like Maria?* Don't blame me, it was the name I was given when I signed up.'

Ella remembered the song from a musical film that her great uncle loved. 'Are you a problem?' she asked, smiling and drained her coffee cup.

'I rather think I am,' said Maria, with a mischievous frown. 'You going in, by the way?'

'I'm not staying,' said Ella. 'I'm actually looking for an elderly relative who's wandered away from home.'

'Oh, now I'm sorry to hear that,' said Maria. 'You thinking he might be in there?'

'Yeah,' replied Ella. 'He's a priest, so I thought he might be here. I'm just going to take a quick look, if someone doesn't shoo me out first.'

'Tell you what,' said Maria. 'I'm heading in there myself. The new mother superior wants us to get more involved in the local community, and so we all have to go to local churches on Sundays now. I got sent here.' She pursed her lips for a moment as she nodded at the church building, and then turning back to Ella, she enquired, 'What's your name, by the way?'

'Ella,'

'Oh, what a pretty name,' responded Maria. She then drew closer and said in a quieter voice, 'To be truthful with you, Ella, it's no bag of laughs in there. I come each Sunday. I comfort myself with the thought that I will be earning at least seven years off purgatory for every one visit.'

Ella laughed out loud, to which Maria said, 'Oh shush. Don't be telling the Vicar I said that! But listen now, mercifully, the service is not too long. Why don't you sit with me? If you see your relative, you can go sit with him, of course.'

She grasped hold of Ella's arm, and despite the fact that Ella had no desire at all to worship in this church, she was enjoying the company of this nun, so she went with her. After entering the church, they made for the back pew. There were not many worshippers in the church, so it did not take long to ascertain that Uncle Sol was not in the congregation.

'He's not here,' whispered Ella to Maria.

'Sensible man,' whispered Maria in return, causing Ella to giggle. 'Why don't you stay with me for the service, and then we can do some looking together after we get released from here?'

Ella agreed to stay. She found that Maria's company transformed her experience of the church service. Maria's sighs, tuttings, and occasional whispers of 'Oh, for the love of God,' made the service very entertaining. And Maria was right - it was not a long service. When the final hymn was put out of its misery, the Vicar (whom Ella found unbearably pompous) gave the blessing. Maria took hold of Ella's sleeve saying, 'Let's make our escape while we can.'

Both women were the first out of the building, despite the Vicar trying to flag down Maria, for he was always keen to make a good impression on the visiting sister. But today he was thwarted in his attempt by the head flower arranger, who intercepted him and demanded his attention regarding a simmering dispute to do with the rota.

'Thank God,' said Maria, as they made their way down the steps. 'Now, I usually go to the Café in the harbour, if it's all right with you. Sunday is *Love a Nun Day*. Or, at least, that's what I tell Sid the owner when I get there, and it always gets me a free coffee. I'll try and get a free one for us both.'

Sure enough, as they entered the busy café, a voice from behind the counter called out, 'Is that my nun visiting us today?'

'That it is, Sid, my lovely,' replied Maria. 'Is there enough love in your heart for the two of us today?'

'Always there is, Maria,' replied Sid.

'More friendly than church, don't you think?' said Maria, as she guided Ella to a table by the window. 'I'm sorry, love, that we didn't find your relative in the church,' she said, removing her coat and placing it on the back of her seat. 'What relative is he?  And how come he's disappeared?' Ella explained the story to Maria, who listened intently. As Ella was finishing the story, Sid appeared and placed two coffees and two large bacon rolls on the table.

After some banter with Sid, Maria turned to Ella and said, 'Thank you, love, for telling me about your Uncle Solomon. I'm so sorry. It must be such a worry for you.'

'Mm,' said Ella, who had just taken a bite out of her roll. 'It is. But I somehow sense he's safe. You know what I mean?'

Maria nodded for some moments and looked very thoughtful as she clutched her bacon roll. She then said, 'I agree with you there, Ella. I expect he is, too.' She reached for the tomato ketchup.

'Mind you,' said Ella. 'I thought I would really have this strong sense of where he was. But I've got to admit now, I haven't a clue where he might be.' She took a bite of her roll, and with her mouth full, she mumbled, 'You weren't very polite about that church service. I thought nuns were supposed to be all holy and well-behaved.'

'Oh, not when they come from Swansea!' replied Maria, dousing her bacon with a large quantity of ketchup. 'I'm pretty sure that's why they called me *Maria* when I joined the Order. They tried hard to get me to behave like Our Lady, but I'm sorry to say there is very little in me that would commend me to the Mother of Our Lord. But, hey ho. Work in progress, I suppose.' She bit into the roll, releasing a stream of ketchup back on to the plate.

Ella was sipping slowly from her coffee, and said, 'Well, to be honest. If you were all holy and that, I don't suppose I'd be drinking coffee with you now.'

'Oh, that's the nicest things anyone's said to me all week,' said Maria, beaming.

Ella smiled and said, 'It's just... That church service: to be honest with you, I thought it was crap. I mean, why do people go to this stuff? What's the point of it? And the Vicar. Well, he was a long way up his...., if you get my meaning.' Despite the obvious earthy nature of her new friend, she still felt the need to edit her language a little.

Maria laughed out loud, then said, 'Yes, lovely. Yes. I think that's a very good way of putting it! But you know, life's tough for clergy these days, so I'm not going to be too hard on the man. But, for my money, I'd want a priest whose feet are firmly planted on this good earth, but whose heart is set on heaven. But some of them nowadays seem not to like this world very much, and have precious little to say about heaven. I think your man down the road there is a bit like that, and it saddens me. I suppose he got lost somewhere, and I pray he'll find his way home one day. What is your great uncle like?'

Ella put her cup down and looked out of the window for a while. 'I don't know honestly,' she said. 'He's such a private man. Don't know what goes on inside him, really. People in the village like him. Don't think anyone understands his sermons, but that doesn't seem to bother them much.' She turned and looked at Maria. 'If he wasn't so... I don't know. Locked up, I suppose. He doesn't allow anyone in. Not even me. If we were allowed to see inside, I think we'd find something precious.'

'Then he's been hurt somewhere down the line,' said Maria. 'People lock themselves up for a reason, Ella. I've learned to respect that.'

'But then we can't really get to know them, can we?' said Ella, raising one of her neatly trimmed eyebrows.

'I agree,' responded Maria, placing her coffee mug carefully on the table. 'But I've learned that you can't prise open a human soul. But who knows what might be going on inside of him while we're supping our coffee here? You know, I think he may well be on his way to being found.'

'By the police, do you mean?' said Ella, raising both eyebrows.

'No, lovely,' replied Maria. 'No. There's more than one way to be found in this world.' She then looked out of the window, for the sun had broken free from the cloud that had been hiding it. 'Why, look at that beautiful Spring day out there,' she said. 'What say we take a walk together for a little time.'

Ella frowned for a moment. 'I'm supposed to be searching for Uncle Sol. But it's useless isn't it? I'm not going to find him, am I? I just needed an excuse to get out of the house really. I live in Tregovenek. I shall probably start walking home along the coastal path. So, you want to walk with me a bit of the way?'

'I'd love that, Ella,' said Maria, her face creasing once again into a smile. 'My convent is roughly in that direction.' In point of fact it was in the opposite direction, but a sense of direction was not one of Maria's strong points.

'Cool,' said Ella. 'Do you think you should...' She was pointing to a large ketchup stain on the front of Maria's habit.'

Maria looked at it and then back at Ella, and started laughing. 'You can't take me anywhere, Ella!' she said. She then called for Sid, who came over with a damp cloth. It appeared he was used to this particular rescue operation. Once clean, the nun and the girl rose from their seats. Sid refused payment, so they made their way out of the café into the warmth of the April sun.

# 12

As Ella and Maria were leaving Sid's café, Matt was making his way down to the harbour. He had endured the most uncomfortable and restless night in his car, which left him with a stiff neck, sore back and deep weariness. He decided to drive his car back to his office, and after having a wash, he recommenced his search for his daughter. He picked up a coffee at the local Costa, then walked towards the harbour. The truth was, he really had no idea where Ella would be. He felt sure she would be in Porthann somewhere. But where? He walked near the church and could hear the strains of a hymn emanating through the open door. He paused for a few moments. Would Ella have gone into the church? She may possibly have peeked in to check if Uncle Solomon was there. He walked up the steps, but on reaching the door, he thought better of it. No, he knew Ella's views on church. There's no way she would be in there. And besides, Matt had no great fondness for church either, and getting near the door was about as much as he could manage. So he briskly walked back down the steps and headed towards the harbour.

It had been a while since Matt had last visited church. He didn't even go with the family to the Christmas Midnight Mass anymore. Somehow, it all seemed just too hypocritical. And he was not into sentimentalism. All those candles and grossly out-of-date hymns and carols. Yes, there was something quaint about dear old Uncle Solomon wheezing his way through the prayers in his trembling voice. But that world really was not for Matthew Micklefield. He had gone off God a long time ago. It was no great crisis. No terrible experience of suffering that put him off. It was more a dose of Richard Dawkins that did it. After reading him, he realised no reasonable human could believe in God. It was OK for the likes of Uncle Solomon, who lived in his own rarefied atmosphere. But for those like Matt, who had to manage the cut and thrust of a demanding business life, God was utterly irrelevant.

He had reached the steep and narrow alleyway that led down to the harbour, and as he did so, he became very aware of walking from the bright sunshine into the dark and cold shadow of the lane that still held the chill of the night. Walking slowly over the uneven cobbles, he recalled his meeting with the girl he called Angel, but who had let slip that her actual name was Jenny. He had been taken aback by the depth of sympathy that he had felt for this girl. She seemed so vulnerable. He felt a deep sense of shame that men - men just like him - had abused her so deeply.

Yet, despite his admiration for Angel, there was one part of her story that was hard to understand: it was her faith in God. As far as he could make out, God had been no use whatsoever to her in her troubled life. She was in the gutter, and God had done absolutely zilch to get her out of it. So what possible use was God to her? And yet she spoke so lovingly of her cathedral of light and her friend called Beatrice. Matt paused for a few moments as he reached the end of the alleyway. He was standing in the shadows, but just one step away was the bright beam of the April sun beckoning him. It seemed he was the only person in this part of town, for it was so quiet. He looked up between the stony margins of the walls of the old houses to the bright azure above him. Even the gulls had fallen quiet, and all Matt could hear was the sighing of the breeze and the occasional crash of a wave against the nearby harbour wall.

He was thinking about Angel and her words about going into her lantern cathedral. He recalled her words, 'It was massive and there was light and colour coming from everywhere.' He remembered that she said it was like Paradise, and she thought she heard angels singing. How could this girl who had fallen on such hard times honestly countenance the presence of a God in this world? He frowned and shook his head, and turned his face away from the bright sky back into the shadows. Against all the odds, she had faith. And perhaps more than that, she also seemed to have hope. 'Will I ever have hope again?' he said out loud as he leaned against the cold stone of a neighbouring house, and studied the cobbles beneath his feet. Much to his shock, a voice near him said, 'Oh, I would think so, lad.'

He had assumed he was on his own, but as he looked up, he beheld a man nearby that he had often seen in town but never spoken to. He was to Matt the archetypal fisherman: a red, weathered face, fringed with a short-cropped and scruffy grey beard; dark eyes shining out beneath the rim of a faded blue woollen beanie hat; ill-fitting yellow dungarees and a stained, dark blue Aran knit jumper.

'Good morning,' said Matt to him.

'Ah, it is that,' said the man. 'You're Matthew, aren't you? The estate agent?'

'That's right,' said Matt.

'Didn't think you worked on a Sunday?' said the man, tucking his thumbs under the straps of his dungarees, and looking hard at Matt. 'Looks like you have some thinking to do.' He nodded his head towards the sea, and started walking in the direction of the harbour wall. Matt followed the fisherman, who walked with a distinct limp. 'It's the knee,' he called. 'In case you were wondering. Doesn't stop me doing my job, though.' He reached a bench that was set beneath the higher part of the sturdy harbour wall and sat heavily upon it. 'Park yourself here for a few minutes, if you have them to spare. Blokes like you are usually too busy for me to get the chance to talk to you.'

Matt felt a little uneasy, fearing he may be trapped into hearing a lengthy account of the fisherman's woes. But he decided to risk it, and sat down next to the man. They were facing into the harbour.

'I never tire of it,' said the fisherman, gazing upwards. 'Such beauty in an April sky. Look at that.' Matt looked up and some bright cumulus clouds were scurrying across their azure backdrop. 'The name's Theodore by the way,' said the fisherman and held out his calloused hand. 'They all call me Theo.'

Matt tentatively shook the rough yet warm hand, and said, 'And most people call me Matt.'

'Aye, they do,' said Theo. He then pointed to a row of terraced houses just a little way down from the harbour, saying, 'I was born in that cottage there, look. The one with the blue door. Though it was green in my day. And a very pretty green at that.'

'Nice place to live,' said Matt, inspecting the property with the eye of an estate agent and considering its value.

'I can't think of a better house to be born in, can you?' said Theo. 'When I was about six years old, I was sitting at that window that you see there next to the door, and I was looking out at the billowing waves of the sea, and I says to my lovely mother, God rest her, "Mother, does the Spirit of God still move over the face of the waters like it did in the beginning?" Well, she knew exactly what I was asking, because she knew her Bible well, you see.'

Matt continued to look at the house, but now listened to Theo instead of calculating the house's value. Theo inhaled sharply and continued his story. 'She said, "Let's go and have ourselves a look," and she wrapped me up in my little oilskin, and we walked to the harbour wall just there.' He pointed to some steps a few yards down from where they were sitting. 'We climbed up to the top of the wall, up those very steps. My, there was a gale blowing hard from the West, and the heavens were bucketing their rain all over us. My mother locked her arm around me and we must have stood together there for about half of an hour, watching the heaving and stirring of the waters. Wild, it were. I watched the waves leaping and frothing to greet the wind, and the salty spray danced and twirled and rose up high into the stormy sky. Neither of us said a word. I felt quite safe. She was a strong woman, my mother. "So?" she says eventually, looking down at me with the wind blustering her hair all over the place. And I says, "I can see it, Mother. The Spirit of God *is* moving on the face of the waters, just like the Good Book says it does."

'"Well, then," she replied. "Now you have your answer." And she took me back home and we got ourselves dry. I still loves to watch the move of the Spirit on the water to this day, Matt. It's a wonder to behold, it surely is.'

Matt was very unsure how to respond, so rather limply he replied, 'Yes.'

'Nothing wrong with the land, mind,' said Theo, folding his arms and looking back to the sprawling buildings of the town that rose up from the harbour to the fields beyond. 'Nothing wrong with it,' he repeated.

'No,' said Matt, very unsure of where the conversation was leading.

They were quiet for a while, then Theo rose from the bench and said, 'Help me up, will you, Matt?' Matt helped up Theo, who steered him to

107

the steps to the higher part of the harbour wall, where once the young Theo had stood with his mother. They climbed up to the wide and unfenced walkway of the wall. When Matt tentatively peered over the edge, he could see that it was a long drop to the mud below that was slowly receiving the incoming tide. He instinctively stepped back.

'You'll be just fine here,' said Theo, and linked his arm into Matt's. Theo was an old man with a bad knee, but his arm was strong. Matt felt safe in the company of this expert of sea and wind. They stood together in silence for a few minutes, and then Theo said, 'My world.' A variety of sea birds were singing and twittering from the muddy shore beneath them, and gulls squawked overhead. With his free hand, Theo pointed over to the horizon that was shimmering in spring sunlight. 'When did you last really look at the sea, Matt?' he asked.

'Er… Well…' stammered Matt. He had never engaged in such a cryptic conversation, and he really did not know how to answer this man's questions. 'We live in Tregovenek, just up there.' Matt nodded to the west. 'And we are fortunate, for our house overlooks the sea.'

'Ah,' said Theo, shaking his head. 'That'll be part of the problem.'

'Sorry?' said Matt, frowning.

'That'll be your problem, Matt,' repeated Theo. 'Folks buy houses near the sea so they can enjoy the view. "Isn't it beautiful?" they cry, and then hurry off to their work. "Look at this beautiful sunrise," they say, or "My, it's stormy today. Look at those waves."

'Yeah. That's just what we say,' confessed Matt. 'We love it.'

'Hm,' said Theo. He was frowning. 'The sea's not for admiring,' he said. 'You have to become friends with it. It's a bit like breaking in a horse, I should think. Or so Freddo tells me up at the stables. You have to get near the sea - and on it - to get to know her character. Her moods and that. You have to know what delights her and what disappoints her. Mind you, it's taken me a lifetime, and there are days when I think we are only just getting acquainted. She's got a stubborn streak, she has. Fancy a coffee?'

Matt was once again taken aback by the sudden change of direction in the conversation, but agreed. He helped Theo down from the wall and they made their way to a van in the small car park that was selling hot drinks. When they reached it, Theo called out, 'Morning to you, Sarah, my love.'

A large and beaming lady appeared, drying her hands on a cloth and said, 'Good morning to you, young Theo.' She looked at Matt and said, 'And to you, sir.' She cocked her head to one side, and said, 'You're the estate agent bloke, aren't you?'

Matt nodded, and for some reason felt guilty at being recognised as such.

'Two coffees,' said Theo.

'Milk and sugar?' said Sarah, reaching for the pot of filter coffee and looking at Matt.

'Just black, please,' replied Matt, still pondering on the fact that these two locals seemed to know him so well. But just what exactly was his reputation among the likes of Theo and Sarah?

They took their coffees, and Theo led Matt to a rough wood picnic table, where they settled.

'You in trouble, Matt?' enquired Theo, after he had taken a sip from his drink. 'Don't mean to be nosy. But I see it in men, I do. Can't help it. And on occasions, I can be of help. All I know comes from the ocean, really, but she teaches me much, she does.' He raised his eyebrows and looked at Matt.

'Yes,' said Matt, surprising himself with his honesty. 'Yes, I am in trouble, Theo,' he continued. 'Business is bad.'

Theo hardly raised his mug from the table, and stooped to slurp from it, then said, 'They don't like you, Matt. When you developed the fisher cottages two year back, well, them's that bought them never live in them. God knows where they are, but we don't see hide nor hair of them, except for a week or two perhaps in the summer. They not even gone in for that Airbnb outfit. Least that ways we get to see some folks. It's not right, you see, Matt. Not right for our towns and villages.'

Matt was very familiar with this complaint from the locals. He had met it with most of his developments which, it was true, were almost all second homes. He had his set answer, which he knew sounded like a politician's response. And he knew that with Theo, such an answer would not work. Again, to his surprise, and against his normal, reliable instinct, he heard himself say, 'I'm sorry, Theo. I have no excuse.'

Theo nodded his head, then said, 'Heard you're trying to develop the old McHenry farmhouse on Crescent Hill up there. Making it into posh apartments, they say. More holiday lets, I suppose?'

Matt was going to answer about tourism being good for the local economy, but again he knew this would cut no ice with the old fisherman. He shocked himself again with his response. 'And this is my downfall, Theo. That farmhouse is going to make me bankrupt. It's my comeuppance. I shall get my just desert, and you'll all be pleased.'

'Oh, dear God, no, Matt,' said the old man, raising his sparse eyebrows. 'I don't want your downfall, lad. Oh, no, no. I don't like to see any man downfalling, I don't. But my guess is you got greedy, and we're all prone to that one.'

Matt had been expecting a stern rebuke and a whole load of 'I told you so.' He was very taken aback by Theo's sympathetic response. He looked into the aquamarine eyes of the seafarer, and said, 'Thank you, Theo. I don't deserve that.' He looked down and played with his coffee mug for a while, then said, 'And my marriage is in trouble. And my daughter's run off.'

Theo chuckled for a few moments, saying, 'Oh my, Matt. You don't have your troubles to seek, do you, lad!' His chuckle revealed his clear lack of dental care, but it was nonetheless a very endearing smile. He then quickly looked serious, sniffed hard and said, 'Where's she gone, then, this daughter of yours?'

'It's a long story,' replied Matt. 'To be honest, I think I lost her a long time ago. I've been too busy with my work and too... Well, the thing is, we have my wife's uncle living with us. He's a priest, and he's gone missing too.'

'Ah, that's the old pastor, who disappeared from the church at Tregovenek, is it?' said Theo.

'Word gets around quickly in these parts, doesn't it?' responded Matt.

'Word like that does,' replied Theo. 'Don't often get news of a missing priest around here. And I hear there was blood on the floor.'

'Yes, apparently,' replied Matt. 'So, Ella, my daughter: she went out searching for him. But we don't know where she is.'

Theo paused for a few moments. 'The girl must love him?'

'I suppose she does,' said Matt. 'But maybe she was just looking for an excuse to get away from home for a while.'

Theo was quiet again and closed his eyes. Matt noticed that his eyes were moving under his thin and wrinkled eyelids. With his eyes still closed, Theo then said, 'The Reverend.'

'Yes?'

'He's safe.'

'How do you know?' said Matt, sitting up straight. 'You've seen him?'

'Well, depends what you mean by "see",' said Theo, opening his eyes and looking at Matt.

'Sorry?'

'There's more than one way of seeing, Matt.'

'Is there?'

'Course there is,' said Theo, and drained his coffee. 'The old Father is safe. More safe than you realise. Now, I have a suggestion.'

'A suggestion?' said Matt, who was feeling constantly outmanoeuvred in this conversation.

'A suggestion,' repeated Theo. 'Would you come out with me on the water? In my old boat. It's quite safe, and it's not rough today. Might help you to see. God's Spirit gets busy on that water.'

Matthew was frowning. He had come to this town to look for his daughter, but so far, he had chatted to a sex worker, spent the night in his car, talked to a quirky old fisherman, but he had not done a great deal of searching for Ella. Could he honestly waste a couple of hours bobbing on the ocean with Theo?'

'She'll be on her way home soon, if that's what you're wondering,' said Theo.

'So, you can "see" her too, can you?' said Matt, hearing the cynicism in his own voice.

'No, Matt,' replied the fisherman. 'But I have had many a conversation with young folks down here. I've got to know what goes on in their souls. Times are tough for our young ones. We need to hear them out more than we do. I reckon I've listened to the likes of your Ella before now. And I reckon she'll be home soon. Don't you fret. So, you coming aboard?'

'Yes, all right,' said Matt, once again surprising himself.

Theo heard the deep weariness in his voice. 'It's a beautiful morning,' he said, as he took hold of Matt's elbow, and steered him towards a jetty at the end of which were tethered several dinghies. They clambered aboard one of them, and chugged out to an aged fishing vessel that was facing out to sea, welcoming the incoming tide.

# 13

As Theo and Matt were making their way out to sea, fifteen hundred years earlier, Solomon was staring out at the same ocean. He had left his room feeling very tender following his vivid recollections of his father. He was going to the chapel for the worship, but paused as he caught sight of the sea. The sun appeared from behind a cloud, and its beams danced brightly on the surface of the glittering water. The beauty of the scene soothed Solomon. He looked down at the simple huts on the water's edge that marked a harbour. These huts were not familiar, but so much about the shape of this coast felt *very* familiar. He knew now for certain that he was from this part of the world and inhabited this region in his native century. But still so much was missing from his story. He knew now about his father, less about his mother. He sensed he had been a priest. There were random snippets of a familiar world that broke into his consciousness. Such snippets of memory simply added to his sense of disorientation. If only he could work out *who* he was. Not knowing his name felt profoundly disturbing. Seanchara was fine, but it was not the name he knew himself by.

And then there was God. He was living in a time that was not his, but among a people who served and worshipped Christ, and he had no doubts that in his normal world, he too worshipped Christ. He knew worship happened in that great stone building where Monnine first found him. Yes, he was sure, he had led worship in such a place as that. But he couldn't remember seeing a gathering of people in that great building. He could remember parts of it. It seemed to him as a large monument of stone, impressive in its own way, and certainly beautiful. It had coloured glass in the windows. He frowned as he tried to remember. Yes, they were pictures made of glass. Pictures of people. But despite the coloured glass and the impressive nature of the building, he could not feel its soul. Or could he? His eyes were fixed on the gently undulating surface of the sea, but his inner eye was on that building. And for a moment or two, this building seemed to him to be a person, and it was a person lost and grieving. 'Ah, you poor dear thing,' he said out loud. 'You were built for so much more. Now look at you. And none of it is your fault.'

'You joining us then, Seanchara?' Monnine's voice shocked Solomon out of his thoughts, and for a few moments he simply looked at Monnine, blinking.

'Sorry,' he said, his countenance lifting. 'It's the brilliance of the light on the water.'

'It is indeed bright today,' she said, and took his arm. Together they walked up to the building, which was no more than a simple, wooden barn. Inside the barn there was a scattering of wooden benches, most of them occupied. Towards the front were gathered a group of children, and in front of them was a table furnished with a cross, a loaf of bread and a flagon of wine and some mugs. A group of people holding lyres came to the front and started strumming a tune. A young woman joined them and she started singing. Solomon listened to the words as best he could, for he could not catch all of them. He could hear that it was a song to do with the gentle Christ, who came to this world, shattering the powers of darkness through his triumphant death on the cross, and conquering the dark of hatred with the brilliance of his love.

He was fascinated by the spirit of the singer. He was mesmerised by her. She seemed to be almost enacting the scenes about which she was singing. She raised her arms high in the air, reaching to the heavens. Then she lowered them, and they hung limply by her side, as her head swayed back and forth apparently in grief. She grasped herself in a tight embrace and then appeared to be cradling a child. All the while her face depicted the drama of her words, and this included tears and laughter. Solomon was sure he had never witnessed such a thing, and knew for certain that a song like this had never been sung in that great building where he was found.

A man who seemed to be as old as Solomon then rose from one of the benches and he began to recite a story from the Bible. 'That's Corman,' whispered Monnine. 'He's our hermit. Rarely visits, he does. It is good that he is here today.'

This hermit was small in stature, with a bald head and fulsome beard. His filmy eyes were the colour of wood smoke, and appeared to work independently of each other. In his husky voice he recited the story from the gospel of John, of Christ meeting with his friends on the seashore in the days following his mighty resurrection from the dead. 'At daybreak,' he said, having memorised the story many decades ago, 'Jesus stood on the beach, but the disciples did not know it was Him...' Solomon listened to a story that he soon realised he knew well. But he felt he was listening in a way that he had not listened before. It was something about this simple chapel; something about the way Corman was reciting it; something about the crack that was breaking open in his soul, letting in a fresh, new air; there was something that was enabling him to hear a familiar story as if for the first time. Christ was appearing on the seashore, but his friends did not recognise him. Solomon sensed in some curious yet comforting way, Christ was appearing to him now, in this very building. But He was appearing in such a way as made him realise that he had never really known Him. He hardly recognised this Jesus. He was so different.

Corman, took a few paces forward, and then, looking straight at Solomon with one of his milky eyes, leaving the other eye fixed to the heavens, he continued the story: 'And Christ said to his bewildered friends, "Children, you have no fish," They answered him, "No". Solomon was looking at the hermit and listening intently. He was being drawn into the story. He was there - in the boat on the surface of a sea that was flickering and sparkling in the early morning sunlight. Like the disciples of old, he too was feeling lost and helpless. He was an old priest, wearily hauling in an empty net, feeling fruitless and so full of failings. With his broken memory, he could not say what those failings were, but he was in no doubt that whatever ministry had been entrusted to him in his normal world, this empty net was a true picture of its sad desolation.

Corman was still looking at Solomon with one eye, and smiled as he repeated the word, 'Children!' With that one word, Solomon was plucked from his gloom. Yes, he had been a child, and the memory of his childhood trauma was as a shard in his soul. Yes, the resentment towards the God who had failed to be a good shepherd was a shadow over him. But here, with these words from Corman, God and child were meeting afresh on a seashore in morning light, with a fragrance of resurrection swirling around them. Solomon felt shard and shadow

115

slipping away as Corman continued his story. 'Then Christ said to them, "Cast your net to the other side, and you will find some fish." Solomon felt the child within him rise up in the boat, and with great delight, hurl the net to the other side of the boat. He felt the strength in his young arms. He felt the tug of the fish. He felt the gripping of the net. There was still life in this sea to be found, and no matter how empty his net had been, here was a burning hope that it could yet haul in a miraculous catch.

Solomon's eyes were closed as Corman related the rest of the story. Far from feeling lost in his thoughts, Solomon felt found in them. But such contemplation was brought to an end, when he heard the young priest, Jowan, say 'We come together to His table now to share in his feast.' Everyone stood and looked towards the table, and Jowan told the story of the Last Supper, and in the brittle memory in Solomon's mind, he recalled that he too used to tell this story at a table. As Jowan spoke, he took the loaf of bread and lifted it high, and as he did so a shaft of sunlight fell on the table. Jowan then took the large pottery goblet that was filled with wine, and he also lifted this high above his head. And Solomon noticed that as he did so, for a time, the face of the priest crumpled in grief, before he cried out, 'Christ is our victor!' and the people gathered in that chapel began to sing a song that felt to Solomon to be expressing both desperate grief and effusive joy.

The people then made their way to the table, and Jowan gave them pieces of the freshly blessed bread, and they supped from the cup of sacred wine. Yes, this rite, Solomon did indeed remember. And yes, he remembered that it had always been so important to him, so precious, so meaningful. But here in this little chapel, the rite had all of those, plus an extra quality. The only name Solomon could find for it was *warmth.* Something thawed within him, as he savoured the strong flavours of baked wheat and fermented grape. As he returned to his bench, he felt the life of the child again: the child within; the child tugging at the net of squirming fish; the child being healed of old wounds; the child at last finding his freedom. As he settled back on his bench, he lifted his closed and dampened eyes to heaven and whispered, '...that we may perfectly love thee, and worthily magnify thy holy name.' Anyone from his own time would have been astonished to see the old

116

priest, sitting on his bench, with his frail arms raised to the rafters like the enduring branches of a wintered tree welcoming the Spring.

*

Ella paused for a few moments on her walk with Sister Maria up the coastal path, and observed a small fishing boat chugging out to sea. As she watched it, she remembered a story that her great uncle had read to her long ago about some children and a mouse sailing across a magical sea that sparkled like this ocean did in the April sunlight. It was sailing towards Paradise, and something about the beauty of the ocean today made her more aware of Paradise than she had done for a long time. 'Look,' she said to Maria, pointing to the boat. 'Do you think there's a mouse in there sailing to the end of the world?'

Maria smiled. 'Ah, *The Voyage of the Dawn Treader*,' she said, a little out of breath from the walking.

'That's the one,' said Ella, delighted to be reminded of the title of a book she had loved.

Maria was catching her breath and shielded her eyes from the sun as she surveyed the scene, and said, 'Well, I suppose those fishermen are just about their normal business, but I do agree with you, Ella. Just at this minute, it looks to me like they are sailing on a silver sea to the boundaries of heaven.' She brought her hand down and said, 'Now, look you, there's a nice spot just down there for us to settle for a few minutes for a little rest and a chat. Then I will need to head back to my convent.'

'Good plan,' said Ella, who was much enjoying the company of her new friend.

As they settled themselves on the grass, Maria pulled off her blue veil, revealing her head of short blonde hair. 'Time to have a break from this blessed thing,' she said.

'Beautiful hair,' said Ella. 'Do you have to wear it?'

'Well, what do you think, Ella?' replied Maria, neatening her ruffled hair. 'If I wore my hair free like this, just think of how all the men in Porthann would be driven mad with desire!'

Both women laughed, then Ella said, 'Back there in the café, you said that there was more than one way to be found in this world. What did you mean?'

'Ah, well,' said Maria, as she folded up her veil. She turned and looked at the girl and said, 'Tell me, Ella. How do you feel? Lost or found?'

Ella squinted in the sunshine and brushed her fair hair from her face. The rings on her fingers caught the sunlight which momentarily dazzled Maria. 'I'm not sure,' she said. 'I feel lost at home, if I'm honest. Mum and Dad... Well, most of my friends seem to have parents who are separated or divorced. I suppose I'm lucky that mine are still together, but I expect once I've left home, they'll separate. In fact, when Dad finds out about Mum, it could happen sooner.'

Maria frowned, and said, 'O love, I'm sorry. Is she... seeing someone?'

Ella nodded and said nothing for a few moments. 'I mean, Dad's no saint, so I don't altogether blame her. He got very messed up with cocaine some time back, and I don't think he's really recovered. He gets very stressed about work and takes it out on Mum and me.' She shrugged her shoulders. 'Expect he'll pick up the habit again before too long.' She pulled at some blades of grass for a moment, then continued, 'Mum's a counsellor actually. She probably needs more counselling than anyone.' She looked up at Maria and smiled. '"Physician, heal thyself." Isn't that in the bible somewhere?' Maria nodded.

'I dunno,' continued Ella, looking back out to sea. 'We were all happy once, a long time ago. Dad said I became a stroppy teenager, and I suppose I did. Mum blamed her moods on the menopause, and kept getting angry with me. Now she's busy bonking some bloke she's met, but it doesn't seem to be making her any happier.' She looked back at Maria. 'We have become the worst versions of ourselves. Why does that happen in a family?'

Maria shrugged her shoulders for a moment, then took her turn picking at the grass. 'My father left home when I was six, and I never saw him again. If my mother's view of him is to be believed then he is Satan incarnate!' She chuckled briefly. 'My mother was a depressive. And my lovely brother.... Well, we lost him.'

Ella furrowed her brow and said, 'Lost him?'

Maria's eyes welled up for a few moments. She sniffed hard, then brushed the skirt of her nun's habit for a few moments. 'Took his life, he did. Poor boy had awful problems. But I loved him more than I have loved any other soul on this earth. He's in heaven now, and I know he's at peace.'

'But you're not at peace,' said Ella.

'Oh, Ella!' said Maria, sniffing again and smiling. 'You're going to be a counsellor like your mother, aren't you?'

'No way!' said Ella. Both women laughed for a time. 'But how come you have faith after all that shitty stuff. Oops, sorry.'

'Oh, don't worry about language,' reassured Maria. 'I learned every swear word there was in my home. In English and Welsh.' She paused for a few moments. 'Swear words are much better in Welsh, actually. You get much more feeling in them. They do the job better, I'd say.'

'So, do you swear in the convent, then?' asked Ella, raising her eyebrows.

'Only in Welsh,' said Maria. 'No-one understands Welsh in the convent!' Both women laughed again. This was the most down-to-earth Christian that Ella had ever met, and she was intrigued. 'And you are correct, Ella,' said Maria. 'I'm not quite at peace about his passing. But that's all right. It's OK to grieve isn't it? And I can grieve about what I've lost on earth, and at the same time rejoice at what my brother gained in Paradise. There's always hope, Ella. And I still believe in God despite the tragedy. I know it turns some people off. But you see, God's my friend. I was grieving so hard, I needed my friends. I needed His love and care, you see. I couldn't turn against Him. Oh, no. And He was my friend, Ella. *Such* a friend at that time.' She reached over and cupped Ella's hand for a few moments, then said, 'And tell me about your uncle'

119

'Great uncle, actually,' said Ella. 'He's the brother of my mum's fanatical born-again mother. But Uncle Sol's not fanatical. At least, I don't think he is. Certainly not in the way Gran is. He's lovely. He's the quietest man you'll ever meet. Lived in our home all my life and hardly said anything during those years.'

'Well, admirable in some respects,' said Maria. 'That would not have been my problem, I can assure you!'

'I think I mentioned he's a priest,' Ella continued. 'His dad was also a priest, and he was the priest of our village many, many years ago. Uncle Sol's been retired for years now. Almost twenty years, I think. He's really old. He's been looking after the church in the village because the actual Vicar has hundreds of churches to look after. Or something like that. I don't know how it works. Anyway, Uncle Sol does the service there every Sunday and goes and says his prayers in the church most days. Seems to enjoy himself there.'

'But it's not your thing,' said Maria.

'Definitely not my thing,' said Ella. 'Much as I love Uncle Sol. I wish I could enjoy it, because I'd like to be there with him actually. But the people there are... Well, let's just say they're not my type. And I'm not into sitting for an hour in a cold building getting a sore bum and being bored out of my mind. Not my thing.'

'What is your thing?' asked Maria.

Ella shrugged her shoulders and replied, 'Dunno. Doing my A levels this summer. Everyone says I'll get A's and should try for one of the grand Universities - you know, Cambridge and Oxford. But that doesn't really do it for me. I'm going to take a year or two out and decide.'

'And what will you do in that year or two?'

Ella looked out to the ocean again, frowning in the sunlight. She smiled through her frown and, throwing her arms in the air, she said, 'Find a ship and sail away!' She looked at Maria and laughed her engaging laugh. 'What do you think I should do?'

Maria paused and said, 'I was about to say something corny.'

'Corny?'

'Oh, you know,' explained Maria, looking a little flustered. 'I was going to say something about finding yourself. But then that sounds banal, doesn't it?'

'Yeah,' agreed Ella.

'Oh, thank you!' said Maria, and smiled a downturned smile.

'Sorry!' said Ella. Both women were quiet for a time. Ella lay back on the grass, and let the warm Spring sun soothe her. 'I had a bit of a moment yesterday.'

'A moment?' enquired Maria.

Ella's eyes were closed as she spoke. 'Dunno, really. I was on the path near here, sitting in the sun like now. And I felt this kinda thing happening in me. Can't really explain it. But I suppose I was sort of aware of God in a way. You know...' She opened her eyes and looked at Maria. 'I'm not a Christian, but I did feel something yesterday. And if it was God, well... Yeah. I suppose He or She did feel like a friend. Like you said.' She closed her eyes again and laid her head back on the grass.

Maria said nothing, but leaned back on her elbows. She was enjoying the fresh air ruffling her veil-free hair, and looked up to the sky. Then she started humming and, after a while, she put words to her tune.

Dyma gariad fel y moroedd,
Tosturiaethau fel y lli:
Twysog Bywyd pur yn marw -
Marw i brynu'n bywyd ni.
Pwy all beidio â chofio amdano?
Pwy all beidio â thraethu'i glod?
Dyma gariad nad â'n angof
Tra fo nefoedd wen yn bod.

Ella had no idea what it was that Maria was singing about, but something about it caused her eyes to moisten. She was aware of strong feelings - something to do with homesickness. When Maria had finished, Ella pulled herself up. She wiped her eyes, and said, 'I don't know that song. It was beautiful. You've got a fab voice.'

'Oh, I'm no Julie Andrews, am I?' said Maria, sitting back up. 'But God made me Welsh and I love singing, I do.'

'Yes, but what was the song? What's it about?'

'It's one my mother used to sing to us when we were little, and it's still one of my favourites. The English sing it to the words, *Here is love, vast as the ocean, lovingkindness as a flood.* Not bad, but the Welsh is much better, of course.'

Ella was sitting up, pulling her knees to herself. She was looking at the little boat that was now far off, making its way down the coast. She then lifted her eyes to the horizon and said, 'The ocean is so vast isn't it? Is there really a love that big?' She frowned as she looked at Maria.

Maria adjusted her position on the grass again and looked at Ella. 'No-one can tell you about the love of God, Ella. You have to find it for yourself. Where did you learn to swim?'

'To swim?' said Ella, taken aback by the question. 'Ok. I learned to swim as a kid. Dad took me down to the sea. But I'd just splash and fool around at first. It was a long time before I really learned to swim.'

'I thought so,' said Maria. 'But then one day you did swim?'

'Yeah, I did. Bit scary, but I did. Dad was with me. I was soon out of my depth, but he'd taught me breaststroke and I soon got the hang of it. Loved it after that.'

'What did you love about it?'

'Being in something so wild and huge. That sense of being held by it. Knowing you were at the edge of something so massive. Feeling the power of the waves. Bit of danger. You know. All that kind of stuff.'

'I know just what you mean,' said Maria, her eyes glinting in the sunlight. 'And I think it's a bit the same with the love of God. You can keep it at a distance, or you can dare get closer to it. And then you start to feel its power and mystery. You realise it is massive, and yet it welcomes you, and holds you. And you splash around and have fun. You feel refreshed by it and invigorated.'

'Yeah, OK,' said Ella. 'But you're a nun, and that's the kind of way you think. It's not how me and my friends work. Love - yeah. But God loving us? I'm not sure. But nice that it works for you.'

122

Maria leaned her head to one side and, looking at Ella, said, 'When I was singing that old Welsh hymn, something touched you didn't it? And it wasn't the quality of my singing, that's for sure.'

Ella chuckled and said. 'You sing great. But yeah, there was something cool about the song.'

'Well,' responded Maria. 'That might just be your toe in the water. But look you, time's moving on, and I should be on my way. They'll all be wondering where I've got to.' She brushed some grass off her habit, then stood up. Ella also stood. 'So where are you going now, Ella? You going home?' she asked, as she attempted to gather her windswept hair into her veil.

'Not sure,' said Ella. 'Here, let me,' she said, as she assisted the nun with her headgear. 'I'm only a mile or two away from home,' she added, securing the veil. 'But I still want to find him - my Uncle Sol.' She put her hand to her forehead and looked around at the gorse-covered hillside. 'Where the hell is he? Would God help me to find him, do you think?'

'Oh, for sure,' said Maria brightly. Then she stepped toward Ella and hugged her tight. 'You're a sweetheart, Ella,' she said, and added as she released her. 'You've made my day.'

'Well, you did say it was *Love a nun day*,' said Ella.

'You've given me more love than you know,' said Maria, making an unsuccessful attempt to straighten her veil. 'I do hope you find your Uncle Sol very soon.'

'Cheers,' said Ella. 'See you around, I hope. Do you know your way back to the convent from here?'

'No,' said Maria, and started her infectious chuckle again. 'But I think it's in this direction. Let's see.' And with that she stomped off back along the coastal path giving Ella a final wave before she disappeared.

Ella decided to remain on the hillside for a time. She had felt considerably cheered up by her time with Maria. She even felt happy, and she wanted to dwell in that happiness for a time. So, she lay down on the warm grass again, and it was not long before she fell into a deep and sun-blessed sleep, her mind suffused with the memory of Maria's

Welsh voice singing to her of a love that was as vast as the glittering blue ocean that stretched before her to a misty horizon.

# 14

Solomon was standing in the area that one day would serve as the small harbour of Tregovenek. After the church service, which included a lunch of fresh bread, honey and beer, he made his way out of the church building intending to have a lie down in his room. However, he found his elbow grasped by Corman, the hermit who had spoken during the church service. And this hermit was now persuading Solomon to take a ride with him in his very insecure looking coracle.

'I built this when the hair was still fresh grown on my chin,' said the husky voice. 'But she's been a faithful craft, and she's taken me over many a rough wave in her time. Brought me across the ocean from Eire.' Despite his look of frailty, he was strong enough to drag the small boat across the sand. Solomon was attempting to help him, though he was still feeling weak from his fall in the church, and was not able to be of much assistance. Corman paused as they drew near the water. He stood up and Solomon guessed he was not much more than five feet tall. His hairless and tanned head shone in the April sun. His gaunt and deeply creased face looked like it was made of leather, and his lips were pale and chapped. The face would have looked almost lifeless had it not been for the animated wood smoke eyes. His left eye seemed to be permanently fixed to heaven, while his right eye surveyed the world around him. There was a whole vocabulary of expressions in these eyes, and if the old man should ever lose his speech, Solomon was convinced that he would communicate quite effectively just with those eyes.

Solomon clambered aboard, and Corman used his paddle expertly, steering the boat over the gentle waves and out to the deeper waters. For some time, the old hermit paddled them over the relatively calm waters, saying nothing. Solomon couldn't even be sure if he had ever been in a boat before, but his initial sense of high insecurity gradually calmed and he found himself clinging less desperately to the sides of the boat.

'I may have been a young'un when I worked the wood and hide of this boat,' said Corman, as he lifted his paddle out of the water and stowed it in the coracle. 'But I built it strong, don't you think?' He smiled a virtually toothless smile.

'Indeed,' said Solomon.

For a few moments, Corman was caught in a seizure of coughing which ended with him spitting a large lump of mucous into the sea. 'I'm better off without that,' he said, wiping his mouth on his sleeve.

'Are you not well?' enquired Solomon with a frown of concern.

'I follow the Christ of the untamed seas,' replied Corman, and apparently that was the answer to Solomon's question. The old hermit leaned forward and, grasping Solomon's hand, said, 'He made us all strong, He did.' The strength of the grip surprised Solomon. Keeping hold of Solomon's hand, Corman adjusted his position on his seat, causing the boat to rock alarmingly for a few moments. He moved closer to Solomon and with his good eye, he examined the elderly face as if he were examining some precious specimen. The other eye remained fixed on the sky. Solomon felt awkward and preferred to look at the rippling water rather than the probing eye.

'So,' said Corman after a few moments, leaning back on his seat. 'You are visiting from another age.' A faint odour of garlic accompanied his words.

'You can tell by my clothes, I expect,' said Solomon, tapping his suit trousers.

'Your soul,' answered Corman. 'You come from the time when humankind has achieved so much, yet destroyed so much.' He dipped his hand in the water, and circled it around for a few moments. 'The waters are so pure and free in our time. You must be pleased to be here.'

Solomon was getting used to being in a fixed state of perplexity, and the latest experience of this was being in the company of one who seemed to have some knowledge of Solomon's time. 'I am pleased,' he answered, with some uncertainty. 'If I may... Do you know much about my time?'

'Time?' said Corman. Both eyes looked up for some moments and scanned the skies. 'Adam and Eve knew time,' he said, then lowered his head. He pulled at his beard for a few moments. 'They walked with God at the time of the evening breeze. Now, that's what I call time!' He grinned again, displaying his one good front tooth. Solomon noticed that his eyes were watery.

'I was with a disciple of Patrick once,' he continued, sitting up straight and grasping both sides of the coracle. ' We were far inland in the folds of his desert place. It was at the time of year when the days are long and the dark of night is a shy thing. We had been fasting all day, and were about to share some bread in the glow of the evening sun. We then heard Him walking. Divine footsteps for sure. No mistaking such a thing. You could see the grass yearning up to him. The trees stopped their swaying and their branches leaned towards him. The larks rose as one in the air and sang more beautifully than an angel choir. Butterflies danced all around us. Oh, we knew He was there, all right. There's no mistaking a Presence like that. I swear the truth of it. You'd think the beat of our hearts would be stilled by the fear of it. But no, our hearts recognised Him, and they leaped like the lambs in Beltane. That was time, my friend. That was time.'

The water was lapping gently against the boat, and the tide was nudging it towards the shore. 'But your time,' said the hermit, as he grasped the paddle and placed it in the water. 'I only saw it the once.'

Solomon, who was both moved and perplexed by the hermit's previous comments, said, 'So, you have visited my time?'

'Aye. It was when I was back in Eire and living in my hollow,' said the hermit, as he worked the paddle into the water. 'I awoke before sunrise. It was before the blackbird started her song. It was a cold morning and I felt the frost under my feet. I left my hollow to empty my bowels, and then washed in the chill stream. When done, I put back my cloak and walked back. But I had scarce taken two steps, when I saw I had trespassed into another world. It was a world I knew not.'

He paused his paddling for a moment and said, 'Once, by a mighty act of grace, I visited Paradise. But I knew this was not Paradise that I had stepped into. Oh, no. Far from it!' He started paddling again, with much deliberation. 'This world was different. It did not have the light of Paradise. I knew not where I was, and I confess I was filled with fear. The world I had walked into was nothing like my own, and yet there was something of mine about it.' Again, he paused the paddling and wiped his nose with his sleeve. He looked at Solomon with his free eye and said, 'God help me, Seanchara, I was so soaked with fear, that if I had not already emptied these bowels of mine before, I'd sure have emptied them there and then.'

The old hermit drew in his lips and sucked at them for a few moments, then looked at Solomon. 'I saw things I had no name for,' he said. The tide was moving them back to shore, so he started to paddle the boat back out to sea again. He drew his rough, bearded chin forward for a few moments, then said, 'It was early morning. I found myself near a track. Not like the tracks of our world. No, this was a blackened, hard track. Not even the old Roman roads looked like this. Then I heard a roaring, and I turned and saw a great wheeled cart, heavy and forged from iron. It was heading down this track towards me. No horse was pulling it. It moved on its own, and it moved so fast - faster than the speed of a fleeing deer. I had to cover my ears for the roar it made. As it passed me, I saw humans trapped inside of it. It took them down the track and out of sight, and then the world was quiet again. Then I heard another roaring. A more distant roaring and it came from above me. I looked up, and there was a winged creature in the sky, flying higher than any eagle would dare to fly. It streaked a thin trail of white cloud across the blue. My soul was heavy with dread. "Spare me, O Lord!" I cried. I was certain I had entered the portals of hell itself. But then He sent me a good angel to hold my hand. He took me away from that dreadful track into a quieter pathway. Such strength did that angel give me. This blessed creature then explained to me that I had stepped into a time that was centuries ahead of mine. And that is how I saw your world.'

'But... But how do you know it was *my* world?' asked Solomon, shifting his position a little as both his seat and the subject matter were distinctly uncomfortable.

'I knew it was your world, because I saw you,' said Corman, now paddling hard out to sea.

'Saw *me*?' said Solomon, pulling back his head in astonishment.

128

'Even though my poor eyes appear to argue with one another, they are not as dim as they appear,' said the hermit. 'That good angel, he steered me along that quiet lane. There were banks of grass either side. As the sun shone its kindly rays upon us, we came to some houses made of stone. Such grand things they were. And then I saw people. Some of the men had no beards, and some of the women had cut their hair short. They wore strange garments.'

'Did they see you?' asked Solomon.

'No, most didn't,' replied Corman. 'But a few of the young children did. They were the ones who had the eyes to see. But you didn't see me. You did not have the eyes.'

'Where did you see me?' asked Solomon. His mouth hung open.

'There was a mighty building. Grey stones climbed up high, with a square tower at one end. There were tall windows, with glass set in them. I'd heard stories of grand castles of high walls of stone, and turrets and towers. So, I guessed I was now laying my eyes on one of these, and thought the people of this village must have feared an enemy and built this great thing to defend themselves.'

As Corman described the building, Solomon saw it clearly in his mind's eye. 'That's my church!' he said. 'You saw my church.'

'Your *church*, you say?' said Corman, raising his eyebrows. 'That is a church? But why would you build a house of God like a castle? A church is a home. It is the house of God where all are welcomed. The church is a place of wonder. Powerful, yes. But tender power. A church is the place you step into and you become royalty. And the royal of the land step inside, and they become a friend to all. The princess kneels next to the beggar as they sup from the wine that is life for all. That's the church I know. But the building I saw in your time - why, only the princess could step in there, surely? But if you say it is a church, Seanchara, I'll believe you, for we are friends.'

Solomon felt strangely guilty. But he was keen to move on, so he asked, 'And that's where you saw me?'

'Aye, I did. I tell no lie. You stepped from the door of the castle - or church, if that's what it was - and walked on a pathway through a field of small standing stones to a gateway. Some of those standing stones had been shaped like our Saviour's cross. I felt better to see those signs of my Saviour. And then you walked on to a large building that I guessed was your home. I called out to you as you passed me, but you did not hear. "He is not awake," said the angel. I could then see that your soul was sleeping as deeply as the wintered hedgehog in its nest. Yes, I saw winter in your soul, my friend, and I yearned for you to feel even a day of Spring sunshine. It seemed to me then that you had slept for a great long time. I said to my angel friend, "That soul fell asleep as a child and he's not roused himself since." That's what I said, Seanchara. That's what happens in our hermit lives, you see. We can't help but see things when we've dwelt for many years in our lonely and hallowed places with Christ.'

Solomon felt shaken by this extraordinary account, but he could not deny the truth of it. He sensed that his soul had endured a long winter. Both men sat silent for a long time as the gulls circled above them, and the seawater lapped their boat. Solomon was staring out at the horizon, his mind trying to make sense of what he was experiencing, but without success. Then, the nagging question emerged again. He turned to look at the old hermit, and asked, 'And did you discover my name?'

'No,' said Corman, and Solomon's head dropped. Corman then added, 'People are known by their names. But they think once they have a name, they are known. But no. You are only known when you let yourself be known by the Heart who created you. Only then does your name have any meaning.'

'I still long to know my name,' said Solomon. His head remained lowered.

Corman placed his calloused hand over Solomon's, and closed his eyes, inhaling a deep breath. Then his husky voice seemed to be transformed into a beautiful baritone of which any choir would have been proud. Keeping his eyes closed, he sang,

'O my Lord in heaven, Thou hast searched for me and Thou dost know me

Thou knowest my downsitting and mine uprising.

From far off, thou knowest the thoughts of the chambers of my heart.

130

Before the word reaches my tongue, Thou knowest it.
Thou art behind me. Thou art before me.
Thy gentle hand rests on me.
Whither shall I flee from thy Spirit?
If I climb up to heaven, Thou art there.
If I descend to the dark hollows of hell and make my bed there
Even there I shall find Thee.
The great dark is not dark to Thee.
The night is as bright as the day.
I will praise Thee, for I am fearfully and wonderfully fashioned.
What wonders thou hast performed.
My soul knoweth this. It knoweth this right well.'

*

Not far away, Monnine was standing on the headland with Jowan, and they were both watching the little coracle on the waters of the sea that held the two elderly men, who were sitting silent and still. 'What think you, priest?' said Monnine.

'Corman will help him to find his tears,' said Jowan.

'Aye,' said Monnine. 'God sent Corman to us today, that's for sure. He's pulled tears from my eyes often enough.'

'And mine too,' said Jowan.

'He's taking him to his isle,' said Monnine, as she watched the boat bobbing its way towards a small island not far from the coast. She then looked beyond the island and studied a strip of cloud that was ambling across the thin clear line of the horizon. She studied it for a long time, then said, 'I still miss it.'

'I know you do,' said Jowan, and he placed an arm around her shoulder. 'Maybe one day He will call you back to your beloved Eire.'

'Maybe,' said Monnine. 'But it is no bad thing to long for home.'

'No,' said Jowan. 'Such longings keep our hearts tender.'

The two friends stayed a while longer, watching the coracle make its unhurried way over the shimmering water towards the verdant island.

131

# 15

Lisa was determined not to get inebriated prior to her parents' arrival for lunch, but she needed support from somewhere, for she was battling with a complex of disturbances. The first, very refreshing glass of Chardonnay seemed to be sharpening her mind. She was sitting at the kitchen table playing with the now empty, yet still cool, glass. The reading of her uncle's journal had troubled her. It was not a bad troubling, for she had discovered beautiful things about this quiet man, who had been living among them for the past nineteen years. But this discovery of the life locked up within him had had the effect of disturbing something that had long been locked up within her. It was not something she could give words to, but she knew it was to do with the core of her true self. This thing wanted recognition. It was the child at the windowpane. The child that wept while she sat in Solomon's study.

This unexpected awakening was triggering another disturbance, and that was to do with this dangerous dalliance with Troy. Overnight she had developed a clear conviction that she did not need this man. It was not so much that she felt guilty about this secret relationship - well, yes, she *did* feel guilty. Especially after the conversation with Ella. But it was not guilt that was causing her to decide to end the relationship. It was much more to do with a determination to listen to whatever this was within her that was now calling for her attention. This new thing coming alive in her was having the effect of somehow reorienting her, and she was starting to see things from a different angle. And from where she stood now, the whole business with Troy had most certainly lost its charm. It was more a strong conviction that if she were to pursue this relationship, she would miss an opportunity that was presenting itself to come alive in a way that she had never known and for which she had possibly always longed.

Quite how she would ever explain this to Troy and bring about an end of the relationship was certainly a challenge. But there were other challenges to face just at the moment, the main one being the thought of her mother's imminent arrival. And it was this challenge that caused her to refill the glass and use the wine's calming ministrations to help her complete the final preparations for her honey mustard chicken bake and her version of an Eton mess. It was therefore a relaxed, if a little lightheaded Lisa, who opened the front door to welcome her parents on this bright Sunday morning.

'Usual, Dad?' she said, as he entered the kitchen following his wife.

'I never say no, Lilly,' said her father, using the nickname that he had long ago adopted.

'Make it a small one,' commanded Jean, as she settled herself noisily at the kitchen table.

Lisa poured a large glass of cider and handed it to her father. 'Orange, Mum?'

'That'll do nicely,' said Jean. Lisa's mother was of medium height and, though she strove to make her appearance tidy, it always seemed that her clothes worked against her rather than for her. Her hair was mostly grey now. It was always marshalled back with various grips, yet it clearly had a mind of its own, and it erred and strayed frequently, much to the annoyance of its owner. Her complexion was ruddy, and her demeanour was one of defiance against all the obstacles that a sinful world had put in her way.

Ted, by contrast, was the kind of man nobody would ever think of arguing with. His face was weather-beaten and cheerful. In his time, he would have been regarded as handsome by many, though being self-effacing by nature, he was never one to receive compliments. Few knew much about his hair as his cloth cap was seldom off his head. He always wore a country check shirt at least one size too big for him, and, much to the annoyance of Jean, his trousers were often held up by bailing twine. He had worked on the same farm all his life, and there was nothing he did not know about sheep and cattle. He was mostly retired now, but he still enjoyed regular visits to the farm to help out when needed.

'Dinner will be ready in ten minutes,' said Lisa.

'Thanks, lovey,' said Ted, grasping the glass of cider with his strong hands. 'Can't wait.'

Lisa took a sip of her wine, looked at her mother, and said, 'Well, Mum. How did you get on with the spirit of unbelief? Can we rest easy in our beds now?'

'I won't have you mocking us, Lisa,' retorted her mother. 'Tell her, Ted. Tell her to respect her mother.'

Ted chuckled and replied, 'I gave up trying that one a long time ago, Jeannie.'

Jean looked disapproving at her husband, and took a sip of her orange, and said to Lisa, 'Greg did a wonderful prayer, if you want to know. Got us all standing up and binding the spirit, he did. But he said that you had to be willing to release it, otherwise it would keep its grip. Do you want to do that now, while we are with you?'

Lisa was draining the vegetables at the sink. She paused, raised her eyebrows and, glaring at her mother said, 'What do you think, Mum? Is that honestly likely?'

Jean sighed. 'I don't know where we went wrong with you, Lisa, I really don't. We brought you up in the faith, and I don't know why you have gone and backslidden like you have.'

'Mum, let's not do this,' appealed Lisa. 'There are more important things to be thinking about today.'

Jean reluctantly let go of the spirit of unbelief problem. 'Yes, Lisa, I know,' she said, softening. 'We're all worried about Solomon. It's so unlike him to do something like this.'

'Well,' said Ted. 'To be fair, I don't suppose the poor old bloke had much choice about what happened to him.'

'Well he should be careful about going out after dark,' countered Jean.

'It wasn't really dark,' corrected Lisa, as she placed a bowl of steaming veg on the table.

'The world's a wicked place, Lisa. And we have to be careful. And that brother of mine is not properly born again, so he doesn't have the protection he should.'

Lisa sighed and said, 'Let's eat now.' She fetched the chicken from the Aga, set it on the table, and served generous helpings to her parents.

Ted always enjoyed his daughter's cooking, which he felt had a vitality about it that was lacking in his wife's. He took a mouthful and, looking at Lisa, said, 'Beautiful, Lilly.'

'Thanks, Dad,' said Lisa, smiling at her gentle father.

'Yes,' said her mother. 'Quite nice. A little over seasoned for my liking. But thank you all the same.'

Lisa glanced at her mother following her version of a compliment. Whether it was the upset of recent events, or maybe the influence of the wine, but for one reason or another, Lisa saw her mother differently. She felt an unusual sense of compassion for her. She reached over and, grasping her mother's forearm, she said, 'I'm so sorry, Mum.'

Jean paused her eating and sat up straight, frowning. 'Sorry?' she said. 'Sorry for what? You don't need to be sorry. The chicken's fine. Just a little too much salt, that's all.'

'No, Mum,' responded Lisa, still holding her arm. 'Not the food. I'm sorry I've been such a disappointment to you.'

Jean's frown deepened. She was focussed on releasing a tenacious piece of chicken from its bone. Glancing briefly at her daughter, she said, 'Whatever do you mean, Lisa?'

'I've been such a disappointment to you with my faith,' replied Lisa. 'Or with my lack of it. I can see how sad you are about it. I really didn't want to make life harder for you.' She looked over to her father, who had paused his eating. 'Or you, Dad. I'm just sorry that I haven't been the kind of Christian you'd have liked me to have been.'

Jean was very taken aback and troubled by this sudden apology. Her daughter was usually belligerent in discussions of this sort, not conciliatory, and certainly not apologetic. 'There's no need to apologise,' she said, stuttering a little. 'I mean it's your choice, of course. It's just...'

'No, Mum,' protested Lisa. 'Don't spoil it. I know you'd like to now think of ways of getting me on to the right path again. But I won't ever be in your way of thinking. It really doesn't suit me. So really please, please don't try and change me. But I'm just saying to you, I'm really sorry I can't be different, and... And a better daughter for you.'

Ted had downed most of his large glass of cider, and was starting to feel the emotion of the conversation. 'Lilly, my love,' he said, reaching out and grasping the shoulder of his daughter. 'Don't you worry yourself about this faith thing. You could never, ever be a disappointment to me. Dear God, you mean everything to me, you do.'

Before Lisa could respond, Jean blurted out, 'And me,' then returned to do battle with the chicken leg. 'Excellent lunch,' she said with her mouth full. 'Must give me the recipe.'

Lisa looked over to her father and smiled warmly, and he smiled back and winked. He then looked more serious as he said, 'We're all worried about Solomon. It's making us all a bit emotional, isn't it?'

'Yes,' agreed Lisa. But as she looked across and saw the kindness in her father's eyes, she was taken by surprise by sudden thoughts about Troy, and realised just how shattering it would be if her father ever got to know about this threatened affair. Now a sense of guilt *did* hit her hard, and she lowered her eyes to her plate.

'So, no more news, I take it,' said Jean, helping herself to more vegetables.

'No,' said Lisa, returning her attention to the matter at hand. 'The Inspector came last night and will probably call in again today. She seemed to think that Uncle Sol fell, got concussed, and has wandered off somewhere.'

'Mm,' said her mother. 'Ted and I think that's the most likely. But it still worries you, though, doesn't it? I mean, he could be lying in a field somewhere. Or...' She paused for a few moments, and then Lisa observed something she had very rarely witnessed in life. Her mother's lip started to tremble, and for a few moments she allowed rare tears to fill her eyes. She quickly rebuked herself. 'Forgive me,' she said, reaching for her handbag and searching for a tissue. 'Don't know what came over

136

me.' She sighed a deep sigh, and pulled her spectacles from her face, and wiped her eyes with her tissue. 'Makes you realise that you care for someone when something like this happens, doesn't it?'

This was the first time either Ted or Lisa had ever witnessed any sign of affection in Jean for her brother. 'So, Mum,' said Lisa, 'Were you and Uncle Solomon close at one time?'

'Ah, well there's a story,' said her mother, returning her handbag to the floor. She paused for a few moments, and then looked up briefly at Lisa and said, 'No, dear. No, we were never really very close. You know the story. How Solomon's father went off to war and never came back. Well that was shattering for both him and his mother, of course. Must have been terrible grief for him. Well, Mum remarried eventually and they had me, and I guess Solomon must have felt a bit pushed out, really. He was ten years older than me, you see, and by the time I was a little kiddy, well, we never saw much of him. He was kindly to me when he was around, but I got the impression that my father didn't care for him much. And Mum never showed him much affection. That can't have been easy for him.'

'So, you never really knew him?'

'No, I dare say I didn't really. I mean, I was very close to Mum and Dad, but he wasn't. As you know, Mum had to move out of the Rectory when Solomon's father died, and she moved to Pedrogwen, where she met Dad. But Solomon would cycle back here to Tregovenek, and I heard from folks later that he used to stand outside the Rectory and spend hours just gazing at the place. And he'd spend long hours in the church too. Either in the church or at the grave. I don't think he ever really got over the death of his father. I did feel a bit sorry for him, I must say.' She scraped the last of the gravy from her plate, and sighed for a few moments, then added, 'Course, our faith was different, and that didn't help. Mum and Dad didn't go to his father's church. Too close to home, I guess, for Mum and Solomon. So, they started going to the new church in Porthann. *Living Light Church*, it was called in them days. They met the Lord there in a wonderful way and were born again. Mum then said she'd never been a proper Christian before, which I believe. But this upset Solomon. I suppose it was disrespectful to his father. Well, I

137

reckon that sent Solomon all high church. In reaction, I suppose. Shame, cos you can't get born again with all that high church mumbo jumbo.'

'Well,' interjected Ted, as he spooned another potato on to his plate. 'We don't know that, love. I think the dear man loves the Lord, I do. He just has a different way of talking about it, that's all.'

'Hm,' responded Jean, unimpressed. 'Well, the point is, he and I were very different. That's the story, Lisa. We chose different paths. And the truth be told, we never really got to understand each other. But blood is thicker, as they say. And when all's said and done, he is my half-brother, and now that he's gone missing, I… Well, you know…' Jean felt the emotion rising again and, for fear of provoking more tears, she said. 'You must give me that recipe, Lisa.'

None of what her mother told her was news to Lisa, but now that she had opened a window on to her uncle's soul through reading his journal, the story carried much more feeling for her. How she wanted him here now, at this table, where she could reach out an arm and hold him. She felt quite acutely the grief and hurt that had been locked in him for so long.

She busied herself for a few moments clearing the first course and bringing in the sweet, and as she placed the bowls on the table, Ted nudged his glass towards Lisa. She took it away and refilled it. As she gave it to her father, he asked, 'Any news from Matt or Ella?'

'Yes, I was wanting to ask that,' said Jean, frowning at Ted who was taking a sip from the refilled glass.

But before Lisa could answer her parents, the doorbell rang. She went to the door, and Ted and Jean heard some animated conversation in the hall. Lisa then returned to the kitchen, and with bright eyes said, 'It's Inspector Littlegown. They've found Uncle Solomon! They're bringing him in now!'

# 16

Jean rose from her chair at the announcement that Solomon had been found. Inspector Littlegown entered the kitchen triumphantly, and stood by the window, with her arms folded over her ample chest, and her chin in its usual prominent position. Lisa introduced her to her parents.

'My Sergeant is just getting him out of the car and will bring him in a jiffy. Just to warn you,' she said in a lowered voice. 'The gentleman's in a bit of dishevelled state. He seems quite well, but I think he may have taken some comfort from the bottle, if you get my meaning.'

'From the bottle?' cried Jean. 'My brother's never been one for drinking!'

'Well, please bear in mind, madam,' explained the Inspector, 'The gentleman has had a very nasty blow to the head, and that can affect behaviour. And I must tell you he is very confused. So please be patient with him.'

'Where did you find him?' asked Lisa.

'Truro, madam.'

'Truro?' cried Lisa. 'How ever did he get there?'

'By bus, I should think,' replied the Inspector. 'Right,' she drawled. 'I think my Sergeant is bringing him in now.' She called through to the hall, 'This way please, Sergeant Wickham.'

Lisa and her parents heard the sound of the front door closing followed by the sound of the metal-tipped footsteps of Sergeant Wickham, and the rather more shuffling footsteps of his companion. The Sergeant appeared in the doorway, and ushered into the kitchen a tall elderly, unshaven man, bald headed save for tufts of tousled hair over his ears, and the clear mark of a recent blood-stained cut on the side of his head. He was wearing torn jeans, a black shirt and a very old tweed blazer, and it was evident from the odour that accompanied him that he had not washed for some time. Open-mouthed, he surveyed the company in the kitchen with a vacant and bewildered look.

'I am pleased to return to you, the Reverend Solomon Ogilvy' proclaimed the Inspector triumphantly. She folded her arms and looked at Lisa.

Lisa and Jean simply stood for a few moments unable to speak. Eventually it was Jean who spoke, saying, 'Inspector, I don't know who that gentleman is, but I can assure you that he is *not* my brother.'

Inspector Littlegown's arms fell gradually from her chest, and she leaned her ear towards Jean, saying 'I beg your pardon?'

Before Jean could respond, Lisa said tersely, 'That creature there is not my uncle!'

'Right...' started the Inspector.

'No, it's not right,' said Lisa. 'What did you think you were doing, dragging this... this wretch over here? And how could you possibly think he was my uncle?'

'With respect, madam,' said Inspector Littlegown, frowning sternly at Lisa. 'You provided no photograph. I have been asking for one and am still waiting for one. So we could only go by your verbal description. And this man does match your description and, as you can see, he has had a blow to his head. And when I asked him if he was the Reverend Ogilvy, he replied very clearly that he most certainly was.' The man in question nodded at this point and smiled a limp smile.

'Well I'm replying very firmly, that he is *not* the Reverend Ogilvy,' protested Lisa. "And he is nothing like the description I gave you!'

Sergeant Wickham shuffled forward and, bowing deferentially towards the Inspector, he said, 'Ma'am, would it be prudent to return this gentleman to the vehicle now?'

The Inspector nodded rapidly to her sergeant, saying, 'Indeed. Straight away. And, Sergeant - make sure the car windows are open - wide.' Sergeant Wickham took the arm of the blinking gentleman, who bowed to the assembled company several times before withdrawing. 'I'm very sorry,' said the Inspector, raising her chin defiantly. 'These things happen.'

'Well they *shouldn't* happen,' declared Jean.

'If you'll excuse me,' said the Inspector, stalling any further protests. 'I'll leave you now and get on with the search for Reverend Ogilvy. We mustn't waste any more time.' Then looking at Lisa, she said, 'And may I please insist, Mrs Micklefield, that you email a photograph of the gentleman to me right away. And by that, I mean without any delay. This will ensure this kind of mistake won't happen again.' She turned, but before she left through the door, she said, 'By the way, has the girl turned up?'

'No,' said Lisa. 'No, she hasn't. But please don't be dragging a drunken, half-witted and foul-smelling seventeen-year old here later, claiming it's her. My husband's out doing the searching, and I think it's best if we leave it to him.'

'Very well,' said the Inspector, and she marched down the corridor and left the house, banging hard the front door behind her.

Ted, who was still seated and had remained quiet throughout these proceedings, emptied his glass, burped, and said, 'Easy mistake to make.' Lisa and her mother looked at one another with raised eyebrows, making no comment.

*

'That's our house,' called Matt, above the roar of the boat's engine. Theo slowed the motor to idle and peered inland. Matt was standing at the side of the boat, pointing to the headland, saying, 'Follow that line of gorse up, and you come to the edge of the village. Do you see that tall yew tree, and the grey stone-built house next to it? That's ours.' The driveway of the house was hidden by trees and shrubs. Had Matt been able to see it, he would have seen a police car rapidly exiting.

'That's a big house, Matt,' said Theo. 'Must have cost you a packet, that must.'

141

'It did,' said Matt.

'Beautiful, though,' said Theo, studying it hard. 'So, now you're in the view you say you look at every day. The whole world looks different when you're on the sea, don't you think?'

Matt was enjoying the gentle bobbing up and down of the boat on the water. He studied the land for a while. He could see the grey tower of the church rising above the trees, and various other houses peeking out from the April green trees and shrubs of the village. He then spent some moments observing his home. He felt a strong affection for it.

Theo stopped the engine and Matt became aware of the simple and delightful melody of lapping water and birdsong. Theo entered his small cabin for a few moments and returned with a pipe and a tobacco pouch. He sat at the stern of the boat and worked at clearing the old tobacco from the pipe. 'You from these parts originally, Matt?' he asked, as he banged the pipe hard on the side of the boat to clear it of debris.

'From St. Austell,' answered Matt, lowering himself to sit on the side of the boat. 'Lisa and I met at Bristol Uni. We moved here after we got married.' He waved his hand in the direction of Tregovenek and added, 'This part of the world feels very much like home now. Lived in that house for over twenty years. God, it does look beautiful from here.'

'It *is* beautiful, Matt,' said Theo, but his attention was now focussed on his pipe, as he rammed shreds of dark tobacco into it with his weathered thumb. 'This is a fine latakia,' he said, sniffing at the tobacco. 'It's been warming me for many years. Only one pipe a day for me, but it's enough to put a gleam in my spirit.'

Both men were quiet for a time. Once Theo had restocked his pipe, he worked on igniting it with the help of several matches. Soon the smell of the briny sea was accompanied by the fragrance of latakia. 'This coast's a wonder, Matt,' he said, gazing towards the shore. 'Look at the birds. I see many ravens in the trees around your house there. The gulls, fulmars, gannets and guillemots all make their homes around here. They're like friends to me. Help me find the fish. They get me all I need to keep me going.'

'How long have you been fishing, Theo?' asked Matt, still keeping his eyes on the headland.

'Over fifty year, I'd say,' answered Theo, after sucking hard on his pipe, an action that released clouds of blue that drifted towards the land. 'Once my mother knew I loved the sea, she let me go.'

'You made a living by fishing from this little boat?' asked Matt.

'Enough,' said Theo. 'Only ever used this one boat, and she's served me well. I've never gone without. Not even in the bad winters.' He used his pipe to point to the sky as he added, 'Him up there looks after us, Matt. Gives us all we need.'

Matt turned and looked at this fisherman in his much-repaired dungarees and oil-stained Aran jumper, and said, 'You didn't make a lot of money, though, did you?'

'Enough, Matt. Enough is all you need,' said the old fisherman, closing his eyes as he savoured the tobacco.

Matt looked down at the salted wood of the boat floor for some time. His feet toyed with the ropes. 'What *is* enough, Theo?' he asked.

'Ah,' said Theo, removing the pipe from his mouth, and pointing the damp and much-chewed end of it to Matt. 'I thought you might be getting round to asking that. I've looked at you, Matt. I seen you walking fast to your office. I seen you all dressed up in that smart suit of yours getting into your posh car. I seen you taking people from the cities off to look at our houses. I seen the look on your face, and it doesn't make me happy, Matt. I looks at you, and I says to myself, "There's a man who never got the sway of what's enough." What is it in a man, that he always wants to grasp more of things, when what he's got is enough to give him happiness?'

Matt smiled a weak smile. 'You know me well, Theo. Didn't know I was being watched.'

'Not watched, Matt. I'd say *loved.*'

'Loved?' said Matt, frowning and turning down his mouth.

'Not like that, Matt!' said Theo. He smiled and rubbed his nose with his sleeve. 'No, long ago I lost my suspicion of my fellow humans. We're

143

all on this planet together for such a short time. Why waste the precious time we've been given hurting each other? Why waste the time hurting *ourselves* for that matter? No, there's more to be gained in life by loving than there is by hating, that's for sure. So I learned to look *into* people rather than *at* them, if you get my meaning.'

Matt was still frowning. 'I'm not sure I do,' he said. 'Sounds a bit nosey, if I'm honest. A bit intrusive.'

'That it is, Matt. That it is,' said Theo, who was now reigniting his pipe.

'Well, I don't like people intruding into my life,' protested Matt.

'Don't you?' said Theo, exhaling large clouds of blue smoke. 'Ah well, please yourself. It all depends on what you do with what you see. I see inside your soul and I take it to the Great Friend up there.' He nodded to the sky.

'You take it to God?' said Matt, holding a frown that was more to do with disapproval than curiosity.

'I do,' said Theo. 'That's where it belongs.'

'So, let me get this right,' said Matt. 'You peer inside my soul. Think you've got the measure of me, and then take it to God. What does God do with it then? I imagine he's pretty horrified. To be fair, I'd rather you left it alone and kept it well away from God.'

'Don't you like what's in your heart, Matt?' asked Theo, leaning his head to one side.

Matt thought he was in the company of a fisherman, yet he was now feeling more in the company of a psychiatrist. 'What's your point, Theo? What are you getting at?'

Theo shook his head, 'I'm sorry, Matt. I've always said it as it is, and it gets me into trouble. Look, I'll keep my mouth shut for the rest of the journey. I just… I dunno. I just like what I see in you, I suppose. If you want my opinion, there is something really dear in that heart of yours, but there's another bit of you that's been obsessed with making money and impressing people and all that stuff, and that's the bit you show to all of us. But by doing that we miss the dear bit of you. That's all. But I'll keep this old mouth shut now. Let's just enjoy the view.'

Theo sucked hard at his pipe, and with teary eyes, stared at the breaking waves on the seashore. Matt felt tantalised. He did not like this kind of conversation, and yet he couldn't deny that Theo had summed him up very accurately. He had lived his life these past twenty years or more by desperately trying to make money and become impressive. And now that brittle edifice was about to come tumbling down.

The April sun was warm on Matt's back, and it shone brightly on his homeland lying a short distance across the sea ahead of him. 'I so don't want to lose it,' he said, not particularly to Theo, but simply because it needed saying.

Theo's pipe had gone out, and he placed it carefully on some ropes on the floor. He walked over to Matt and sat beside him, rocking the boat precariously. Then for a few moments, he put an arm around his shoulder and said nothing. Matt could smell the mix of fish, tobacco and diesel that was seeped into the fisherman's clothes. The strength of the old man's arm felt wonderfully reassuring. 'Matt,' said Theo. 'Never be without hope. There's always a way.'

'Is there?' said Matt, who was now feeling a vulnerability he had seldom known.

'There is,' said the gentle voice of the fisherman.

A larger boat passed not far from them, and Theo turned and waved to the occupants of the boat, who seemed to be friends of his. For a time, Theo's boat bobbed and bounced on the wash from the passing boat, and then the waters stilled again.

'I met a girl last night, Theo,' said Matt, now looking up at the sky, squinting his eyes in the brightness. 'She's a prostitute. Don't worry,' he said, glancing briefly at Theo. 'I didn't get up to anything. But we talked for ages. She told me about her life. Poor soul, she's been to hell and back. And still on the game and can't get off it. And drugs. And yet I saw something in her that was far stronger than anything that's ever been in me.'

'Did she give you her name?'

145

'She didn't mean to, but it slipped out. She's called Jenny.'

'Ah, I know the lass. She also told me her name when we got talking a year back now. Sweet girl, she is. It's sad, Matt, isn't it? Dreadful sad. But I know what you mean about that strength. I seen it in her too, and it brought tears to my tired old eyes, it surely did. She has a fine spirit. In another world, she'd have been a queen, sat on a throne of pearl.'

'She would,' said Matt. 'She would.' And for reasons he could not comprehend, he started to sob like a child. 'Sorry, sorry,' he kept saying, as waves of stress and grief poured from him. His weeping was accompanied by the cries of gulls and guillemots, the cool breeze of the Atlantic, and the gentle thud of the rippling waters of the incoming tide against the side of the boat. Theo remained still beside him, every now and again placing a firm hand on Matt's back, patiently waiting for this discharge of emotion to run its course. And eventually it did. Matt's sobbing stuttered to a close, the birds above swooped away from the boat to the land, and the breeze dropped and the world was stilled.

'If I get through all this bloody mess I've got myself in,' he said eventually. 'I will live differently, Theo.'

'I know, lad. I know,' said Theo. He inhaled through his nose slowly and gazed out to the sun-bathed coastline. After a while, he said, 'See what I mean about the Spirit of God on the face of the waters? It gets working on you out here. There are some words my mother used to speak to me. I don't rightly know where they are from, but they say, "He sees into the oceans and the human heart, and He knows the secrets of both." That's why we are here, Matt. The oceans and the human heart. They have a lot in common. And the Great Friend knows the secrets of them both. He loves being where the secrets are. That's where He feels at home. That's what my mother told me, and I see no reason to doubt her. Anyhow, time we were on our way.'

On the journey back both men were quiet except when they passed a small island that was mostly rocky, but topped with a scattering of shrubs and trees. 'Not really noticed that island before,' cried Matt to Theo above the roar of the engine.

'No,' replied Theo. 'You'd only see the edge of it from your house. But the fishermen around here know it well.'

'Does it have a name?'

'It does,' said Theo, slowing the engine for a moment. 'It's called Corrie Island. They say it got its name from an old soul called Corman, who was one of the holy saints of God who chose to live his life out there. Got no reason to doubt that, Matt.'

'Can't have been much fun in rough weather, though,' said Matt chuckling.

'I expect that's when they loved it the most,' said Theo, and increased the speed of the boat as they headed for the harbour over the face of the sea that glittered excitedly under the brightness of the noonday sun.

# 17

Fifteen centuries before Matt was being taken out to sea in Theo's boat, Solomon found himself in a coracle, travelling towards the very same island that Theo and Matt had passed. Corman was steering them towards the island's small sandy beach. Both men had been quiet for some time, but the Irish tones of the old hermit's voice still resonated in Solomon's mind. Corman had sung the psalm that Solomon had known well. *Lord, thou hast searched for me, and thou dost know me.* He was feeling searched for. There was this sense that someone valued him so much, that they were searching high and low for him. Solomon was aware that so much of him had been hidden from sight - even from his own sight. But now he felt that something divine had caught sight of the inner workings of his soul. The thought of a divine glimpse into his soul might have been enough to freeze him into a new dormancy. But no. Far from it. Through the companionship of this strange hermit, Solomon was feeling quite the opposite. The God whom Corman worshipped was not a God who was probing the hearts of humans for faults. The gaze of this God was not wintering his soul, but thawing it into something that felt much more like springtime.

For some reason, Solomon felt less anxious to recapture his name now. He would settle for being known as Seanchara for the time being. In this centuries-old world that he was visiting, in which he had felt profoundly displaced, he was coming to a comforting sense that even if *he* did not know who he was, there was One who did. He was known by the One from whom no secrets were hidden. He was known by the One who had access to all the chambers of his soul.

'What is this island?' asked Solomon, as he clambered awkwardly out of the boat on to the seaweed-draped shore.

Corman grasped the coracle and pulled it up above the high tide mark, then said, 'This is where I stand and talk to my friends, the guillemots. Dressed in their black coats and crimson boots, they launch themselves from the cliffs to come and see old Corman.' He beckoned Solomon to follow him on a well-trodden path that snaked its way through a coppice. Sunlight flickered through the brilliant green of the emerging hazel leaves. He walked in front of Solomon, but continued to speak. 'There was one dear bird that would feed from my hand. I had known her since she was a chick. Her mother was dead, so she chose me for her nurse, despite my sins. She left her homeland of the crags, and she dwelt with me here on my island.' He stopped walking and turned to Solomon, saying, 'All through the cold of a sharp winter she stayed here. At the coming of the dark she would come and settle her downy self on my lap. We would admire the beauty of the shining stars together. In Lent I entered the water every day for my purging and my prayer, and she joined me. She would nuzzle her downy head against my bare chest and lift her beak to the skies. And there we praised and sang together. I swear, that bird had more Holy Ghost in her than even blessed Anthony himself. And that godly Spirit spun out from her, so it did. I was on fire in those waters. His angels have many forms, Seanchara.'

Corman closed his eyes and nodded as he recalled the memory. Then he opened them brightly again and said 'Come.' He turned and walked on at a brisk pace. Though the two men were of a similar age, Solomon recognised that Corman was much the fitter, and it was hard keeping up with him. He was grateful for his stick, not least because he could use it to beat back the nettles and brambles that intruded onto the rough track. The uphill path emerged from the hazel coppice to a small grass-covered clearing. To one side of the clearing was a simple hut, and to the other there grazed a cow. Corman led Solomon towards the hut.

'Is this your home?' asked a breathless Solomon.

'I had travelled the world,' said Corman, as he arrived at the hut. 'Then He told me to stop the travelling and start my adventuring here in this my desert home. Wait here.' He opened the creaking door of his hut and entered its dark confines. He returned with a couple of simple wooden stools and directed Solomon to seat himself on one of them. He then fetched from his hut some mugs, a flagon of milk and a loaf of bread. And so the two men sat together in the warm April sun, refreshing themselves with Corman's simple fare.

'I like your island,' said Solomon, as he chewed a bit of tasty, if a little stale, bread.

'I'll need to free her from her milk soon,' said Corman, glancing towards the cow. 'She provides for me so well, that she does.' He then turned and, with his left eye, as ever, fastened on the heavens, he fixed his right eye on Solomon. 'Tell me what you remember of yourself, my friend,' he said, and bit off a chunk of bread.

Solomon placed his mug carefully on the ground, and held his bread with both hands. 'I fear I remember very little...' he started.

Corman interrupted by saying, 'It is time to stop the fearing, Seanchara.'

Solomon looked at the kindly and weathered face of the old hermit and said, 'I think I have been afraid all my life. Of course, I don't know. There is so little of it I remember.'

'Tell me what it is that you recall today.'

'I know that my father was a priest,' said Solomon. He closed his eyes and turned his face to the warm rays of the sun. 'I think he was a very, very good man. And I loved him. And I think he loved me.'

'What became of him?' enquired Corman, his mouth full of bread.

'He left us,' said Solomon, and for a few moments his lip quivered. He opened his eyes, and looking at Corman, he said, 'In my former world, I don't believe I ever wept. These tears...' He touched his eyes, and inspected the moisture on his fingertips. 'Where have they been?'

'Tears are a treasure for sharing, not for keeping,' said Corman. 'Many a time has this island received the waters from my eyes. It knows how to hold them. Your tears are safe here, Seanchara.' He was quiet for a few moments. His tanned and wrinkled hand was gripping his mug of milk. He drank from the mug, then looked at Solomon and, raising his wispy eyebrows, he said, 'I once felt the tears of Christ.'

Solomon looked stunned for a few moments. 'The tears of Christ? How did you feel them?' he enquired.

'I made pilgrimage to the city of Jerusalem,' said Corman. 'I was not yet forty years on this earth, and I had the strength in my limbs. So, I walked the long pilgrim journey to the holy city of David. My, that is a city to see, it surely is.' He shook his head, his good eye looking across the clearing to the grazing cow. 'There are such grand buildings in that city - so grand they would stop the breath in your lungs as you beheld them. There were ruins as well. Ancient stones, the size of my poor hut here, stacked one upon the other. I saw the place where the great temple of Herod once stood. And a few steps from there, I visited the sacred place of Christ's suffering. They took me to Pilate's palace, where our beloved Saviour received His wounds when they flogged Him. They showed me the very stones that were once sprinkled with His crimson blood. I wept to see such things.'

Corman adjusted his position on his stool, and said 'They showed me the place where they say He died. It is now hidden by the shade of a great building. But I felt no presence of a Saviour's cross in that place. I came upon a woman dressed in black. Her body was bent with age, but her spirit was as straight and strong as an arrow. She placed an old, cracked hand in mine, and begged me to follow her. She led me to a place beyond the wall of the city. A dry place, it was. A lonely place. A place of stones and sand. She released my hand and pointed to the ground and said, "Here." It was the only word she spoke. She covered her head with her shawl, and was gone.'

Corman's brow furrowed and he closed his eyes as he said, 'A sombre cloud stole away the rays of the sun, and a darkness fell heavy upon me like a shroud. I fell to the ground, and lay my cheek on that sand, with my arms outstretched before me. You could not stand in that place.' Corman lifted the back of his hand to his dampened face, and held it there. 'I knew that I was lying in the very place where He suffered. There was no doubt. And then... Then He was there.'

Solomon observed the water leak from beneath the clamped eyelids. In a whisper, he said, 'You mean...?'

'Aye,' replied Corman, anticipating the question. 'Despite my sins - and they are many - He chose to make me His guest in that place. I held my eyes tight shut, for I knew that if I were to behold Him, my soul would be sucked clear from this mortal body. I heard the sound of his sandaled feet scuff the sand close to my outstretched hand. I knew He

151

was leaning over me. That blessed face leaned over my own. I heard the breath in His nostrils. Then two precious drops of Paradise fell on my face here.' Corman stroked his cheek as he said, 'I lay there with one cheek pressed to the hardened earth of this world, and the other was host to the warm tears of Heaven.'

He opened his eyes and fixed his right eye on Solomon, and said, 'A man is never the same after a moment like that. There will always be a madness. But a wondrous madness, that's for sure.'

A light breeze danced around the men for a few moments and neither spoke. Solomon sipped from his mug, then said, 'I don't believe I ever knew such moments. But your words evoke a longing in me.'

Corman smiled such a warm smile that Solomon wanted to weep again. He removed his spectacles and dabbed his eyes with a handkerchief that he had pulled from his trouser pocket. Corman then asked, 'What else do you know, my friend?'

Solomon closed his eyes, inhaled deeply, then said, 'I know that my father died when I was still a child. He died at the hands of violent men, even though he would never cause harm to another. He died, so I was told, trying to protect a friend. When we got the news, my mother and I clung to each other. I remember that so clearly. How I loved her. We were bound together by a terrible grief. We were so close for those few years as we cared for each other. Then she took to another man... And we were no longer close.' He paused and frowned while his mind searched earnestly for information about his life that had been so hard to come by this past day or two. 'Yes,' he continued opening his eyes. 'Yes, they married and a girl was born. Much younger than me...' He paused again, then added. 'Her name was... Jean.' Some secure barrier in his mind was giving way, allowing more memories to pass through to his conscious self. 'Yes, I have a sister called Jean. I thought she was the dearest thing, you know. But I... I am not sure I ever really knew her. I was alone then.'

Solomon's gaunt face peered down at the ground for some moments. Then he drew his hand to his neck as he said, 'And in time I became a priest, like my father. Yes, I was a priest.' He nodded slowly, drawing his finger around his neck depicting the clerical collar. 'Maybe I was a priest of that church you saw when you came to my world?' His frown returned. 'Maybe not? No, I think I was the priest of another church for many years.' He shook his head. 'That's all that I know at the moment.' He looked somewhat forlornly up at Corman. 'Perhaps I was a hermit? Maybe that's why I've met you? Do you know what I was? What I did with my life? Do you know why I'm here?'

Corman heard the desperation in the questions. 'I don't know why you're here, Seanchara,' he said, and pulled off a piece of bread from the loaf and chewed it. 'But I do know that you're meant to be here. There can be no doubt about that.'

'Do you know if I will return?' asked Solomon.

'Do you want to?'

'I don't know. It depends what life was like back there. If it was good, then, yes, I do. But the few things I remember about that world make me sad. Perhaps I have been rescued from a very sad world? Perhaps I'm here now for the rest of my days. Perhaps I have died and this is the first stage of my journey onwards.'

'No,' said Corman with conviction. 'This is not a valley of death, my friend. But it is, I think, a tomb. Like Lazarus, you have been bound tight. He will call you forth. We are the friends to do the unbinding. But there is work to do before you step back into that world.'

'What work?'

'You will see. And whatever it is, it will be a work of grace. The stream that flowed from your eyes tells me there's a work of grace happening. You let it happen. That's my advice.' He took a sip from his milk, then said, 'But tell me something. That big building I saw you walk from?'

'Yes,' said Solomon. 'I do remember that church. I know that church well.' He frowned deeply as he trawled the fragments of his memory. 'Yes, I know my father was the priest there and I feel sure that I serve there now. Yes, I am sure I do. I think the church you saw must have been the church where I fell. Where Monnine found me.'

'So, tell me,' said Corman. 'In your world, do all God's people gather in such grand buildings?'

The question nudged more memories from Solomon's bruised mind. 'There are thousands of buildings like that all over the country. But there are other denominations with different buildings.'

'Dominations?' said Corman, his face creased in concern. 'They dominate people?'

Solomon was about to explain, but he could not ignore Corman's mishearing. 'I rather think that's right,' he said. 'I think probably the priests - some of them - probably me - have dominated the faithful. Yes, I rather think the church has sought to dominate the people. I am sure we have not been a church like Monnine's community over there.' He glanced over to the headland.

'There was a priest who visited us once,' said Corman, dipping a piece of bread into his milk. 'He had been trained at a grand place in France, so he said. And he came to us wearing a gorgeous robe that looked like a garment belonging to royalty. Beautiful embroidery and such colours. It was very fine. His head was shaved differently to the monks here - well, those that still boast of hair on their heads, that is!' Corman stroked his hairless head and chuckled. 'And that priest told us that we must start building our churches with stone, and that we had to start making money out of our farming. He rebuked us for not having a fine gold cross and proper stone altar and things like that. He didn't dwell long with us. I think he was very lost.' He shook his head. 'The desire for gold has hardened the hearts of even the finest of God's children.'

'Is there no silver and gold in your community, then?' asked Solomon.

'We get given gifts,' replied Corman, slowly nodding his head. 'We've had some grand gifts in our time, so we have. But we sell most of them, and use the money for God's purposes. Usually for buying slaves their freedom. It was Patrick who taught us that. Poor blessed Patrick, who suffered so much as a slave. But God freed him, and so we free others.'

Both men were quiet for a time, then Corman added. 'But some gifts we have kept.' His right eye turned to Solomon, and his face creased with a smile.

'You have?'

'We have. In our community over there, we have a hoard of treasure. Plenty of silver and gold in it. We call it the progeny gift.'

'A progeny gift? I don't think we have such things in my world. What is a progeny gift?'

Corman's smile faded as he explained, 'A nobleman came to our community in great distress. His son was fearfully sick. He carried him in his arms, and the pallor of death was on the lad. Monnine took him into the chapel, and laying him before the altar, she prayed healing prayers. Our God of wonders raised that dear child, and the nobleman was so grateful that he wanted to express his thanks to Almighty God through a gift to the community. He was a wealthy man - a *very* wealthy man - and he decided to give half his fortune to the community. He brought it in a cart drawn by an ox. Such beautiful things were in that cart: pendants and brooches decorated with carnelian and jasper; a sword with a great ruby set in the pommel; finely crafted cups of gold and silver; precious ornaments from the time of the Romans. I saw the cart myself with all its treasures, and marvelled at the sight of them. Oh, yes, even old Corman felt temptation rising as he beheld the gold. Monnine thanked the man, then asked all the community to listen to Christ, seeking His counsel about the use of such a gift.'

Corman leaned forward, and clasped his knees. 'One of the girls in the community - a young lass she was at the time. Not more than ten years on this earth, I'd say. Well, the morning after Monnine had asked the community to listen, this lass awoke from a dream that was as clear in her mind as the water springing from the well. An angel had come to her in the dream, so she said, holding all these beautiful things in his hands. All the treasures brought by the grateful nobleman. And in this dream, the angel of God says to the young girl, "This treasure is a true gift from your heavenly Father. But it is not for your keeping. It is for you to entrust to the earth, to be received by ones who will come after you." Well, as you can imagine, as soon as Monnine heard this, she was clear that it was a prophecy from heaven. This was God wanting the community to store up some treasure that would be needed by those coming after us. It is a good thing to leave gifts for our children. So, she called it the progeny gift.'

155

Solomon's frown was fixed throughout this conversation. 'So...' he said, 'your community decided to bury the treasure in the ground?'

'They did, and I expect the breath will be long gone from my body before the day comes when it is needed. In fact, it would be better for me not to see it again, for I did not like the way my eyes were gladdened by the sight of it.' He then leaned forward, resting a forearm on his knee, and said, 'But there are many more treasures than gold and silver in this world, Seanchara, and much finer ones. Did our Lord not tell a story about the treasure hidden in a field? And the man who found it sold all he had to buy the field, so he could dig up that treasure. Our Christ had no interest in gold or silver. He was speaking about the treasure of his kingdom. That's a treasure of the heart. We must dig for these treasures, Seanchara. We must dig in the dark of our own souls and see what Christ has hidden there from before the foundation of the worlds.'

Solomon's frown betrayed his confusion. 'Are you saying that I may have some treasure buried in my heart? If so, what could it be?'

'You have, my friend,' said Corman. 'Your wounds have been as a heavy stone sealing the real treasure of your life. But it is time to set it free. Think of what life this will bring to those whom our Father has called you to love!' The hermit smiled again, then supped from his mug. Solomon's brow remained furrowed, and he played with the edge of his smock. He still had very little knowledge of how he had lived up until now, but he was developing a strong suspicion that the life he had lived in his other world was only a shadow of the real thing. He sensed that there was something within him that had indeed been buried for too long. His mind could not grasp all that he was experiencing at this moment, but he knew that Corman had moved over the surface of his soul with some sensory equivalent of a divining rod, and had located something so valuable, that Solomon knew that whatever years were left to him, he, like the man in the parable, had to give all he had to finding it.

He started to feel self-conscious about this inspection of his inner life, so he returned the conversation to the original subject and said, 'So this treasure in the community. You must have had to hide it well?'

156

'No. Not at all,' replied Corman. 'Monnine told me that most of the community were there the day they buried it. Jowan prayed blessings upon it, before several of the strong men of the community shifted a large boulder over it. You can't miss it. It's in the compound, not far from the guest room where you are staying. It's that large, round stone with a cross engraved on it. Take a look at it, when you return. You'll see people there from time to time. It has become the place for praying for future generations. We gather there to pray for our children and their children. And we pray for our spiritual descendants, the ones who will carry the story of the Christ of suffering love, long after we are resting in the ground.'

Solomon's brow was deeply lined again as he said, 'But aren't people tempted to steal it?'

Corman blinked for a few moments, then smiled his crooked smile and, chuckling, said, 'They'd have to shift the bolder first!' He then added, 'But it's not in our nature to do stealing. We've been given so much, so why should we? But I am more taken by what lies in the secret chambers of our souls. As I say, this is where the true treasure lies, Seanchara.'

Solomon was straining to understand such a level of trust. He was sure that in his world, buried treasure would be far from safe if its location were known. 'I think your world is very different from mine,' he said.

'Oh, no, Seanchara,' said Corman. 'Don't get me wrong. There's plenty of stealing, and murder and all kinds of hideous crimes in this world, so there is. But in the gathering of God's people, we have had our hearts healed, you see. Yes, we have our temptations. Mine rage within me at times, and tire and wound me. But it is not our way to hide from our temptations. When I am at war with myself, I cross the waters and spend time in the company of Monnine, Jowan and the others. That's where I find my healing. We don't keep secrets. People only keep secrets when they carry shame. There's no place for shame when hearts are alive with love. And I suppose if I were gripped with a longing for a goblet of gold, well, I'd ask Monnine to step with me in prayer to the portals of heaven.

157

There's no attraction for the shine of gold when we glimpse the beauty of God.'

Solomon could not answer. He knew his Christianity had been made of a very different metal. 'I am not at all sure I have ever really known that beauty,' he answered.

Corman nodded for a few moments, then asked, 'Do you not have hermits in your world?'

'We do have monasteries and convents,' answered Solomon, remembering. 'I am not at all sure about hermits. To my knowledge, you are the first that I have met.'

Corman continued to nod his head. 'That may be the problem,' he said, his left eye as usual, surveying the skies. 'Many of us are called to these desert places to do the praying. None of us are worthy, but we know we must put down our anchor in our wild place of quiet. When I'm not visiting the community, I'm here at prayer. When I'm not entertaining friends like you, that is.' His right eye glanced at Solomon, then he continued, 'That's my calling now. This is a broken world, and the mending comes through prayer. My Master went off to his lonely place to pray, and I have to do the same. He battled with Satan in the desert, and I do the same. Oh, I've had some fearful battles on this isle, you would not believe it. But battle I must. My prayers are poor, but God is all grace, and so even my poor prayers unlock the casements of heaven, they surely do. That's when holy grace pours out untamed and free to renew the face of this troubled world. That is why we are here. And you my friend. You may not be a hermit, but He called you to be a priest.' The right eye was back on Solomon again.

Solomon felt taken aback by this last comment. He was very sure that whatever it was he did in his ministry, he did very little opening of heaven's windows through his prayers. 'I don't think I was a very good priest,' he said, so quietly that Corman only just heard it.

The old hermit now shuffled to his feet, and came and stood by Solomon. 'It's not who we once were that counts for anything,' he said, laying his hand on Solomon's shoulder. 'It's who we are now. And who we might become, if only we would adventure in our spirits. Let me pray for you now, my brother.'

158

'I would like that,' said Solomon. He knelt on the earth, and felt the sharpness of the stones as his knees pressed the ground. Corman's robe brushed Solomon's shoulder as he laid his hands on the head of the old priest. 'Breathe in, my brother,' said Corman. 'Breathe in the air of this world. Breathe in the eddying currents of the Holy Spirit. Breathe it in to the chancel of your heart.'

Corman then lifted his head to the scurrying clouds above and prayed, 'O Lord God Almighty, craftsman of the heavens, founder of the seas, I call upon Thee now to send the holy rays of thy son, Jesus, into the heart of this beloved child of grace. Open a casement of paradise, that celestial life may now flow like a refreshing stream into the droughted and hidden garden of his soul. Sweep over the contours of his troubled mind, so that the bruises of grief might find their mending. I thank Thee, Father, that you have brought this dear brother to my little isle. May it be an island of grace and freshness for him, as it has been for me. May he return soon to his world, unbound and abundant in life. May his remaining days be radiant ones and his nights be hallowed with blessed dreams. May his faith be as sturdy as the rocks of Kernow; may his hope be as sure as the incoming tide; and may his love be the love of dear, tear-soaked Calvary. And on the day of his rising, shed him of all his wounds, and let him break free into his eternal destiny.'

Both men remained still for many moments. Solomon's knees no longer ached against the stony ground. He knew he was experiencing a peace in his soul that was permeating throughout his body. He felt it strengthening every part of him. If ever he was to find himself beneath an open window of heaven, this was it. So, he raised his hands high to the sky to welcome the new daylight into his once shadowed soul. Then he lowered his hands and slowly made the sign of the cross, the sign of the wounds of his Saviour, the sign of resurrection hope that no longer felt like an elusive dream. A great boulder had been lifted from his soul. Corman had helped him to find the once buried treasure, and this treasure was now being raised from the dark to be shared with others in the clear light of day. This was his progeny gift. Not a treasure to keep buried, but one that needed raising to the light to bring life to the future to which he was returning.

Corman helped him to his feet, and together the two men made their way back to the coracle in a silence of contentment.

# 18

A particularly noisy gull woke Ella from her slumbers. She had been asleep for at least an hour. The sun was slipping behind a ribbon of thin cloud that crested the horizon. She did not have her phone with her, so she had no idea of the time, but she guessed it was getting near the time when normally, when she was at home, she would be having tea with her parents. She did feel hungry. And she was reluctantly starting to acknowledge that her search for her great uncle was not going to result in her finding him. In many ways, she always knew that. She had just needed to get out of the house. And she wanted to do something to help with the finding of the old man. Despite the failure of her search, she was feeling considerably stronger. Somehow the unexpected meetings with both Rahab and Sister Maria had reset something within her. She felt calmer and more together. Less tangled. Less stressed.

The breeze was starting to feel chilly and she knew she must either head back into town to continue her search, go and stay with a friend, or go home. Home? How would it be seeing her mother again? Would her mother have confessed yet to her dad? Had there been a dramatic row? Had one or other of them now left home? Had they decided this affair marked the end of their brittle marriage? And Uncle Sol: maybe he had now returned? And if he had, he would be needing her. Her curiosity, combined with her need for food, and fresh clothing, and her concern for her great uncle, all conspired to convince her that she needed to head for home. And she was missing her phone more than she liked to admit.

So it was, after an hour or so, she found herself trudging up the familiar gravel driveway with crows squawking in the yew trees overhead. She had not taken her keys with her when she hurried out yesterday (was it only yesterday?), so she had to ring the doorbell. She waited anxiously, then heard the familiar sounds of the door being unlocked. It was her mother who opened it. Ella noticed there was redness around her mother's eyes, and she was looking more defenceless than she had ever seen her.

'Oh, Ella,' she said, and her eyes filled with water. She went to hug Ella, but Ella was unable to respond. She was still filled with a deep sense of disappointment and indignation at her mother's unfaithfulness.

'Have they found him?' asked Ella, throwing her bag on the chair in the hall.

'No,' said Lisa. 'Tea?'

'Sure,' said Ella. 'You got any food? I'm famished.'

'There's some chicken from lunch,' said Lisa. 'Grandad and Gran were here.'

'Hm,' said Ella, sitting down at the kitchen table. 'Where's Dad?'

Lisa then explained about Matt's rushing off to find her. 'Ah, he's a softy, isn't he?' said Ella. Lisa made her a cup of tea and placed it in front of her. 'Can you text him to let him know I'm back?'

'Will do,' answered Lisa, putting some of the lunch on a plate and placing it in the Aga. 'I got a text just now to say he was staying another night at the office. When he knows you're back, he may return this evening.'

'You told him? You know, about…' asked Ella. There was accusation in her tone.

Lisa sat down at the table. 'No, I didn't get the chance. He rushed out as soon as he discovered you had gone. Anyway, the Inspector was here and… well.'

'You've got to tell him, Mum.'

'I know, love. I know.'

'Warn me before you do. He'll go ape.' She warmed her hands around the mug of tea.

Lisa looked at her daughter and said, 'I've just been on the phone to… to the man.'

'The one you been bonking?'

'To the one I've been *seeing*,' corrected Lisa. 'It never got to bonking, if you must know. But if I'm honest, it got pretty close.' Her head was lowered under the heavy burden of guilt and shame. She then looked up at her daughter and said, 'I've told him it's off. I've finished it.'

'Good,' said Ella. 'But the damage has been done, hasn't it?'

'Yes,' said Lisa wearily. 'And it wasn't much fun hearing his reaction, either. Seems like he'd invested much more in the relationship than I had. But it felt a relief to do it.' She looked at her daughter. 'Ella, darl.. Ella, sweetheart. I can't tell you how sorry I am about it all. I can never excuse myself. I don't know what the hell I thought I was doing. I'm just sorry. I'm sorry it has to affect you. Nothing in me would ever want to hurt you.'

'Bit late for all that, mother,' said Ella, drinking more of her tea as she looked out of the window. Her mother may have had her reasons for this unfaithful dalliance, but the fact was, this act of betrayal was almost certainly going to break up the family. Ella was in no mood to simply forgive and forget.

Lisa was struggling to find words. She wanted to find a new way of communicating with her daughter that did not end in a row. 'I'm… I'm glad you overheard my phone call. It was good that you did.'

'Hm,' said Ella. 'Good for you, maybe.'

Lisa realised that any further conversation about her disastrous romance was not going to help either of them. She reached into the oven, and collected the dinner. 'Here, you're probably ready for this,' she said, putting the plate on the table. 'So where did you get to?'

'Thanks,' said Ella, pulling the plate before her. Whatever her current feelings about her mother, she couldn't deny that there were few things she enjoyed more than her mum's cooking. 'Went into town,' she said.

'I wondered,' said Lisa. 'We checked with some of your friends.'

'Told you not to,' said Ella. She attacked the food hungrily.

'I know,' conceded her mother. 'Dad was really worried for you.'

'I'm nearly eighteen, for Christ's sake.'

'I told him that.'

163

'There's something going on with him, Ella,' said Lisa. 'He's been so uptight lately. I think things aren't good with the business. He should never have bought that property on Crescent Hill. I so wish he hadn't. I tried to warn him.'

'Said it would make him millions, didn't he?'

'He did.'

Ella paused her eating for a moment and said, 'He's not back on the stuff again, is he?'

'I hope not,' replied her mother.

Both women were quiet for a few moments. 'Great chicken,' said Ella, then added, 'I met a refugee.'

'You did?'

'Refugee or Asylum-seeker. Can't remember which. Met her on the coastal path. Said her name was Rahab.'

'Where was she from?'

'Some place in Africa, I think. Forget where now. Told her to call in though. Nice girl. Also met a nun.'

'A nun?'

'Yeah. A real nun. She was cool actually. Hundred percent genuine. Called Sister Maria. Swears in Welsh.'

'Does she give lessons?' asked Lisa, and for a moment both women laughed together.

Ella put her fork down for a moment and said, 'Mum, I'm really missing Uncle Sol. What do you think has happened to him?'

Lisa sighed and said, 'Well, you won't believe it, but this morning that ridiculous Inspector - who drives me mad with the way she says, "Ri....ight" all the time, when things are clearly far from all right. Well...' Lisa giggled for a few moments, then said, 'She came in triumphantly claiming to have found Uncle Sol, and promptly introduced a deranged old alky she'd found in Truro! He was nothing like Uncle Sol!'

'What? You kidding!' Both women laughed again.

'But seriously, Mum. This will be his third night away from home. It's cold out there. Suppose he's in a field somewhere. He might have broken his leg or something.'

'I know, love. But - and I know this sounds a bit spooky - but I have a strong sense that he's OK, even though I've really no idea what could have happened to him.'

'Yeah,' said Ella, frowning. 'Both Rahab and Sister Maria said they felt the same. Don't know how they could possibly tell, though. But I suppose I feel the same. Maybe it's wishful thinking?'

'Yes - could be. The whole village is talking about it,' said Lisa.

'I bet they are,' said Ella. She was making fast work of her mother's chicken pie.

'I know this bloody thing with my work colleague is really big,' said Lisa. 'But the most important thing at the moment is to get Uncle Sol back home safely.'

'Agreed,' said Ella. 'Nice supper, Mum. I'm going to get a shower.'

Lisa watched Ella leave the room, and felt relief. Relief that her daughter was home. But even more relief that, despite everything, there were signs of warmth from her daughter.

*

Down at the Pilchard Inn, there was no shortage of speculation about the missing priest. It was undoubtedly one of the most exciting things to have happened in the village for a long time. Ethel Cairns had become the new village celebrity, as the one who had actually discovered the blood on the floor of the church, and she had now recounted her story to most households in the village. It was a story that was a little enhanced with every telling, so that her reports of the amount of blood in the church would now suggest a massacre rather than an accident. Various theories were continuing to emerge as explanations for the blood on the floor, the smashed money box, the discarded dog collar and the utterly uncharacteristic disappearance of the old priest.

Ethel had never been a regular at The Pilchard, but by becoming the great discoverer of the Disappearance, she was expected to be present in the pub every evening until the missing priest was found, and the mystery solved. On Saturday evening, more cider flowed through her delicate constitution than it had for a long time, and she was feeling its effects on Sunday. However, dutifully she made her way to the pub on Sunday evening, where several had already gathered to discuss the latest theories regarding the disappearance. On Saturday Daniel Moody had not shown up, but he was there Sunday evening, and he introduced some new information that considerably spiced up the story of the missing priest. Daniel was well known in the village, for he had worked all his working life in the community as painter, decorator, gardener, drains clearer, repairer of roofs (including thatches), clocks and mowing machines.

Daniel settled himself next to Ethel near the fireplace and he started chatting to her and to the small group who were gathered near the fire. He then reported a tale which stunned the group.

'So, you are saying,' said Leo, 'That you actually saw the old Father leaving the church on Friday evening. This was before Ethel had gone into the church.'

'I don't knows what time it was that Ethel got herself into that place,' said Daniel, his old, tanned face creasing in concentration. 'But as I said, when I got there, it was getting dark. The bats were fluttering all over the place. I'd just had my usual glass of Rattlers here at the pub…'

'Ah, that will be the problem, I reckon,' said the sceptical Charles.

'It was nothing to do with the cider, Charlie,' insisted Daniel. 'Oh, no. I saw what I saw. It weren't the cider.'

'Well, it can have its effect on you,' slurred Ethel.

'Well go on, tell us more,' said Teresa. 'Did you really see the old man. Was he injured?'

'Slowly, slowly,' said Daniel, who was never known to do anything in a hurry. 'I was coming up the lane towards the church. It were a bit drizzly and getting dark. And then I saw a brilliant light coming out of the church porch. I mean it were no light you'd find in this world, I can tell you. I mean, it didn't blind you like a car headlight. It was just different.'

'It's true,' said Ethel, keen to remind the group of her crucial role in the drama. 'The lights were on when I went in.'

'No,' protested Daniel. 'It weren't no normal light I saw, Eth. This light were different.'

'What you mean *different?*' asked Teresa.

'Different,' replied Daniel. 'And that's when I saw them.'

'So, that's when you saw the Reverend leaving the church, did you?' said Leo, who had just collected his beer from the bar, and came and joined the conversation.

'That I did, Leo,' said Daniel. 'He were walking with another creature.'

'What do you mean by a creature, Daniel?' said Teresa.

'It were different,' said Daniel. 'Different - that's the truth.'

'Oh, for God's sakes, Dan,' appealed Teresa. 'Can't you bloody give us a bit more detail on this. How was this creature different? I mean, was it the kind of thing you'd see on Star Wars?'

'Maybe,' said Daniel. 'It had two legs, I think. But it were dressed in a kind of cloak, like. Right down to its feet. So I can't be sure. It were smaller than the Reverend, though.'

'Let's return to planet Earth for a moment,' said Leo. 'I think we can safely assume it was a normal human being, wearing a cloak.'

'No,' said Daniel with conviction. 'Don't mean to disagree with you, Leo. But it didn't look like anyone from this world to me. I mean, at one level, yes. It could have been a normal person wearing a cloak, I grant you. But you don't normally gets to see through a normal person, do you?'

'So, you're saying this person was a see-through person, Dan?' said Teresa.

'It were a see-through person, Teresa. That it was. Saw right through them.'

167

'Well, that doesn't sound natural to me,' said Ethel, trying her best to place her glass on a nearby table. 'You don't expect to have see-through people wandering around the church, that's for sure. The church is for respectable people.'

'Ah, Ethel, that's true,' said Leo, helping Ethel get her glass to the table. 'But I think it's becoming clear what we're talking about now. We're not talking extra-terrestrial and space ships here. We are talking *ghosts*.' Several in the group flinched at this mention of the dead. 'Whether we like the idea or not, our Reverend's been in the company of a ghost.'

'I have to disagree with you again, Leo,' said Daniel. 'That were no ghost.'

'How do you know?' said Theresa sharply. 'You seen many? You a bloody expert?'

'I seen several,' claimed Daniel. 'And none looked like that.'

'You seen ghosts, Daniel?' called Jan, serving another customer at the bar. 'Good God!'

'That I have, Jan,' said Daniel. 'And I don't want no seeing of them again, I can tell you. Scared me shitless they did.'

'So, this… whatever it was - that took the Father. He didn't scare you, then?' said Charles.

'Oh, God, no,' said Daniel.

'Well it sounds pretty scary to me, Dan,' said Charles. 'I mean if I saw someone being taken out of the church by a half invisible being, I'd be wetting meself, I would.'

'That's your age,' called Jan.

'Look,' said Daniel. 'You asked me and I'm telling you. I wasn't scared by what I saw. Quite the opposite, if you must know. There was something about that creature that was… well, comforting, I suppose. Looked kind, it did.'

'I see. We're all clear now,' said Leo, raising his eyebrows. 'We're talking about a see-through spectre of the night, who specialises in beaming a bright light wherever it goes, enjoys the company of elderly priests, and is unusually kind.'

'Well, I suppose that's more or less it, Leo,' said Daniel.

'But what about the Reverend?' said Teresa. 'How was he looking?'

'He looked dazed.'

'Not surprised,' said Charles

'But couldn't see much wrong with the gentleman, apart from that,' added Daniel. 'He seemed to be walking all right. But he was clinging on to this robed thing, whatever it was. He didn't seem to mind it being there.'

'So, what happened? asked Teresa. 'Where did they go?'

'Well, that were a bit weird, if you ask me, Teresa.' said Daniel. 'Cos, they both thinned.'

'They thinned?' said Leo, with a clear note of scepticism in his voice.

'Thinned,' repeated Daniel.

'You mean they got thinner?' said Charles.

'That's what thinning normally means, don't it?'

'Yeah, Dan,' said Teresa. 'But the point is, people don't normally thin just like that, do they? So, tell us. What the hell *do* you mean?'

'I mean, they just sort of thinned into nothing,' said Daniel. 'I saw them come out of the church in all this light. They walked a few paces on the path, and then they thinned. And the light disappeared. And that's the sum of it.' He took a long swig from his glass.

'And what did you do?' asked Charles.

'Came back down to the pub, course,' said Daniel. 'Needed another pint after seeing something like that. Wouldn't you?'

'Well, you didn't mention it when you came here,' said Jan from the bar.

'No,' said Daniel. 'Not the kind of thing you blab about is it? Needed time to think about it, I did. It felt special. You know, like... Like I'd been given something very special. Needed to keep it to myself for a bit.'

'But you're telling us now,' said Charles.

'I am,' said Daniel. 'Feels proper to tell you now.'

'You going to the police with this?' asked Teresa.

'Nah,' said Daniel. 'They already think I'm tiddlywinks in the brain. They'd never listen to a yarn like that, would they?'

No-one could deny that Daniel had a point. This was a man who would take some believing at the best of times. They were all quiet for a moment until Jan called from the bar. 'Looks like you need some refills there,' and that precipitated a change of conversation.

By the end of the evening, most were working with the theory that Daniel had seen something all right, but in a cider-hazed way, and they decided that the explanation for the priest's disappearance was abduction either by alien or ghost. And they came to the sad and reluctant conclusion that Father Solomon Ogilvy would not be seen again in Tregovenek, and would either now be a ghost himself, or supping with the aliens on some distant planet.

# 19

As Corman paddled the coracle away from his island in late afternoon sunlight, Solomon savoured the powerful sense of peace that had arrived in his soul following the hermit's prayer for him. Neither men spoke as they traversed the waters back to the simple harbour. 'It is time for me to say farewell, Seanchara,' said Corman, as he helped Solomon out of his boat. They both paused for a few moments as they heard the sound of the curlews in the estuary. Both the priest and the hermit shared the same love for the song of the curlew.

'We have only known each other for such a short time,' said Solomon. 'But it feels sad to bid this farewell.' He became aware that his voice was sounding less tremulous than usual. He heard a strength in it.

Corman came towards him and embraced him for a few moments. 'I return to my desert place,' he said. 'And tomorrow you will return to your people.'

'Tomorrow? How do you know this?' asked Solomon.

'Hermits know things,' said Corman. And with that, he collected a sack of provisions that had been left for him on the shore, and returned to his coracle. Solomon watched him paddle back out to sea, back to his island, back to his home. Though Solomon had been deeply impressed by Corman, he had had no experience of people prophesying and predicting things, so he was far from certain if he really would be somehow transported back to his own time tomorrow. But nonetheless, hearing the words of the hermit gave him renewed hope that before too long he might make his way home. Wherever home was.

That evening there was another meal in the dining barn, and Solomon surprised himself by feeling increasingly at ease in the customs and culture of this community that so recently had been completely alien to him. At the end of the meal, when the parents left to settle the children, Monnine grasped Solomon by the arm, saying, 'It's a mild night, but let's pick up a sheepskin before we leave.'

Dutifully Solomon grasped a lush sheepskin from a bench by the door, as did Monnine, and they stepped out into the compound. A wooden fire had been lit near Solomon's hut, and he and Monnine settled on the bench next to it. The night was quiet except for the distant hoot of an owl and the occasional bark of a fox.

'Corman says I will return tomorrow,' said Solomon to Monnine.

'Then you will,' she replied.

'But, how will I?' asked Solomon, lifting the sheepskin more securely over his shoulder.

Monnine assisted him for a few moments, then said, 'You don't need to know that. But you do need to recover more of your memory before you return.'

'Indeed,' said Solomon. 'I need to remember a great deal more. My name for a start. And where I live. And who I live with, if any. And…'

'No,' interrupted Monnine, smiling. 'You only need to remember enough.'

Solomon nodded his head, then looked at her and said, 'Such as?'

Monnine replied, 'Och, that's not for me to say. That's for God to give.'

'But…' said Solomon, 'If I may. How will God give me back my memories?'

'You will dream,' said Monnine. 'You will sleep out here tonight by this fire. There is a little cloud, but in the main, the sky will be clear and you can let the stars beam upon you. They are ready messengers of their master. They will speak.'

Solomon looked up at the night sky. As he did so, the slender moon slid out from behind a wispy cloud. They both watched as the clouds parted, and more of the grand night sky was revealed. As Solomon gazed above him, he recalled some scripture and spoke it out loud: 'There are also celestial bodies, and bodies terrestrial: but the glory of the celestial is one, and the glory of the terrestrial is another. There is one glory of the sun, and another glory of the moon, and another glory of the stars: for one star differeth from another star in glory.'

'The words of blessed Paul,' said Monnine, nodding her head. 'I know well his words.' She mused for a few moments. Then, gazing above her, she continued the Scripture that she also knew by heart, 'So also is the resurrection of the dead. It is sown in corruption; it is raised in incorruption.'

Solomon lowered his head, and surveyed the soil beneath his feet. 'I feel the frailty of this old body, Monnine. I fear there are not many days before it will be sown in the ground.'

'Whatever days you have, Seanchara,' said Monnine. 'Let them be good ones.' She then stood and said, 'Now it is time for sleep. I will fetch your mattress and pillow, and stoke the fire.'

Solomon was far from certain that he was facing a comfortable night. It seemed a quite ludicrous plan for a man of his age to sleep under the stars on a cold night like this. And yet, he couldn't deny that there was a part of him that was looking forward to it. He poked at the fire with a stick, then, chuckling to himself, said, 'At last, I am open to adventure.'

'Indeed, you are,' said Monnine, overhearing him. She was carrying his mattress, and pillow that she had collected from his hut. 'Your father had the adventure in him, if I'm not mistaken?' she said, as she laid the mattress on the ground.

'Yes, he did,' said Solomon. His demeanour then became serious as he said, 'And I suppose that was his undoing.'

'You think so?' said Monnine, puffing up his downy pillow. 'I'm far from sure about that. But what I suspect is that you became wary of adventure all your life because of it.'

Solomon's mouth fell open for a few moments before he said, very slowly. 'I do believe you are right, Monnine.' It was true - he had always shied away from adventure, for in his old way of thinking, it was adventure that had stolen his father from him.

'You settle yourself when you're ready,' said Monnine, placing some wood near the fire for Solomon to replenish as needed. 'I'll check the fire from time to time. Keep that sheepskin over you. You'll not be cold with all that wool covering you. He was a big sheep, that one.'

'Thank you, Monnine,' he said, standing as she left. 'God bless you.'

173

'And His blessing on you, Seanchara,' she said, disappearing into the dark.

Solomon returned to his hut for a few moments to make use of his chamber pot, and then returned to settle himself on his mattress, pulling the warm sheepskin over him. As far as he knew, he had never slept out under the stars before, except perhaps... Yes, he could now remember. In the expansive garden of his Rectory home.... Yes, he and his father, lying close together under a blanket. Both of them laughing and pointing to the vast sea of star-sprinkled blue above them. And as he recalled so vividly that starlit memory, he drifted into sleep.

Whether it was the stars, the effects of his time with Corman, or because of Monnine's prayers in the chapel that were uttered for Seanchara until dawn, but the night did indeed hold the light of revelation for Solomon. During the hours of darkness, his pilgrim dreams unlocked so many memories. The childhood home, his University and College training, the precious love he abandoned for the sake of his calling, the large empty Rectory and the three village churches that were his care for close on forty years. And then... And then, it came to him. He dreamed of Tregovenek. The name of his village returned to him, and he knew that he lived there in the twenty-first century. And he saw the gravel path leading to the large house called Altarnun House. And in this dream, he peered through the kitchen window, and there was his niece, Lisa and her husband, Matt. And there also was Ella - beloved Ella. He saw her look up from the table and smile at him, and he smiled back. This he knew was his home, but in the knowing was the remembrance that it was a troubled home. His delight was tempered with sorrow.

He then saw the church, the place where Monnine had first found him. He saw the congregation scattered bleakly among the dark oak pews. He even saw himself, standing at the front of the church, in his cassock and surplice, his face long, his brow furrowed, his soul heavy. He peered at the pale and wrinkled face and saw such emptiness. The stone building looked cold. Life had been hollowed out, leaving only a rind that had little to commend it. In the dream he grieved for how life had drained from this church. He shuddered at the sight of himself looking so bound, locked in some lonely darkness. In the dream he

174

searched and searched for adventure in his face, and in the faces of the congregation scattered thinly among the pews. But alas, he found none, and he felt dismayed.

Just before dawn he had one final dream. He was a child again with his father. It was Christmas - there was torn paper on the floor. He could smell the strong fragrance of pine needles from the Christmas tree that was decorated with just a few coloured baubles. A warm fire crackled in the grate. He and his father were sitting on the floor, and he was clasping a small pewter mug. On it was beautifully engraved the words *Solomon David Ogilvy 9 March 1937.* In this dream he held the mug as if he had found a great treasure. 'The date of my baptism, Father,' he said.

His father beamed down at him and said, 'Yes, my boy. I wanted to get this done for the baptism, but it has taken me a long time to get around to it. But better late than never.'

'Thank you, father,' said the boy, and hugged him tight. He then sat back and said, 'But father, why did you name me *Solomon.* I know he was in the Bible, and he was a king. But I'm not going to be a king.'

'No, my boy,' replied his father. 'The main reason I chose that name for you is because my name is David, and in the bible, David's son is called Solomon. And Solomon was very, very wise.'

'Like his father.'

'Even wiser.'

'Will I be wise, father?'

'Of course,' said his father. 'And the older you get, the wiser you will be.'

'So, when I am an old, old man, I will be very, very wise,' said the boy.

'You will be,' said the father.

And that was the end of the dream.

*

In the twenty-first century, in the manager's office of *Matthew Micklefield Estate Agents*, the proprietor was trying to get some sleep. This was the office from where he oversaw the work of the successful estate agency. It was also the office from which he devised and planned the recently very unsuccessful development operations. Two years ago, when the business was going well, he carpeted his office with a fine Axminster. Whilst it proved very comfortable as a carpet for his office, it was proving far less comfortable as a bed. But it was not the lack of a comfortable mattress that was keeping Matt awake. It was the lack of peace in his mind. He was recalling the surprising meetings with Jenny and Theo. Two more different people were hard to imagine, and yet each in their own way had touched something very tender in him. As he lay on the carpet, gazing at the ceiling panels, and with his coat failing to properly cover him, he stroked his unshaven chin and thought about the young girl that he had called Angel, but who had let slip that her name was Jenny. From poor beginnings, he had worked hard in his life to earn enough money to clear himself from the degradation of poverty. He nursed a belief that any sensible person could lift themselves off from that fatal floor if they worked hard enough. But now he met Jenny, and she was disturbing his hitherto safe worldview. How could he possibly blame her for the degrading lifestyle in which she was trapped? Life had just dealt her a very bad hand.

How had he managed to become so hard? How come he had never really stopped to think about the likes of Jenny before? Why had he not been more compassionate during his life? Why did he never open his eyes sufficiently to be able to see the world as Theo saw it? He kept hearing Theo's words, 'In another world, she'd have been a queen, sat on a throne of pearl.' Yes, Matt was in no doubt that there was something regal in the girl's spirit, and in another very different world to this one, where life was completely fair, that regal spirit would indeed be honoured. But she did not live in that world. She lived in this shady world, where far too much was unfair. And for Jenny, rather than dining with royalty, she was trapped into this life of prostitution and drugs, where she was forced to pander to the lusts of men. And men who were no worse than Matthew Micklefield. He had never been with a prostitute, but he knew he was capable of it, and he knew that if he did consort with such a girl, then like the rest of her despicable customers, he would have treated her as less than human. He felt so ashamed.

And then there was Theo. Again, a man that only a few days ago, he would have judged as having nothing useful to offer a prominent businessman. Matt Micklefield was developing his prosperous business, so chatting to an old fisherman was a serious distraction and waste of valuable time. But today Matt had climbed out of his ego chariot, and sauntered for several hours with this sage of the sea, and learned more true wisdom in these hours than in all his days of business. The crises he was facing both at home and in the business had weakened his defences, allowing both Jenny and Theo to gain access to a hitherto hidden part of his soul, and their presence there was releasing a confusing set of emotions.

He was sorry not to have found Ella. Searching for her made him realise just how fond he was of her. He had so easily allowed her teenage temperament to annoy him, and he had spent so little time with her lately. No wonder she was aloof. He was relieved to get the text from Lisa that their daughter was home and safe. And Lisa? What about Lisa? What was happening in her life? Were all those late-night crisis meetings really to do with work clients? He was sure he could smell aftershave on her pillow when she returned. But he did not dare challenge her. It would be hard to bear the pain. But it was also a sense of guilt. He surprised himself that he was not angry with her. His guilt was running so deep in him. Guilt from the days of the dope. Days when he was so cruel to both Lisa and Ella. If it came to a sin competition, he won hands down. And besides, if she was rushing off into the arms of another man, then could he honestly blame her? He had hardly been much of a husband to her of late. It was months since they had known any kind of intimacy. The stresses at work and the threat of losing everything for which he had slogged so hard had rendered him all but impotent.

Matt sighed and tried to get himself more comfortable. He turned his gaze to the window. A drizzle was distorting the image of the world behind the glass that was lit by the pale light of the street lamp. A hundred yards down that very street stood the granite sturdiness of the bank building, and in that building tomorrow he would endure the meeting that he could defer no longer. Sheila Farnley, the manager, had

177

become a good friend, but she had retired over a year ago. Her replacement, a rather sinister, thin young man called Iain Slipp, was efficient, slick and most definitely not generous. Matt knew there was no leeway with this manager. Not only was he going to deny Matt another loan, but he would call in the other huge debt. It was long overdue, and he had made it very clear that the deadline had passed. Matt would have to sell his grand plan property at a hideous loss, and all his dreams of fabulous wealth would become a nightmare of humiliation. He would have to have a terrible conversation with Lisa, Ella and Solomon about putting up Altarnun House for sale. At least that would sell well, and he could clear the debts. They would just have to rent a very much smaller house on one of the outer estates of the town. He was far from sure if they could afford a three-bed house. If so, what would happen to Uncle Solomon? Maybe it would be a good thing if the old man had been bumped off. One less problem to worry about. And that dark thought oozed into the cavity of his soul that was already thick with guilt and shame.

Eventually Matt fell into a troubled and restless sleep, and when daylight started to filter through the misted window, Matt was fairly convinced that he had not slept at all. He heaved his aching body off the floor and cleared the mist from the window with his sleeve. He saw a world dampened by cold and squally showers. He breathed hard on the glass and the view of the street dimmed. But there was nothing he could do to dim the fact that Monday 16 April had arrived, and soon he would need to walk down that rain-rinsed street to his ominous appointment.

# 20

Matthew Micklefield was known in Porthann as the lad who had done very well for himself. He had grown up in the south of the county and, from time to time, when chatting to locals over a pint in the pub after work, he would tell tales of a considerably misspent youth, which apparently had included his being expelled from his school at the age of fifteen. He never gave the reason why. However, at some time in his late teens, his fortunes changed with one very lucky break when he got a job at an Estate Agents in Bodmin. It was a short-term job to help them set up a new computer system. But he presented as a very confident young man, who soon showed an aptness for the house buying and letting business. He was taken on as one of the office staff, and within a couple of years he had become one of the best, with a talent for gaining good sales for some of the most unpromising properties. He then moved to the north coast and set up his own business in the middle of Porthann. Though a young man at the time, his business quickly flourished and his soon became the most respected estate agent in town.

It was in those early years that he met the young and pretty Lisa Hancock from Pedrogwen, and not long after they were married, he bought Altarnun House, the very desirable property in the nearby village of Tregovenek. Generally, Matt was well liked and respected in Porthann, but in recent years the mood towards him was definitely changing. He was prone to selling properties at highly inflated prices that attracted only the wealthy buy-to-let purchasers. Furthermore, he had taken up a new line in development, converting some fine old family homes into holiday flats. However, in the main, his affable character and winsome ways meant that he had not made too many enemies.

What most people in the town did not see however, was the anxiety that lay behind the confident exterior. Matt was a natural risk-taker, and generally his risks paid off. But one thing he could not tolerate in himself was failure. He had to succeed, and, as he saw it, the clear evidence of that success was prosperity. Hence the house, the car and the suits. And it was important that people should know that it was all due to his hard work, and his entrepreneurial skills. He enjoyed his reputation of being one of the wealthy people of the community. But from time to time, the business had faltered at great cost to Matt's emotional wellbeing. Any sense of failure caused a most oppressive darkness to shroud his soul. On two occasions, this dark had caused him to revert to his teenage practice of taking cocaine. But that habit had nearly cost him his sanity and his marriage, and he vowed never to go down that road again.

On this particular April Monday morning, the same troubling dark was glooming over Matt's soul, as dark as the rain-laden clouds that were hanging menacingly over the coast. None of the staff had yet arrived at the office. He made himself a black coffee and sat at his desk. The appointment with the bank was at eleven o'clock. This would be the meeting to trigger his downfall. His mind went back for the thousandth time over the plans he had made for this farmhouse. He knew that taking on the McHenry farmhouse was a risk, especially in the current economic climate. But the architect had come up with such wonderful ideas. With her ambitious and contemporary plans, she would transform this semi derelict farmhouse and outbuildings into six beautiful holiday lets with indoor heated pool and gym. He had poured all his capital plus a loan into the project, certain that the end result would make him a very handsome profit. But there had been so many unexpected costs. He could blame Brexit, the pandemic, and the government, but he knew that the chief person to blame was himself. He had become too cocky and had not done proper research. In his preparation, he had cut too many corners in his eagerness to make a quick profit. And, if the truth be told, he had become greedy.

He pulled out a pencil from his overcrowded pen pot, and started doodling on a notepad. He pressed hard on the pencil, indenting the random black lines into the pad until the lead broke. He hurled the pencil across the room and got up from his chair and looked out the window at the drizzle dampening the street below. He was starting to feel the desperate heaviness of the crisis in which he found himself. However, for a few moments, his mind wandered to the missing Uncle Solomon. Matt was fairly certain now that the old priest was dead. No doubt, he had staggered out of the church after falling, and collapsed somewhere. The last couple of nights had been cold, and it was unlikely a man of his age could survive.

'What wonderful faith,' he said out loud. He surprised himself, and was not entirely sure quite why he said it. But as this curious statement echoed in his mind, it became clear to him why he suddenly blurted it out. He regarded Solomon's life as a very desolate life, and a life that had achieved very little, and certainly had made very little money. Solomon had none of Matt's ambition and drive, and Matt had always assumed that the old man must have lived with a mountain of disappointments, regrets and unfulfilled hopes. So, to achieve faith in that lonely and empty world, was by Matt's reckoning, something really quite impressive. He felt a growing sense of grief that Solomon was probably dead. In a way that he had never even contemplated before, Matt found himself wishing that the old man was back at home, in his room, and sitting in his chair by the window. Matt imagined that he would go and knock on the door of the room of this quiet priest, and ask him for wisdom. Why had he never thought to do this before when times were tough? He didn't know. But he was sure that, if the old man had been around now, Matt would have knocked on his door. Yes, he was sure that somewhere in that serene soul there was a fount of wisdom to help Matt through this difficult time. He might even lay his hand on Matt and say a blessing. It might even be a moment for Matt to open his heart and mind to the possibility of the existence of God. It might be Matt's Lantern Cathedral moment. He sighed deeply and emptied his coffee mug. A light-filled cathedral just at this moment seemed so much more attractive than the gloomy philosophy of Dawkins.

But he knew that today there would be no conversations with Solomon, and no visits to bright cathedrals. 'Fairy tales,' he said out loud as he returned from the rain-streaked window to his desk, where he sat down limply in the chair. 'Back to reality, Matthew. Face it. In a few hours all this will have crashed down. You will be sitting red-faced and humiliated before the gaunt face of the predatory Mr Slipp, and you will be declared bankrupt.'

'Or dead,' he heard himself answer.

So, it had returned.

That nagging voice, which most of the time he had managed to stifle, had abruptly made itself heard. It was the voice that declared he was a failure as a businessman; a failure as a husband; a failure as a father; and a failure as a man. This was not the first time such sinister thoughts broke free from the depths into his consciousness. But it had not come with such force before. And never before had it sounded - what was it? *Comforting* was the word. Yes, it was a comforting thought. Why not? He could just step out of this hell and walk into oblivion. Such a thought felt like a liberation. He even chuckled as he thought of the bank manager with his tight smile and heavy glasses, tapping his lean fingers on his desk, waiting for the late Matthew Micklefield to arrive. And yes, by then, he could well be the late Matthew Micklefield. That would wipe the smile off the sly face of young Mr Iain Slipp. Matt reached down to the bottom drawer and pulled out a half-full bottle of cider brandy that he kept for special occasions. This *was* a special occasion.

Within fifteen minutes, the empty bottle was in the wastepaper basket, and Matt was out of the building and making his way unsteadily to his car. He knew exactly where he must make for. He started the car with much revving. Determination was strong in him as he drove erratically out of Porthann towards the high place the locals called Gerhard's Leap. It was named after a young, half German man, who was living in Porthann when War broke out in 1914. He was hounded by locals after the sinking of the Lusitania, and so stressed was he by this hostility that he ended it all by throwing himself off the cliffs. No-one was hounding Matthew, save for the accusing voices from within his own soul. Nonetheless, Gerhard felt like good company today. Gerhard would understand.

The clouds had darkened and the drizzle turned to rain by the time he was parking the car in a small lay-by. To access Gerhard's Leap, he needed to walk a short way along the coastal path. He duly walked the well-worn, slippery path with resolute steps. The wind buffeted him as the path drew him closer to the cliff edge, the pellets of rain sharp against his face. He was wearing no coat, and his clothes were quickly becoming sodden. He refused to entertain any thoughts of Lisa or Ella. He wanted nothing to stop his mission now, and he knew any thoughts of those he loved would prevent him from doing what he needed to do.

What occupied his mind most was an appalling sense of his own uselessness. There was no further use for Matthew Micklefield in this world, and there was now only one thing to be done.

There was no signpost marking the spot, but all the locals knew the place where over a hundred years ago, the young German freed himself of his woes. Matt reached this spot, and his cobalt eyes looked through the veil of rain to the heaving, grey sea. The brandy was making Matt feel unsteady, but he wished he had another bottle with him to give him the courage to do what he needed to do. He was now only two steps away from his freedom. He noticed a weathered sign nearby warning people to keep back from the cliff edge. But such a sign did not apply to one with his clear intention. He thought how, for people like him and Gerhard, there should have been a sign saying "This way".

He stepped nervously forward and peered over the edge. It was high tide, and he saw the white water breaking against the jagged rocks at the foot of the cliff. The vertigo he felt caused him to instinctively step back several paces. The thought of falling was horrifying. And yet, it would not take long. What a relief it would be to reach those rocks, welcoming him into the bliss of oblivion. Those blessed waves would wash over his mangled remains, cleansing the world of Matthew Micklefield and his many failures. All he had to do now was to take those three steps to the edge, open his arms like a bird on the wing, and fly to his freedom.

He was finding it hard to stand still in the buffeting wind. He took one step forward. He was a few inches nearer that fateful and beckoning edge. For a moment, he looked to the sky, and saw that it had lightened, for the dark, sombre clouds had passed, taking their rain with them. He then drew his eyes down to the few inches of turf between him and the edge. Just a couple more steps. But then, just as he was about to step forward another pace, the wind abruptly dropped, and the world that had been so full of noise and storm became disturbingly quiet. It felt to Matt that creation had noticed this figure on the cliff top and had decided to stop and spectate, holding its breath, waiting to see if this anguished human was going to take those two further fatal steps. Even the gulls were silent, maybe waiting to see if they would witness another wingless human trying to fly from the cliff top. Matt's feet seemed to be

183

fastened to the soggy ground beneath him. How hard it had become to walk. He clenched his fists and looked up again to the skimming clouds. He pulled back his lips, grimacing to the skies. He hated the insipid indecision within him. Why couldn't he just do what needed to be done. Then, in desperation he yelled out, 'Don't be such a bloody coward!'

His scream gave him the courage he needed, and he was on the point of taking those two vital steps when he was arrested by a voice behind him, which called out, 'You'd be a bloody coward to do it!' It was a girl's voice. A Scouse voice. Matt turned around, and there was the sodden figure of Jenny walking towards him.

'Angel!' he said, using his name for her. 'What the hell are you doing here?'

'Saving you, by the look of it' she answered, brushing a clump of wet hair from her face. Her platinum eyes were fixed on him. 'Look at the state of yer.'

'But… But how did you know I'd be here?'

'I didn't,' she said, placing her hands on her hips, and tilting her head to one side.

'So why *are* you here?'

'I'll only tell you, if you get yourself away from that edge,' said Jenny. 'You're scaring me shitless, you are. I can't stand heights at the best of times.'

Matt was now in a state of profound confusion. He still wanted to hurl himself over the edge, but there was no way he could do it with an audience. So, reluctantly he stepped away from the cliff edge back to the path. He wiped the rain from his eyes that had been blurring his sight, so that he could see the girl more clearly. Like him, she was also drenched. She seemed so thin and frail in her faded sweatshirt and torn jeans, and yet the expression on her face was one of determination and… And what? Her face was communicating something that he knew he could not bear to witness, so he looked quickly away. With his head still turned, he said, 'So, come on, tell me. What *are* doing you here in this godforsaken place? Did you follow me out here?'

'I didn't follow yer,' she said, shaking her head. 'Honest to God, I didn't.'

'Well, go on. What the hell are you doing walking along the cliff path in the pelting rain?' Matt was feeling a mix of anger at being thwarted from his vital mission, and shame at being found out.

'I was just walking over to Tregovenek,' she cried. The wind was roused again and a rain-laden cloud glowered over them.

'Why?' called Matt.

Jenny could hear the anger and desperation in his voice, and she knew why. A few years ago, she had been prevented from doing something similar, and she remembered how much she had resented it. But now, more than at any time in her life, she was so grateful that someone had turned up to stop her. Now she could do the same for someone else. Someone who most likely would resent her for preventing him doing his deadly deed. But stop him she must. And here was a moment in her life where she could do something special - even heroic. Something awesome. Something life-saving. In this moment, she felt more alive than she had ever done, and her face glowed with her conviction. Without any doubt, she knew that it was God who had called her here, the God of her colour-filled, hope-seeped, lantern cathedral had called her to save a life.

Matt was standing a few feet away from the girl. She could see the desperation in his face. He was stooped, with his arms hanging limply at this side, with water dripping from his outstretched hands. He was shaking and looked like a wild creature caught in a trap. She felt such compassion for the man, and she risked walking over to him and briefly placed her hand on his forearm. The sky was lightening and the gulls were starting to call again. 'I knew I just had to go to Tregovenek,' she said. 'That's all.' She put her hand in the pocket of her sodden jeans.

'What?' said Matt, frowning. 'In this weather?'

'I knew I had to,' she repeated.

'What do you mean you had to?'

Jenny chewed her bottom lip for a few moments. Then, returning to look at Matt, she said, 'I just wanted to see yer house. That's all. The rain

185

didn't put me off. I been out in rain plenty of times. I just wanted to see yer house.' She shrugged her shoulders and raised her eyebrows as she looked at Matt, blinking as the falling water from her hair brushed her eyelashes.

'My house?' said Matt, his face still contorted with pain and confusion. 'You... You wanted to see my house? What do you mean?' Matt was now aware of the cold and hugged his arms around himself.

Jenny nodded. She was feeling triumphant that she had managed to draw Matt away from that fearful cliff edge. But she now felt embarrassed by her reason for making this journey to Tregovenek. She looked briefly at Matt, and said, 'Sorry. I just...' She sighed, shrugged her shoulders again, then continued, 'It's just... The thing is, you were the kindest person I'd met since Beatrice in the Cathedral. I just wanted to see yer home, that's all. I wanted to imagine what it would be like to live in such a great home as you lived in. I wanted to try and see your daughter. You know, the one you were looking for. I was sure she'd be back home by now, and I wanted to see her. Perhaps I'd see her through a window, or something. I wanted to try and imagine what it would be like to live in that home, and how great it would be. I mean, I know you said your life was a helluva mess, but I still reckoned your home would be ace.' She frowned for a few moments and said, 'I wouldn't have knocked on the door, or anything. I'd have just looked at it from the road, like. I wouldn't have shamed yer, honest. So that's what I'm doing here. I didn't follow you. Honest to God, I didn't. I never thought I'd bump into yer up here. And not in a million years did I think you'd be... you know. Didn't realise you were that sad.'

Matt was now feeling very cold. He had no coat, and his jumper was soaked through. He was still hugging his arms tightly. He swallowed several times. 'You thought... You thought our home would be like that?' he said.

'I did. But I guess... Well... Sorry.'

Neither said a word for a few moments, then Jenny said, 'I were your angel, though, weren't I? Looks like I were meant to be here. I mean, what were the chances?' She smiled a vulnerable and beautiful smile that touched Matt so deeply that he could no longer hold back the sobs that had threatened to erupt throughout the conversation.

He pulled his hand up to his face, and for a few moments patted his mouth. Then, smiling and frowning, he looked at Jenny, and with a strangulated voice, said, 'You were meant to be here, Jenny. You are my angel sent from God.' She stepped forward and, for a long time, the two saturated friends held each other tight as a thin ray of spring sunshine filtered through the parting clouds, and flickered as highlights on the soaked surface of Jenny's blonde hair. Matt could now put a name to the expression he saw on Jenny's face earlier: it was love. It was one of the clearest expressions of love that he had ever witnessed. It was not romantic love that he saw. Rather it was an expression of utter goodwill of one human towards another; it was an exceptionally generous understanding of another's need; it was, perhaps above all, a profound yearning for the other to be well. It was a love that had been forged in the shadowlands of a desperately bruised heart.

Matt stepped back for a moment and said, 'Is it ok if I call you *Jenny*?'

'Course,' said Jenny. 'We're friends now, aren't we? But can I still be your angel?'

'Definitely,' said Matt.

'I'm bloody freezing,' she said, as she released him. She wrapped her slender arms around herself and said, 'You got your car here?'

'I have,' said Matt, grasping Jenny's arm.

'Can we go find somewhere warm, then? We'll both be dead from cold in a few minutes.'

'You wanted to see my house,' said Matt, as he steered Jenny along the path back to his car. 'I'm taking you home.'

*

A long, long way away in terms of time, yet not far in terms of distance, Solomon was awake after his night under the stars. The blackbird had woken him early. Despite the chilly air, the sheepskin had

187

kept him warm. And someone, presumably Monnine, had clearly been over to put fresh wood on the fire, as it was glowing contentedly. From somewhere across the compound he heard the crying of a baby, and there were other muffled sounds of members of the community waking to a new day. He pulled himself up and felt some stiffness. And then he remembered.

He remembered the dream.

More than that. He remembered everything.

'Tregovenek,' he said quietly to himself. It was so good to hear the name of his village again. 'Ella,' he said out loud. 'Lisa, Matt... And Jean and Ted... And...'. He smiled a warm smile. 'And yes... Solomon. Reverend Solomon David Ogilvy.' He had finally come to himself after what seemed like years of being away. With a little difficulty, he stood up and, grasping the sheepskin, he moved over to a bench and sat on it, pulling the sheepskin around his shoulders. So, his brain had finally healed sufficiently to bring back this all-important knowledge.

He grasped a stick and leaned forward to push an escaping piece of wood back on to the fire. He was feeling a profound sense of reassurance from knowing his name again. He uttered it out loud several times and had a curious sense that it sounded different. Something had been filled in that had previously been missing. Indeed, it was fair to say, much that had been hidden within him had been brought out into the light during his time with Monnine and her community. Some outer coating had been gently stripped back revealing parts of his soul which had not seen the light of day since his childhood.

'Christ's joy to you this morning,' called a voice to his left. He recognised it at once as Monnine's. She had just emerged from her watch in the chapel. She was pulling her cloak tight around her shoulders as she walked towards him.

'Good morning to you, Monnine,' said Solomon, and stood to welcome his friend to the fireside.

'Did the fire and sheep's coat keep you warm, Seanchara?' she asked, as she settled on the bench beside him.

'Most warm under this sheepskin, thank you,' replied Solomon.

'So, how did it go, sleeping beneath the quiet of the stars?' enquired Monnine.

Solomon recounted the dreams of the night, and the information they imparted to him.

'So your name is Solomon, is it?' said Monnine thoughtfully. 'Did your father hope you'd gather the wealth or the wisdom? Or both maybe?'

'Well, I never had the wealth,' said Solomon. 'And judging by how I find myself at the moment, I doubt I have had much wisdom either.'

'Solomon had his dream,' said Monnine, and closed her eyes. 'Let me recall the story in that book of Kings. Remember the man also fell asleep, and he dreamed the kind of dream that you knew under the stars last night. It was an open dream.' She frowned as she recalled a passage of scripture that she had committed to memory. 'The memory fails me these days, but let me try... Yes, here it is: the Almighty Father has stepped into the dream and speaks to him saying, "Lo, I have given thee a wise and an understanding heart; so that there was none like thee before thee, neither after thee shall any arise like unto thee. And I have also given thee that which thou hast not asked, both riches, and honour. And if thou wilt walk in my ways, to keep my statutes and my commandments, as thy father David did walk, then I will lengthen thy days. And Solomon awoke; and, behold, it was a dream." 'After quoting the scripture, Monnine opened her eyes and looked at the old man saying, 'You have the wise and understanding heart for sure, my friend. When you return to your people, that heart will be a happy channel for the wisdom from above. You will see.'

'Hm,' said Solomon, not entirely convinced.

Before he could say more, Monnine leaned towards him saying, 'And don't be surprised if you get the others too.'

'The others?'

'Aye,' she replied. 'I'm thinking about the riches, and the honour and the length of days.'

Solomon frowned for some moments as he heard these words. Returning to his memory during the night was his conviction that Matt's business was in far deeper trouble than Matt was letting on, and he therefore seriously doubted this prediction of wealth. The honour and length of days also seemed highly unlikely, for he had felt none too strong these past few months. But he did not want to disrespect his friend, so he stretched out his hand, grasping hers and replied, 'Thank you, Monnine.'

'And do you remember the name of the place where you live?' asked Monnine.

Solomon's brow furrowed briefly, and then he smiled and said, 'Yes, I do. The name of my village is Tregovenek.'

'Is that so?' said Monnine, raising her eyes briefly to the skies. She then looked back at Solomon, and said, 'That makes much sense to me.'

'It does?'

'It's in the language of the people here in Kernow,' she said. 'You live in the homestead of hope. That's the meaning of the name.'

'Well, well...' said Solomon. 'That I did not know.'

But listen,' she said, rising from the bench. 'Come and let's have some warm milk to start our day.'

Solomon duly rose from his seat, and they made their way to the dining hall. There they found a pot of milk by the cooking fire. Monnine poured them two mugs and passed one to Solomon. 'So, you are Solomon,' she said, as they settled on a nearby table. She fixed her green eyes on Solomon and added, 'But how much of Solomon have you become, I wonder?'

Solomon knew that this was the kind of question he had been avoiding all his life.

# 21

Ella slept well that Sunday night and she was awoken by the sound of rain splattering on the window. She remembered that today was a revision day. Quite why she had decided to choose biology as an A level was still a mystery to her. However, she had been doing well at it, and was predicted an A. Nonetheless, the thought of going over her notes on pectin, lipids and enzymes was not enough to get her out of bed, and she pulled her duvet over her. But she couldn't get back to sleep. There was too much turmoil inside her. Her mother had been having something pretty close to an affair. Her father was behaving weirdly. Her great uncle had now had three nights away from home and she had failed to find him. But, on the bright side, she had met two very interesting people over the weekend. An African asylum-seeker called Rahab, and an entertaining nun called Maria. It was the remembering of those two that gave Ella the energy to get out of bed and get started on the day.

'Delightful morning,' she said sarcastically as she made it down for breakfast. Her mother was sitting at the kitchen table reading the paper.

'Morning, love,' she said to her daughter.

'Not going into work?' said Ella, as she filled the kettle.

'No clients today,' lied Lisa. She had cancelled her three clients earlier. She knew Troy was in the office today and she was not ready to have a face to face meeting with him, so she called in sick.

'More coffee?' enquired Ella.

'Please.'

'Dad been in touch?'

'No,' said Lisa. 'I've tried texting him several times, but he's not got back to me.'

'Not like him.'

'No, but...' Lisa sighed and looked round at her daughter. 'There's something going really bad with that new development. He's been so stressed about it. And he did mention he had a meeting with the bank manager today. He'll be really worried about that.'

'How serious is it?' asked Ella, filling the cafetière.

Lisa shrugged her shoulders and pushed her chin forward.

'It's serious, isn't it?' said Ella. She brought the steaming cafetière to the table.

'I think it could be,' said Lisa. 'He's not said so, but I'm pretty sure we're going to be losing this house.'

'God.'

'I know.' Lisa sighed. 'You know, he really is a good man, Ella, isn't he?'

Ella nodded her head, and was about to say something when she was interrupted by the sound of a car on the drive followed by the doorbell. 'I'll go,' Lisa said, and departed to the hall.

Ella heard conversation in the hall, the sound of the strenuous wiping of feet, and her mother returned followed by the distinctive figure of Inspector Littlegown.

'This is the Inspector,' said Lisa wearily.

'Hi,' said Ella, then went to the cupboard to fetch some cereal.

'You the girl that went missing?' enquired the Inspector.

Ella raised her eyebrows, said nothing and fetched a bowl and spoon.

'Yes, she is,' said Lisa. 'But all's well, as you can see. Do sit. Coffee?'

'It will be tea with one sugar, if you please. Not milky,' replied the Inspector. 'Just as I said,' she continued, as she removed her cap and sat down. 'Young people. Told you she'd be back.'

Lisa chose to ignore the comments about her daughter, and said, 'So, what progress are you making with my uncle?' She placed a milky tea in front of the Inspector, who appeared to wince. Lisa passed her sugar.

'Right,' said the Inspector as she helped herself to a generous spoonful of sugar. 'Apologies again for the unfortunate wrong identity yesterday.' Ella looked at her mother and winked. Inspector Littlegown took a lengthy swig from her mug, almost emptying it. 'So,' she continued as she unsuccessfully attempted to disguise a burp. 'We do believe we have a new piece of evidence.'

'You do?' said Lisa. Ella paused eating her muesli, and looked at the Inspector.

'We do,' replied the Inspector, then drained her mug.

'And?' said Lisa, lowering her head, peering at the Inspector.

'Right,' said the Inspector slowly. 'We received a report from the Methodist Minister in Porthann. And a gentleman who matches the description you gave me attended worship at her church yesterday evening.'

'She did?'

'She did. She said he left early before she had a chance to speak with him. But I'm afraid we can't progress this until I have a photograph of your uncle.' She started to bang her substantial finger on the table as she continued, 'I can't emphasise enough that I need a photograph of your uncle. We urgently need a photograph, and that is why I have come here today. I've even come armed with a memory stick, if the only photo you have is on your computer.' She produced a memory stick from her pocket and waved it at them, then added, 'But surely you have one on your phones? In which case, please would you text it to me now.'

Lisa looked at Ella and said, 'I'm sure you have one, Ella.'

Ella reached for her phone, but she was very doubtful if there was one.

'You have one I can use, miss?' enquired the Inspector, failing to hide her growing irritation.

'Well,' said Ella, who picked up her phone and started to scroll through her photos. But she knew full well that she had no photographic record of the old man, whom she loved so dearly. How come she had never thought to take a photo of him?

Just at that moment, there was the sound of another vehicle on the drive. Ella got up from her seat and peered out of the kitchen window. 'It's Dad,' she said.

'But it can't be,' responded Lisa, frowning. 'He's got this crucial meeting with the bank manager this morning. He won't be missing that.'

'Well it *is* him,' said Ella, peering through the window at the drive. 'And he's got a girl with him!'

'A girl?' said both Lisa and the Inspector together.

But before anyone could say more, Matt and his companion had come into the house and entered the kitchen. Lisa and Ella both stood up as they entered. The Inspector stayed seated, her hands folded around her empty mug.

'We're drenched,' said Matt. 'And Jenny here is freezing to death. We need to get her a towel and some warm clothes.'

The arrival was so sudden, and the appearance of the girl so surprising, that no-one quite knew what to say for a few moments. It was Lisa who simply managed, 'Jenny?'

'Oh, sorry,' said Matt. 'This is Jenny. I met her in town last night.'

The Inspector took one look at the girl, and was in no doubt as to her trade. Both the Inspector's eyebrows were raised as she stared at the table in front of her, sucking in her cheeks.

Then Ella said, 'I saw you on Saturday night, didn't I?'

'Yeah,' said Jenny through chattering teeth. 'I remember. Fancy.'

'You did?' said Matt.

Lisa, still bewildered, but filled with concern for the girl, said, 'Ella, for God's sake take the girl upstairs. Let her use your bathroom, and see if you can find some dry clothes to lend her.'

'Cool,' said Ella, and went over to the girl. 'I'm Ella,' she said.

'I guessed,' said Jenny.

'Hear you went out looking for me, Dad,' said Ella, glancing at her father, before leaving the room. Matt smiled a limp smile at his

194

daughter. 'Thanks,' she said as she kissed him lightly on his damp cheek. Then she shepherded Jenny up to her room.

'You should get changed as well,' said Lisa to Matt.

'I'd love a hot coffee, first,' replied Matt, as he moved towards the welcome heat of the Aga.

'Right,' said the Inspector, rising from her seat and grasping her cap. 'It appears that I'll not be receiving the photograph while I'm here.' Firing a fierce stare at Lisa, she said, 'I'm going to have to tell you straight, that we will be making no progress on this case until I receive that photograph. You must have one somewhere. As soon as you send it to me, I can check it with the minister in Porthann, and we can get the photo out on the local news. Somebody will recognise him, for sure. So, the photo: as soon as you can, please. I'll see myself out.' With that she left the kitchen, and Matt and Lisa heard her firmly shut the front door.

Lisa found a towel and gave it to her husband, who gratefully dried his face and hair, then she refilled the cafetière.

'So… The girl?' she said, tipping her head to one side.

'Oh, the girl,' said Matt. 'Yes. Er… Well, I called her Angel. But actually, her name's Jenny.'

'Angel? Jenny? Who in Christ's name is she? And why is she here? And why aren't you at the bank, for that matter?'

'Oh, sorry,' said Matt. The events of the morning had been so deeply troubling to Matt, that he felt completely disorientated. He was trying to haul his mind into some kind of coherence, but he could not stop it from revisiting the rain-soaked cliff edge. Had his angel not turned up, he could well be splattered into several pieces on the shore by now. And, apart from all of that, Lisa was right. It was now approaching the time when he should be with the bank manager. His phone would soon be ringing. He placed it on the table.

'Matt?' said Lisa, who was waiting for an answer. 'The girl?' She poured a coffee for her husband.

'Oh, sorry,' repeated Matt. He remained by the Aga to keep warm and sipped gently at the welcome coffee. He then told Lisa about his meeting with Jenny on the Saturday night.

Lisa listened carefully and was aware of the fragile nature of her husband's mind.

'Ok,' said Lisa, as she sat at the table. She had refilled her cup, and took a sip from it. 'So, you were out looking for Ella, but instead you met a sex worker called Jenny, whom you called Angel - God knows why. You decided not to sleep with her - for which I'm grateful - but you bought her a McDonalds instead.'

'Yes,' agreed Matt, still pressing himself to the warmth of the Aga.

'But,' Lisa said. 'That doesn't explain why she's turned up here this morning with you.'

'Er, no,' said Matt. He felt a little warmer now, and came and sat across the table from his wife.

'Were you with her all yesterday as well?'

'No, no,' said Matt. 'No, yesterday I was with Theo.'

'Theo?' said Lisa, wincing in confusion. 'Who the hell's Theo?'

'Oh, you don't know him?'

'No I don't,' said Lisa, her impatience growing.

'No, well,' said Matt, who was now starting to doubt his own story. None of it sounded very convincing to him. 'He's a fisherman and he took me out on his boat.'

'On his boat? But you were supposed to be looking for Ella!'

'Yes, I was, wasn't I?' Matt sighed and looked down into his coffee. 'Sorry.' His face slowly crumpled and he began to shake. He put down the mug and hid his face in his hands.

'Darling?' said Lisa, surprising herself with the depth of affection and compassion that she felt for her husband. She reached across the table and grasped his hands.

Matt recovered himself and, red-eyed, he looked to Lisa. She had never seen him look so forlorn. At that moment, they were interrupted by the sharp ringtone of his phone. The name of the bank glared out at him. He noted the time - ten past eleven. He switched the phone to silent, then looked up at Lisa. His face crumpled as he said several times, 'I'm so sorry....'

*

'You got your own shower and loo!' exclaimed Jenny, as Ella showed her into her room.

For a moment, Ella felt a little guilty regarding her ensuite room that she took very much for granted. 'Help yourself,' she said, guiding Jenny to the brightly-coloured bathroom. She pulled a couple of fresh towels from the cupboard and handed them to her. 'I'll look out some clothes that you can borrow.'

Jenny took the towels and drew them to her cheek. 'So soft,' she said, and Ella noticed that it was not just the rain that was moistening her face. She reached out her hand and briefly squeezed the thin elbow of the girl. Her dyed blonde hair, that was still sodden from the rain, framed her delicate face. She saw in the platinum eyes a remarkable quality of defiance against the misfortunes that had clearly come her way. But dark shadows lay around those eyes, betraying the effects of drugs. Ella knew the signs well.

When Jenny eventually emerged from the bathroom with one towel wrapped around her slender frame, and the other acting as a turban, Ella had laid out some possible clothes for her on her bed. Jenny quickly chose some and, though Ella was of a slightly different build to Jenny, nonetheless, Jenny was delighted to put them on and insisted they fitted perfectly. 'Must be like heaven living here,' she said, pulling on her top.

'Yeah,' said Ella unconvincingly.

Jenny spent some time drying her hair and Ella watched her. Now that Jenny was out of her bedraggled state, Ella saw more clearly both strength and beauty in the girl. Was it this that drew her dad to befriend her? She sat on the bed next to her and leaned her head to one side saying, 'What do you do? Are you what I think you are?'

'A whore?' said Jenny.

'I wasn't going to use that word,' said Ella.

'Well, seeing's you asked,' replied Jenny, defiant again. 'Yeah I am. You shocked?'

'No,' said Ella, and Jenny could see she wasn't. 'In fact, I was just talking to one on Saturday. One from Africa.'

'You did?'

'Mm,' said Ella. Then she looked at Jenny and said, 'So did you sleep with my dad, then?'

Jenny was now brushing her hair and smiled a winsome smile for a few moments. She paused the brushing and, frowning, said, 'No, he didn't want to. Not very flattering is it? I mean, I don't look that bad. I got the right shape and that.' She clutched her ample bosom.

Ella chuckled, then said, 'So why? Why are you with him?'

Jenny spoke openly about the evening meeting and the shared meal in the car. But she was much more cautious about the meeting on the cliff top. She was certain Matt would not want the family to know of his intentions that morning. So, she simply said she was out for a run and bumped into him. Ella sensed this was not the whole truth but decided not to push it.

'You found the old man you been searching for?' asked Jenny, changing the subject. Ella shook her head and pursed her lips. 'You worried?' asked Jenny.

'Yeah,' said Ella. 'I mean, I get everyone saying he's probably OK. But, he's eighty-five, for God's sake.' She looked out of the window. 'He's been gone since Friday night. It's a long time to be on your own out there at that age.'

'I prayed for him,' said Jenny, placing the brush neatly on the bed.

'Yeah?' said Ella. She felt some anxiety. Here was yet another person who had a thing about God.

'Yer, I did,' said Jenny confidently.

Ella shrugged her shoulders, and said, 'I'm not... you know. God's not really my thing. Sorry.' She didn't want another conversation about religion. The discussions with Rahab and Sister Maria were quite enough.

'Oh, that's a pity,' said Jenny.

'Is it?' said Ella, now staring out of the window.

'Yeah,' replied Jenny. 'I wouldn't be without God, I wouldn't.' She then leaned back and lay her head on the soft pillow. 'I love this bed,' she added.

Ella was starting to feel annoyed with all these religious people she was meeting, and was finding it extraordinary to be meeting another *religious* sex worker in the space of a few days. Both women had clearly had really hard lives, and had to engage in a profession that must have been the last thing they would have wanted. And yet here was Jenny talking about God in her life. So she turned to Jenny and said, 'Well, if you don't mind me saying so, God's not done you much good in your life, has he?'

Jenny sat up and said, 'He's done me a power of good, He has. Just because I'm a prozzie, doesn't mean God's forgotten me.'

To Ella, it most definitely *did* sound as if God had forgotten her. However, she didn't want to argue with the girl. But there was another problem. 'Ok, if you say so. But then, he can't exactly approve of what you do. My gran's a born-again Christian, and if you told her you were a prostitute, she'd say you were being led by the devil and you'd be going to hell.'

'Would she?' said Jenny, lying back on the pillow again. 'That's sad, isn't it? Poor thing. I'd say she's got a helluva lot to learn about the kind of people that God's fond of, don't you think? Some people get God so wrong, they do.'

Ella started to laugh.

'You laughing at me?' asked Jenny, raising her head from the pillow.

'No, no,' assured Ella. 'I'm laughing at what you said about my gran. Be fab to see you tell her that she's got God completely wrong! I'd love to see her face!' Her laughter was so infectious that Jenny joined in. Ella lay back on the bed next to her new friend, and both girls were caught in a time of delighted and shared mirth. Both, for different reasons, felt a welcome sense of freedom.

# 22

Monnine and Solomon found a table in the dining hall. Others entered the dining hall that Monday morning to gather their breakfast, but they could see from the intensity of expressions on the faces of Monnine and Solomon that they needed some privacy, so they ate at different tables.

'I do not understand your question,' said Solomon, who was both anxious and curious.

Monnine supped from her mug. 'The milk is rich today,' she said. 'There has been blessing on our cows of late, there surely has. There's a drop of Paradise in this milk, don't you think?'

Solomon drank from his mug and, without doubt, there was a quality about the milk that he knew he had never experienced. 'They have put honey in this milk, surely?'

'No,' said Monnine. 'There is no honey in it. Just Paradise.' She drank again from her mug, then placed it carefully on the table. 'So, the question I asked you: how much of Solomon have you become?' She ran her finger up and down the mug for a few moments, then looked at Solomon and said, 'Three nights ago, I was at prayer in the chapel. I was drawn into such an intensity of prayer. More than I have known before.' She frowned. 'It was as though a great and beautiful storm raged through my mind. Not a storm that destroys, but one that clears the path. And for a blessed few moments, the path was clear, and I could see all along it. I saw everything.'

'Everything?'

'Everything that I needed to see.' She was now looking away from him towards the door. 'The Apostle Paul told us that once he was transported to the chambers of Heaven. For my sins, I thought that I should never see such a thing while my feet are planted on this earth. But, by the gentle grace of God, I was allowed to catch sight of the marvels to come.' She shook her head. 'It is a tender thing to have your mind so clear, that your eyes are truly open. All you hope for by faith is given to you in sight. You hear sounds that could never be caught by the ear of our mortal frames. Oh, the sweetness of those sounds.' She turned back to him, her eyes glistening as they reflected the flame of the nearby fire. 'We have much to look forward to, my friend. So much.' She beamed her endearing smile.

Solomon, who, at best, always had a fairly limp view of the afterlife, furrowed his brow in an attempt to understand what he was being told. Monnine unclasped her cloak. Whether it was the warmth of the nearby fire, or the glow of the memory, she was feeling a heat rising in her as she related her experience. 'I knew at that moment,' she continued, 'that I only had to take one step, and I would cease breathing the air of this world, and would begin to inhale the dear airs of that world opened to us by our Saviour. How I longed to step over. How I longed.' She sighed. 'I shall be homesick now for the rest of my days on this earth.'

She stopped talking. Her mind had moved to another world. 'If I may,' said Solomon. 'Why did you not take that step?'

Monnine blinked for a moment, then looked back at Solomon, and said, 'Oh, well now... Oh, I knew. I knew it was not the appointed time. But so kind of Him who loves us, to give me that precious glimpse. But now, listen,' she continued, returning her focus to Solomon. 'This is the point of my story. I then saw time.'

'You saw time?' said Solomon, the lines of his forehead deepening. 'Corman also spoke to me of time.'

'Aye,' said Monnine. 'That man knows more about time than any of us.'

'But you say that you actually *saw* it,' said Solomon, struggling to grasp such mysteries.

'I saw it,' replied Monnine. 'Magnificent it was. Quite magnificent.'

"How... How did it look?'

Monnine raised her eyebrows and looked back out through the doorway again. 'How it should,' she said. She turned back to Solomon and said, 'Do you know that time is also beloved? It's a great comfort that, isn't it?'

'I suppose so,' said Solomon, though far from convinced that it was a comfort.

'*Now* is only a small part of it,' said Monnine. 'He blessed us humans with the power to remember. When we remember, our minds take a journey back through time. Our memories can lift us or they can weigh us down. But you, my friend, you arrived here with very little past to remember. You were unbuckled from it, so you could walk with a lighter step, for the weight of your past had become too heavy for you. For the first time in your life, you were free of it. Is that not a special gift?'

'It is,' agreed Solomon, his grey eyes blinking slowly behind his spectacles.

'But you were not free of fear,' said Monnine. 'You arrived carrying your fear.'

'Yes, I cannot deny that my fears burden me,' said Solomon, who was feeling the heaviness of them as he admitted them.

'When your yesterdays are healed, your shame falls away,' said Monnine. 'And when your tomorrows are healed, your fears are dispelled. We all need the healing of time if we are to live free in each of the todays that we are given in this life.'

'But how can I be relieved of my fears?' asked Solomon.

Monnine looked at this man, who had come to them from the future. She saw the frailty in his eyes as he asked this searching question.

'What do our Scriptures tell us?' replied Monnine. 'It is the perfect love that casts the fear out of us. Our fears can be our friends, you see. They drive us to seek out that perfect love, the love that shone radiant from our Saviour when he walked among us. So, while fear is there, our quest is there. We will not rest 'til our fears are at rest. Our fears will only rest when we find His love. That's the nature of perfect love.'

'Then,' said Solomon, resting his eyes for some moments on the glowing logs in the fireplace. 'I will indeed search for that love for the rest of my days.' The two were quiet for a few moments, then Solomon leaned towards Monnine and said, 'You felt that love three nights ago?'

'I did. And my fears dissolved like cold flakes of snow under the gaze of the morning sun.'

'So, was it from that reverie that you stepped into my time and found my fear-bound soul?'

'Yes,' said Monnine. 'Let me return to that story.' She shifted her position on her seat, and leant her arms on the table. 'So, I was looking at time, admiring it in a way I had never admired it before. And in my gazing into the future years, I saw a statue of our Christ on the cross. Carved in marble, it was. I have seen such statues of the Roman gods, but not of our Saviour. It was attached to a wall of stone. I saw the sad face, the white marble eyes looking downwards in pity. Above the stone wall that held the stature was another wall made of glass. Glorious colours of glass. Quite beautiful it was. And beneath the figure of our Christ was a large table. A fine, white garment was placed over it, as if it was prepared for a banquet. All this I saw to be inside a large and high-roofed hall. There were grey stone pillars supporting the grand wooden roof, and in every wall, there were more splendid windows of colour. At first, I did not know what all this was, but then I came to understand that this was how the people of the future built their churches. I then saw some dark wooden benches, and seated on one of those benches was you. There you were, Solomon, sitting alone on that bench. Your hand pink with blood was cupping the crown of your head. You were, without doubt, a wounded and lost man, and I knew I had been called to aid you.'

'Wounded and lost? Yes, indeed,' said Solomon, as he drained the last of his warm milk. 'And how did my world seem to you, Monnine, as you stepped into it?'

'It also felt wounded and lost,' replied Monnine. 'You and your world - the same. I knew I had travelled many years forward from my own time, and strangely it all felt quite normal. The sounds of Paradise were still sounding in the chambers of my soul, but they faded as I walked into that grand building. The building was indeed glorious, but it had the feel of winter about it, and I felt a gnawing emptiness under that high, high ceiling. It seemed to me that there had been no radiance in the place for many a year. But the sight of my Saviour carved in marble gave me comfort.'

'And then you came over to me,' said Solomon, as his demeanour brightened. 'And you took my hand and led me here.'

'I did. I led you through the mystery of time to my community here. I knew this was to be your tomb.'

'My tomb?' said Solomon, somewhat startled.

'Lazarus.'

'Ah, Corman spoke of this.'

'Corman saw it,' said Monnine. 'He sees such things.'

'So, I have died in this tomb?'

'Och, no. The tomb of Lazarus is where you come alive! I and Corman and all the others here are the friends to unbind you. You came to us as one with a soul so wrapped in shrouds we scarce could find the gleam of life. But gleam there was. Enough to catch the eye of Christ. He saw the sweetness in your spirit, and the unspoken longing in your soul. And He has called you to come forth. You have stepped forth. You are unbound. You will return alive, my friend.'

Solomon's eyelids closed for a few moments, and he said quietly, 'Yes, I do feel unbound. But I fear it is all too late. I only have a short time left on this earth.'

'Well, now,' said Monnine. 'If your days are few, then let them be days filled with wonder. Live as you have never lived before. It is better to be fully alive for even one day in this dear world, than to spend all your days in a life half-lived. Some people never come out of their hibernation. But for you, Solomon, the Spring sun is rising. The earth around your soul is getting warm. You have the chance to live at least some of your days as the person you were created to be.'

Solomon felt Monnine's words evoke a new energy within him. 'It is true, Monnine,' he said. 'Mine has been a hibernated life. But it is time for me to emerge from my hiding. I sense that what you say is true, even though my poor mind cannot grasp the half of this. But will they

205

recognise me? I think some will be deeply troubled to see me so changed.'

'Aye, there are some,' cautioned Monnine, 'whose wounds and fears have so reduced their dreams that they have forgotten how to find the realms of hope. And others, who for sad, sad reasons have preferred the dark to the light. Yes, there will be some who will not understand. But the light that beams from the skies of heaven is both vigorous and tender. Let it shine from you, and I think more shadows than you think will flee from its rays.'

A young man came over to their table with a loaf of freshly baked bread. Monnine tore off a steaming chunk away from the loaf and offered it to Solomon, which he gratefully received. He closed his eyes for a few moments, savouring the taste. Then he said, 'Monnine, I shall miss you. I shall miss you all. I am feeling sad. I have not felt this sorrow of parting for many years.'

'I know,' said Monnine. 'This is the cost of the open heart. And we shall miss you, too. You have gifted us more than you know.'

'That is hard for me to believe,' said Solomon. Then he added, 'But tell me, how do I return to my world? How do I step through a boundary I once believed to be impossible to cross?'

Monnine was chewing hard on a piece of the bread, and when she eventually swallowed it, she said, 'Was it not His friend, Peter, who said, 'But, beloved, be not ignorant of this one thing, that one day is with the Lord as a thousand years, and a thousand years as one day.'

'I believe it was,' said Solomon, who knew and loved his scriptures.

'Then you have your answer.'

'I do?'

Monnine, with her mouth still partly full, called across to the young lad who had brought the loaf to them, 'Marcus, you have baked us a treat today. Thank you.' The lad waved an acknowledgement. Turning to Solomon, she said, 'He only learned to bake last week, but he is making a good job of it. So, where were we? Ah, yes, a thousand years and that. Your time would be more than a thousand year's distant from our time, I think?'

'Yes, much more, I am sure.'

'It's a grand mystery, it sure is. But the clue is in those words "with the Lord". With Him, all time exists. That means beginnings, middles and endings. Even eternity is in there. They are all with the Lord, and He may lead his children through any of the doors of time, whenever He should choose. He can pull the future into the present, and the past is always within His reach. But the kind of travelling you have done is not very common.'

Solomon was taken aback by how matter of fact Monnine seemed to be by the concept of this movement between times. His face was a grimace of concentration as he asked, 'So it is not very common for one like me to come from the future to visit you?'

'Very rare,' replied Monnine, reaching for more bread. 'I doubt any of us here will see someone like yourself stepping into our time again. It will be a story for our children and their children, that is for sure. But I do know this: our world here is not your home, and so you cannot stay here. Much as we've grown to love you, this is not your place of belonging, and if you stay here too long, you'd start to suffer. We shall go to the chapel soon. It's where I was when I was sent to your world. I expect that will be your place of departing.' She tilted her head to one side as she looked at him and asked, 'Do you feel ready to return?'

'I think so,' said Solomon, who was feeling some nervousness about the thought of seeing his family and parishioners again. 'But how do I explain to my people what has happened? Who is going to believe me when I say I have travelled through time to your community here?'

'They don't need to believe it,' said Monnine. 'Those whose eyesight of the heart is sharp will see. And those whose eyes are dim, will simply think you have done some vivid dreaming when you had that bang on your head.'

'I suppose so,' said Solomon. Then he looked at Monnine and said, 'But what sort of a priest shall I be when I return?'

'Different,' said Monnine.

'I'm thinking I should no longer carry out my ministry in the church,' said Solomon.

207

'Nonsense!' exclaimed Monnine. 'The church in your time is in trouble. Even my brief visit told me that. And Corman has had his glimpse too, and he felt the same. He told me so. Made him fearful sad, it did. No, you must serve them as a priest for more days yet, because your soul has awoken, and you can help them to wake up.'

'But...'

'It's not about "buts",' said Monnine. 'It's about love, don't you see? I know what you are thinking, my friend. You think you will have to return, and labour hard to cajole them to life. You think you will have to plan great gatherings in that barn of a place where your people come for worship. That building with its glass of many colours looks mighty beautiful and is grand in its own way. But what you will be building will have nothing to do with stone and glass. Neither will it demand the sweat from your brow. No, you will be building with the laughter and the tears of Christ. Build what we have here. Look at it. Look at the lives of these dear people. Each and every one lit by the glowing fire of Christ. All you need to do is light His fire, and watch the people warm themselves by it.'

Solomon was still doubting very much that he had it in him to touch the hearts of people in the way that Monnine was suggesting. But he could not deny that something was stirring in him. Though he was feeling the tiredness of his years, he also felt an almost youthful energy of inspiration rising from the healed part of his soul. He turned and gazed out of the door of the dining hall. He could see that the compound was busy with animated life. Men, women and children were busy about their various occupations. 'Your community,' he said almost dreamily.

'Yes?'

'Your people... It feels like you are all so united. So, at one. There's a peace.'

'Not always,' said Monnine, now munching her last piece of bread. 'I've had to break up a few fights. There's no-one who's perfect here, I can tell you that, for sure!' She chuckled.

'Ah,' said Solomon. But he knew that the church communities of which he had been part were nothing like the community he was experiencing here.

'The thing is,' said Monnine, now brushing crumbs from her gown. 'We are united, even if we do have our fights from time to time. But that doesn't mean we have settled down as a nice happy family fixed to this home. Oh, no. Each one of us here has been caught by a breeze that has a habit of blowing us to new waters. It is a wild breeze, it is. Remember the words of John, in his lovely book: *The wind bloweth where it listeth, and thou hearest the sound thereof, but canst not tell whence it cometh, and whither it goeth: so is every one that is born of the Spirit.* That's the wind of heaven, and there's no better wind than that. I've seen even the dampest heart catch light in that wind. It doesn't cure all our problems, but it does set us on adventures. Take Marcus there.' She nodded in the direction of the young baker. 'He was taken as a slave when he was a young'un. But, thank God, we found him and freed him. My, when the Spirit sparked life in that wounded soul, it was a wonder to see. He'll be adventuring soon, I have no doubt. He'll be baking bread on a different shore before the year is out.'

'Why? Why all the travelling?' asked Solomon, his eyebrows furrowing.

'Because when you have been given so much, you want to search out the wasted places of humanity, and there kneel before the beloved people, offering them the bread of life. Marcus longs to share that kind of bread, he sure does. Many will feed from his table. And besides, did you not tell me that your own father heard the call to go to another land?'

Solomon looked down at the table and picked at a piece of rough wood. 'Yes, he did,' he said. 'And it cost him his life.'

'I know, I know,' said Monnine, and placed her hand over his. 'But, listen my friend. Who knows what life he lived in those days, and what life he shared? If he had not gone, then something within him would have died.'

'Instead, we died,' said Solomon, who turned his hand over so that he could clasp Monnine's. He drew strength from it.

Monnine grasped his hand firmly and said, 'Walk free of your past, Solomon. Don't let it hold you back from living. Your father would not have wanted that. Live while you now have the chance. Don't be held back by past sorrows.'

Solomon's demeanour lifted, and he smiled a kindly smile at Monnine, saying 'I believe I have lived in the shadow of grief all my life, and I am weary of it. You are right. It is time to move on.'

'It is indeed,' replied Monnine. 'Now come, let me gather the others and we will say our farewells.' And with that, the two rose from the table. Solomon still had little clue as to how he was going to take the mysterious voyage back to his own time, but he rested in Monnine's confidence, and together they walked out into the compound as the rays of the morning sun slipped through the parting veil of April clouds.

# 23

Matt's phone lit up again. This was the third missed call. Each one from the bank. Each call left a message. Each time Matt did not check the message. Instead, he was trying to explain himself to his wife, but only managed a random jumble of thoughts. He did not want her to know the drastic action he was so close to taking just a few hours previously.

'So, you're not going to the meeting now?' enquired Lisa, as she observed Matt refusing to take the calls.

Matt shook his head.

'Just how bad is it?' asked Lisa. She knew much lay in the answer to her question. Matt said nothing. He was sitting at the table. The palms of his hands were clasping his forehead, and all Lisa could see were his pale fingers pressed on to his damp hair. She knew that if she could see his face, it would be grimaced in pain. His lack of answer confirmed her fears. 'We can get through this, Matt,' she said quietly.

For some time, he didn't move, and then he inhaled deeply and looked up at her through his reddened eyes. 'I'm so, so sorry, Lis,' he said. He could not bear to see the anxious face of his wife, and he looked out through the window. The world outside looked distorted as a fresh shower of rain was splattering against the glass.

Lisa had been all set to break to Matt the appalling news of her fling with Troy. But how could she, when he was in this state? And the romance looked so much more appalling now. Somehow, when Matt was his usual brash self, occupied in his work and apparently with very little need of anyone, her clandestine meetings with Troy seemed somehow understandable. If discovered, as she knew she would be one day, she could argue that she had good reason to be going off to find the affection and a listening ear that she wasn't getting at home. But now things looked very different as she was confronted with this undefended Matt. She had imagined breaking the news to him during one of their rows, where the admission of her romantic dalliance would be the necessary coup de grâce for the marriage. But angry as she had been with Matt, there was no way she could deal a blow to the wounded figure opposite her.

For some moments she recoiled from the vulnerability that she saw in him. She felt annoyed. He had emotionally upstaged her. But then she became aware of this other, unfamiliar part of herself: this once dormant part of herself, the child that had awoken since the disappearance of her uncle. And this part of herself was not experiencing annoyance, but something quite different. Had she been able to find a name, it would have been something like *compassion*. Not a patronising 'there, there' compassion, but the true sense of the word - a suffering *with*. She became very aware that she and Matt were in this mess together, a mess that was both of their making. The disaster that had been looming for a while was now happening, and no amount of finger-pointing and point-scoring would make it go away. She felt an overwhelming sense that the only way to overcome this problem was by being tender with each other, and by facing it together. She reached forward and plucked the damp fingers from the tousled hair and held them tight as she said, 'Matt, let's do this together.'

He raised his reddened face to hers and nodded very slowly. 'It's been a long time,' he said in a whisper.

'What happened?' she asked.

'I got lost,' he answered.

'Me too.'

They were both quiet for a while, then Matt looked toward the kitchen door and said, 'That girl upstairs.'

'Your angel?' The idea of the girl being likened to an angel was still a mystery to Lisa, but she recognised that for some reason this is how her husband viewed her.

Matt smiled a weak smile. He looked down at Lisa's hand stroking his and said, 'She's had such a broken life. You know what old Theo said?'

'What did he say?'

212

Matt's face crumpled for a few moments. He then steadied himself and replied, 'He said that in another world that girl would have been a queen, sat on a throne of pearl.' For reasons Matt could never understand, these words caused tears to run freely from his eyes. Lisa had never seen him weep like this. Not even in his penitential phase following the cocaine episodes. A very different current was flowing through the soul of her husband. Matt released his hands from his wife's and found a handkerchief in his pocket. Though damp from the rain, he nonetheless used it to mop his eyes, then blew his nose. 'She loves Cathedrals.'

'She does?'

'Well, one in particular. It's in Liverpool.' Matt sniffed, then chuckled briefly and said, 'She called it *Paddy's Wigwam.*' Lisa smiled an uncertain smile. Matt then frowned again as he stuffed his handkerchief back in his pocket. 'Theo was a character too.'

'You went out in his boat?'

'Yeah - he invited me to go with him. Just a short trip. But he took me out there.' Matt nodded in the direction of the ocean behind him. 'Our house looks very different from there...'. His lip started its trembling again, but he controlled the emotion and continued. 'I asked how he could make a living from fishing. You could tell he'd not got a lot of money.' Matt looked up at Lisa and said, 'You know, that old guy has scarcely two bob to rub together, but he's so much happier than I've been with my million. What have I been doing with my life, Lis?'

Lisa was unable to respond to such a searching question, yet knew this was the question that had the potential to change the course of her husband's life. 'I think I've been asking the same of myself, Matt,' she said, almost in a whisper, as she was only just daring to acknowledge the lostness she was feeling.

'We were in the boat, looking up at our house,' said Matt, not hearing his wife's response. 'He told me straight that he and loads of the locals disapproved of the development work I've been doing, and all the selling of properties to wealthy Londoners and so on.' Matt shook his head, then looked back at Lisa. 'I knew they all thought that but, you know, for the first time I actually felt a bit guilty about it all.'

'You shouldn't,' said Lisa, yet was not convinced.

'I should, Lis,' said Matt. 'You know, I went off on Saturday to search for Ella. I knew she'd be all right, but I suppose I just needed to get out of the house. So much was at breaking point in me. But I now realise it wasn't Ella who was lost. I was the one that was lost. And I have been for a long time.'

'So...' said Lisa, who felt she was walking on delicate ground. 'Are you now found?'

Matt pulled his lips back into a forced smile, then said, 'More, *found out*, I think.' He nodded his head slowly. 'You've not married a very nice man, Lisa. Theo said he saw into my heart. Sounds pretentious, doesn't it? But coming from him, it actually felt real. I think the old guy did get a glimpse of the inside of me. And what he saw wasn't nice. He saw a man intent on making money, who'd push aside anyone who got in his way. And he was right.'

'That's a bit harsh.'

'Yeah. Harsh but true. And you know it is.' He looked at Lisa briefly and said, 'I'm not the guy you married, Lis. I've... I dunno... I can see now how hard it must have been for you living with me. Don't know why I never saw it sooner.' Again, he glanced briefly at his wife. 'Must have been hellishly lonely for you at times. And...' He paused for a few moments. He knew that what he was about to say was very risky. But so much was chaos now, why not create a bit more? So, he continued, 'I've not been a proper husband to you for a long time now and...Well, I just want to say that if you have decided to see someone else, then I don't blame you. I don't need to know much... I just... I just want to say, I don't blame you, Lis.'

Lisa felt as if something had slammed into her midriff, and she experienced a temporary physical and emotional paralysis. Matt wasn't looking at her. She knew, despite his assurance, that he was hoping it was not true. She could spare him further pain. She could try and make out that she had just had some idle yet dangerous thoughts; a fantasy or a minor flirtation. She could find ways to soften the blow. She was skilful like that. But she knew that she could now be nothing but honest, and said, 'You're right.' She inhaled deeply, and he slowly turned his gaze to

214

her. She said, 'He's a man I met at work. Nothing serious happened. You know... We've not been to bed. But we kissed, and the damage is done. It didn't last long and it's over now. But yes, it happened. So yes, you do need to blame me, Matt. I've betrayed you, and there's no excuse.'

She could feel the powerful emotion surging in her. She had prepared a fine speech for this moment, but she could remember none of it. She looked at her husband with eyes glistening with remorse and said, 'Blame me, Matt, for God's sake. Don't be nice about this. I've betrayed you terribly...' Skilled as she was at controlling her emotions, this emotion was now more than she could handle, and she dropped her head to her arms that were resting on the table.

Matt looked across at the broken, sobbing figure opposite her. So, his hunch was right. She had been seeing someone. But how could he condemn her, when he was feeling that his crimes were far more serious? He had messed up big time. He was responsible for losing everything they had worked for. Yes, she was right. Her seeing someone else was a betrayal. Yes, it should be the nail in the coffin of their marriage. It certainly hurt to think of her kissing another man. And yes, if he met the guy he'd want to knock his brains out. For a few moments he felt the anger flare up within him. And yet, as he looked at the bedraggled figure in front of him, he found he was loving his wife as much now as in those first happy years of their marriage. This love was dousing the flames of indignation and hurt. Their sins had found them both out, and neither was in any position to judge the other.

Only a few hours ago, Matt had been contemplating hurling himself off a cliff to the rocks below. Now he realised that much in his life had come crashing down, and so had much in Lisa's. They were both lying bruised and battered from their fall, but Matt was experiencing an acute sense that, though they fell for different reasons, they had landed remarkably close together, and the rocks where they lay felt like holy ground, with a gentle and healing sea caressing their wounds.

He got up from his seat and slumped next to his wife and grasped her tight. 'Don't,' Lisa cried. 'For God's sake, Matthew. Don't bloody go kind on me. I don't deserve that. It's worse than your business problems. I've betrayed you. I've betrayed our marriage, and I've decided I'll move out!' His kindness and love in the face of her confession was far more disturbing than the anger and rebuke she was expecting and deserved. The cold judgemental spirituality of her mother was rising up in her. She could hear it now - the stern, reprimanding voice of her mother berating her for committing adultery in her heart, and that she was heading for hell. And yet, the strong arms of her wounded husband were wrapped around her so tight, she could not have run from that kitchen even if she had wanted to. And besides, she had no strength to fight. She had to surrender.

She turned her face to the shoulder of her husband. In those moments, Matt knew some extraordinary transformation was taking place. He had indeed reached the most terrible and frightening low point, and yet he knew that something about his meetings with Jenny and Theo had worked a profound change within him. The trauma of the clifftop and the rescue by Jenny had shocked him sufficiently into seeing his life from a very different perspective. But it had taken these moments with Lisa for him to fully see it. The love for his wife, that had been so strong in their early years, had been reactivated with surprising force, and it was that love that was now changing everything.

He remembered those moments on the ocean with Theo: the gentle bobbing of the boat; the sturdy arm around him; the smell of tobacco, fish and diesel; and Theo's words, 'Never be without hope. There's always a way.' As he heard the old fisherman's voice in his mind, he had a curious sense also of the presence of the One that Theo called 'the Great Friend up there.' Only, He wasn't 'up there'. This Great Friend felt surprisingly close down here - close enough to infuse even the battered soul of Matthew Micklefield with a powerful flow of hope. In these moments, he knew that some menacing darkness to do with his drive to succeed had lifted from him. He felt released from its grip. And he knew that, whatever was to happen to the house and his lost fortune, somehow or other, he and Lisa were going to mend, and they would be able to walk the path ahead, no matter how steep or rugged it turned out to be.

How long they stayed there, neither knew, but at some point, Lisa became aware of the kitchen door opening, then closing. She pulled herself away from Matt, and whispered, 'I think Ella just looked in.'

216

Matt leaned back and wiped the dampened hair from Lisa's face, then, smiling, said, 'I wonder what she made of that?'

As he got up from the floor and made his way to a chair, Lisa said, 'Ella knows, by the way. She heard me speaking to the man on the phone. It's why she ran away.'

Matt nodded for a few moments, then said, 'She must have hated hearing that. Poor Ella. We've been crap parents, haven't we?'

Lisa shrugged her shoulders, and said, 'We have. Poor girl.' She then looked to the door and called, 'Ella?'

After a few moments, Ella opened the door and came in and, behind her, walked Jenny, dressed in a pair of Ella's favourite jeans and a sky-blue top. Her freshly-washed hair was tied back with clips, and the air was filled with the fragrance of shampoo and perfume. 'You both look beautiful!' exclaimed Lisa, trying hard to wipe away the evidence of the strong emotions from her eyes.

'And you both look like shit,' said Ella. 'What's been happening?'

Matt rose from the table saying, 'I'll be back in a minute.' He left the room and they heard him going down to the cellar.

As the girls sat down at the table, Ella leaned over to her mother and said, 'You told him yet?' Then added, 'It's OK. Jen knows.'

Lisa was shaken that Ella should have confided such a thing in this girl they hardly knew, but by now all her defences had been broken down, and she felt she had very little to lose, and said, 'I'm sorry Jenny. You didn't need to see all this.' She found a tissue and blew her nose hard.

'Och, don't you fuss,' said Jenny. 'I seen a lorra worse stuff, I have. Makes me feel at home, to be truthful. I couldn't stay long in the house if you were all perfect, that's for sure.'

'So? You told him?' said Ella, with some urgency, for she could hear the footsteps of her father coming back up the cellar steps.

'Yes,' said Lisa. 'He knows everything.'

'Is he leaving you?' Ella asked, her eyes betraying her anxiety.

But before Lisa could answer, Matt's voice came from the cellar steps saying, 'No, he's not, and he never will.' As he came into the room, he said, 'It's her who should be leaving me.' He then produced a bottle of Brut Imperial Champagne that he had gathered from the cellar wine rack. 'Ella,' he said, as he started to unbuckle the cork, 'You have the worst parents in the world, but I think today is marking the day when we are going to make a new start. Can you get the glasses?'

'Christ!' said Ella, rising from her chair and going to the cupboard. This was the last thing she was expecting.

Not long ago, Jenny had seen Matt in a very different state. The sudden change was indeed astonishing. And yet, she sensed that the crisis on that rain-soaked cliff top had triggered the start of a recovery in Matt. She looked at the bottle that Matt was clutching and said, 'That's real bloody champagne, that is! I never thought I'd be drinking a glass of that!'

The champagne cork broke free with a bang, causing Jenny to squeal. Ella thrust a glass under the bottle and caught the effervescent liquid. 'What the hell's been happening, Mum?' asked Ella, as Matt filled the glasses.

'Look,' said Matt, as he settled at the table. 'I don't want to be melodramatic, but this champagne is because I'm just so happy to be alive. I hit a very dark place earlier, but...' He looked across to Jenny briefly, then turned back to Ella and said, 'But today I have seen more clearly than I've ever seen before, that I have two incredible gifts in you and your mum. I know it sounds hellishly corny, but it's real. I just wanted to celebrate that.'

Lisa was still feeling very fragile, and was still unsure whether what was happening in Matt was a sign of recovery or breakdown. She decided to go with the recovery option for the moment, and rather limply raised her glass, then drained it.

'God, this is smashing,' said Jenny, who had also drained her glass. 'Better than that Prosecco, eh? Gor' any more in that bottle?'

Matt refilled her glass, then said, 'It's not all good news today. I've got to be honest with you, Ella. My business is in real trouble. Mum knows.'

'We losing the house?' said Ella, sitting down near her father.

'Yes,' said Matt. 'We will be.' He held up his hands and said, 'It's my fault. I've been a total arse. I got greedy. I'm so sorry.'

'Well. 'S'only a house, isn't it?' said Ella, not quite convincingly, for she loved the house more than she could say.

'It's a bloody brilliant house,' said Jenny, who had almost finished her second glass.

'What will happen, Dad?' said Ella. 'Just how bad is it? Will we go into social housing? Or can we get a flat or something in Porthann.'

'I'll look into all of that,' replied Matt.

'And what about your uncle?' said Jenny. 'The old bloke who's missing? You gorra find a place for him when he comes back.'

'Uncle Solomon...' said Lisa, who had only drunk a little of her glass. 'Of course. I'd forgotten about him. We shouldn't be drinking champagne while he's still missing.'

'Well, I don't know the old bloke,' said Jenny. 'But from what Ella tells me, I don't think he'd mind us having a drink. If I was lost, I'd rather come home to a happy home than a miserable one.'

'Well said,' responded Matt. But all of them, including Jenny, felt some anxiety that it had now been three nights since Uncle Solomon had disappeared, and there was still no sign of him. No-one dared admit it - but all felt it - there was a growing likelihood that they would not see the old man alive again.

# 24

'It's not been right in that house for a long time now,' said Jean, as she wiped the misted front window and then did her usual examination of how the village of Pedrogwen was waking up.

'Which house is that?' said Ted, as he attempted to marshal the pages of his newspaper.

'*Their* house of course, silly,' said Jean, opening the window for a moment, so she could observe more clearly some activity by the chemist just down the street.

Ted finally got his paper under control and said, 'You mean Lisa and Matt's house, I suppose.' He placed the paper in front of him on the table, and lifted his slice of toast to his mouth, carefully balancing the large supply of marmalade that was resting on it.

'She'll be getting something for her bad head, I'll bet,' said Jean, now straining to examine the person entering the chemist. 'It's Monday morning, and she's usually the first in the queue on Mondays. She'll have been down at that pub again all weekend, I have no doubt.'

'I expect so…' said Ted, whose attention was now with his paper.

'I've spoken to her about this. I've told her about the evils of drink. I've told her about the Lord, and how he could free her from the alcohol. But would she listen to me? Course not. Why don't people listen?'

'Mmm,' mumbled Ted, not listening to his wife.

Jean closed the window and returned to the kitchen table. She dusted her hands on her apron and sat down at the table with her husband. Ted was munching his toast and was studying an article on new, eco-friendly ways of farming beef cattle. 'It'll never work,' he said, shaking his head. 'You can't produce good beef like that. It'll taste of nothing.'

'The marmalade's falling! Careful!' cried his wife, but it was too late as a large lump of the sticky orange plopped onto the much-stained pine table. Jean swiftly returned it to the plate with her plump finger, and went to fetch a cloth. 'Anyway, as I say,' she said, returning and wiping the table hard. 'It's not been right in that house for too long.'

'No,' said Ted dreamily, his eyes still fixed on the paper.

Jean washed out the cloth, took another glance out of the window to check the chemist, and then came back to the table. 'Matthew's not right again,' she said, grasping tightly her mug of tea.

'No.'

'No, he's not,' said Jean, now looking towards the rain on the window. 'He's not been right for a while, I'd say. I can see trouble in his eyes. Shifty eyes, if you ask me. I shouldn't be surprised if he's taking that coke stuff again, Ted.'

'Mm.'

'Terrible what he put Lisa through last time. And then there's Ella. Did you see that skirt she was wearing when we last saw her? Shocking it was, Ted. You could almost see her knickers. I tell you, she wouldn't have been allowed into our church on Sunday wearing a skirt like that. No, she wouldn't. She'll be getting herself into trouble before too long, you mark my words. I can't think why they're not worried sick about her being out alone in Porthann all night. It's not healthy for a girl of that age, Ted.'

'No.'

'Are you listening to me, Edward Hancock?'

'Of course,' said Ted, reluctantly hauling his eyes away from his paper and turning his attention to his wife. 'I expect it will turn out all right,' he said. 'Ella's a sensible girl.'

'No, she's not,' protested Jean. 'She's got very little sense in her, I'd say.'

'It is strange about your brother, though,' said Ted, changing the subject. He never liked discussions about his daughter's family. He and his wife shared very different opinions about them.

Jean took a sip of her tea and replied, 'Yes, it is. Very strange. It's not like him at all, is it? Going off like that. He's never done anything like that before. One thing I will say about Solomon is that he has always

221

been dependable. He's never been given to this kind of thing. I don't know what to make of it, I really don't.'

'I didn't like to say it yesterday at lunch,' said Ted. 'But I don't think all that blood in the church is a good sign, do you?'

'No,' agreed Jean. 'That, and the smashed box and the dog collar they found under the pew. There was violence there, Ted. That much is clear. Poor old Solomon. I hope he wasn't hurt too badly. Dear Lord, do look after him, please.'

Ted reached his calloused hand over to his wife's, and said, 'You care for him, don't you, love?'

'I do, Ted,' Jean replied. Unwelcome tears were threatening, but she quickly stalled them by blinking hard, and said, 'If only he'd truly put his trust in the Lord, he'd have had the protection.'

Ted carefully folded up his paper, and moved it away from him. He inhaled deeply and looked searchingly at his wife. He sensed an opportunity to say something that he had been longing to say for a while. 'Look, love,' he said, leaning towards his wife. 'When will you stop all this?'

'Stop all what?' said Jean, pouting her lip.

Ted sighed, and said, 'I know religion's important to you.'

'It's very important to *you*, Ted Hancock. Don't you start backsliding now. Not at this stage of your life.'

'Jean, love,' said Ted, again taking her hand. 'I do love the Lord. Course I do. But I do it differently from you. I don't get as excited about it as you do, and I don't have all the fixed and definite views that you do.'

'You are not going all liberal on me are you, Ted? Not now, when we've got a family crisis on. This is not a good time to choose to go heading down that dark road of sin.'

'I'm not going liberal, Jean. I'm just saying that we have to love God in our own way. There's your way, there's my way, and there's your brother's way. And his way is just a bit more private than yours.'

'I don't agree with you there, Ted,' said Jean, pulling her hand away from her husband's. 'You know as well as I do that he is not properly born again...'

'But how do you know that, Jean?' said Ted, interrupting her.

'I just do.'

'No, you don't. Only God knows that kind of thing. You trying to play God now, are you?'

'Stop this, Ted, you're starting to upset me.'

'Well, maybe it's time to start getting upset about some things.'

'What sort of things?'

Ted saw the fierce look in Jean's eye. It had been a long time since they had had a disagreement like this, for Ted usually put a good deal of effort into avoiding any conflict with his wife. The atmosphere in the kitchen was tenser than it had been for a long time. The rain was now coming down hard, the wind beating it against the window pane. Ted felt himself shaking a little, but he did not want to waste this opportunity that had suddenly presented itself for talking honestly about their religion, so he continued. 'Look,' he said. 'I know how important religion is to you, love, and I'm not wanting to get rid of it. Honest I'm not. I'm just saying, I've gone along with your ways all our married life, but the truth is, I'm not quite like you. I've got a different way of doing it, and I have a right to. As has Solomon. And I don't think you should be judging either of us for it.'

'I'm not judging anyone.'

'You are. Well, you certainly will be judging me if I tell you what I *really* think.'

'What *do* you really think?' Jean was starting to feel that a hitherto very secure foundation of her life was showing serious signs of giving way. 'Come on, let's have it out.'

'I am a Christian, Jean. You know that. But I don't like to go around shoving God down people's throats.'

'Neither do I.'

223

'Well, you can be just a bit forceful with your views, love. I've heard the way you speak to Lisa, for example. The way you tell her that God is offended by her behaviour. All that blasted business about a spirit of unbelief over their house. What's all that about, then? I didn't like the way that pastor prayed for them in church yesterday. He made the family out to be a bunch of wild heathens that we should all keep well clear of. I should have hated my poor Lilly to have hard all that stuff. To be honest with you, Jean, I don't take to this new pastor we got. I'm not so sure he's the saintly chap he makes himself out to be. Seems a bit too keen on money, for one thing. Anyhow, we'll see. The point is, I just think all that spirit of unbelief stuff is frankly a load of baloney. Sorry, but I do.'

'It's not baloney, Ted. You're wrong there, again. There's no question. That house needs delivering, it does. You can tell it a mile off. And that's what's afflicting them all. It's their doing, mind. If they'd lived by God's rules, it would have gone long ago.'

'Oh, I don't know, I don't know,' said Ted wearily. 'I just think you get further with things by caring and loving, not by hammering and shouting the way that pastor does. It's not my cup of tea, Jean. And it wasn't kind the way you told our Lisa about it all. You could see she was upset.'

'She wasn't upset, she was defiant. You saw that.'

Ted sighed. 'She was defiant because she was upset. Look, we needn't argue about it. All I'm trying to say is that I, for one, actually quite like the way old Sol goes about his faith. It's peaceful. Grant you, the odd time I've heard him preach, I couldn't make sense of what he was on about. Sounds like few do. And I dare say that, for a minister, he's a bit too shy when it comes to telling us all about God. But that doesn't mean he's a heathen and an unbeliever, does it? And I don't think Lisa, Matt or Ella are as far away from God as you say they are.'

Jean held her look of indignation for some time, and did not know what to say. It was bad enough having her daughter's family living in rebellion against God. But now there were signs that her own husband was weakening. But the worst of it was, she found there was a part of herself, a very secret and hitherto well protected part of herself, that was ruffled by Ted's comments, daring even to suppose that he may have a point. She winced at this subversive thought, and to combat it, quickly said, 'I don't like to hear you talk like this, Ted. It's not like you.'

'Jeannie, it *is* like me,' said Ted, reaching towards his wife again. 'That's what I'm telling you. I'm just trying to be honest with you. And I know you. You're a kind soul at heart. But your kindness doesn't shine out when you talk about God. I'll be honest, you come over quite hard. As does that pastor. And a fair few of the people in the church, I might say.'

'Oh, look who's judging now?' Jean tightened her lips, and thrust her jaw forward.

'Pardon me, if I am,' replied Ted. 'But I'm tired of it, Jeannie. I'm tired of trying to force our ways on others. Why can't we just let them be?'

'Because, Ted, we have to preach the gospel. It's a very rebellious world out there. Sin abounds and Satan's on the prowl...'

'Oh, stop it Jean. I don't want any sermons. I've had to suffer more sermons in my lifetime than any decent man deserves.'

'I'm not preaching at you.'

'No,' said Ted, sighing again. 'No. I shouldn't have raised the subject.' His already ruddy face was flushed, and he could feel his heart racing. So, to calm things, he said, 'Any more tea in the pot?'

Jean reached for the teapot and refilled both their mugs. Ted reached for the paper and studied it again. After a long pause, Jean said in a quiet voice, 'Maybe I do get a bit preachy. I'm sorry.'

'It's all right, love,' said Ted, lifting his eyes from the paper. 'As you said, we shouldn't be fighting at a time like this. Let's keep praying that the good Lord brings your brother home to us soon, safe and sound.'

Jean nodded and took a sip from her mug. 'You know, Ted, I'd really miss him if he left us. If he is.... you know.... I'd grieve something terrible, I would.'

Ted moved his paper away for the second time. This subject felt like it might be less contentious. And he saw tenderness in his wife. 'You would, love, I'm sure. But as you said, there's never really been closeness between the two of you.'

'No, but then I think I'd grieve for what we never had. I'd be grieving for the fact that I was ever so loved by Mum and Dad, but I don't think he was, you see. And as I got older, I could have helped him, Ted.' She turned her mournful eyes to Ted, and he could see her welling up. 'I could have helped him, but I never did. I just kept my distance. I could have been a good sister. And you're right, Ted. I'll admit it. I can be a little bit judgemental at times.'

'Oh, but...'

'No, Ted. Let me finish. I got to admit, you do have a point. I can be pushy about my religion.' She was daring to give space to the honest, inner part of herself that was awakened by Ted's comments. It felt highly risky, but she continued. 'I don't know why I do it. I suppose I saw Mum and Dad behave that way. They drummed it in to me that we had to... I dunno. We had to make sure that people got to thinking the right way. You know, got their salvation the proper way. To think any different to this... Well, it feels like a betrayal, really. I'd be betraying Mum and Dad, and all that they stood for. I can't do that, Ted. I can't let them down. But...' Her right hand was squeezing hard the fingers of her left, reddening the fingertips. She sighed a brief sigh and said, 'But maybe they hadn't got everything right. Maybe they were a bit hard. And I think that's rubbed off on me. I've taken the same view, and perhaps it's not always been the best. I don't know.' She then looked up at Ted, her tired and damp eyes glistening under the kitchen light. 'But I don't want to let the Lord down, Ted. I'm just trying to do the right thing. That's all.'

Ted had seldom seen his wife look so undefended, and he reached over and took her hand again. Tears had finally broken through her defences and were making their way down the substantial valley between her nose and her cheeks. 'I'm sorry, love,' he said. 'I really didn't mean to upset you.'

'No, no, Ted. It's not you doing the upsetting,' she said, and sniffed hard. Ted watched her trying to control the powerful emotion that was surging in her, and he rubbed his thumb tenderly over the hand he was holding. After a while, Jean sniffed hard again, stood up and said, 'Come on now, I've got to do the bed, and then it's time we were off to Asda.'

'So, it is, love,' said Ted. 'So, it is.'

*

In the village of Tregovenek, as the church clock was striking its twelve dolorous tones, the clouds were retreating briskly inland, leaving the village bathed in warm sunshine, causing steam to rise from the rooftops. Just down the road from the church, in the large and spacious kitchen of Altarnun House, three women were enjoying a cup of coffee to steady themselves after the champagne.

'So, Dad's phoning the bank now?' said Ella.

'I think he is,' said Lisa.

Ella nodded her head, and said, 'It's been a cool house, hasn't it?'

'I can't imagine living in a such a grand place as this,' said Jenny.

'Where do you live?' asked Lisa.

'In Porthann,' said Jenny. 'In a pokey hole with a few other girls. Don't really know them. They don't speak much English. It's a horrid damp place - especially in winter. Can't wait for the summer.'

'I hope you don't mind me asking,' said Lisa cautiously. 'But I've not met a sex worker before, and I don't know anything about your world. But do you keep the money you make from your clients?'

'I wish!' said Jenny. 'No. I gorra pimp. We give the dosh to him and he pays us.' She sipped from her coffee.

'God, I expect he's a snake,' said Ella.

'You not wrong there,' replied Jenny. Both Lisa and Ella noticed a deep weariness in the girl.

'Does he give you enough to get clothes and stuff?' said Ella.

'Not really,' said Jenny. 'Hardly got anything in my cupboard.'

'So where's home?' asked Lisa.

Jenny raised her shoulders and eyebrows.

'Will you have to be back to work soon?' said Ella.

'S'pose,' said Jenny. 'There'll be hell if I don't. And...' She paused for a few moments, then, with her head bowed, she lifted her eyes to Lisa, and said, 'Sorry, but I take... you know... stuff. And he supplies it for us. I'm hooked on it.'

Ella moved her seat nearer to Jenny, and wrapped her arm around her. 'We understand,' she said.

'Doubt you do,' said Jenny.

'Oh, we do,' said Lisa. 'Take it from me. But you *can* get off it. We know much more than we'd like to about it. Let's talk about it sometime.'

'God, that'd be great. I so wanna ger'off it.' She sighed. 'But yeah, I need to get back now. They'll be wondering where I got to. Been bloody wonderful being here, though.'

'What if you just didn't go back?' said Ella.

Jenny laughed a tense laugh, then said, 'He'd explode. Then he'd give me hell when he found me. Then he'd probably get a new girl and kick me out. Seen that happen to other girls. I don't want any of that, so I'd best be going now. Besides, I need the money and I need the dope. Sorry.'

She rose to go, but Lisa reached out and grasped her arm, pulling her back to her seat. She said, 'Don't go back, Jenny. You can stay here with us for a while. Till you get yourself sorted.'

'Yes,' agreed Ella. It was just what she was thinking. 'Stay here. Please. And Mum and Dad really do know how to get off the drugs.'

'Christ,' said Jenny. She was struggling to comprehend why these two women should want to invite someone like her into their home.' You don't want me living here, honest!' she protested. She felt almost overwhelmed by emotion. 'I.... God, I don't know what to say,' she stammered. 'I can't stay in a place like this. You'd...You'd have to hide me. You couldn't have people seeing me here. You'd be ashamed, you would. And what would the old priest think when he gets back? He

228

couldn't come back to a prozzie living in his house. Don't think that would suit him at all, do you?'

'He'd be delighted,' said Ella. 'I know him. He'd be super cool about it. He would love you.'

'*Love* me?' said Jenny. '*Love?*' she repeated. Her eyes anxiously darted from Ella's to Lisa's. 'I only ever been loved by one person, and that were a long time ago, back in Liverpool. I don't... I don't think anyone would wanna love me. Not as I am now. Not the old priest. Not you. Not nobody. Not when you get to know me, like. I'm not the sort that any decent person should love, honest. And if I stayed here, I would just be a problem to you. And it sounds like you got enough problems of your own to be getting on with.'

'That's settled, then,' said Lisa, ignoring the girl's protest. 'Today, Jenny, you start a new life. Ella, show her the spare room. Then we'll need to go into town to find some clothes.'

'Oh, God. Not Porthann,' said Jenny. Everyone knows me there.'

'We'll find another town,' said Ella.

'Sorry,' said Jenny. 'I've gorra find a loo. All this is too much for me. I can't believe what's happening. Is there one downstairs?'

'In the hall - just near the front door,' said Ella pointing the way. Jenny rushed off.

'What will Dad say?' said Ella quietly to her mother.

'Well, he was the one who brought her here,' replied Lisa.

'True.'

'Problem is, we shan't be living here much longer. Then, I don't know what we'll do.'

'Good point.' Ella then checked they were still alone in the room and asked in a low voice, 'How did Dad take your news?'

Lisa just shook her head and said, 'He was incredible, Ella. I... He was far too nice. I really can't explain it. I think he's so upset about his business and this house, it sort of seemed the lesser of the two evils, I suppose. Perhaps it will suddenly hit him and then he may go ballistic. He's every right to.'

'Well, to be fair, Mum,' said Ella. 'He's not really got a leg to stand on, has he?'

'He's not been with another woman, though, has he? I can't help thinking my crime is far worse than his. He must be so hurt. It would be far easier if he wasn't being nice. Then we could have a proper row about it'

Both women chortled, and then were quiet for a while. They heard the sound of the downstairs toilet flushing. 'What a weekend it's turning out to be, Mum,' said Ella.

'What a weekend indeed,' said Lisa. 'I'm exhausted.'

When Jenny returned she said, 'I opened the bog window to have a peek outside and I saw an old gent in a weird top sitting on the bench in the drive. That wouldn't be him would it?'

'What?' cried Ella and Lisa together.

# 25

Although he had only dwelt in Monnine's community for less than three days, the compound where Solomon had been staying now felt very familiar. Monnine was leading him towards the building that served as a chapel. He paused for a few moments and said to Monnine, 'If I'm leaving today, I need to return this top to you and go and collect my jacket. And you must have this stick back too.'

'They are yours, if you will have them,' said Monnine.

'Well, thank you,' said Solomon, who was now feeling that the smock was far more comfortable than his suit. 'Then you must keep my jacket.'

'Well, it's not a garment that will be of use to us,' said Monnine, smiling. 'But the children will love dressing up with it. And it will be a reminder of our very special visitor.'

Solomon's elderly face creased into a smile. Monnine was about to say more, but she heard the voice of Jowan calling to her from a nearby hut. Solomon couldn't hear what he said, but Monnine gestured to him. Then she turned to Solomon saying, 'I told Jowan that today you'd be leaving us, and he wants a gathering before you go.'

'But Monnine,' said Solomon, his brow furrowing again. 'How do I leave? How do I possibly travel across the centuries back to my time? I'm sorry to keep asking. It's just that it's bothering me.'

'There will be a way,' said Monnine confidently. 'Don't worry about that, now. Come.'

A small group of the community had gathered around Jowan, and Monnine took Solomon's arm and steered him toward the group. When they arrived, Monnine said, 'Before you all depart for today's labours, I have one thing to say to you, and it is both sad and joyful.' She then pulled Solomon closer to herself and said, 'Three nights ago, our Lord sent us a new friend.'

She turned to Solomon and said, 'Seanchara, God has sent you for a short while into our time, and you have been most welcome.' She then looked to the others and said, 'Last night, the Holy Spirit of all wisdom, unlocked the memory of this our friend.' There were lots of smiles and words of appreciation. 'So,' said Monnine, 'Seanchara, would you please now tell us what is the name given to you when you were washed in the waters of baptism.'

Solomon appeared a little shy, but he stood tall and said, 'My name is Solomon.'

'Why, that's a fine name,' said one.

'It's a blessed name, that is for sure,' said another.

'Could you tell me where you keep your concubines!' quipped a young man, which drew laughter from most, but a stern rebuke from his mother standing near him.

Monnine raised her hand, and said, 'My beloved friends, we believe that today Solomon will leave us.' And before too many voices could protest, she quickly said, 'He must return to his home and his family. And he is a priest in the service of the Good Shepherd, so he must return to his flock.' She then turned and cupped the face of Solomon, saying. 'Solomon, child of God, and known to us as Seanchara during your time by our hearth. Thank you for visiting us. You will always be in our hearts. You must return now to your people. But go back with your soul mended. Go back with the gusts of God's glorious Spirit filling your sails. Go back and tell the people of the God who walks alongside them. Never be afraid again. Let faith be the strength that binds you. Let hope be the wings that lift you. May love be the fire that warms all who come near you. Go blessed, dear friend. Go blessed.'

With that she embraced him, and the others in the group gathered close and wished him well. Men, women and children came and hugged him as if he were one of their family. Since his early days of enjoying the closeness to his parents, the only person he had ever allowed to come this physically close before was his great niece, Ella. But here, people he hardly knew were grasping hold of him and embracing him. He knew without doubt that the old Solomon would have recoiled in embarrassment and fear at such intimacy. But on this day, following this extraordinary sojourn with this community, he welcomed each embrace with unashamed delight. He was allowing a ray of love to enter the hitherto unlit place of his soul. It was human love. And yet, he was sure that radiant in this human love, shone the divine love for which he had searched all his lonely life. For the first time for as long as he could remember, Solomon Ogilvy felt alive. And his tears were as the baptismal waters of the new life that had cried itself awake in the fold of this ancient community.

With the last embrace, Monnine led Solomon towards the chapel. As they approached the door, they heard a husky cry from the gateway to the compound. They turned and saw the stooped figure of Corman walking towards them.

'I thought he might come,' said Monnine, waving to the old man. 'He's left his island twice in two days. You are honoured, Solomon!'

'I was awake before sunrise,' said the old hermit a little breathlessly as he approached them. 'I was stirred to pray for you, my friend. In the night, I went down to the water's edge, and facing the land, I prayed for your journey. As the dawn came, I knew your mind had been healed, and all that had been lost had been returned. Not long after, the sun broke through the cloud, and then a guillemot flew from its crag toward me. You recall my guillemot?' Solomon nodded a response. 'Well this was another one inspired of the Spirit, and It flew above me, encircling me seven times. Then it flew towards the community. It was my summons to be with you as you journey on today, Seanchara. And so here I am.'

'I am much comforted by your presence, my dear friend,' said Solomon, who took hold of Corman's arm. 'And let me tell you. I have found my name.'

'Tell me,' said Corman.

'My name is Solomon.' His face creased into a smile.

Corman nodded saying, 'Of course... Of course.'

'Come,' said Monnine, and led the two elderly men into the chapel. Bright sunlight was now beaming through its few windows. A large candle flickered near the altar. 'Here?' said Monnine, looking at the simple altar.

'Indeed,' said Corman. 'This has to be the place.'

'Sit yourself for a moment,' said Monnine, and Solomon sat on a plain wooden bench. Corman sat next to him. The chapel floor was mostly made of hardened earth, but Monnine stepped on to an area of smooth stone that was situated in front of the altar. 'Will you tell the story?' said Monnine.

Corman nodded. He turned his right eye to Solomon, while his left remained drawn to the heavens. He said, 'The Spirit had blown me here about a year before Monnine and her friends arrived. I knew I was being called to build a home of light for this land, but I was not sure exactly where. So I walked up and down this coastline.' He turned and fixed his eye on Solomon. 'Do you know what I was searching for?' he asked.

'No,' said Solomon, intrigued.

'Evil,' said Corman.

'Evil?' exclaimed Solomon. 'Why ever evil?'

'The land is wounded,' said Corman, his face darkening. 'Do you not hear its cries?'

'I don't think I do,' confessed Solomon.

'It is our way,' said Monnine. 'We learned long ago to listen to the heart cry of the land. When humankind acts with violence, the land is always bruised by it. Abel's blood cried from the land after he was murdered by his brother. Such brutal acts cut into the soul of the earth. If a human causes its wounding, then a human must bring about its cure.'

'But how?' asked Solomon. Such concepts were completely new to him.

'By prayer and fasting, of course,' said Corman.

'So,' said Solomon, straining to understand, 'Do you mean you deliberately sought out wounded land so you could pray for its healing?'

'Definitely,' said Monnine.

'It is in the book of the prophet Isaiah,' said Corman. '*The parched ground shall become a pool, And the thirsty land springs of water; In the habitation of jackals, where each lay, There shall be grass with reeds and rushes.* I walked the beaches; I walked the hills; I walked the plains.

All the while, I listened. So much was blessed. How I praised God for this good land. But then I came here to this rock, and oh, my heart broke. For five days and nights I lay with my ear pressed against this dear stone.' A tear eased its way out of the corner of the hermit's eye. 'The jackals had indeed prowled and devoured. I heard this, Solomon. I heard it all, and saw it with the eye of my heart. I understand not why humans can be so cruel to each other. Life was taken here for despicable reasons. The blood of the innocent cried out as loudly as the cries of the blood of Abel. This place needed to be cured.'

'But this dear friend of ours offered his prayers to God,' said Monnine. 'It is over fifteen years ago now that he cleansed this site. So, the wound was healed, and... You tell them, old man.'

Corman's face, that had been in anguish, now became wreathed in delight. 'That Easter Sunday, after all my praying, I was still alone on this rock. But, this I swear to you, Solomon. When the sun lifted itself over the hills on that blessed morning of resurrection, clear water started to pour forth only twenty paces from here.'

'It is where we draw our water now,' added Monnine, nodding in the direction of the well.

'Even reeds started to grow there,' said Corman. 'Had the prophet himself been here that day, I believe he would have danced with me, as I did dance. It was the land's way of celebrating. I am convinced.'

Hitherto, Solomon had never imagined such things could have been possible, but in these past two days, his imagination had been so activated, that he was now finding no difficulty in believing such a story. 'And so, this had to be the place for the chapel,' he said.

'Indeed,' said Monnine. 'It was the first of our buildings.'

Solomon looked to Monnine, and asked, 'So, is this the place where you were at prayer on the day you stepped into my world?'

'It is,' said Monnine.

'And so, from here I depart,' he said, looking at the smooth, flat surface of the rock on which Monnine was standing. 'It makes sense.'

'Do not think of it as a door of time, my brother,' said Corman, patting Solomon's arm. 'See it more like one of the great conjunctions of the planets.'

Solomon's frown betrayed his question.

'This is a place of power, without question,' said Monnine. 'But there would be those who would want it to be a place of magic. A place where you stand and find yourself flung to far off places and far off times. But it is no magic door. It is a place of being drawn into the heart of God. Because with God, all power is about love.'

'And the planets?' asked Solomon.

'Imagine our world here in this time as one planet,' said Corman, now rising to his feet. 'And your world in your time is another. Three evenings back, when you walked into that great building that you call your church, you were close to the end of your days. Your heart failed as you fell but, as it failed, it cried out to its Creator.'

'My heart failed?'

'Oh, yes,' confirmed Monnine. 'It stopped for a few moments, then it rallied.'

'I knew none of that,' said Solomon. 'And I do not recall any such crying out.'

'No, you did not cry out with your voice,' said Corman. 'It was your failing heart that cried. It yearned and it wept, my brother. It wept for all the years unlived. It wept for all the loves unloved. It wept for all the days left empty. It wept for all the prayers unuttered. It wept for all the tears unshed. It wept for all the joy unlaughed. It wept, Solomon. It surely wept. And it was over this very stone that you fell. In your great building it is covered by wood and more stone. It used to support the altar until they made your building even greater. They then moved the altar away from the stone, and they forgot its story. But dig under the place where you fell, and you will find this very stone.' Corman now joined Monnine on the stone, and said, 'It was the strength of that weeping that caused your soul to hear the call of Monnine's prayer. You and she were on this rock in different times, but the yearning and the prayer, the longing and the pain were as planets aligned. The yearning

236

of her prayer, and the yearning of your heart is what brought you together. Monnine was taken to your time, but she knew that your healing could only happen here in our time.'

'Did you know all this?' asked Solomon, looking at Monnine.

'I knew all about the stone, of course,' said Monnine. 'But I knew not where my prayer would take me that day. That is the mystery of prayer.'

'It is a mystery indeed,' said Solomon, his eyes wide with wonder. He then asked, 'So how do I return?'

'The planets are still aligned,' said Corman. 'But the longings are different. You now have a longing for home. And those in your home are longing for you - more than you realise. And because we love you, we too yearn for you to be where you belong. You must travel while the longings can carry you.'

Solomon grasped his stick, and stood up saying, 'Yes. It is time I returned to my home.' He stepped forward and joined them on the stone.

'You are free, dear brother,' said Corman. 'You are free.' And these were the last words Solomon Ogilvy heard in the world of that ancient time, for the next thing he knew was that he was back in the village of Tregovenek lying on the floor of his parish church, just where he had fallen three days previously. He placed the palm of his hand on the floor tiles that were now cleaned of his blood. They felt warm - unusually warm. He lay his cheek against the tiled floor and heard a humming sound that very gradually grew fainter, until it finally faded from his hearing. He pulled himself up and moved to a nearby pew where he sat.

The building felt large and cold. He found himself weeping, which developed into a sobbing. So many emotions passed through him in these moments, not least a deep sorrow at his parting from a place and a people that he had come to love so much. But after some time, the emotion of grief was replaced by an unusual serenity. He pulled from his trousers a handkerchief and mopped his face. Sunlight was breaking through the coloured glass. The swaying of the yew tree outside was causing the rays of light to flicker on the floor in front of him.

He cast his eye around the building, once so familiar to him, but now feeling more alien. He had no doubt that the chapel of fifteen hundred years ago that he had just left was in exactly the same location as this church. Faithful people generation after generation had built upon the work that Monnine and her people had started. He pulled himself up from the pew. He was clutching the oak staff that Monnine had given him. He was wearing the woollen smock. Never before had he entered this church so casually dressed. He walked towards the altar and placed his hand on the beautifully embroidered white altar frontal. He thought of all the times he had lifted the host at this place, beckoning the people, who would shuffle forward in their orderly, hushed way to receive the arid wafer on their tongues, and take their sip of *Vino Sacro* from the sterile silver chalice. And then he remembered the young Jowan, ablaze with sunlight and Holy Spirit, his eyes moist with emotion, lifting with trembling hands the bronzed, freshly-baked bread.

He stood for a while in the chancel and surveyed the dark oak and well-polished pews, and thought of his meagre choir straining to sing a setting of the psalm for the day. And then he thought of the young woman in the barn, who enchanted the congregation through her singing of the song about the Christ she so clearly adored. And he saw her again, her arms raised above her flaxen hair, her sleek fingers pointing to the heavens, and through her melody and tone of heart, beckoning the love of heaven to touch the hearts on earth. He remembered how his heart was indeed so touched.

He then moved to the pulpit and thought of the many, many times he had wearily yet dutifully climbed the staircase of worn sandstone into the wooden chamber, from where he delivered his sermons to the tired and lifeless faces spread before him. And then he thought of Corman with his stooped shoulders and husky voice, fixing him with his right eye, while the left pointed to heaven. He remembered his telling of the gospel story of the morning lakeside. 'Children, you have no fish.' He heard the words again. Words he had spoken so many times in his reading of the Easter stories. And yet in that world, spoken by this curious hermit, the words had broken free, scurrying to the unlit places of Solomon's soul, animating them with resurrection fire.

And so Father Solomon Ogilvy wandered around the church he had known since his own father served here in the days when his country was at war. He paused as the memory came alive for him so clearly. His father, dressed in his black cassock, and white preaching tabs, laughing with parishioners at the back of this very church. His father, who had heard the call to serve the soldiers in that far-off land. He was remembering his father's leaving, and marvelled at *how* he was remembering. He was remembering without the weight of it pressing upon him. Yes, he grieved, but no, the grief did not pin him down like it used to. He felt lighter. He felt freedom, and in response, he lifted his arms high in the air as he stood at the back of the church. Though his arms ached at the holding, he left them there for some time. It felt the only appropriate action for conveying his thanks.

He then lowered his arms and looked to the door of the church, which was open, letting in the dappled Spring sunshine. He remembered his last journey out of this building, in the dark, with Monnine supporting him. On that occasion he was walking back in time, but now he was walking forward to his future. He walked through the swallow-swooping porch out into the churchyard, and felt the warmth of the sun on his aged face. But he no longer felt so old. Something was eastering up in him. His friends from the time past had unbound him, and he was being called to walk in a new light. He may not have long to live, but what days he had left, he was determined to live well. Then, as he made his way along the uneven paving, past the graves of the dead, he remembered the living. He thought of his family. Ella was the first to come to mind, and his eyes filled with moisture. He looked forward so much to seeing her again. And Lisa, his niece. He frowned for a few moments. When he last saw her, she looked so lost. And Matt, her husband. Why was he so afraid? He must listen to them all, not lock himself away, hiding from them anymore. He tripped on one of the paving stones and steadied himself with his stick. He thought of his sister, Jean. He smiled as he thought of her. He remembered her as the little toddler with whom he loved to play. But his smile faded as he thought of their estrangement and her fierce faith, which so often had felt like an attack on his shy faith. But now it looked different and far less threatening. And more than anything, he knew that he loved his sister deeply.

He made his way down the path and noticed some torn police tape littering the area by the lichgate. He gathered it up, and tucked it in his pocket. He walked down the lane to Altarnun House, his home for almost two decades. On his way he passed a cottage, with an uncollected newspaper resting on the doormat. He stepped closer and studied the date. The date assured him that he had been away the same three days that he had spent in Monnine and Corman's world. Only a few yards before reaching his home, he passed the small stone arch set into the grassy bank, built several centuries ago to house the ancient well that had been bubbling up with fresh water for generations. It was now called St. Non's well, for at some time during its long history, it had been named after the Welsh saint. How often he had walked passed this without giving it a second thought. But today the well held new meaning for him, as he remembered Corman's story of his cleansing of the land that had caused the waters to erupt here in this very place.

And so he arrived at his home. He stood by the gate studying the robust grey stone building with its generous windows and steep, gabled roof. He looked up at his bedroom window. He recalled his room so vividly, yet it was a room that represented a world and a life that now seemed so far removed from the person he was becoming. Nonetheless, he experienced a strong sense of affection for the house as he looked upon it. Yes, this was his home, and he felt most fortunate to dwell here.

He crunched across the gravel, and was going to make for the front door, when some seagulls squawked above him, causing him to glance towards the sea. There was little wind, and the ocean was a calm blue. Some years back, Matt had placed a bench on the lawn facing the sea, and he decided to take a few moments resting there before entering the house. He assumed nobody was in, so there was no hurry. He sat on the bench, and gazed out at the very same ocean that he had seen in the world of distant time from which he had only just stepped. The memory of that world was still glowing warm within him. He looked to the headland to his left and, to his delight, he could just make out the edge of Corman's island. He rested his arm on the back of the bench, and gazed at the scene for a long time. How he loved that little island. How he loved his conversation with Corman. What a wonder he had been granted.

He would have stayed there longer had his thoughts not been interrupted by the sound of a downstairs window shutting abruptly. So, somebody was in. He guessed it would be Ella, so he got up from the bench and, clutching his stick, he made his way to the front door.

# 26

When the family first moved into Altarnun House, Matt adopted the corner upstairs room as his study. Though a small room, it accommodated his few books, his cricket gear, school trophies, his father's drink's cabinet, and a sizeable desk. Sitting at this desk he could survey the back garden with its lawn and apple tree, with the wild area beyond of some exposed bedrock and a tangle of shrubs, gorse bushes and trees. He was sitting at his desk this Monday morning and watching the April sunlight periodically breaking free of the cloud, and brightening the verdant lawn. If he leaned forward on his desk, he could catch a good view of the sea that was as calm as it had been yesterday, when he was taken by old Theo on his unexpected and strange adventure.

He was still holding his phone. It had only been a short conversation with the bank manager, and yet it was the kind of conversation that held all the portent of the judge donning the black cap. The conversation marked the end of Matt's life as a successful businessman. Today, his life as a bankrupt failure would begin. The world was strangely quiet in response to this news. The rocks at the end of the garden did not split in two. No birds fell from the sky. No violent storm erupted from the West. Apart from the murmur of voices from the kitchen, the world was taking this news very quietly indeed. 'I suppose you've seen it all before,' said Matt to the world in general.

He placed his phone carefully and neatly on his desk, then ran his hands over the smooth, polished surface. He turned and looked around the room and up at the ceiling. This would be the last time that he could say that this home was his. Soon the For Sale boards would be up, and a flow of wealthy strangers would be doing their tours of the house, and he and Lisa would be doing their best to enthuse brightly about the place, all the while resenting every person who dared presume ownership of this their home. But, if he could persuade them to part with more money than the house was worth, then maybe he and the family might end up in not too bad a place in Porthann.

He sighed as he looked back out of the window. He was feeling dizzy with emotion. It was not yet lunchtime, yet it felt like he had lived through several days since he awoke at sunrise with deeper feelings of despair than he had ever known. Despite the wonderful conversations with Jenny and Theo, he had come to the very clear conclusion that the world would be much better off without him. Or was it *because* of his meeting with Jenny and Theo? They were such good people, and his life, by contrast, was so very bad. It had been a very clear conviction: he had to remove himself from this world. Get out of the way before he could do more damage. And so he made his way to the cliff. Would he have had the courage to leap off that dreadful edge? The brandy had given him the confidence to get pretty close. He would never know. As it was, his angel turned up. How glad he was that she had come. How deep his gratitude to the girl. Quite probably, he now owed his life to her. And something about those moments with her in the drenching rain on that clifftop was the crisis that changed things. He would never know how to explain it, but it did.

Then he came back to this home with Jenny. He felt he came back as someone different. As he said to Lisa, he had found himself - a more honest and wiser piece of himself, that had been hidden in some discreet place, and took a mighty crisis to release. He thought of how this newly discovered expression of himself was seeing everything now in a different light. He was even seeing his wife in a different light. This wife, whom he had once so adored, yet in recent years had more ignored than adored. Lisa, so competent and assured. Someone he so easily took for granted. The one who had stood by him when he went through his terrible times with the drugs. The one who, frankly, he just pushed to one side as he pursued his career and hunted for his fortune. And she was the one who had had enough of being taken for granted, and was seeking comfort with someone who noticed and valued her in a way that her husband did not.

Yes, this was a shock. He had suspected it, but it was still hard to hear of it nonetheless. He picked up a pencil from his desk and played with it in his hands. His frown deepened and something darkened in his soul. It really *had* happened, then. She was the one to have the affair. He always feared it would be him. But no, it was Lisa. Good, upright,

243

everyone's friend, Lisa. His wife had kissed another man and was close to bedding him. He felt an old anger stir in him. An indignation was aroused. A line of argument developed in his mind that was about defending him and accusing her. He was jarred out of his thoughts by the pencil snapping in his hands, and he looked down at the sharp and jagged remains. Carefully and deliberately, he joined the two pieces back together again.

He looked out of the window. A row of gulls was standing to attention on the summer house roof, all peering out to sea. His mind went back to Theo, the kindly, thoughtful simple-living fisherman. He felt himself back on the boat again and could smell the tobacco breath that conveyed such searching words to him. *We're all on this planet together for such a short time. Why waste this precious gift hurting each other? Why waste the precious time hurting ourselves for that matter? No, there's more to be gained in life by loving than there is by hating, that's for sure.*

This is what got hold of him in the kitchen just now. He was tired of blaming and accusing and punishing Lisa. He had seen her in a completely different way when he was with her just now. He was aware of such a strong conviction, that there was more to be gained by rescuing his marriage than by walking away from it. *There's more to be gained by loving than hurting.* Maybe the Great Friend, as Theo called him, was having some influence in his life. Maybe He was finally nudging Richard Dawkins off his perch. Matt had proudly placed Dawkins there long ago, but he didn't look much use to him now. No, something greater than Dawkins was happening, and Matt wanted to be part of it.

The seagulls decided it was time to take to the air again, and they soared skyward, high above the garden, and then back out to sea. *Never be without hope. There's always a way.* He heard those words from Theo when he was hugging his distraught wife in the kitchen. He heard them again now. *Never be without hope.* It was the memory of those words that caused him to rush to the cellar and return with champagne. If he had stopped and thought about it, such an action was absurd, crazy. His marriage and his business were being threatened with collapse. What was he thinking of, breaking open the champagne? 'You were thinking of hope, Matthew,' he said out loud to himself.

He rose from his chair, and wandered aimlessly around his study for a few moments, then returned to sit again at his desk. He stared back out of the window. The breeze caught some of the blossom of the apple tree, causing it to dance erratically before being scattered across the lawn. 'So, this is hope,' he said out loud. 'So much is torn from us and falls to the ground, but look what it produces.' He watched more of the blossom flutter around the garden, then looked back to the tree. Without any doubt, he knew that the buds on the tree were strong, and the blossom would give way, in time, to the apples that the family loved. The family would not be here to enjoy them this autumn, but nonetheless, the apples would still be there for someone.

He felt again, that surprising energy that he had felt earlier in the kitchen. He felt this powerful conviction that, even though so much that was beautiful was being lost, it could be - and would be - replaced by something even more wonderful. He leaned back in his chair, nodding his head. Yes, this was a change. The old Matt was a desperate man: desperate to impress; desperate to make his millions; desperate to make his mark; desperate to *be* someone. And this *someone* that he was so desperate to become, was a person who was happy to cast to one side the locals who suffered through his property deals; the lives of those like Jenny who, before this weekend, he judged as losers; and the old fishermen like Theo that, until yesterday, he would have happily branded as worthless eccentrics that were best avoided. And, he was not far off casting aside even his own family in this vain pursuit. Even the strange Uncle Solomon, the old pious priest, who lived his reclusive life in this home.

Matt stood up and made his way to the door. It was time to go and join the family. But just before he took to the stairs, he noticed the door of Solomon's room slightly ajar. He went to it, and gently pushed open the door. It was literally years since he had last stepped into this room. He went no further than the doorway, but standing there he cast his eye around the room. There was something endearing about it: the two walls lined with a library of very carefully ordered and catalogued books; the neatly-made bed that, with sheets and blankets rather than duvet, appeared to be from another time; the worn armchair set in the window; the beautiful leather-topped desk on which was placed a

245

notebook and pen. Matt studied all this carefully, and would have stayed longer had he not been interrupted by the sound of the front door being flung open and footsteps running on the drive.

He moved swiftly to the landing window and looked out to the drive. There, he was astonished to see the distinctive figure of Uncle Solomon rising from the bench with the help of a sturdy wooden stick. He watched Ella running fast towards the old man, who threw his stick to one side as the two greeted each other in a long embrace. Matt raced downstairs.

'It *is* him, then,' said Jenny, as Matt arrived in the hallway.

'Yes, it is,' cried Lisa, who was standing next to her. All three watched Solomon and Ella have a brief conversation. Ella then picked up the stick from the driveway, and they made their way to the door.

'Welcome home, Uncle,' said Lisa, as Solomon stepped out of the sunlight into the hallway. Lisa, who had never embraced her uncle out of respect for his shyness, did not know quite how to greet him. But the decision was taken from her as the priest stepped towards her. With his grey eyes glistening and face creased in a smile, he lifted his arms and grasped Lisa's shoulders. His thumbs gently massaged her shoulders as he fixed his eyes on her for a brief time, and Lisa could see that a disturbing yet also wonderful change had taken place in her uncle. 'My dear Lisa,' he said in a voice that sounded stronger, less tremulous and more sure than usual. He then pulled her towards him, and for the first time in his life, he hugged his niece. Lisa lightly clasped the back of the woollen smock. This closeness felt awkward to her, but not to him. He then released her and looked at Matt.

Matt was far less sure about hugging, and reached out his hands to grasp Solomon's. 'Welcome home, Uncle Sol,' he said. Then he looked at Jenny and said, 'This is Jenny, a friend of ours.'

Solomon turned and stepped towards the girl, who was standing in the light of the doorway. Her eyebrows were fixed in an expression of surprise and delight. Her arms were hanging at her sides. Solomon observed both her frailty and strength. He reached out and pulled her hands from her sides and, to everyone's surprise, he pulled them to his lips and gently kissed them. Then he held them tight and said, 'How very nice to meet you, young lady,' and released them.

'Likewise,' said Jenny, as she stroked the place on her hand where the kiss had landed. She dipped her head and smiled. She had never known anyone to treat her with such respect.

'Come out of the draught,' said Lisa, as she shut the door, and led them into the kitchen. She sat Solomon at the chair nearest the Aga and put on the kettle. The others sat at the kitchen table. Solomon placed the palms of his hands on the table in front of him, and cast his eyes around the kitchen with a look of deep appreciation.

It was Jenny who said what all the others were thinking. 'They've all been out searching for you, they have. Where've you been hiding?'

'And where did you get that cool smock?' asked Ella.

'And that stick,' said Matt. 'Beautifully carved handle.'

'Are you growing a beard?' asked Ella. 'It suits you.'

'Let him catch his breath, poor man,' said Lisa. She placed a hot mug of tea in front of her uncle.

'It's good to be home,' said Solomon, as he wrapped his fingers around the mug, revealing the prominent purple veins on the backs of his hands. 'Where have I been hiding?' he said, repeating Jenny's question. He nodded his head and said, 'That is a very good question, Jennifer. And not one I can easily answer. Nor is it easy to tell you where I got this smock, Ella. Nor this stick, Matt. No, it's all been a little bit strange.'

'Doesn't matter, uncle Sol,' said Ella. 'The important thing is you're home.' She reached out and stroked the back of the veined hand, and added, 'I came looking for you.'

'You did, Ella?' said Solomon. 'Bless you. There was no need.'

'The police have been searching for you,' said Matt.

'Oh, my,' said Solomon, and chuckled briefly.

'Yes, not very effectively,' added Lisa.

247

Solomon kept looking around the kitchen and said, 'Everything is looking different. Very beautiful. Yes, very beautiful.'

No-one knew how to respond to this, but when Solomon looked down at his tea, he revealed the cut on his head. 'Your head,' said Lisa. 'You've hurt yourself.'

'Ah,' said Solomon, after he took a welcome sip of the tea. He reached up and dabbed his finger against the wound which was still tender. 'Yes, I fell in the church, you see. But it's not serious. It bled a bit, but it's fine now. I must have slipped. Monnine says it knocked me out for a time.'

'Monnine?' asked Ella and Lisa together.

'Oh, Monnine,' said Solomon. He was quickly becoming aware that the sheer joy of being back in his home was going to be tempered somewhat by having to explain his most unusual experience. However, his task of having to embark on this explanation was happily delayed by the sound of the doorbell.

'I'll go,' said Ella, and hurried off along the corridor to the front door. Those in the kitchen listened with interest as the door opened. They heard Ella cry out, 'Rahab!'

Matt and Lisa looked at each other and both said, 'Rahab?'

Solomon lifted his eyes to the ceiling and, quoting a scripture, he said 'By faith the harlot Rahab perished not with them that believed not, when she had received the spies with peace.'

'Another harlot?' said Jenny. 'Cool.'

# 27

Ella returned to the kitchen in the company of a tall, slim and dark-skinned girl of a similar age to her, who was wearing a white top, floral skirt and draped around her shoulders was a large orange and red patterned shawl. Her hair was braided and carefully threaded with beads. Her smile radiated brilliant white from her dark-skinned and finely-featured face.

'This is Rahab,' said Ella casually. 'Met her on Saturday.'

Solomon rose from his seat and, stretching out his hand to grasp Rahab's, said, 'I am most pleased to meet you.'

Lisa, who was still struggling to adjust to this dramatically different extravert version of her uncle, also reached out her hand and simply said, 'Hello.'

'My great uncle, and my mum and dad,' said Ella to Rahab. 'And my friend, Jen.'

Jenny waved her hand to Rahab, and Rahab smiled her gleaming smile back at Jenny.

'So, your mother's uncle has returned,' said Rahab, smiling at Solomon.

'I have indeed,' replied Solomon.

'Rahab knew you were safe, Uncle Sol,' said Ella. She then looked at her mother and said, 'Mum, could she stop for lunch?'

'Er, yes,' said Lisa, who was now feeling distinctly disorientated by the rush of surprises that the morning was bringing. 'It's just soup and cheese and things.'

'That's fine,' said Ella. 'I'll help you fix it.' And so, Ella and Lisa busied themselves for a time collecting food, crockery and cutlery and preparing a lunch for the assembled group. Matt also felt distinctly put out. He had been busy preparing a speech to explain to his family that the house agent would be arriving the next day to erect the For Sale board, and he wanted to start sharing his thoughts about the kind of house they might be able to afford. But with the old man's return, and Rahab's arrival, all those plans flew out the window. He was too confused to embark on a normal conversation, so he excused himself from the company.

So, Solomon, Jenny and Rahab were left sitting at the table. Quite uncharacteristically, Solomon was now quite enjoying a life that had become profoundly unpredictable. It felt remarkably refreshing. 'Tell me about yourself,' he said to Rahab.

'I now live in Porthann,' she said, brushing the jangling beaded hair from her face. 'I have lived there about two years now, and I have been looking for work.'

'Thought I'd seen you there,' said Jenny.

'Ah, do you work in Porthann, then?' said Rahab.

'You could say that,' said Jenny.

Rahab looked at her more closely, and quickly understood why she was cautious. She recognised the signs. She had no intention of embarrassing Jenny, for she recalled how hard it was to live with that same identity. She reached across to Jenny and briefly tapped her hand and said, 'I really like your top. It suits you.'

'Ta,' said Jenny. She then reached out and stroked Rahab's hair and enquired, 'Are they hair extensions?'

'No,' replied Rahab, her white teeth gleaming. 'All of it is the hair God gave me.'

'But, tell me, if you don't mind my asking,' said Solomon, interrupting the girls' discussion on hair, and leaning a little towards Rahab. 'Where is your family?'

Rahab smiled and said, 'My family home is Eritrea,'

'Where's that then?' said Jenny. 'Never heard of the place. Somewhere in London, is it?'

'No,' replied Rahab. 'It's a country in Africa.'

'God, you come a long way, haven't yer?' said Jenny

250

'I have,' said Rahab, nodding her head.

'Your parents got work here, then?' asked Jenny

Ella was putting some plates of cheese and meats on the table, and said, 'Jen, she came here seeking asylum.' She was worried that Jenny's line of questioning could turn out to be uncomfortable for Rahab.

'Oh, I met refugees,' said Jenny. And indeed, she had in her sad trade. 'Sorry,' she added. 'Not alorra fun that, is it?'

'No,' said Rahab. 'But God has been with me.'

At this moment, Lisa delivered bowls of soup to the table, and announced that they could all start eating. 'Ella, call your father, would you?' She then turned to the others, and said, "It's just a home-made soup. There's cheese and meats as well.'

Solomon looked down at the steaming bowl and, leaning towards it, inhaled deeply. Since returning from his other world, all his senses seemed to have been sharpened. He noticed it walking down the lane from the church. Every colour was richer, every sound clearer. The fragrance of the blossoms and the freshly-mown grass smelt heavenly - perhaps literally. And the fragrance of this soup smelt like he was about to eat something delectable, and as soon as his spoon touched his lips, he knew he was not wrong. Jenny also drew her spoon to her mouth with great care. She had not eaten a meal in a warm home like this for as long as she could remember. The beautiful crockery, the daffodils on the table, the range of cheeses, the kindness in the room, the respect that the old man had given her. She marvelled at how by some miracle she managed to find herself here. She sipped from the soup and looked up to Lisa and, in a husky voice, she said, 'It's bloody brilliant soup, this is, Lisa.'

'I agree' said Solomon.

'Good one, Mum,' said Ella, as her father arrived and joined the table.

For a while, the conversation centred on the food: where it came from; how much it cost; who liked what; what they ate in Liverpool; what they ate in Eritrea. Throughout all of this, Solomon was silent until he finished his soup. Then, as he was slowly spreading some butter on his bread, he said, 'I have visited another time.'

'You whar?' said Jenny, who had just helped herself to a large chunk of cheddar.

'May I have the salami, please, Matt?' said Solomon, reaching out his hand.

'Sorry, Uncle' said Lisa. 'Did you say you visited another *time*?' Such a comment was distinctly disturbing. She had been suspecting that his fall had affected the state of her uncle's mind.

Solomon calmly made up a sandwich of salami and brie, and as he pressed the slices of bread together, he said, 'Did you know that fifteen hundred years ago, a woman called Monnine came over from Ireland and planted a community of Christ here. Right here where we are living.' He munched at a piece of his sandwich.

'No,' said Matt. 'No, I didn't. Pickled onions please, Lis.'

Solomon nodded until he swallowed his mouthful, then said, 'A hermit called Corman was here first. He started off by rooting out some horrible evil through his prayers, and then he blessed the place.' He nodded towards the church. 'Just up there. Where the church is now. That's what he blessed, and Monnine built the chapel there. Corman didn't stay with them. He went and lived on that little island that you can just see from the front garden.'

'I know the one,' said Matt. 'I saw it yesterday when I was out in the boat with my friend, Theo.'

'Out in a boat?' cried Ella. 'And who's Theo?'

'Friend,' answered Matt. 'Theo called it Corrie's isle. But he said it was named after an old saint called Corman. When did you find that out, Sol? Strange you should mention it.'

'I went there,' said Solomon. 'Corman took me there.'

'Oh, so you *were* in town, then,' said Ella. 'And you bumped into a guy called Corman, who decided to take you out to the island named after someone who happened to have the same name as him?'

'No, Ella,' said Solomon. 'It was *the* Corman who took me there.'

'Well,' said Matt, who had paused eating and was looking anxiously at Lisa and Ella. 'Theo told me that *the* Corman lived fifteen hundred

252

years ago, Sol. I know you're getting on, but I don't think you're that old!' There was a moment of light laughter.

Solomon picked up his serviette and wiped his mouth, then looked at Matt and said, 'You are correct, Matthew. I was visiting his time.' He paused for a few moments, then quoted, '*But, beloved, be not ignorant of this one thing, that one day is with the Lord as a thousand years, and a thousand years as one day.*'

'That is in our Scriptures,' said Rahab, as she reached for another piece of bread.

'Indeed, it is, my dear friend,' said Solomon.

'I think I understand,' said Rahab. 'My people would understand this. It is how they see time. You see it very differently here in England. A very dull way of seeing it. In Eritrea, we understand that time can bend.'

'I met plenty of bent people,' said Jenny with her mouth half full. 'But never heard about bent time. Sounds crackers to me.'

'I'm sorry,' said Lisa, feeling the need to take charge of a conversation that, in her view, was gaining in eccentricity by the minute. 'Just *exactly* where have you been this weekend, Uncle Solomon? It's really important that we know.'

Solomon was about to attempt to answer this question, when they heard the sound of a vehicle on the gravel. Ella looked out the window and said, 'Looks like a police car.'

'Oh, God!' cried Lisa. 'That's all we need.' She got up to go to the door.

'It'll be that police lady, I'll bet,' said Jenny.

She was right. Lisa returned with the cumbersome Police Inspector close behind her. 'As you can see,' Lisa said wearily to the Inspector. 'All is well. Reverend Ogilvy has returned.' She looked at her uncle and said, 'Uncle Solomon, this is Inspector Littlegown.'

Solomon rose from the table, and said, 'I'm delighted to meet you, Inspector.'

The Inspector was wearing her most disapproving look, and bending her head back she said, 'Right...' She pursed her lips, then said, 'I'm pleased to see you safe and sound, sir. But might I ask where you have been these past few days? And I'd be grateful if you could give me an account of what took place in your church on Friday night that resulted in your disappearance?'

'Inspector,' said Lisa. 'The poor man has only just got back. Can't this wait?'

'No, madam,' said the Inspector. She had spent a good many hours on this case, and was being made to look a fool. She wanted an answer, and she wanted it quickly. She thrust her chin forward and said, 'Just tell me please, sir.'

'Do you want a seat?' asked Matt.

'No thank you, sir. I'll just hear what the Reverend has to say, then I'll take my leave, and I won't need to bother you anymore.' Then looking at Solomon, and taking out her notebook she said, 'Sir? If I may?'

'Yes, of course,' said Solomon, adjusting his serviette on his lap. 'I went into the church on Friday evening and it seems I slipped on the floor and fell. It appears I knocked my head. I must have been unconscious for a time and I'm told my heart may have stopped for a short while.'

'Oh, no,' said Lisa.

'It's all right,' continued Solomon. 'It was only for a few moments. I remember coming around and going to sit in the choir stalls. Then a lady called Monnine arrived. She wasn't from our time, but from fifteen centuries ago.'

'I beg your pardon, sir?' said the Inspector, turning her head and aiming her good ear at the priest.

'He was concussed,' said Lisa. 'That might explain...'

'Lisa,' interrupted Matt. 'Let Solomon give his account.'

'I'd be grateful if you could, sir,' said the Inspector, her ear still aimed in the direction of Solomon. She was holding her pad and pen prominently.

'Yes,' said Solomon. 'It's quite simple really, though I know it is a little difficult to believe. I was telling the others about it just now, and our young friend from Eritrea here was kindly explaining about how her people understand time.'

The Inspector raised one eyebrow and turned her attention briefly to Rahab. 'From Eritrea, miss?'

'Yes,' replied Rahab brightly.

'Right,' replied the Inspector in her usual slow manner. She studied the young woman for a few moments, before returning her attention to Solomon. 'Please continue, sir,' she said.

'So, Monnine,' said Solomon with animated eyes. 'She's the lady from Ireland who planted Christ's community here around fifteen centuries ago. A very fine lady, if I may say so. Well, it was she who led me out of the church.'

'Pardon me, sir' said the Inspector, who was not writing in her notebook. She looked sternly at Solomon, saying 'Am I to understand that you are claiming that a lady from fifteen hundred years previous to our time, chose to visit you in the church last Friday evening?'

'Yes,' said Solomon. 'Quite extraordinary isn't it? It took me a while to accept it, I must admit. Nothing like this has happened to me before. But the thing is, Inspector, she then led me back to her time.'

The Inspector's chin shifted forward again. 'You travelled to her time, sir? Fifteen hundred years back, you say?' Her hands holding her pen and pad were frozen in mid-air.

'Yes,' said Solomon. 'As you can imagine, this part of the world looked quite different in their time. None of our buildings, of course. Just a compound of huts, really. But it was most interesting meeting the wonderful people there. And I was telling the others that the hermit, Corman, took me over to his island...'

'Thank you, sir,' said the Inspector, whose impatience was starting to get the better of her. Her hands mobilised again, and she vigorously crossed something out in her notebook. 'Could you now please tell me how you managed to get back here this morning.'

'Indeed, I can,' said Solomon, who was feeling relieved at the opportunity to tell something of his story. 'I was very unsure how it would all work. I mean it's not every day that you step through time, is it, Inspector? But there is a stone, you see, near the sanctuary steps in our church. You can't see it, as it's under the floorboards now. But it's where Corman prayed and fasted. Well, you know how the planets sometimes align...'

'If I could just have the brief version, please, sir,' said the Inspector. Her face was reddening.

'Well,' said Solomon, his face now beaming. 'One moment we were standing on the rock in their time, and the next moment I was back in our church in our time. I was a little sad to leave my new friends actually, but it was also wonderful to be back. I walked from the church to the house, and I had forgotten just how beautiful our world is. The birdsong was quite stunning...'

Again, the Inspector interrupted. She had had enough. She slammed her notebook closed and said, 'Thank you very much indeed, sir. Thank you all. I don't think I need to discuss this any further. But could I remind you that police time is very valuable. *Very* valuable. So, if any of you should be thinking of stepping into another time, or heading out to another planet to meet up with aliens, or getting yourselves lost in any kind of way, could I please beg you *not* to involve the police. I shall see myself out.' With that she firmly replaced her cap, left the house, slamming the door behind her. Moments later, the family could hear the sound of sprayed gravel as the car sped out of the drive.

'Oh dear,' said Solomon.

'Right,' said Lisa. Then everyone at the table erupted in laughter.

# 28

As the family cleared the lunch table, Lisa said to Solomon, 'Uncle Sol, I'm sure you'll be tired. Do go and rest.'

'Yes, Lisa,' agreed Solomon. 'It has indeed been quite a morning, and I'd be glad of a little rest now.'

He was about to go when Ella said, 'Uncle Sol, where did you get that top?'

'Oh, this,' said Solomon, pulling the edge of the smock forward. 'Monnine found it for me. I've rather taken to it.'

'And the stick?' added Matt. 'It's beautifully carved.'

'Yes, that was a gift too.'

'So,' said Ella, as a frown deepened on her face, 'that smock and stick are fifteen hundred years old?'

'Hm,' said Solomon, blinking hard. 'I suppose they are in one sense. But in another sense, they have only been recently made. Funny old world isn't it?' And with that he left the room.

After he departed, Lisa said, 'I'm so glad he's back. But what *did* happen to him over the weekend? We're none the wiser, are we? Obviously, he didn't travel through time, though he clearly believes he did.'

'Don't see why he shouldn't have a little ride through time,' said Jenny, reaching for a piece of cheese before Ella could pack it away. 'I've always thought that there's a real Doctor Who somewhere in the world. The old man probably got picked up by a Tardis.'

Matt was thoughtful and, ignoring Jenny's theory, said, 'Obviously he hasn't travelled through time, but I think it's only kind to go with him on this. He's somehow managed to imagine the whole thing. But to be fair, whatever it was that did happen to him, it seems to have done him a power of good.'

'His mind seems totally fine,' said Ella. 'In fact, he seems brighter now than I've ever known him.'

'I agree, Ella,' said Lisa. 'I've never known him so chatty and… sort of *with* us. And he gave me a hug! He's never done that in all the years I've known him.'

'I suspect we'll never really know the truth of what's happened to him this weekend,' said Matt, as he placed the crockery into the dishwasher. 'I think it's obvious he had a really bad knock on the head, walked out of the church half-concussed and has been wandering around somewhere over the weekend and enjoying these rather sweet delusions of being back in a bygone age.'

'Yes, I think it has to be something like that,' said Lisa, as she dried her hands on one of the several towels hanging by the Aga.

'Well, if I may say so, I agree with Jenny,' said Rahab. 'I believe him. I don't know about Doctor Who, but it is clear to me that time has shifted and the Father has been allowed to visit his ancestors and learned much from them. He's bringing their wisdom back for us. We are blessed.' She radiated a smile into the room.

Lisa and Matt looked at each other quizzically. Neither wanted to offend their new guest. Ella could see the conversation was not going to go anywhere more productive, so she invited Jenny and Rahab out into the garden, and it wasn't long before the three were sprawled on the back lawn chatting together under a warm April sun. The sound of their laughter echoed around the grounds and found its way through the open window of Solomon's room. He smiled and nodded as he heard the happy sound. He was used to Ella bringing her friends into the house, but these two new friends seemed rather different to the others. Very different. And he liked them very much.

He had been sitting in his familiar armchair that overlooked the sea, and remembered Corman's little coracle bobbing over the waters. He closed his eyes to try and catch his forty winks but, try as he might, not even one wink was forthcoming. There was too much running around in his mind, so he rose from his sea-view chair and walked around his room for a few moments. He opened the door. He no longer wanted the very private world he had once occupied. Something had opened up in his soul, and it had much more room for people. He thought of going out into the garden to join the conversation on the lawn, but then his eye caught sight of his journal that was neatly placed on his desk.

He moved over and sat at his desk and lifted the book. This was where he recorded his private thoughts. Some of them very private. He opened the pages, with the care a historian might use when opening an ancient manuscript, and turned to the most recent entry. He remembered so clearly the last time he had sat there. It had been on Friday, which was only a few days ago, and yet which felt like a lifetime. In these pages were recorded the thoughts of a tired and aged priest, who was lonely and very lost.

He opened the entry for last Wednesday. It was less than a week ago, yet the writing could have belonged to another man. He ran his finger over the opening lines: *I suspect this will be one of my last entries. My days are numbered, I am sure. I'm feeling my age.* Yes, he couldn't deny he was still feeling old, yet somehow, not quite so old. Maybe there was something in what Monnine said when she quoted from the book of Kings and spoke of the biblical Solomon's long life. Maybe his days would be long. Certainly he felt a strength in his bones today that he had not felt for many years.

His eyes returned to his writing again, and he read about his regrets and his fears and his memories of that early love that he had abandoned for the sake of his calling. He felt the sorrow of it again, and yet it carried less weight. He read his comments about the family: *I don't understand why they are so unhappy. They have so much. This beautiful home in this blessed part of Cornwall. They have work that they enjoy (though I do wonder if Matt's work is too stressful?). But more than anything they have Ella. Dear, sweet Ella.* Yes, he had indeed left a troubled home on Friday evening. He was still worried for them, and yet he perceived there had been something of change in them also. Both Matt and Lisa seemed less trapped. He noticed tenderness between them. And Ella? Dearest Ella. How wonderful it was to not only see her again, but for the first time to take hold of her in his arms. His old self was far too afraid and shut off to even think of hugging. But whatever work of grace it was that had happened in the deeper parts of his soul over the weekend, it was having the happy consequence that at last he could convey his affection to his great niece.

He then turned to the most recent entry in his journal. Friday 13th April, written only an hour or so before his fall in the church. Slowly he read the words of St. Augustine that were written out in his elegant handwriting: *Late have I loved Thee, O Beauty so ancient and so new; late have I loved Thee! For behold Thou were within me, and I outside; and I sought Thee outside and in my unloveliness fell upon those lovely things that Thou hast made... Thou didst call and cry to me and break open my deafness: and Thou didst send forth Thy beams and shine upon me and chase away my blindness.*

He was weeping again. He was not accustomed to tears, yet he knew now that tears were friends. How different these words of Augustine looked to him now. On Friday he recorded them with sadness. These words only reminded him of his many failings. And yet now he could read them as a description of his actual experience. Yes, late, very late, was his heart opening to his Lord. He had visited an ancient time and had gained something so new. He could see it with great clarity. Once he had lived as a child out in the cold, looking in at a home so warm. He had looked in through the window of the world of human love, but had not entered it. He had looked at the world of the divine love, yet remained outside. His grief and his fear had locked him out. But Monnine, Corman and the others had taken him by the hand, and led him over the threshold to the most wonderful hearth, and by that hearth he started to hear things he had never heard, and see things he had never seen. 'Late have I loved Thee,' he said out loud. 'But better late than never.'

He then read the final words of his entry, *How will I ever forget Father's final words to me on that day when he left for War. 'Solomon, my son. Three things remain: faith, hope and charity. But the greatest is charity. Be on the watch for these three things, and you will be well and you will do well.'* These were the three precious gifts his father entrusted to him: faith, hope and love. These were the qualities he had always admired when he had seen them in others, yet he so seldom experienced in his own heart. But, in these last few days, faith had been rekindled, hope had become real and, more than anything, a dark and frozen part

260

of him had thawed and at last he was finding a freedom to love. He leaned back in his chair and said, 'Thank you.'

He was going to say more, but there was a knock at his door. He turned around and saw Matt standing in the doorway. "Matthew, come in,' he said. Up until now, Ella had been the only person he had invited into his room, but it now felt safe for others to enter. Matt tentatively closed the door behind him. 'Pull that seat from the window and sit down,' said Solomon, who remained in his desk chair.

'It's really good to have you back,' said Matt.

'It is very good to be back,' said Solomon. 'I'm so sorry I caused you all so much worry.'

'No, not at all,' said Matt, who was sitting on the edge of the chair, clasping his hands.

Solomon noticed the tension, and said, 'What is it, Matthew? Something is troubling you.'

Matt nodded. 'Yes, Uncle Sol, I'm afraid it is.' He eased himself a little further on to the chair, but still clasped his hands together. 'This has been our home for many years…'

Solomon noticed Matt's lip quiver. He guessed what was coming and said, 'Matthew, I think I can guess. The business is bad, isn't it?'

'It is,' said Matt. He breathed in deeply and controlled the swell of feelings within. 'And to be honest with you, Sol, it's my fault. I can't blame anyone else.' He looked up at Solomon and, for a moment, was taken aback by the expression of such extraordinary kindness that he saw in the old man's eyes. Such kindness made it easier to convey the bad news. 'We are going to have to sell. I'm so sorry.'

'But why apologise, Matthew?' said Solomon. 'You have given me nineteen wonderful years in your beautiful home. You should have moved me out a long time ago. It is high time I found a place of my own.'

'Oh, no, no,' protested Matt. 'We would never do that. You are part of us now. No, you will stay with us. And, hopefully, I will be able to find a smaller place in Porthann, and there will be a room for you. You must stay with us.' Matthew attempted to convey confidence by a rapid nodding of his head.

'You are far too kind,' said Solomon. He then added, 'You will miss this lovely home, Matthew. I am so sorry. You say it is all your fault, but you mustn't blame yourself too much. We've all made mistakes, but the main thing is to learn from them.'

'I don't think you've made many mistakes, Sol,' said Matt, now relaxing back into his seat.

'I have made many, Matthew,' said Solomon, furrowing his brow. 'My main mistake was to only live half a life. I can't do much about that now, but I am determined to live fully in whatever days are left to me.'

Matthew was also frowning, as he said, 'I rather think I'm in the same boat. My life has probably been less than half lived. Perhaps somehow, out of this mess, I can learn to live a better life.' He then inhaled quickly and said, 'Corrie's Island?'

'Yes?'

'You say you went there.'

'I did. With Corman.'

'What was the island like?'

Solomon paused for some moments and looked past Matthew out of the window, and rested his eyes on the bank of cumulus clouds that had settled over the ocean. 'Corman was a funny old chap. One eye looked at you and the other seemed fixed on heaven. But I liked him. Liked him very much, actually.' He chuckled briefly then, turning his head a little, he said, 'He loved a guillemot, and they prayed together. Fascinating. Well, he took me up to his hut, you see, and gave me bread and warm milk from his cow. He kept a cow on the island. We had such a nice conversation. A life-changing conversation for me, as it turned out.'

'Uncle Sol,' said Matt. His hands were gripping each other again. 'I hope you will forgive me if I say I can't quite believe this time travelling. It's just. Well, you know it doesn't really happen, does it? So, do you think maybe you were concussed and so - the island, Corman and all the things you told the Inspector - do you think it was a sort of dream or hallucination while you were concussed?'

'Yes, possibly,' said Solomon. 'You see, for me, Matt, it doesn't really matter how it all happened. The fact is that, one way or another, I visited a place and time which is different to ours, and I saw things that woke me up. A kind of healing took place in my soul there. Things that had weighed so heavily on me during my life left me. I was part of this community and was... well... very happy there, that's all I can say. I saw people living as they were meant to live. Simply, kindly, openly. I saw them worshipping God in such a lovely way. They came to life when they took their Communion. You should have seen them. It set their hearts on fire. It sparked adventures in them, Matthew. Quite different to how I've done church all my life. No-one ever set off on a wild adventure after one of my sermons! No, I have to tell you, I liked their way better. But whether all that was in a dream or, by some mystery I travelled there, I don't know. I just know I could not have asked for a more wonderful gift, and I shall be forever grateful.'

Matthew smiled at Solomon and said, 'I'm really happy for you, Sol. I'm just sorry you have had to return to such bad news.'

'It may not be as bad as you think, Matthew,' said Solomon. He then added, 'But tell me. While I was away, you have made two new friends. There's Jenny, who is now out in the garden with Ella. And you met a man called Theo, who took you in his boat. These sound like interesting meetings.'

Matt eased himself back in his seat again. He was feeling more relaxed, partly because Solomon was taking the bad news so well, and partly because there was now a clear explanation for the old man's stories of time travel. It was apparent that he had enjoyed a wonderfully inspiring dream while he was concussed. And thankfully, wherever it was that his body had lain these past three nights, it had not harmed him. So, feeling more relaxed, Matt said, 'Yes, they are special people. On Saturday Ella decided to go off and look for you, and when I heard the news, I was worried for her and went out to search for her.'

'Oh, I think that young lady knows how to look after herself,' said Solomon. 'But if I had been her father, I think I would have done the same.'

'Well, I know Ella and I have had our fights, but I do love her,' replied Matt. 'Anyway, it was a fruitless search. I never did find her. Instead, I came across Jenny. Sorry if this shocks you, but she's a sex worker, and she tried to offer her services to me on Saturday night.'

'Not much shocks me nowadays, Matthew,' reassured Solomon.

'Actually, I was very low on Saturday night when I met her,' continued Matt. 'I felt horrified at first and I wanted to run away. But then I saw something really quite sweet in her, and I felt for her. Compassion, I suppose it was. I've not often had much time for that before now. I took her to McDonalds and we had a meal together, sitting in my car. I wept buckets after she left. I thought of all the good fortune I had in my life and all the bad fortune that had happened in hers. But despite that, she was a far better person than me. Old Theo said that in another world she would have been a queen. And I agree.'

Solomon was leaning forward in his chair, listening intently to Matt. He had never heard him speak in this way before. He had always presented so brash and confident. Even in his bad days of the drugs, he still presented with plenty of bravado. But this was a different Matthew, and in Solomon's view, a much nicer one. 'And Theo?' he said.

'Ah, well, that was yesterday morning,' replied Matt, as he picked at the threads in the worn arms of the chair. 'A funny old bloke. A fisherman. And at first, he took me to the harbour. He said that when he was a child, his mother took him to the harbour wall because he wanted to know if he could see the Spirit of God moving on the face of the waters, like it says it does in the bible. Funny thing for a kid to say, wasn't it?'

'I would say it was a very good thing to say,' said Solomon. 'Since my visit to Monnine's community, I've had different eyes, and I've very much enjoyed watching the Spirit move on the face of the sea. Most exciting, it is.'

Matt lifted his eyebrows for a moment, then continued. 'Well, he took me out in his boat, and I guess we might have been near the island at a similar time to you. Or... You know... how you imagined the island when you were, er...'

'Keep going,' said Solomon, who had accepted that Matt was struggling to understand what had happened to him.

'Well, we had a long chat in his boat. He made me realise that much of my business has not been good for the local people, and for the first time I... Well, I suppose I had a bit of a conscience about it. But it wasn't just about that. He sort of looked into my heart.' Matt was surprising himself, for he had never had this level of conversation with Solomon before. And yet he was now finding Solomon to be an excellent listener. He continued, 'Old Theo spoke straight to me, which is probably what I needed. He said there's this bit of me that's obsessed with making money and trying to impress people. He certainly didn't mince his words! But then he said that, because I was always trying to impress people with my grand business and that, I didn't show people the better part of myself. I remember his saying, "But by doing that, we miss the dear bit of you." It really moved me, that. I dunno, I just came back from that boat ride wanting to live differently.'

'Sounds like you were in the company of the Spirit of God on those waters.'

'Maybe.'

'You felt better?'

'Well, I did for a short time. But I went back to the office that evening and tried to sleep on the floor. All through the night I kept thinking of what a failure I was, and I really doubted that I could ever live a different and better life.' He looked up at Solomon. 'I was reaching the end, you see. There was an appointment at the bank this morning, and I knew that the manager would be telling me that I would have to sell this house to release the funds to repay the debt.' He looked down and said, 'I was in the pits and drank some brandy and I suppose...'. He looked up at Solomon and said, 'I've not said anything to Lisa or Ella about this. They don't really need to know. I just couldn't face that bank manager telling me what a mess I'd made of things, and I knew I couldn't go to the meeting. The truth is, I honestly came to the conclusion that life would be a great deal simpler for everyone if I wasn't around. I went to Gerhard's Leap and thought about... You know... doing it. Maybe I would've. Maybe I wouldn't. I'll never know, because by some miracle, Jenny happened to be walking along the coast path this morning and she saw me. I'd called her *Angel* when I first met her. And this morning, she really was my angel. She knew what I was thinking. She was great actually. It was tipping it down at the time and we were both drenched, and so I brought her back here to get dry.'

Solomon was now straining forward in his chair, anxious to catch every word. His brow was deeply furrowed, conveying his concentration, and his moist eyes spoke of his compassion. Matthew glanced at him briefly, then sighed and said, 'It was a bit of a weird time this morning in the kitchen, to be honest. Surreal. When I came into the kitchen, I saw Lisa in such a different way. I'm not sure what it was, really. Being so desperate, perhaps. She looked just so... so nice. And I felt I'd been such a poor husband to her. Well, as it happens she... Well, she's made some mistakes too. Anyway, to cut a long story short, despite how bad we've been, we both just realised we couldn't do without each other. Amazing, really. I know this sounds mad, but I just felt so elated. So elated at being alive. So elated to be close to Lisa again. So, I got out a bottle of champagne!' Solomon raised his eyebrows in appreciation. 'And all the time I was sipping champagne, the bank manager was there in his office wondering where I was! Well, I did phone him and I agreed to put the house on the market. So that, Solomon, is what's been happening since you've been away. Quite a lot, really.'

Solomon's eyes were shining behind his spectacles as he said, 'I'm so glad you didn't jump, Matthew. Thank God! How I would have missed you. And you would have missed your chance of being alive in a new way. You had a choice - to die or to live. And you chose to live. Anyone who has made that choice, will live in quite a different way. To use Theo's words, the *dear bit of you* can now breathe.'

Matthew nodded and said, 'Old Theo talked about his Great Friend. It's his name for God. I'm starting to think that there may be a Great Friend around who might want to be on friendly terms with even the likes of me.'

'And the likes of me,' said Solomon. 'Maybe we can both start to get to know Him.'

'Maybe we can,' said Matt. He nodded his head slowly for a few moments, then rose from his seat. Solomon also stood. Matt was about to leave the room, when he turned and walked back to Solomon. 'I'm so glad you've come back,' he said, and both men did what they never imagined they would do. They grasped each other in a long embrace.

# 29

There was a gentle warmth in the April sun as it beamed on the group of the three women that were gathered on the lawn of Altarnun House. Rahab and Jenny were engaged in animated conversation. It did not take long for both women to discuss their distressing stories of being coerced into the sex industry. As Ella listened, she experienced a range of feelings that included both horror and admiration. She was indeed horrified to hear about the appalling world of sexual exploitation, and at times she had to work hard to control her feelings of distress and anger. But the stronger feeling was undoubtedly that of admiration. She was in the company of two people, who had suffered so much, and yet demonstrated such remarkable courage. She had never felt so inspired by her fellow humans. She was certain that if she had had to suffer even a small part of what these girls had gone through (and in Jenny's case, were still going through), she was certain that she would not have come through with the dignity that these two possessed.

A light breeze shook the tree, and the three were sprinkled with a confetti of apple blossom. As Rahab brushed the petals from her face, she said to Jenny, 'So, my sister, today is your first day of freedom.'

'Yeah, I guess so,' said Jenny, smiling her vulnerable smile. 'God knows what I'll do with myself, though. No-one's gonna wanna employ an ex-prozzie, are they?'

'Course they will,' protested Ella.

'You don't know the world like I do,' said Jenny. 'People are not kind to the likes of me.'

'Well, some are,' said Rahab. 'Today God has led you to kind people.'

Jenny studied Rahab for a moment, then said, 'You're fond of God, aren't yer?'

'I've always loved God,' replied Rahab, as more apple blossom fell on her.

'I didn't used to like him,' said Ella. 'But...' She shrugged her shoulders, then added, 'But I think I might be giving him another chance.'

'Oh, yeah?' said Jenny.

'Odd thing,' Ella said, as she shifted her position on the grass. 'Met a nun yesterday.'

'A nun?' said Jenny. 'Cool.'

'Yeah, it was kinda cool, actually,' replied Ella. 'I mean, she wasn't your all-holy, mother superior kind of nun. She was really funny actually.' She laughed and said, 'We went to church yesterday morning together in town.'

'That big ugly one with the posh Vicar?' said Jenny.

'That's the one,' replied Ella. 'Sister Maria was the name of this nun. You know, like in that old movie, *Sound of Music*. Well, you'd think nuns would behave in church, wouldn't you? But she didn't! She got really fed up with the stuffiness of the church and the vicar. It was hilarious listening to her!'

'I have never met a nun like that,' said Rahab. 'But I think I would like her.'

'Oh, you would, for sure,' replied Ella. 'We went for a coffee together after church, and then walked up on the headland for a time. We did chat about God. She really likes Him.'

'Well, she's gorra, hasn't she?' said Jenny. 'She's a nun, for God's sake.'

'Yeah, I suppose,' said Ella. 'But I got the feeling that she liked God, almost *despite* the fact she's a nun.'

'Yeah? Well, I sorta get that,' said Jenny. 'I not met any nuns, but I met a lady in a great Cathedral in Liverpool. She was like a nun to me.'

'She wore the nun's clothes?' asked Rahab.

'God, no,' said Jenny. 'No, she wore trad stuff and smelled of mothballs. But she was a love. We got two Cathedrals in Liverpool, and I met her in the good one. Bright and colour and everything. And we just became friends. She was called Beatrice. Really old-fashioned name, isn't? But she was a grand lass.' She looked at Ella and said, 'Told

269

your dad all about it. It nearly made him cry, it did. Said he wanted to go there.'

'My dad doesn't do crying,' said Ella.

'Yeah, he does,' said Jenny. 'I really like your dad. You're a lucky girl, Ell. I'd have loved a dad like that.'

Not since she was a child did Ella believe she was lucky to have Matthew Micklefield as her dad. 'Hm,' she replied. 'It's not been easy in our home, Jen. I won't bore you with the details, but mum and dad have had lots of fights.'

'I'm sorry, my sister,' said Rahab. 'The battles that take place in the home are some of the saddest.'

Ella had been absorbed in thoughts of her own home, but when Rahab said this, she was reminded of the terrible murder of Rahab's parents in the Eritrean village, and she said, 'God, Rahab. I'm sorry. You must wonder why I'm complaining, when you... When you lost your parents.'

Rahab picked at a few daisies on the grass and said, 'Yes, I do envy you, Ella.' She looked up. 'Every day I think of my mother and my father, and I feel the sorrow. It is a pain that never leaves me. They were very good parents and they didn't fight. They loved each other very much. We were very poor, but my dad knew lots of children's stories. He even knew the Western ones from the Disney films - you know, *the Little Mermaid* and *Aladdin*.' She smiled briefly. 'We could never see the films, but my dad knew the stories, and he would tell them so wonderfully. He would make me laugh so much.' She smiled a radiant smile at the memory. She then looked at Ella, and, changing the subject, she said, 'So your great uncle is home. You must be so pleased he has been found.'

'Yeah,' said Ella, now kneeling on the grass, the tops of her bare knees peeking out from the fashionable holes in her jeans. 'He seems OK, doesn't he?'

'Seems like a really nice old gent to me,' said Jenny.

'He has been on a sacred journey,' said Rahab.

Ella frowned. She was also now plucking daisies. 'What do you really make of all that stuff about him turning up in another time? You

270

seem to think people can do that. But...Let's be honest, it really doesn't happen, does it?'

'We say things don't happen until they do,' replied Rahab. 'I have found it best not to be too certain about some things.'

'Yeah, but...'

'The proof of the pudding,' said Jenny. 'He's been to a pretty nice place by the sound of it. Doesn't really matter where it is, does it? He says it were a good place. Well, if it was as good as he says it was, it will make a good mark on him, won't it? I expect after a while you'll get to believe him.'

Ella was still very unconvinced. Rahab tilted her head for a moment, and some of her beaded braids fell across her face. 'Ella, you love your Uncle Solomon very much, don't you?'

'Yeah,' said Ella. 'Always loved him. But I don't think I really know him. I mean he's always been so quiet. That is, until today. He's probably said more today than in all the years I've known him.'

'I never stop talking, I don't,' said Jenny. 'Can't keep my gob shut.' All three of the girls laughed.

Ella looked at Jenny, and said, 'Jen, you met my dad this morning before you arrived at our house. How was he? You know. What kind of state was he in? He's been acting really weird since he got home.'

Jenny felt awkward. She knew she had witnessed Ella's father nearly taking a very drastic action. But she was also certain that this was not her story to tell. So, she said, 'Yeah, he were a bir upset. Think he's got business problems, by the sound of it.'

'So, he was just out walking?' said Ella. 'In the pouring rain?'

'Yeah,' said Jenny. 'And I was out too, when I bumped into him.' She frowned for a moment. 'He didn't seem too bad.'

Ella adjusted her position on the lawn, and she was now sitting with her arms folded around her knees. Several petals of blossom fluttered on to her ash blonde hair. She looked around at the garden, and over her shoulder to the large house. 'Sounds like we'll have to move from here,' she said, and sighed.

'God, that's so sad,' said Jenny. 'It's such a beautiful house. It's a palace.'

'I know,' said Ella. 'My dad's... Well, he's always taken a few risks. My guess is that he's taken one too many.'

'Are you sure about this?' asked Rahab.

'He's not said anything, but I've seen the signs,' said Ella. 'He's been really anxious and twitchy these last few weeks and had so many fights with mum.'

'How is your mother?' asked Rahab.

The question caught out Ella. She knew only too well that all was not well with her mother, but how could she answer these relative strangers? 'She's OK,' she lied.

She was about to say something else, but was stalled by a call from the open living room window. It was her mother who called out, saying, 'Ella? Your grandparents are coming over soon to see Uncle Sol. Thought you'd like to be warned.'

'Oh, God,' said Ella. 'That's another whole story.' She looked to her new friends and said, 'If you get to meet them, just keep the subject well away from religion. Let's go for a wander around the village and I'll show you the harbour.' And with that, the three young women rose from the grass, and sauntered out of the grounds of Altarnun House.

*

'So, he's back then,' said Jean, as she marched into the kitchen. 'Where is he?'

'He's up in his room,' said Lisa. 'I told him you were coming around, and I expect he will have heard you drive in.'

Ted and Jean sat themselves at the kitchen table, while Lisa put on the kettle. 'Matt and Ella around?' enquired Jean.

'Yes,' said Lisa. 'Matt's in his office. You've just missed Ella. She's gone for a walk with friends, but I expect she'll be back soon.'

'Knowing that young lady, she'll wait 'til we're gone,' said Jean.

'Oh, come on, love,' said Ted.

'Sorry,' said Jean. 'It's just that I've been a bit tetchy since my brother disappeared.'

'A bit!' said Ted.

'Well, it's not every day that your brother disappears from a church leaving his blood behind him, is it?' barked Jean.

'All right. All right,' said Ted, raising his hands with palms facing his wife.

'So, how is he, Lisa?' asked Jean, looking up at her daughter. 'Is he? You know. How is his mind? You said he's been concussed. Do you know where he's been? Does *he* know where he's been?'

'Er,' said Lisa. This was going to be a question that she would be asked often in the coming days, but she had not yet worked out how she would provide an answer that was respectful of her uncle, yet did not make him - or her - out to be completely deranged.

'I expect the old chap will tell us when he's ready,' said Ted, reaching out to receive the steaming cup of tea that Lisa passed to him. 'Ta, Lilly, love,' he said, smiling a reassuring smile to his daughter.

'Yes, but he's getting on,' said Jean. 'And there have been signs of... you know.'

'You know what?' said Ted curtly.

'Well, people can lose their minds at that age, and...'

'Most don't,' replied her husband.

At that moment, the door opened and Solomon walked into the room.

'Well, there you are, brother,' said Jean, remaining in her seat and offering him a faint smile.

'Here I am, sister,' said Solomon.

Ted put down his mug, stood up and reached out his hand to Solomon, who shook it firmly. 'Good to see you back, Sol,' said Ted. 'We ain't half been worried for you.'

'I am so sorry to have bothered you all,' said Solomon, sitting at the table next to his sister. He looked to her and reached out his hand and placed it over hers and said, 'It is good to see you again, Jean. Very good.'

Jean's mouth tightened, and she looked across to Ted. This new friendliness was disturbing. 'Good to see you, too,' she said to Solomon, still looking at Ted. She then turned to her brother, saying, 'So, where have you been, then, these past few days? You've had us fearful worried, you have.'

'In a sense, I've been here,' said Solomon. Lisa tightened as she could see trouble if Solomon should try and spin the time-travelling yarn.

'That were a nasty knock you took to your head, Sol,' said Ted.

'Indeed,' said Solomon, reaching his hand to the wound. 'Clean knocked me out for a time. But, if the truth be told, it was a most gracious gift.'

'A gift, you say?' enquired Jean, as she reached for the tin of biscuits that Lisa had placed on the table.

'Oh, yes,' said Solomon. 'Most definitely.'

Jean looked at Ted again and said, 'You don't normally get people saying that a nasty knock on the head is a gracious gift.' She munched hard at her biscuit.

Solomon reached across to his sister for the second time, resting his hand on her forearm. 'It's all right, Jean. I'm not losing my marbles.'

Jean felt she should be the judge of such things, but she did have to concede that, though he was acting strangely, there was, so far, no real signs of dementia. Until, that is, he said, 'I found myself back in the original Christian community that was established here.'

'What's that, you say?' said Jean, withdrawing her arm away from her brother's clasp.

'I don't think I will ever be able to explain it to you,' said Solomon, beaming a kindly smile to his sister. 'But the important thing is that a very deep wound has been healed in my soul.'

Jean was still suspicious. Lisa was anxious. Any moment now, her mother was likely to open fire with her plentiful supply of evangelical ammunition, and she felt protective of her uncle. 'That's wonderful, Uncle Sol,' she said. Jean said nothing.

'Go on,' said Ted, keen to hear more.

Solomon looked at his sister and said, 'Jean, I'm sorry.'

'Sorry for what?' replied Jean, looking at her mug of tea.

'I'm sorry I've not been a better brother to you.'

274

'Nonsense,' protested Jean. She still did not look at her brother, and took a large swig of tea from her mug. Lisa and Ted knew that Solomon had led them on to some very delicate ground. Both brother and sister had strenuously avoided any significant discussion of their childhood. It was an unwritten family law. It was a law that, for some reason, Solomon was choosing to break now.

'When you were born,' said Solomon, 'I thought you were the most beautiful thing I'd ever seen.' Lisa noticed her mother rubbing hard the handle of her mug. 'I was a reasonably happy ten-year-old,' continued Solomon, 'though I know now, I was still deeply grieving the loss of my father.'

Jean still rubbed the handle. Her lips were pursed. 'Mum and Dad were very good parents to us both,' she said. She felt the need to send a pre-emptive strike, lest her brother launch an attack on their parents. She turned and looked briefly at Solomon and said, 'They were godly parents, they were. They followed the scriptures and brought us up proper. We can have no complaints in that department.'

'They did love us,' agreed Solomon. He was realising that it was going to be far from easy to explain to his sister the essence of the profound healing he had experienced over the weekend. He looked briefly at Lisa, who gave him a reassuring smile.

'Let me hazard a guess about this,' said Ted, who was experiencing less tension than his wife or daughter. 'I've often thought about this, Sol. You lost your pa, and it must have been terrible sad for you. God knows what you must have gone through, you poor soul. Then your ma goes and finds herself another man. All well and good for her, maybe. But for you? Well, you find another man in the house, who tells you that he's your father now. That can't have been easy. Then a little babe comes along, and they make a big fuss of her. So you get edged to one side, so to speak. You're grieving your pa, and you're losing the love of your ma, too. Not an easy time for you. That's how I see it, Sol.'

'It was nothing like that,' protested Jean, putting her mug so firmly back on the table, that tea spilt from it.

'Well, maybe not to you, love,' said Ted. 'But think of how it was for your brother, here.'

'He was fine,' said Jean. 'He had nothing to complain of.'

'Mum,' said Lisa, feeling an old anger rising in her. 'Don't be so bloody selfish.'

'Don't you go using that language...'

'It's my house and I'll use whatever bloody language I like, thank you very much,' said Lisa. 'You are being selfish. You are not thinking what it must have been like for your brother. Dad's right, I'm sure. Isn't he, Uncle Sol?'

Solomon, untroubled by his sister's response, nodded, 'Yes, he summed it up very well.' Then he looked across to Jean and said, 'Jean, don't be angry about this. I'm not complaining about our parents. I'm simply telling you that it was a wound in my soul. There's no right or wrong about it. It just happened. I'm not accusing Mum and Dad. In fact, I can well understand it was difficult for them. I'm so glad that *you* were so well loved. The problem is that this wound kept me locked up. You know that. I have lived my life in a kind of prison. I'm not blaming Mum or Dad or anyone. I'm simply saying that a deep grief has bound me for most of my life, but now I am free. *If the Son shall set you free, you shall be free indeed.* Isn't that what our scriptures say?'

Jean felt ambushed. Countless times had she quoted scripture to her brother, but never before had he quoted scripture to her. This was her weapon, not his. She felt profoundly confused. She was very aware that the company around the table were much more with Solomon than they were with her. She felt cornered. She breathed in to prepare herself for combat. So, it was down to using scriptures was it? She closed her eyes, seeking inspiration. God always showed her just the right scripture to use in situations like this. But nothing came. Just when she really needed Him, God had gone quiet on her.

She opened her eyes and looked at her brother. Usually he looked so old and frail to her, yet today there was a noticeable difference. There was a light blazing in those soft grey eyes. There was vitality in the tiny movements of the wispy eyebrows above them. There was a strength in the line of his jaw that she had not seen before. And more than anything, she could not deny that this familiar face sitting next to her was a face of intense kindness. So, with some reluctance, she conceded, 'Yes, Solomon, you are right. Our Scriptures do say that. Yes... Yes, they do.'

276

She nibbled at her biscuit briefly, then saw an opportunity to address what to her was a more important issue. 'So, now you've had this special experience,' she said, shifting her jaw forward, 'Are you giving up all your high church malarkey?'

'Oh, Mother!' exclaimed Lisa.

'No, Lisa' said Solomon, raising his hand and tilting his head a little. 'This has been very difficult for my sister.' He planted his elbows on the table, drawing his hands to his chin, and said to Jean, 'I am so sorry if the way I have followed God has been offensive to you. It was my way, Jean. My way of loving Him. I am so sorry you never saw that. You only saw the ritual, and it offended you.'

Jean was feeling intensely uncomfortable, not least because such a personal level of conversation was taking place in front of the family. There was also something about the way Solomon was speaking that made her far less sure of her ground – a ground of which she was once so sure. 'Let's discuss this another time,' she said, hoping to close the matter.

'No, Jeannie,' said Ted. 'Let your brother speak. This is important.'

With reluctance, Jean said, 'Very well,' and fixed her eyes on her mug.

'Jean,' said Solomon, 'You were right to be critical of some of my ways. I think now there has been so much wrong in the way I have lived my faith. And indeed, so much wrong in the way I have been a shepherd in God's church. In fact, I have been a very poor shepherd...'

'Oh, no, Uncle,' interrupted Lisa. She had never felt such love and compassion for him as she did in these moments. She had caught a glimpse into the deeper layers of his soul when she had read his journal. But now he was sharing with his family matters that previously he had only ever shared in the privacy of the journal. She was feeling anxious and protective of him.

'No, no, Lisa,' said Solomon. 'No-one would claim that I have been a very good priest. But that's not important. I am not burdened by it. It's happened and I can't go back. But I have experienced things these past few days that make me see things differently.' He then turned to his sister and said, 'I wish you had been with me, Jean. I think you would also now be seeing things differently.'

277

'There's nothing wrong with how I see things,' protested Jean.

Lisa and Ted both sighed.

'No,' said Solomon, leaning back in his chair, and repeated again, 'No,' and smiled at his sister, who was biting her lips. He did not want to push her.

At that moment, the door opened and Matt came into the room. 'Hi Jean, Ted.' He then looked at Lisa and said, 'I expect the girls will be back soon, and I just wonder if I might go and fetch some pizzas for us all. You'll stay, won't you?' He addressed the question to Jean, who was just about to reply in the negative, when Ted intervened and said, 'That would be wonderful, Matt. Can I come with you?'

'And could I come, too?' said Solomon, rising from his chair.

'That would be great,' said Matt. 'And over supper, perhaps we can start making plans about where we might move to.' And with that, the three men left the kitchen.

'Where you can move to?' asked Jean, fixing a stare at her daughter. 'Move from this house? Has it got that bad?'

'Yes,' said Lisa, gathering the empty mugs. 'It has.'

# 30

During the winter months, the rays of the sun seldom shone upon the grey stone walls and large sash windows of the rear of Altarnun House. This was due to the steep hill that rose up behind the village. However, by mid-April the sun had gained enough height to clear the hill by the early morning, thus beaming its light onto the east-facing window of Matt and Lisa's bedroom. And on this Tuesday morning the sunlight was piercing its way through the blinds, casting narrow strips of brilliance on the carpet. So bright were those strips that they awoke Lisa from a restless sleep. She checked her phone and decided it was time to get up.

She slipped on her gown and slippers, and made her way down to the kitchen. Ella had also woken early and was at the kitchen table, clutching a mug of mint tea. Mother and daughter sleepily greeted each other and, as she refilled the kettle, Lisa asked, 'Did Rahab stop the night?'

'Yeah,' said Ella, yawning. 'She's with Jenny in the spare room. Said she's going home today.'

'Nice girl,' said Lisa, as she tossed a tea bag into her mug.

'Yeah,' said Ella again. She then looked at her mother and said, 'Dad took the news much better than I thought he would.'

'Much better than he should've,' replied Lisa.

'Agreed,' said Ella. 'But then he's different, isn't he?'

'Incredibly different,' said Lisa, as she filled her mug. She prodded at the teabag for a while, then said, 'The pressure's been building up for months, to be honest. I was expecting him to either have a breakdown, or go back to the coke.'

'Hm,' said Ella. 'Well according to Jen, he was in a pretty desperate place yesterday morning. I guess he could be a bit up and down now.'

Lisa sat down at the table and said, 'I know. I was thinking that. He went from very low to very high yesterday. And yes, I told him about... You know... the man. We've still got a hell of a lot of work to do. But I do think we will get through this, don't you?'

Ella felt an unfamiliar sense of role reversal. Her mother seemed to be the child in need of the reassurance of a parent. She reached out her hand to her mother's and said, 'Sure. I think it will all be super cool. Might just take time.'

Lisa smiled. She looked at her daughter, and not for the first time recently, she saw not the teenager, but the young woman that Lisa was fast becoming. 'You know, Ella, you are becoming such a truly lovely young woman.'

'Steady, mum,' said Ella, and drank from her mug. She looked up and said, 'I'm going to miss this place, though. Aren't you?'

'Very much,' said Lisa. 'I'm amazed how well Gran took it last night.'

'I was expecting a lecture,' said Ella. 'You know - how all this was due to us offending God and all that judgement stuff she dishes out. But she left off all that, which was a brilliant relief.'

'Hm. I expect that's yet to come.' Lisa was holding the rim of her mug to her lip. 'Grandad was sad though, wasn't he?'

'Yeah, bless him.'

'Uncle Sol didn't seem to mind us having to move.'

'No. What a change in him, Mum. He's so different.'

'I can't believe it,' replied Lisa. 'Did you see the way he talked to his sister? He was so direct with her. It really knocked the wind out of her sails.'

'Yeah. You could see she was pretty disturbed.'

'Yes,' agreed Lisa. 'But I think it wasn't just disturbance. I think she was really touched, actually. I caught sight of her looking towards him when he was cutting into his pizza, and - it's the first time I have ever seen this - but it really looked like she loved him.'

Ella nodded and said, 'It would be really nice if they could get on better.'

At that moment, Matt came into the kitchen, yawning and scratching his head. Both his wife and daughter greeted him, then Lisa said, 'What time you going in to work?'

Matt went to make himself his cup of tea, and said, 'I'm not going in this morning, because I want to be here when the guys come to put up the For Sale board.'

'God, it's happening that quick is it, Dad?' said Ella.

'I'm afraid so, Ella,' said Matt. 'The sooner we get this place sold, the sooner I can clear the debt and all the interest that's piling up.'

'Sorry I can't earn a load of dosh to help you out,' said Ella, and smiled a kind smile at her father.

Matt would have apologised again, but over the pizza supper the previous evening, he was told in no uncertain terms to finish his apologising.

'What are you girls doing?' said Matt to Ella.

'Not sure,' replied Ella. 'Rahab's going back soon. Then I want to sit down with Jenny and go online to check out what support we need to find for her. You know, social security and all that.'

'Thanks, Ella. That's really good of you.'

'And Dad,' said Ella. 'She was starting to... You know... get really anxious last night. She's not had any dope for a couple of days now.'

'Ah, ok,' said Matt. 'I've still got some medication left over that will help a bit. Mum and I can chat to her after breakfast. We'll get an appointment fixed for her.'

It was not long before the rest of the household were awake, and by the time the church clock was striking nine, all were dressed and breakfasted. Matt was outside, waiting by the gate for his colleagues to come and erect the For Sale board. Rahab was on her way to return to her household, promising to come back before too long. Jenny was showing clear signs of her withdrawal, and Lisa took her into the lounge. Twice in recent years, Lisa had acted as the pilot steering her husband through the stormy waters back to sobriety. She was glad to share her knowledge and experience with this new friend. Solomon opted for a stroll up to the church.

Ella was supposed to do more revision, but her mind was far too distracted. And besides, this April morning had brought a cloudless sky, and the sun was shining so bright and warm. She sauntered into the garden, wandering around it slowly. The birds were full of song as they

281

busied themselves with feeding and nest-building. Ella was now viewing the house and garden as if it were a terminal patient with not long to go, and she was aware of the emergence of a strong grief welling up within her. Despite the family storms, this home had nonetheless been a safe haven. How many hours had she come into this garden as a child and either play on the swing and trampoline that used to be on the lawn, or enjoy imaginary adventure games amongst the trees and shrubs at the end of the garden?

She made her way slowly toward the overgrown end of the garden that was beyond the apple tree. She sat on the dewy grass, leaning back against the lump of protuberant grey rock that marked the boundary between the well-tamed section of garden with its lawn and flower beds, and the wild section that was left to the designs of nature. Her father had always said this rock was part of exposed bedrock, but in her childhood it had been far more than that. It was at times the top of a whale emerging from the sea, and upon that back she travelled all over the world. It was also a magic stone that had the power to change the fortunes of anyone who stood on it. They had to stand very still for five whole minutes, and if they managed to do this without moving a muscle, then they could become anyone they wanted. Usually she became a music or movie star, but just occasionally it was someone from history, such as Elizabeth 1. There was just something loveable, not to say mystical, about this rock. Its power had launched her on so many adventures of the imagination. She looked upon it on this Tuesday morning, at its lichen-covered and gull-splattered surface, and as she did so, she could hear the sound of the For Sale board being hammered into place somewhere near the front gate. She gazed up at the dappled light flickering through the vivid green leaves of the branches above her.

She closed her eyes, and for a short time drifted off into more memories and imaginings, until she was roused by a voice saying, 'May I join you?'

'Oh, Uncle Sol,' said Ella, delighted to see her great uncle. 'Of course.' She shifted her position. With some difficulty, he sat down on the rock. It was far from comfortable, but it would do, for he was so happy to be in the company of Ella. He stretched his arm out and rested it on Ella's shoulder. She immediately reached out her hand and grasped it. She turned and looked up at Solomon. 'I'm so glad you're back, Uncle Sol. I really missed you.'

'Dearest Ella,' said Solomon. 'And how I missed you.'

Both of them looked out to sea for a while. Ella was still grasping Solomon's hand and she said, 'Thank you, Uncle Sol.'

'For what?'

'For all those times you let me come into your room.' She looked back up to him, and said, 'And you'd put your hand where it is now. You'll never know how much that helped me.'

'Ah... And I think you will never know how much you meant to me.' replied Solomon, admiring the pale face looking up at him. 'Those were such precious times. But, my dear Ella, I had no words for my feelings in those days. I'm sorry I did not give you more.'

'I didn't need words. You gave me all I needed.' Ella was starting to feel the dampness rising from the grass, so she shifted her position and sat on the rock next to her great uncle. 'Tell me, Uncle Sol,' she said, reaching out and grasping his hand again. 'Where *did* you go over the weekend?'

'Ah...' said Solomon again. So much was becoming difficult to explain!

Ella said, 'You know when that Inspector was here?' Both of them chuckled for a moment. 'Why did you make out you had travelled through time? Was it because you just wanted to get rid?'

'Oh, no,' said Solomon, who was cherishing the clasp of Ella's hand in his. 'No, I told her all that, because it was true. I know no-one will believe me. Although I think maybe your friend Rahab might have.'

'I think she did.'

'You don't have to believe it, Ella. And I know everyone will think it is because I'm an old man, and they will probably see it as the first stage of dementia. But I can only say what I experienced. And what I experienced was very real and very special.'

Ella was frowning deeply. 'It's not exactly easy to believe, Uncle Sol,' she said, raising one eyebrow high above her hazel eye. 'But I think I sort of get it. So, you say that this lady - what was her name?'

'Monnine.'

'Monnine. Nice name. So, she travelled from the past and arrived at the church, and then led you back to her time. But in the same place. In this village here. Only fifteen hundred years earlier?'

'Yes, after a while, I came to realise that. But you see, when I first arrived there, I had completely lost my memory. I couldn't even remember my own name. It was very frightening, to be honest with you, Ella. I was aware that I was from a different time - a time a long way into their future - but only little fragments of memory came back to me. But I see now that it was better that I lost my memory. I had to wipe my mind clean in order to discover new things. I discovered myself in a whole new way. And I beheld the world very differently. And the church *very* differently indeed. And I became acquainted with God in a refreshingly new way. I met a people there, whose faith was formed from a different material to mine. It was so special, Ella. I think you would have loved it there.'

'So, what was this place, then?'

'Oh, Monnine, you see, was an Irish lady. Lovely character. She felt called away from her homeland. She boarded a small boat one day, put up the sail, and the currents and winds drew her here to Cornwall. And here she planted a Christian community.'

'You mean you got to meet the first people who settled here.'

'Well, I'm sure other people had lived in these parts before. But this group I met was the beginning of the village as we know it.'

'Did it have a harbour then?'

'Yes, but not like it is now, of course. It was a very simple harbour. That's where my friend Corman docked his boat.'

'Oh, yeah. And he took you over to his island.'

'He did. That was very special.'

Ella paused for a time. Her great uncle was sounding so reasonable and so in control of his faculties. He did not sound like a man suffering from dementia. She looked at him, and screwed up her eyes as the light was bright over the sea. She said, 'You've changed a lot, Uncle Sol.'

'I know I have, Ella. It's all very strange.' His aged eyes looked at his great niece and said, 'I'm so sorry if it's a bit of a shock for you.'

'No, not at all.'

284

'But you have changed too.'

'Yeah, I think I have.'

'Thank you for trying to search for me.'

'Silly wasn't it?' She smiled her beguiling smile at Solomon.

'Not at all,' he said. 'It touches me so deeply that you should even think of looking for me.'

'If I'd known you'd fallen through time fifteen hundred years, I would certainly have come after you. It sounds fab there!' They both laughed.

And,' said Solomon, his brow furrowing again. 'You have also made some new friends. With dear Rahab. And a nun, you say?'

'Oh, lovely Sister Maria,' said Ella, beaming her bright smile. She then looked out to the bright sea for a moment and said, 'She sang me a most beautiful hymn. She sang it in Welsh. It was so sweet.'

'Do you remember what hymn it was.'

'Yes, it was something like, *here is love, as big as the ocean.*'

'I know the one,' said Solomon. He straightened his body and inhaled deeply, and then sang the first verse. Ella listened to the old man's quavering voice, and she noticed a trickle of water running down the side of his nose as he sang. It was so different to Sister Maria's rendition of the same hymn, but it was also full of soul. When he had finished the verse, he opened his moistened eyes, and said, 'It's the most important thing, Ella. The love of God. Vast as the ocean. That's pretty big.' He paused for a few moments, then said, 'I'm sorry. I don't like getting preachy. Forgive me.'

'No,' said Ella. 'It's not preachy. I felt it actually. When Sister Maria sang it, and now, when you sang it. I felt that love. It's special Uncle Sol. And I've seen it. In you; in Maria; in Jenny and in Rahab.'

'Yes, I saw it in Rahab and Jenny, definitely,' agreed Solomon.

Both were quiet for a few moments, then Ella said, 'But, I'm sorry to say, I don't see it in Gran.'

Solomon chuckled, 'Ah, yes. My dear sister! She tries so hard, doesn't she? I think she will thaw out one day. Let's give her time.'

285

While they were speaking, Ella was rubbing her fingers along the surface of the rock that was roughened by the colourful lichen. As she did so, she realised that her fingers were tracing a marking on the rock. She looked down and saw a long line that appeared to be neatly carved into the stone. Then, almost indistinct, was another short line bisecting it. 'Look, Uncle Sol,' she said. 'I never noticed it before. But look at this.' She picked at some of the lichen to make the mark clearer. 'Isn't that curious?' she remarked. 'This mark looks like it is the shape of a cross. Is it a natural mark, or do you think someone has deliberately carved it?'

She was waiting for her great uncle to make some comment, but he was saying nothing. She looked at him and saw his face was frozen in a look of astonishment. He also traced the mark of the cross with his finger, and then he clambered off the rock and stepped back a few paces and surveyed the contours of the stone. He pulled some ivy away from it, so he could see it more clearly. Ella was slightly alarmed by the intensity of his expression. His eyes were wide, as if he had received a terrible shock. His mouth was open and moving slightly. 'What is it, Uncle Sol? You're worrying me.' She also stood up.

'Er...' said Solomon. 'I know this rock. I *know* it. I have seen it before.'

'Yes, you do know it. It's always been in the garden here. It's the one I used to play on...'

'No, no... I saw it when I was with Monnine. Corman told me all about it. It was near my room. I saw it. I saw it, you see.' His hands were quivering at his side. He looked beseechingly at Ella and said, 'Ella, my dear. We need to move this rock.'

'Move it?' She was feeling disappointed. She had come to believe that there was nothing wrong with her great uncle's mind, but this behaviour was deeply disturbing. She said, 'Shall we go inside now and have a cup of coffee, Uncle Sol?' She was adopting the tone of a care assistant.

'I'm not mad, Ella,' said Solomon, now pointing at the rock. The quivering had stopped and his tone had become assertive. 'If your father can shift this rock, there might be something very valuable underneath it.'

'How do you know this?' asked Ella.

286

'It's the progeny rock,' said Solomon, as if that explained everything. 'I am certain of it.' He turned around to look at the house. He tried to imagine the distance from where he was now standing and the well, and the church. Yes, the distance was about right. This had to be the rock. There could be no doubt. Admittedly, Vikings may have discovered it or other treasure-seekers in years gone by, and there could be nothing there. But, on the other hand, the stone looked very undisturbed. He would not be able to rest until he had checked what was buried under it. 'We must check it, Ella. We must,' he said.

'Let's go and find Dad,' said Ella. She was still very unsure about Solomon's state of mind. Yet she could see a powerful and lucid conviction in the old man. As they made their way back to the house, Solomon filled in Ella about the story of the buried treasure. Ella was surprised by the strength and speed of Solomon's steps. It was clear he was either becoming alive in a new and remarkable way. Or this was a spurt of madness that was the herald of a sad and disturbing decline. As she clutched his hand, she decided to opt for the former explanation, and with that choice came an almost overwhelming sense of exuberance. Maybe the rock that she had loved from childhood really was touched with the magic she always imagined it possessed.

# 31

Matt was reasonably happy with the positioning of the For Sale board. However, the truth was that he hated the idea of this sign. It was such a public admission of his failures. Within hours, the whole village would know that he was selling up. The board might as well have said, 'Here marks the spot where Matthew Micklefield was publicly shamed and humiliated. Let all those who are greedy be warned."

Yet, something was shifting in his heart and mind that was giving him the confidence to face this. He was very encouraged to find that, despite the huge disturbance of this sale, he found no need to return to the old methods of comfort that had caused such problems in the past. No, things were changing. That which he had dreaded had come upon him, and yet, he was finding a steadiness and strength to cope with it. Jenny, Theo, Lisa, Ella and Solomon, each in their own way, had induced a change in the deeper strata of his soul. It was as if they were beckoning to life a new, tender yet also tougher, and certainly truer part of himself. Even as his colleague, Ken, was hammering the For Sale board post into place, he felt this newly discovered part of himself opening its lungs and inhaling the fresh air of something very much like faith. For a few moments, as he held the rough wooden post for Ken, and felt the thud, thud, thud of the lump hammer, he had a curious sense of being connected with the old bible story of the Messiah being hammered to a cross. At one point, a sharp edge of wood cut his metacarpus, and he watched the blood trickling to the base of his thumb. Just for a few moments, he had a most unexpected sense that he was standing in some liminal space - a space that held the story of a stream of divine love spurting forth from rough-hewn timber.

Ken checked the board was secure, then drove off. Matt hardly noticed nor acknowledged his departure, and strolled back to the house, dabbing his hand with a handkerchief. He paused by the garden seat on which Solomon had sat the previous day. He looked out to sea and remembered the chugging engine of Theo's little boat. Once again, there was this curious sense that the Great Friend was reaching out a wounded hand for friendship with him. If such a divine Friend did exist, Matt had always assumed that the look in that celestial eye toward one such as he, would always be one of disapproval. And yet he couldn't get away from a strong sense that the look was one of understanding and compassion. To be in the line of such a gaze was almost as uncomfortable. And yet it was not a gaze from which to flee - of that much, Matt was sure.

He shook his head as these unfamiliar religious thoughts occupied his mind. He was roused from these thoughts by the unexpected sight of Uncle Solomon almost running towards him along the west lawn. Close beside him was Ella, and it wasn't long before they both reached Matt.

'Matthew,' said Solomon, heaving in a lungful of air after the exertion of his speedy journey. 'The stone, Matthew. On the south lawn by the wild area. We need to move it.'

'What?' said Matt, his upper lip curling in puzzlement.

'It could be important, Dad,' said Ella, anticipating his objection.

'Important for what?' enquired Matt. Thus, there followed a stuttered conversation, in which both Solomon and Ella attempted to explain, what seemed to Matt, a highly improbable and fanciful idea that there was a large stone in his garden that covered a secret hoard of treasure.

'But, Uncle Sol,' pleaded Matt. 'That's not a stone. It's the exposed part of the rock on which this house is built.'

'If I may,' said Solomon, his hands twitching at his sides. 'I think that if you dig at the foundations, you will find it is a large and separate stone.' Matt sighed and looked at Ella. It was clear that the old man's mind really was going. The story of time travelling and now this absurd tale of a stone in his garden covering treasure was clearly the imaginings of a brain in serious decline.

'I think we should at least have a look,' said Ella, brushing her hair from her eyes. 'We've nothing to lose, have we?'

Matt curtly replied 'Apart from our currently healthy backs and several hours of valuable time. And leaving a hell of a mess in a garden that's got to look good for a sale.'

'Get one of your diggers,' said Ella. 'It will save time. And we can soon make good.'

289

'A digger?' said Matt, removing his cap and running his hand through his thick hair.

'Yeah,' said Ella. 'You told me you've used them. Mini diggers you called them. You could drive it across the west lawn to the back garden. Should be ok.'

'It's important, Matthew,' said Solomon. 'I really think it is.'

Matt felt that his was the only sane voice in this conversation, and was very unsure how to handle this ridiculous request. 'Look,' he said. 'Let me get a spade, and I'll soon show you it's not a separate stone, but definitely part of the bedrock.'

Ella and Solomon wandered back to the rock, while Matt reluctantly made his way to his shed to gather a couple of spades. When they all assembled at the stone, Matt started digging, muttering various complaints as he did so. He was expecting to soon find evidence that this stone was the tip of a far greater mass of rock, but somewhat to his dismay, his digging soon gave ample evidence that this was indeed a lone rock, sitting heavily and sturdily upon the earth. So, the theory that this was a secure capstone to some ancient treasure had become a technical possibility.

Red faced and perspiring, Matt sat down on the stone, and used his blood-stained handkerchief to mop his brow.

'You're bleeding, Dad,' said Ella.

'Just a scratch,' said Matt, who studied the wound on his hand. It had stopped bleeding, but the stain of blood again reminded him of the wounded Messiah. He tried to rid himself of these religious thoughts that were confusing him. He needed to find a way to steer away from this fanciful notion of buried treasure, and listen instead to the steady voice of reason. But the blood seemed to be diverting his attention away from the reason voice to the very unfamiliar voice of instinct. He looked up at Solomon. A light breeze was causing the apple blossom to flutter around him. He was standing upright, with his head slightly angled. His searching eyes, peering through his steel-rimmed spectacles that were glinting in the sunlight, were those of a man awaiting the judgement of a magistrate. His right thumb was massaging the palm of his left hand. Alongside the old man stood his daughter. This young lady, whose heart he was breaking by selling the house she loved. As she stood under the dappled light of the trees, with

290

her hair dancing in the breeze, her soft brown eyebrows furrowed in anticipation, he thought she looked more beautiful than he had ever seen her. Seeing these two people standing before him left Matt no choice. 'I'll phone for a digger,' he said, and walked to the house without saying anything else.

'You better be right, Uncle Sol,' said Ella, as they turned to follow Matt back to the house.

Solomon was now experiencing some doubts. 'I know, Ella,' he said. 'I may be well off the mark. Perhaps I really am going doolally and I *did* imagine it all. Or maybe I didn't imagine it and it *was* there, but later it was found by Viking raiders. No, I have to admit, there is a real possibility of no treasure being down there. But we will never know unless we try.'

'What did they say about the treasure, then?' asked Ella, as they walked over the lawn under warm sunshine. 'What sort of treasure was it?'

'Do you know, I can't remember much about it,' said Solomon. 'It was Corman who told me.'

'The old hermit?'

'Yes, the old hermit,' replied Solomon. He paused as he closed his eyes for a few moments, then said, 'He wasn't really so interested in this treasure in the ground. In fact nobody in that community seemed to have any care for wealth and money. No, he was more interested in the treasure that was buried in me.'

'In you?'

'Yes.' Solomon was frowning as he delved back into the memory of the conversation with Corman on his isle. 'He said that God's business was to search after the treasure in each one of us and bring it into the light, Ella.' His frown dropped, and he looked at Ella and said, 'I asked him, "What is *my* buried treasure, then?" And he answered me, "It is the life fully lived. That life is the sap rising in the bark of the tree; it is the cry of the babe taking its first breath of life; it is the song of the thrush welcoming the dawn." Yes, I do remember it all so clearly. I remember it all clearly because it is so very important.'

Ella was listening carefully. 'Has your life not been fully lived, Uncle Sol?' she asked, as the breeze brushed her hair over her eyes for a few moments.

Solomon looked at a face partly hidden by the fall of hair. His frown returned as he said, 'I am afraid not, Ella, dear. I am sorry to have to confess this so late in life. But now, God has dug into my soul and together we have found the treasure. I have returned from my curious adventure determined to fully live whatever days I have left on this earth.

Ella's attempt to brush her hair behind her ear was not successful, so, still through partly hidden eyes she looked up to her great uncle and said, 'I can see that treasure, Uncle Sol. I have always seen it. It wasn't hidden from me.' She took his hand.

Solomon's eyes glistened as he looked upon the young woman. She noticed the trembling of his lip as he thought of saying something, but the emotion prevented anything from being said. He simply nodded and took her hand, and together they returned to the house.

*

'It will be sad seeing that old house go,' said Ted, as he carefully carried the pan of steaming milk over to the coffee mugs.

'I never took to it much,' replied Jean. 'It's too big. Did you let the milk boil?'

'No, I did not,' replied Ted, carefully pouring the hot liquid into the mugs.

Jean was sitting at her kitchen table. Her hands were clasped. Her lower lip was pushed forward. As Ted passed her the coffee, she made no acknowledgement.

'Don't mention it,' said Ted sarcastically.

'Still,' said Jean, clasping her hot mug with her plump hands. 'They shouldn't have to move. He shouldn't have got them into this mess. It's him I blame.'

292

'Oh, come on, Jean,' said Ted. 'This is hardly a time for blaming. Matt's worked hard, he has. He made a bad investment, that's all. Could've happened to anyone.'

'Hm,' said Jean. She sniffed her coffee and inspected it, saying, 'Smells like the milk boiled.'

'It didn't' said Ted, and to prevent Jean investigating his milk-warming skills further, he quickly said, 'But wasn't it good to see your brother? He looked well, didn't he?'

'Very odd,' replied Jean. She sipped at her coffee and grimaced at the mug. She looked back to Ted, and said, 'It's not natural, that story he told of him being transported off to another time. You know what I think, don't you?'

'Oh, no, don't go down that road, Jean,' said Ted with a sigh. 'Don't you go telling me that some nasty old demon got hold of your brother and deceived him...'

'Stop disrespecting our faith, Ted,' said Jean. Her jaw tightened. 'You have to admit. It's not natural. God did not intend for us to go visiting different times in history.'

'Well, tell me if I'm wrong, but didn't Moses and Elijah turn up to meet with Jesus once? They had to skip over a few centuries to do that.'

'That's different!'

Ted was never interested in theological arguments, and, reaching out his bronzed hand to his wife, he said, 'What is it, love?'

Jean took a sip of her coffee. 'I'm sorry, Ted,' she said. She looked at him, and he saw the strain in her face. 'It's just that I had found a way of managing my brother as he was. I know, I never approved of all that high church nonsense, but I accepted it. I didn't like it, but in a way, it kept everything safe. It kept a distance between us, if you get my meaning. Also, he never said much, so we never had to talk about the thing that really troubled us both. And what troubled us is to do with our past. As you know, we were brought up by very loving parents.' She took another swig from her mug, which left her with a thin white moustache.

'Yes, but you heard what he said, love,' said Ted. 'It clearly wasn't much fun for him in your home. He wasn't complaining about your parents. Just said it wasn't comfortable for him. And I don't suppose it was.'

Jean's eyes started to fill with unfamiliar pools of water. She looked towards Ted, and said, 'I know, Ted. I know it wasn't good for him.' She shook her head, and momentarily rebuked herself saying, 'Silly woman. Stop this.' She drew a handkerchief from her sleeve and blew her nose hard. Still wiping it, she said, 'I really loved him, you know. Looked up to him as my older brother. I always thought he was so gentle. And so handsome. Was sure he would marry, I was.' She looked at Ted, and said, 'It's the way he looked at me last night. He was so tender, he was. So compassionate. I remember seeing that look in him when I was little. Last night he looked like he used to look. It unsettled me to see that. It took me right back to how things used to be.'

She scratched at the table for a few moments, then said, 'My parents were very good parents, as I've said. I don't want you arguing with that, Ted. But, if the truth be told, I could see they were not as kind as they might have been toward Solomon.' She started sniffing again. 'I could see that, Ted. I saw that, when I was a little'un. To tell the truth, I used to cry in my bed at night. Felt so sorry for him.' The emotion started to get the better of her, and she pulled the handkerchief to her face. 'Stop this, you foolish woman.'

Ted reached out and stroked her shoulder. 'Come on, Jean. It's best to let those tears go. They've been wanting out for some time, I'd say.'

She sniffed hard and, after more extensive nose blowing, she said, 'If you want the honest truth, Ted, it was a pain I couldn't bear. I just had to stop myself loving him, and so I did.' Again, her face crumpled.

'Dear God,' said Ted. 'I never knew all that, love. I just thought you never took to him.'

Jean just shook her head for a while. Powerful feelings from years of buried pain were forcing their way into the open and, try as she might, she was unable to stop them. Her sobbing alarmed Ted for a time. He had never seen her like this. She had always been so strong and determined not to give way to emotion. He drew his chair close to hers, and she leaned her head onto his shoulder. For several moments, all she could manage were several exclamations of 'I'm sorry'.

Eventually the storm of emotion subsided, and she inhaled deeply. Mopping her face once again, she blinked several times. Her reddened eyes turned to Ted, and she said, 'Do you know, Ted, I've never admitted all of that to no-one. To be honest, not even to myself.'

'I know why, love,' said Ted.

'You do?'

'Now, don't go getting angry with me, but it's to do with your ma and pa. I know they were great parents, and very religious and all that. But they would not let you speak the way you've just done. They wouldn't have liked it. They thought that kind of thing offended God.'

To Ted's surprise, Jean did not protest, but simply nodded her head. 'You're right,' she whispered. 'I was afraid of them, really. Didn't want to upset them. Thought that if I upset them, God would be upset with me. And I saw how they treated Solomon, and couldn't bear to think of them treating me the same way, I suppose.' She paused for some more nose rubbing. 'Never admitted that before, Ted.' She turned to him, and he saw the anxiety in her face. 'Am I offending the Lord speaking in this way, Ted? I've lost my bearings on this one. You must tell me.'

'No, love,' reassured Ted, stroking her back. 'No, quite the opposite. What does the good book say? Something about Him seeking truth in the inward parts?'

Jean paused and pushed her damp handkerchief back up her sleeve. '*Behold, thou desirest truth in the inward parts*,' she quoted. She closed her eyes and continued, '*Purge me with hyssop and I shall be clean*. King David's words.'

'That they are, love,' said Ted. 'And don't they go on something like, *Create in me a clean heart, O God, and renew a right spirit within me?*

'That they do, Ted,' said Jean, sighing. 'Maybe He's doing just that. Renewing a right spirit in all of us.'

Ted pulled his seat back to its original place, and took hold of his coffee. 'Well, He's certainly doing something like that for old Sol. And as far as I can make out, He's doing some work of grace in you, too. And in me, for that matter.'

Again, Jean nodded. 'So, it seems,' she said. She was quiet for a while. Things were becoming clearer. She then looked to her husband through her bleary eyes and said, 'I know what I have to do, Ted.'

'What is that, love?'

'I have to ask him to forgive me.'

'Oh, I'm sure he wouldn't be wanting you to do that.'

'No,' agreed Jean. 'No, looking at how he is now, I don't think he would be wanting that. But I know that I need to do it. I need to clear the air. I've let my brother down, Ted. I could have helped him in his loneliness, and I haven't. I've always known that. It's just that the more time went on, the harder it felt to do anything about it. Much easier to brush it under the carpet. But it feels like the good Lord has lifted up that carpet now, so I best deal with what's hiding there. No secrets from Him, Ted, are there?'

'Oh, no, love,' agreed Ted. 'From Him, no secrets are hidden, that's for sure.'

'You know something, Ted?' said Jean after a few moments. She was now staring into her half-drunk coffee.

'What's that, love?'

She looked up at him, and said, 'I know that I said things just now about his travelling... You know - through time and that.'

'You did, love.'

'Well - now, don't go thinking I've lost my marbles, Ted - but, if I'm honest, I'm now wondering if maybe he *was* telling the truth. Maybe he did somehow manage to... You know. Slip into another time and that. I don't know how, but what does that matter? I don't know anything. I was touched by what he said, Ted. He told me that he wished I had seen what he had seen. He's been somewhere special, that's for sure. And it's done him a power of good. I think maybe it's doing all of us some good. It's getting to me, as you can see. I like the sound of where he's been, Ted. I think if I'd been there, I'd also be seeing things quite different now.'

'Well, I'm never going to understand any of this, Jean,' said Ted, looking at his undrunk coffee. He then looked at Jean and said, 'You've got such a simple, down-to-earth bloke as your husband, and he'll never get his head around most things, let alone folks travelling through time. But what I do know is what I see, Jean. And I see changes in your brother that I didn't think possible. And I see a change in you this morning that I never thought I'd live to see. And they are changes

296

I like. Changes that I like very much. So that, my Jeannie, makes your husband a very happy man, it does.'

To his surprise, Jean's blotched face creased into a smile, and the smile turned into a chuckle. 'God bless you, Edward Hancock. What would I do without you?' She leaned forward and kissed him, and Ted cupped her damp face with his hand, and held her cheek to his for a few moments, before she leaned back in her chair and sighed a long sigh.

She took a sip of her coffee, then frowning, said, 'That milk. It *did* boil, didn't it?'

Ted nodded slowly, and said, 'It did, love. Yes, it did.'

She looked sternly at him for a few moments, then laughed with a freedom that Ted had not seen for many years.

# 32

'You've ordered a *what*?' said Lisa, as she was washing her hands.

Matt was setting the table for lunch. 'A digger,' he said. 'Only a mini digger.'

Lisa dried her hands with some vigour, and stared at her husband. 'Listen, Matt. Are you losing your faculties too? It's hard enough trying to manage Uncle Sol's weird behaviour. But you've also been acting really strange since you arrived back home soaked to the skin yesterday morning. Sobbing one minute, and then cracking open champagne the next. You're not right, Matt. This is really, really strange behaviour.'

Matt ignored the accusation, and opened the fridge door. He pulled out a selection of cheese and meats and placed them on the table. 'I realise it does sound strange, Lis, but the old man might well be on to something. It won't do any harm just checking.'

Lisa's face was reddening. 'One moment, you are your usual hard-nosed businessman, selling off this property to clear your debts, and the next you are believing the lunatic tale of an old man, who is clearly suffering from concussion and possibly dementia, who says that there is a whole heap of treasure lying at the bottom of our garden just waiting to be found. You must admit, Matthew, this is not the behaviour of a sane man.'

At that moment, the kitchen door opened, and Jenny walked in. 'Sorry,' she said, as she sensed the tension. 'Shall I come back later?'

'No,' said Lisa, sighing. 'Come on in. We're just getting lunch.'

'What's this about treasure?' she asked, as she sat at the table.

'You mind cutting this into slices?' said Lisa, placing a large loaf of bread in front of her. 'I picked it up fresh this morning.'

Jenny leaned towards the bread and inhaled deeply. 'God, I love the smell of fresh bread, don't you?'

Lisa returned to the pressing subject and said, 'So what time's it coming? This digger thing?'

'About two,' replied Matt quietly.

'And how are you planning to get it into the back garden?'

'Along the west lawn.'

'I mowed it at the weekend. And it's been raining. A heavy digger will ruin it.'

'No, honestly, Lis. It won't. It's quite light.'

'What's happening, then?' asked Jenny, as she carefully sliced through the soft bread.

'Matthew wants to... Oh, you tell her,' said Lisa, and thumped a bowl of fruit on the table.

At that moment, Ella arrived. 'When's the digger coming?' she asked, as she went to the sink and started washing her hands.

'Oh, God,' said Lisa.

'You don't like the idea, Mum?' said Ella.

'Oh, yes,' replied Lisa. 'I love the idea of a digger tearing up the lawns, then digging a bloody great hole in the back garden, just when we are trying to make it look good for a sale. Yes. Fabulous idea.'

'But Mum, just suppose...'

'It's all right, Ella,' said Lisa. 'I know I have slipped into a parallel universe, where husbands turn up drenched in the company of... of young ladies; where old men claim they are travelling through time; where houses we have lived in and loved for over twenty years have to be sold; and where people decide to follow the crazy visions and go digging for treasure at the bottom of their gardens. It's OK. I'm hoping one day to return to a world of relative sanity. And if it doesn't happen soon, I shall probably join the ranks of the insane myself.'

Ella went up to her mother, and stood before her with her arms open. 'Sorry Mum,' she said. 'I think it will turn out OK. Honestly.'

Lisa looked at her daughter, and saw in her just the calmness and strength she needed, and she stepped forward and welcomed the warm hug.

'Ah, bless,' said Jenny, chewing at a piece of bread.

Solomon then entered the room, and looking to Matt, said, 'Ordered the digger?' For reasons he found hard to understand, his question set off a shaking laughter in the mother and daughter, who were hugging one another.

*

Ethel Cairns was just on her way back to her shop after her lunch break, when she was arrested by the unusual activity at the gateway of Altarnun House. A lorry was leaving the property in a billow of diesel fumes and was growling its way up the hill. Ethel hastened to the gateway, and saw on the gravel drive a small digger. She stood in the road for a few moments, frowning in puzzlement. Her frown deepened further when she observed Matthew Micklefield emerging from the side of the house with a slim young lady, who was not Ella. They were both laughing and, as they walked, he reached out his arm and pulled her to himself.

Ethel moved nearer the gate, hiding herself behind some greenery, so she could study the strange goings on without being noticed. She watched Matt clambering into the digger and drive it onto the lawn where, with some violent jerks and puffs of smoke, it disappeared to the back garden. The young lady eagerly followed him. Ethel continued to stand there for some moments, her open mouth inhaling the final whiffs of diesel fumes from the lorry. She eventually turned away, but as she did so, she noticed the For Sale board. She jerked her head back at the sight of it. She read it carefully several times, then continued to stand in the road for a few moments gaping at it. She had seen plenty of murder mysteries to know that in this world, there were unscrupulous people, who would casually bump off relatives, and then bury their bodies in the garden. Then they would sell up and move away as far as possible, usually in the company of a young woman, who is the cause and inspiration of the crime. In her mind it was clear: Matthew was now burying the body of Father Solomon, who had probably objected to his behaviour with this girl. Quite where Lisa and Ella sat in this conspiracy was hard to tell. But that conundrum did not deter Ethel from her excited speculations.

She was in no doubt she had just been a key witness to a piece of evidence that would soon be vital to police enquiries. Never before had she been party to such drama and intrigue. The excitement of it put a

300

new spring in her step, and she hurried back to her shop. She would have much to tell her customers this afternoon.

*

'Tell me again, Uncle Sol,' said Lisa. 'You say this Morraine...'

'Monnine is her name,' said Solomon, raising his voice above the roar of the digger.

'Sorry. *Monnine*,' continued Lisa, also raising her voice. 'So, she buried treasure in this spot and a girl had a dream saying it was for future generations.'

'That's it,' said Solomon.

'They called it a progeny gift,' said Ella.

'And do you know what exactly they buried there?' asked Lisa.

'Corman did tell me,' answered Solomon. 'But I'm damned if I can remember. I was really thinking about other things at the time.' It was getting warm in the back garden that was now bathed in afternoon sunshine, so Solomon pulled off his smock over his head, revealing his uncollared black shirt underneath.

'Right,' said Matt from the cab of the digger. 'I've got the bucket under what I think is the edge of the rock. Just pray that the hydraulics will be strong enough. Ella, can you watch the front there, and let me know if the bucket looks like it's slipping.'

'Will do,' said Ella, and moved to the back of the rock.

Then with a roar of the engine and more plumes of diesel smoke, the digger went to work on the boulder. For a few moments, the rock resisted the force of the digger, but then it showed signs of shifting. The bucket of the digger succeeded in gripping the back of the rock and tipping it, so that after a few moments, the great stone had rolled over, crushing the grass and brambles that once lay beside it.

Matt stopped the engine and leaped from his cab, and all moved to see what was revealed in the place where the rock had once stood. They beheld an oblong of compressed earth with a few dazed worms and millipedes attempting to wriggle their way to safety.

'No sign of treasure there,' said Jenny.

Matthew turned to Solomon and said, 'Did this Monnine say anything about how far down the treasure was buried?'

'Er, no,' said Solomon. He was becoming very uncertain about this whole enterprise now, and he was feeling rather foolish.

'Well, it's bound to be a way down,' said Ella. 'They'd want it to be safe.'

Lisa was far from sure about any of this, but she nonetheless ventured, 'Look, you've got to dig down. We won't know for sure unless you go down a few feet.'

'True,' said Matt. 'I'll just shift the rock a bit further away, and then I'll get digging.'

So Matt climbed back into the cab, and rolled the large rock onto the lawn, which provoked a disapproving frown from Lisa. He then moved the digger to near the newly exposed earth and lowered the clanking bucket and started scraping away the earth. Lisa, Ella, Jenny and Solomon all watched intently. Each one of them experienced the uncomfortable mix of doubt and hope. 'What's that?' cried Jenny. They all rushed forward but were disappointed to see that the bucket had simply cut in two a small rock that was lit up by the sunlight.

Matt went back to work. 'Can't you dig a bit deeper?' asked Ella.

'I don't want to harm anything,' called back Matt. He had often used a digger, but never for these purposes. He thought of the *Time Team* programmes he had watched, with archaeologists using a digger with great skill to skim off thin slices of earth for fear of damaging any buried artefacts. So, to the onlookers' frustration, he dug into the soil inch by laborious inch. After an hour of digging the hole was over two feet deep. Solomon had fetched one of the garden chairs and was sitting on it. He was no longer looking at the hole but was simply looking down at his knees. He was feeling terrible, and was now seriously doubting everything that had happened to him these past few days. He knew others were assuming that either he had hallucinated following concussion, or that he was entering the bewildering world of dementia. And yet, within his doubts, he also felt a longing now to return to the very world that he and others were questioning.

Matt stopped the engine. He needed a break. He walked towards the now gaping hole and stood beside it. He realised how much he had invested a hope in this possibility of the discovery of treasure that could potentially rescue him and this house. But he was now reluctantly concluding that such a hope was a forlorn one. He looked at the crumpled figure of Solomon, and went over to him, placing a hand on his shoulder. 'We were right to try, Sol. We had to try anything.'

'I'm so sorry, Matt,' said Solomon, cupping his hand over Matt's. 'Maybe I really was imagining it all. It was so kind of you to believe me.'

Matt was about to respond, when he heard Jenny's voice. She was lying beside the hole, leaning down into it with her arm extended. In a constricted voice she said, 'What's this thing here?'

Matt went over to the hole and looked in. 'I can't see anything, Jenny,' he said.

Jenny craned her head up to Matt, and said, 'I've always had good eyesight, I have, and I swear to you, I can see something here. You got a spade or something?'

Matt was still very unsure, but he went over to a pile of tools that he had assembled nearby, and fetched a trowel. Lisa and Ella were now peering into the hole. Jenny took the trowel and scraped at the earth. After a while, it became clear that she was indeed unearthing a small object. Nobody spoke as she continued to carefully chip away at the compacted earth, and soon everyone in the group realised that they were looking at a sight that they hardly dared believe.

'What...What is it, Jenny?' asked Lisa, breaking the almost reverential silence.

'I think I gor'it,' said Jenny, as she eased something small away from the earth. She pulled herself up from the hole and knelt by the group of keen onlookers. She opened her hand and, lying in it, was an object that filled Jenny's slender palm.

By now, Solomon was standing up and also observing carefully, his lavish eyebrows twitching wildly. 'It's in the shape of a small cross,' he said. 'The metal is so delicate.'

'That metal,' said Ella. 'Is it...?'

'It's too murky for gold, surely?' said Lisa.

303

'Can I have a look?' said Matt, and Jenny passed him the object. He licked his thumb and used it to carefully rub away dirt and grime from the metal. They could all then see in the heart of the object, an amber stone, bound by intricate metalwork.

'Dear Lord,' said Solomon. 'There is no doubt. This little creature is made of gold and holds at its centre a most beautiful carnelian.'

The whole group was silent for a few moments, for no-one knew quite what to say. It was Jenny, who broke the silence by saying, 'Shall I see if there is anything else down there?'

Matt said, 'I think we are supposed to tell someone first.'

'We need to be sure,' said Ella.

Before anyone could say anything else, Jenny was back, lying on the ground and reaching into the hole. The others peered into the hole, giving her advice as she scraped away and, sure enough, it was not long before she found another piece of metal. 'Here's something,' she called. She scraped away at the soil.

Matt was now kneeling at the edge of the hole. 'It's a pommel!' cried Matt.

'You wha?' called Jenny.

'A pommel,' replied Matt. 'You know - the top of a sword hilt.'

'My God,' said Lisa. She was experiencing a strange mix of delight and shock.

'Well, it's a lot bigger than the last thing,' said Jenny. Matt now lay on the ground and stretched into the hole, assisting Jenny with the delicate scraping away of the soil. Soon the two of them were very carefully raising to the surface a large and splendid handle of a sword with a partially corrupted blade. Everyone gathered around, as Jenny held the object in her two hands, while Matt gently removed pieces of the earth that had held fast the treasure for centuries. Solomon reached over, and with a dampened forefinger, he gently rubbed the pommel, revealing a stunning ruby.

'What... Whatever do we do with this?' asked Lisa, who was now visibly shaking.

'We have to call the police,' said Matt.

'Oh, no,' said Lisa. 'Not her again.'

'I'm afraid so,' said Matt. 'We've found enough to know there almost certainly is a hoard here. Now we have to hand it all over to the experts.'

'Sorry to be blunt,' said Ella. 'But isn't this stuff valuable? Who gets the money for it?'

'It's your land,' said Jenny. 'Should be yours by rights. Surely?'

'I'm not sure it's as simple as that,' said Matt.

'But it might be,' said Solomon. He smiled and put an arm around Ella. 'It just might be,' he repeated.

*

It was early evening by the time an irritable and bemused Inspector Littlegown was at the end of the garden with Matt and Solomon, standing by the gaping hole.

'Right....' she said, even more slowly than usual. She inspected the sword that was laid out on the ground alongside the small cross. Her lip was curled, as if she was smelling something unpleasant. 'It certainly looks like treasure, doesn't it?' she conceded.

'We think there could well be more down there,' said Matt.

'I dare say, sir,' said the Inspector. 'May I ask what led you to start digging a hole in this part of your garden?'

Matt and Solomon looked at each other for a few moments.

'I suggested they look here,' said Solomon, turning to the Inspector. 'I had heard about the hiding of the treasure when I visited the original community that settled here, you see. I was told it was hidden under that rock over there. It used to sit over this hole until Matthew moved it earlier.'

The Inspector lifted her substantial chin and looked along her nose at the old man. Before she could say anything, Solomon said, 'I appreciate, Inspector, that you will never believe me when I say I visited the community that originally dwelt here. So, I think you will simply have to put it down to me having a vision, or a mystical experience. Or that I used divination or some such. You will have to

305

find some way of understanding it. All I can say is that when I was visiting Monnine's community, I heard about the great rock that covered the treasure. And when I returned here, I discovered that this rock happened to be in the garden of our home. That's why I asked Matthew to look beneath it.'

Inspector Littlegown's chin was still raised, and she had sucked in her cheeks. She opened her mouth with a click and said, 'Very well,' then made a note in her book.

'So, what happens next?' asked Matt.

'Good question, sir,' answered the Inspector. 'Good question. There's a procedure we must follow. We shall send the archaeologists in to do a proper search. All items discovered will then be passed to the Coroner. I would think these artefacts will end up in a museum.'

'And...' started Matt.

'I think I know your next question, sir,' said the Inspector. 'Will there be any reward money?'

'Will there?' asked Matt, scratching his head with his muddy hand.

'I'm no expert, sir, but my guess is that if there are other items down there similar to these two objects, then this find will be of considerable value. The coroner and the Secretary of State all have a say in determining if you receive reward money. But I did check out previous similar finds after I got your call, and I would say you stand a very good chance of receiving a reward.'

'Oh, there are some more swords and silver and gold chalices in there,' said Solomon, who was now remembering Corman's description of the treasure. 'And pendants and brooches. The nobleman who entrusted the treasure to Monnine's community was very wealthy.'

'With respect, sir,' said the Inspector, leaning back her head again. 'I don't believe you have actually investigated this particular plot of land yet. So, I don't think any of us can say for sure what is in there. Let's see what the archaeologists find, shall we? I expect them to be along tomorrow. In the meantime, I must ask you all to keep well away from this area. I'll get my sergeant to come down and cordon it off.' Solomon nodded. But he knew he was right about the contents of this hoard. This most definitely was the treasure that Corman had spoken of, and no Viking or thief had found it in all the intervening years. His

306

family was the progeny and the proper recipients of this delightful gift. He knew that Monnine would have been delighted with his finding this treasure. In fact, he sensed she possibly knew that he and his family would be the recipient of this gift. She was that kind of person.

The Inspector, Matt and Solomon walked around to the front of the house. The Inspector gave them various instructions and warnings about the find. Then, before entering her car, she removed her cap, and said, 'To be honest with you, these past few days have been among the most puzzling of my career.' She looked at Solomon and said, 'I rightly can't make head nor tail of what's happened to you, sir. But all I can say is, that if what you have been telling me has even a grain of truth in it, then I've got a lot of thinking to do. The world maybe isn't quite what I thought it was. Good evening to you, sir.'

As her car crunched its way out of the driveway, Matt reached out his arm and wrapped it around the bony shoulders of his wife's uncle. 'And the same goes for me,' he said. 'The world certainly is not what I thought it was.'

Solomon reached his arm around Matthew's back and said, 'And the same also goes for me too, Matthew. The world is not what I thought it was, either. It is so much bigger, so much more mysterious, and so much brighter.'

The two of them looked out over the sea and, for several moments, they watched the hazy sun ease its way towards its rest, and listened to the sounds of the seabirds singing their evening hymns of praise.

# 33

The next few days saw a hive of activity in Altarnun House. A team of archaeologists were making use of the digger that Matt had hired, and already the hole at the end of the garden had expanded significantly. As Solomon predicted, they discovered further cups, swords, coins, brooches, pendants, crosses and ornaments. It was proving a significant find. In his study, Matt was making extensive enquiries regarding the proper processes regarding the discovery of buried treasure. From what the archaeologists were telling him, the find was already exceeding a million pounds in value, and these artefacts would be in demand from museums all over the country - particularly those in the West Country. His research was also assuring him that he and Lisa, as owners of the property and finders of the treasure, would be entitled to reward money. Although it was early days, by Friday he had secured enough confidence in this probability to arrange a meeting with his bank. Somewhat begrudgingly, Iain Slipp acknowledged that Matt was eligible for reward money from the find, and so agreed for a deferment for the debt repayment, thus meaning that Matt could take Altarnun House off the market.

Ethel Cairn's theory about murder and burial did excite many in the village for a couple of days, until Thursday, when Father Solomon Ogilvy happened to enter her shop to buy the local newspaper. She was somewhat reluctant to acknowledge that the parish priest was undeniably alive and well. Thereafter, the story had to be significantly amended to something far less entertaining. However, she could report that the priest was behaving very oddly and out of character, even making amicable and humorous conversation. Moreover, he was actually seen walking around the village *without* his clerical collar, and wearing a scruffy fisherman's smock. Clearly something very strange had happened to him since his knock on the head in the church. And there was the puzzling presence of the For Sale board that appeared outside Altarnun House for less than a day. Furthermore, Ethel had to report a hive of activity at the house in recent days, and more than once, she had observed people in high viz jackets making their way round to the back garden. It was most inconvenient that she could not find any vantage point from which to view the back garden, so she

308

could only speculate what all the fuss was about. Of her several theories, buried treasure was not one of them. She was drawn again to human remains to do with the crimes of previous occupants. In itself this was interesting, but did not have the appeal of a real live up-to-date drama.

Her grocery store had become the epicentre for the considerable conversation and speculation that all this activity produced. Business had never been so good at her shop. Discussion was largely focussed on two issues: if Ethel's theory was correct that the police were exhuming a body, then who might have met an untimely and violent death at Altarnun House in its history? And the second issue was to do with the parish priest. Quite what strange thing might he do or say next? His erratic behaviour was profoundly disturbing to the well-established villagers, especially the few church goers. Dementia was an obvious explanation for the old priest's behaviour, but because most of the church congregation feared this fate for themselves or their spouses, they were quick to look for alternative explanations. Such explanations were hard to come by, so as soon as it was discovered that Father Solomon would be returning to church on Sunday, it seemed that most in the village had decided to attend church to make a closer inspection of the priest, and come to an agreed explanation for the disturbing behaviour.

On Friday afternoon, Lisa (who had taken the week off work) drove Solomon to his sister's house in Pedrogwen. It had been Jean's suggestion. She had been greatly unsettled by the conversation with her brother. He had opened a door into a room containing their shared history, that hitherto they had both kept firmly shut and bolted. And yet she knew that this part of their lives needed addressing and, despite the great turmoil of visiting this once hidden part of their shared story, there felt to be a potential for a necessary healing. It was to this end that she invited him over for a coffee.

As Lisa navigated her Range Rover down the narrow lanes to the neighbouring village, she said, 'It's been almost a week since your accident in the church, Uncle Sol.'

'Yes, Lisa, it is,' replied Solomon, who had reached up to grasp the handle above the car door. Lisa's driving was always a little too fast for his comfort.

'I...' Lisa hesitated. She was unsure how to say what she wanted to say, for what she wanted to say was something that was so utterly implausible. She tried again, 'Uncle Sol, you knew exactly what would be under that rock in the garden, didn't you?'

'Yes,' agreed Solomon. 'My only doubt was that others would have found the treasure trove a long time ago. I thought the Vikings may have found it. But it was so well hidden wasn't it?'

'Yes,' said Lisa, as she slowed for a T junction. 'But you knew treasure had been buried there. You somehow knew it.'

'I had no reason to doubt Corman and Monnine. They were honourable people.' As the car stopped at the junction, he leaned forward and pronounced, 'Nothing coming on the left.'

Lisa moved out and accelerated. 'But, you see. I'm sorry to put it this way, but the fact that there really *was* treasure there, proves that you really *did*... You know, somehow or other, go back in... Well, in time.'

Solomon turned and looked at his niece, and said, 'I know, Lisa. It's impossible isn't it? I have given up trying to work out how it happened. All I know is that what I experienced was very real. And I feel extraordinarily blessed. I'm not expecting many people to believe me. In fact, it would be much easier if they didn't. I shudder to think what the tabloids would do with it. But if you believe me, Lisa, it would mean a great deal to me. But for most of the world, I think it's best to go with the concussion story, don't you?'

Lisa looked briefly across to her uncle and smiled warmly at him. 'You're right,' she said. 'We must make sure your privacy is protected with this find of the treasure.' She turned her attention back to the narrow road, and said, 'Matt and I will make sure of that.'

Solomon was quiet for a few moments, then said, 'You and Matt... You seem happier.'

A tractor was approaching, and for a few moments Lisa's attention was taken up with negotiating the car along the very tight passage between tractor and grass bank. Solomon had closed his eyes during the passing manoeuvre, but opened them when they were clear of the tractor. Lisa said, 'Yes, Uncle Sol. Much happened when you were away.'

'So I hear.'

'I've... I've not really been myself. I...was nearly very foolish.'

'You don't need to tell me.'

'I'm beginning to realise you notice much more than I thought.' She turned and smiled briefly at her uncle.

'I really don't want to interfere,' said Solomon. 'But I was worried about what you would do with your loneliness. But I think you are less lonely now?'

'I am. Yes, I am.' Solomon eased his hand from the handle and lowered it to his knees. He fixed his eyes on the narrow lane in front of him, but in his heart, he was giving thanks to God for the answer to the many prayers he had offered up for his niece.

He would have been surprised to know that Lisa was also, in her own way, giving thanks to a God who, in recent days, had surprised her by making His presence felt in her life. Not the angry and easily-offended God of her mother. Nor the distant and remote God of her uncle - as he was. She was becoming aware of the presence of a different sort of God. He was still a shadowy figure in the mists of her own confusion, but she felt sure that whoever this God was, He or She was something to do with the new energy and life that she now witnessed in her uncle.

As she drove her uncle down the narrow lanes, she was becoming aware of the same energy and life bubbling up in her. The child was no longer knocking at the window, but was out in the fresh air, playing in the meadows. She was experiencing moments of being aware of an infant joy that kept taking her by surprise. And there was also a longing. The more Solomon talked about Monnine's community, the more she knew she would also have loved to have visited it. Her regular sensible self would have put aside such silly notions. But that voice was no longer the dominant voice of her soul. Now real imagination was possible, and with this released imagination, she sensed that she would have loved Monnine. She felt that Monnine would have been a spiritual mother to her in a way that her own mother had never been. How she would have loved to have lived in that community, to have raised Ella there, even to have worshipped in that little chapel. Something about it felt like a true home. Indeed, she was starting to feel homesick for it, despite the fact that she knew so little about it.

'Next right, I think,' called Solomon. Lisa had been lost in her thoughts, and she suddenly realised that the turn to Pedrogwen was upon her. She braked hard, and managed to negotiate the turn to the village without colliding with the oncoming car.

Solomon's hand had returned to the handle and was gripping it hard. 'Sorry!' said Lisa.

'Kept me awake,' responded Solomon, blinking hard.

*

'You sure you're not stopping?' said Jean to her daughter.

'No,' replied Lisa. 'I just need to pop into Asda. I'll be back in about an hour?'

'Course,' said Jean. 'Your dad's out fixing someone's mower, but he may be in when you come back.'

Lisa grasped her bundle of keys and left. Jean put a pan of milk on the hob, while Solomon sat down at the large pine kitchen table. Jean fetched some mugs from the cupboard, and as she returned to her sideboard, she turned to her brother and said, 'Where did you get that smock? It's not like you to go wearing that kind of thing.'

'Oh, this?' said Solomon, reaching out his arm and stroking the sleeve.

'Yes, that thing,' said Jean, spooning some instant coffee into the mugs.

'Monnine,' said Solomon. 'She said I could keep it. And I left them my jacket. Don't think I'll be needing it now. And they found it very amusing.'

'Not needing your jacket?' protested Jean, now filling the mugs with hot milk. 'You always wear your jacket. I don't think I've ever seen you out of it.'

'I know,' said Solomon.

'It's disturbing, Solomon,' said Jean, placing a steaming mug in front of her brother. 'I mean, your behaviour. You know... You're not yourself.'

312

Solomon looked up to Jean, who was opening a packet of chocolate digestives. 'I disagree,' he said. 'I am more myself now than I have ever been.'

Jean frowned as she struggled to open the packet. Eventually, it sprang open releasing a pile of broken biscuits to the table. 'Darn the thing,' she said, as she proceeded to fish out a complete biscuit, and handed it to Solomon.

Neither spoke for a few moments, until Solomon said, 'What did you want to talk to me about, Jean? You wanted us to meet this morning.'

'I did,' said Jean. She was struggling to know how to start the conversation. But the door to that secret room of their shared family history was ajar. She took hold of its handle by asking, 'Tell me. What was your pa like?'

Solomon broke his biscuit in two, and drew a half to his lips. He paused for some moments, then his thin hand returned to the table. He looked at his sister, and said, 'He was a tall man, as I am. I loved being lifted up by him and seeing the world from his height. He smelled of eau de cologne and tobacco. He had grey eyes like mine. He used Brylcreem on his jet-black hair that was always brushed smartly back, leaving his forehead gleaming. I always remember him in a suit, except in the summer when he wore a white jacket. He took it off when we played catch on the lawn. I used to love those games.'

Jean was munching her biscuit, but managed to say, 'Sounds like he was a good pa to you.'

Solomon nodded. He was still clutching the two halves of his biscuit and the chocolate was melting on his fingers. 'I loved him more than I can say, Jean,' he said, and looked up to the ceiling for a few moments. 'We lost him, though. He felt this call, you see. It was the war, and I think he was feeling bad that he wasn't fighting, like many of his friends were. He felt that being a priest of a small village wasn't enough. So, he went off to the Far East. Admirable in so many ways. But for Mummy and I - it was devastating. Especially when we got that fatal news.' He turned to Jean, as he said, 'I thought she'd never recover. She was perfectly lost without him. I've never seen a woman so distraught.'

'Until she met Dad,' said Jean.

313

'Yes,' said Solomon. 'It was good that she met him. She had been so lonely.' He finally took a bite from his biscuit, and after chewing at it for a few moments, added, 'And I got a new sister.' He beamed at Jean.

Jean had long finished her biscuit, and was gathering the broken pieces back into the packet. She looked briefly at Solomon, then said, 'Did you blame God for losing your pa?'

'I did,' said Solomon. 'But only in the last few days have I admitted it. I was angry with God for stealing my father from me. I know that now. And yet I am also now resolved to it.' He placed the final piece of digestive in his mouth and chewed it slowly. 'I made a friend when I was away. Corman was his name. A hermit.' Jean noticed his chocolate-stained fingertips tapping each other. She got up and fetched a paper towel. 'He had been to Jerusalem' continued Solomon. 'He had been to the very place where our Lord died.' Solomon was looking straight ahead of him, and his brow furrowed a little. 'Made a great impression on him.' His brow relaxed as he looked at Jean. 'His story made a great impression on me, actually. We talk so much about the Cross, don't we? But few of us are really touched by it. Well, he was. And I was, as he spoke to me. Something lifted in me as he spoke about his experience at Calvary. I knew that I was changing. A sort of thawing out, I suppose.'

Jean had never heard her brother speak so personally before. He was so much more present than he had ever been. He was not speaking as a theologian or a priest, but much more as a friend. She passed him the paper towel. 'You need this,' she said, nodding at his fingers. She watched him make slow use of it. Then an old familiar part of herself rose up and enquired, 'So, would you say you've been born again now?'

Solomon angled his head for a few moments, and studied the tired eyes that peered at him over the plump cheeks. They were the eyes of the secondary school teacher that she had once been. The eyes that were always on the lookout for errors. He was aware of a feeling that he had often harboured, yet not quite owned, of being grateful that he had never been one of her pupils. But this censorious look did not prevent him from speaking honestly, for that was his language now. 'I feel like Lazarus, Jean,' he said, cupping his now clean hands around his mug. 'Not so much born again, but more coming back to life. That life I used to live appears to me now as one lived in a dark tomb. But

314

Christ has called me forth. I'm slowly getting used to the light. The friends I met last week helped to unbind me. I shall be forever grateful.'

This did not compute with Jean's spirituality. You were either born again or you weren't. Coming out of tombs was not part of the deal. She wanted to correct her brother. Get him to the point of admitting that he had never been properly born again, and to now become a proper Christian, as she saw it. But another force was at work, competing with the usual familiar drive of correct Christian procedures. It was unsettling to experience it, yet also a little exciting. For a time, she simply stared at her brother in silence. He seemed to be absorbed in his own thoughts, smiling and staring into his empty coffee mug. She felt she was at a dangerous pivotal point in her life. Tip one way, and she would be back in the safe world of clear Christian doctrines and behaviours that were easily understood and obeyed. Tip the other way, and she would fall into uncharted waters that held many risks. A land of uncut and undried. A land of fewer certainties, and yet a land of new discoveries. An adventurous land of possibilities and maybes. She had a disturbing sense of destiny about this present moment. The choice she was about to make would determine the direction she would take for the rest of her life.

She never consciously made the choice. Something within her seemed to do it, for she found herself saying, 'I always wanted to question Mum and Dad about their faith. They were so darn certain about everything. But I never dared speak to them like that.' She frowned as she spoke, and felt she had made a statement of terrible betrayal. 'I mean,' she said hastily, trying to make amends, 'I respected them, of course. And they were honouring the Lord...'

She was interrupted by her brother, who stretched out his hand, and clasped hers saying, 'It's all right, Jean. It's all right. You were a good daughter to them. You were a much better daughter to them than I was a son.'

'I've tried to honour them, and their faith.'

'You have.'

'We've been to church regularly, Ted and I.'

'You have.'

315

Both brother and sister were quiet for a few moments. Solomon attempted to withdraw his hand, but Jean kept hold of it. 'I'm sorry, Solomon,' she said, and looked at her brother with a look that conveyed both fear and shame.

'You have nothing to be sorry for...' started Solomon.

'No, I have,' said Jean. 'I've judged you. I even told people you weren't a proper Christian.'

'I probably wasn't...'

'Course you were,' said Jean. 'You loved God. That was always clear. I was just too silly and pig-headed to believe that your way of loving Him was proper and right.' She sighed and said, 'Let's be honest, I've got myself lost, Solomon. I've never admitted it before. Not even to myself. I've been hiding, I have. In my own little world, where I thought I had it all buttoned up. But look what I've done: I've kept my family at arm's length, and that's not right. Lisa, Matt and Ella: look how they frown at me every time I open my mouth to tell them about God. I even got the church praying for their house to be delivered of a spirit of unbelief last weekend, would you believe? It's not kind that, is it?'

'I'm sure...'

'No, hear me out, brother. I don't rightly know what's going on in me just at the minute. All I know is that when you went missing, something was set off inside of me. A voice in me - I don't mean spirits or that kind of thing - I mean the voice of the *real* me. Well, it started speaking to me, if you get my meaning. It started asking questions of the track I'd put myself on all these years. You see, I... I missed you, Solomon, when you went missing.' She looked at her brother through her now watery eyes. 'I thought to myself that if you were gone... You know - properly gone - how much I would grieve you. But not just grieve you. I'd grieve what we never had. I realised that there had been this great gap between us all these years, and it wasn't proper. And I realised that the gap was of my making. So, this is why I asked you round here. I just wanted... Well, I just wanted to say how sorry I am. I just wanted to say sorry.' She felt she had not expressed herself at all well, but she also felt a keen sense of relief.

They were still clasping each other's hands. Solomon reached over and stroked his sister's cheek. It was the first time he had done it since she had been a toddler. They were both a little taken aback. 'Thank

316

you,' he said. 'But it is I who should apologise. It is I who should have looked out for you, Jean. But we don't want to spend the rest of our lives apologising. Instead, let's make the most of the days we have left. I think perhaps in some special way, we are both being born again. We are being given another chance.'

Jean was pursing her lips to contain her emotion, and was nodding hard. She inhaled deeply, and said, 'Well now. Ted will be in soon. How about another cup?'

'I would like that very much,' said Solomon, reaching for the packet in front of him, and drawing out a piece of broken biscuit. Everything was tasting so much better since his return.

# 34

'How did the old man get on with his sister?' asked Matt, as he slumped into the sofa following the evening meal. Ella and Jenny had gone down to the pub with a couple of Ella's friends, and Solomon was in his room preparing his sermon for Sunday. Lisa pulled a bottle of Chardonnay from the cooler and filled two glasses.

'He said very little on the way home,' she replied, as she passed her husband the chilled glass.

'She seemed pretty rattled by him yesterday,' said Matt.

'I know,' said Lisa, settling in the armchair next to the sofa. Both were silent for several moments. Their eyes were fixed on the window that overlooked the view of the large tarpaulin that was fixed over the site of the dig at the end of the garden. The scene was slowly fading with the setting of the sun, and when Lisa turned on the table lamp, it disappeared and was replaced by a ghostly reflection on the window of the couple sipping their wine. 'How sure are you about the reward money?' she asked, as she rose from the sofa to close the curtains.

'It's definite we will get something,' said Matt. 'The only question is, how much.'

'So you've been rescued?' said Lisa, as she returned to her seat.

'I have,' said Matt. 'Yes, I know. I don't deserve it, if that's what you are thinking.'

'No, Matt. I'm not thinking that,' said Lisa. She crossed her elegant legs, and looked up to the ceiling for a few moments. 'We've both been fools. Neither of us deserve anything.'

They were silent for a few moments, then Matt ventured, 'The man... You know, the guy you were drawn to...'

'Troy was his name,' interjected Lisa. She was now staring ahead of her. 'Silly name, isn't it?' She smiled a half-hearted smile.

'Did you.... Were you in love with him?'

'Yes,' said Lisa, still staring ahead of her. 'Well, I *believed* I was.' She turned and looked at Matt, who seemed to her to have the look of a wounded child. 'But I know now, it wasn't love, Matt. It was a kind of escapist infatuation. I feel so embarrassed about it now. I feel like I've been a silly schoolgirl.' She bit her lip for a few moments. 'He's a nice guy, actually. Been divorced for a while. Lonely. Wounded. Unpleasant ex. All that stuff. I suppose I was a bit sorry for him at first. But as we got talking, I started to talk about myself. He was really interested in me. He listened, Matt.'

'And I didn't,' confessed Matt.

'No, you didn't,' agreed Lisa. 'And, to be honest, I don't think I really listened to you, either.'

'How did we drift apart, Lis?' asked Matt.

Lisa raised her eyebrows, pursed her lips, and shook her head slowly.

Matt was resting his glass on the arm of his chair. He stared at it for a few moments and said, 'I think my mistress was money.'

Lisa smiled, and said, 'Ironic therefore, that you should discover some buried treasure!'

Matt sighed a laugh, then said, 'The irony is that I discovered it just when I've come to the conclusion that it's money that nearly killed me.' He looked at Lisa and added, 'And nearly killed our marriage.'

'Maybe you could only find that treasure after you had come to that conclusion.'

'Maybe,' agreed Matt. 'But you and I. I think we can mend, don't you?'

'I think we can,' said Lisa, and smiled at her husband.

It had been a long time since he had seen her smile at him in this way. He felt both delighted and awkward. He looked back to his glass and said, 'Such a weird story, isn't it? The old man going back in time like that.' He looked up at his wife, and asked, 'Do you believe him, Lis?'

'Actually,' said Lisa. 'I do. What was it that Hamlet said?'

'If I remember right, something like, "There are more things in heaven and earth, Horatio, than are dreamt of in your philosophy."'

'Hm. Impressive,' said Lisa, still holding her smile. She turned and rested her eyes on the saffron curtains, and added, 'Maybe life is about having to change your philosophy from time to time.'

'My philosophy has certainly had a seismic shift these past few days.'

Lisa sipped from her glass, her gaze still on the calm of the curtains. 'As you know, Mum put me off religion.' Turning to Matt, she said, 'By the way, did you hear she got her church to rid our house of a spirit of unbelief!'

Matt chuckled, and said, 'Well, I guess we've not been the most believing of households.'

'Uncle Solomon has,' said Lisa.

'Yup,' agreed Matt, and finally took a first sip from his glass. 'I never really understood his way of believing, if I'm honest. I mean, with your mother, it was all in your face and there was never any doubt about her beliefs. But with your uncle, none of us had a clue really what he believed. No one understood his sermons.'

'No,' agreed Lisa. 'But when you were away, and he was missing, I had a look into his room and found a diary of his.'

'Oh, yeah?'

'Mm. I shouldn't have read it really, because it was personal. But it was beautiful, actually. I only read a page or two, but I realised what a sweet man he is. And what a tender faith he had.'

'Tender?'

'Yes. Raw somehow. Well, that was before all this. I'd say he is very different now. He's able to talk now, for one thing. And now he can talk, we are getting to know so much more about him.'

'Agreed,' said Matt, stretching out his legs, and putting his hand behind his head. He turned and looked at his wife and said, 'So are you getting more religious now?'

Lisa frowned, and tilted her head slowly. 'Yes, I think maybe I am. But don't worry, not like my mother.'

'Praise the Lord,' said Matt, imitating his mother-in-law. He then added, 'More like Uncle Sol?'

'Perhaps,' said Lisa. She drained her glass, and placed it carefully on the side table. 'It's strange, but when he talked about that community he visited, led by this Monnine person, I felt... Well, I felt I should have loved to have visited it. I think I would have had a strong faith there.'

Matt returned his gaze to the ceiling, and said, 'Yeah, I should have liked to have gone to that place too.' He turned and looked back to Lisa. 'It was Jenny that got me thinking about religion actually.'

'Is she religious?'

'Yep. Bit strange, I grant you, for a girl of her profession. She's had a hell of a life, but nonetheless there's a strong faith in that girl. And...Well...' Lisa noticed a struggle going on in her husband.

'What is it, Matt?'

He sighed, and looked briefly at Lisa, then turned away and said, 'On Monday, when I came in. And Jenny was with me.'

'Yes?'

'I think... I believe that God sent her to stop me...'

'Stop you?'

Matt leaned forward on the sofa and clasped his hands. 'On Monday morning, before I came home, I was at Gerhard's Leap. I was feeling just so... so bad about myself. And I...You know.' Lisa was now sitting upright, clutching the arm of her chair. Matt pursed his lips for a moment, then said, 'Whether I would really have had the courage to do it, I don't know. But just as I was thinking about it, Jenny turns up. I had actually called her *Angel* when I met her on Saturday night. She didn't tell me her name at first, and that's the one I gave her for some reason. Well, on Monday morning she was my saving angel. And I had this real sense that God had sent her to stop me doing anything stupid. And if God sent her to do that, then... Well, God mustn't think too badly of me, must he?'

Lisa reached out her hand and grasped Matt's, and said, 'I thank God you didn't do anything stupid, Matt. I thank God for Jenny too, if she was the one sent to stop you.'

Matt was strengthened by the clasp of her hand, and smiled. 'It all feels like a new start, doesn't it?'

'It does,' said Lisa. 'Let me refill the glasses.'

321

*

Ella had not found the visit to the pub easy. That evening Jenny had been hit hard by strong withdrawal symptoms, and she became highly agitated. She was shaking for most of the evening, and was unable to concentrate on the conversation with Ella's friends, occasionally erupting in angry responses. Ella also had to stop her drinking, which resulted in more angry protests. She recognised the signs from when her father had gone through the same withdrawal symptoms, and these were not comfortable memories for her. She eventually persuaded Jenny to come back home, and both girls fell into bed exhausted. Ella was awake early, but Jenny was still in bed at lunch time. Lisa went to her room, and managed to persuade her to get up and come downstairs to join them for lunch. She looked a wreck, and said little, but did manage to eat something.

After taking some food, she started to feel steadier. Ella suggested a walk up to the church, and Jenny agreed. 'How is it?' asked Ella, as they ambled their way the short distance to the church.

'It's easing,' said Jenny. She winced, as a jet of pain darted through her head. 'I'm not craving the stuff this morning. It's evil, in't it?'

'It is,' agreed Ella. Long ago she had come to the same conclusion.

As they walked over the broken paving stones to the church, Jenny took Ella's arm to steady herself. The sun emerged from behind a cloud just before they entered the porch. Jenny paused and turned her face to its warmth. 'That's better,' she said. She was definitely feeling the crisis was passing, and her strength was returning. The shots of pain were less frequent.

The old oak door of the church was open and they wandered down the centre aisle. Jenny unhooked her arm from Ella's, and ran her hand over the ancient oak of the pews. 'I love these places,' she said, now casting her eye around the building. A stream of sunlight had filtered its way through the branches of the yew tree in the churchyard, and was piercing the coloured glass of one of the south facing windows, illuminating one of the pews in a mix of reds, oranges and purples.

Jenny sat in the coloured light, and smiled. She looked to Ella, who had joined her, and said, 'This is special.'

Both women sat in the brightness of the colourful rays for a time without speaking, until Jenny said, 'I told your dad about my cathedral in Liverpool.'

'Yeah?'

'It was special, it was. Coloured light like this, but all over the shop. The whole place filled with colour, it was. That's how I think of God, don't you?'

'To be honest with you,' said Ella, 'Until the past few days, I've not given much thought to God in my life. My gran was a bit fierce with her religion, which put me off. I loved Uncle Sol, and he was obviously a believer, and so I always kept an open mind. I mean, if he loved God, there had to be something in it.'

'I met a few Goddy types,' said Jenny. 'I once passed a man on the street with a big bible in his hand. He could see I was a prozzie, so he started shouting bits of the bible to me. Judgement stuff, you know. Told me I was going to hell, and that. You could see he had a mean streak in him.'

'I don't know why some people are like that,' said Ella, and she felt the sadness as she said it.

'I told him to go and f himself,' said Jenny. 'And more. That slowed him down a bit.' Both girls laughed.

'Rahab's amazing, isn't she?' said Ella.

'She's a jewel,' said Jenny. 'You said you met a nun too.'

'Yeah. Sister Maria was her name. She sang to me. I told Uncle Sol about her, and he said, if ever she turns up at church he will ask her to sing.'

'That would be cool.'

'It would be beautiful,' said Ella.

The girls were quiet again for a while. 'Can I ask you something?' said Jenny. She bent her head and looked searchingly up at Ella.

'Sure,' said Ella.

'Do you think your nun friend would think that God could ever... you know. Could he well... like a person like me? I mean, how I've lived would shock most nuns, don't you think? I can't see many of them approving of me. My life's been screwed from the moment I was born.'

Ella reached out and took Jenny's hand. 'I know what she would say to you, Jenny. She would say that God loved you with all of His heart, and is sorry that your life has been screwed. That's the kind of God she worships.'

Jenny's eyes watered, and she looked away for a while. Then she said, 'But your gran. From what you say, she'd have me burning in hell for all the sins I've committed.'

Ella sighed. 'I suppose she would,' she said. 'But, you know, there are times when I have seen a softer side to my gran. Uncle Sol went to see her yesterday. I asked him how he got on, and he said something strange.'

'Yeah?'

'He said that for the first time since she was little, he stroked her face and she started to cry.' Jenny turned down her mouth, and raised her eyebrows. 'I know,' continued Ella. 'It's a bit weird. But, you see, Uncle Sol has never, ever touched anyone, apart from once or twice he patted my shoulders.'

'Patted your shoulders?'

'Yeah, when I was really sad or frightened.' Ella put her hand on her shoulder, where on occasions she had received the tender touch of her great uncle. 'It meant everything. But that's all he could manage in those days.' She looked at Jenny. 'So if he stroked his sister's face, well, that's revolutionary! They have never shown any affection to each other. And she didn't stop him, so he said. So I'm thinking, maybe the change in him will be changing her in some way too. I hope so.'

'Well, I never met the lady,' replied Jenny. 'But from what you tell me, she needs to change.'

'Hundred per cent,' replied Ella.

'So what about you?' said Jenny. 'Everyone seems to be changing.'

'Hm,' said Ella, frowning. A breeze in the churchyard caused the coloured light to tremble on the faces of the girls for a moment. 'When

I left home last Saturday to go and search for my great uncle, I went into town along the coast path and stopped and sat for a while in the sun. All the time, I was thinking about Uncle Sol - wondering what had happened to him. But also, remembering things about him. And the thing I kept remembering was seeing him praying here in this church. In that stall just there.' She pointed to the clergy stall ahead of them.

'I bet he was good at praying,' said Jenny.

'Yes, I think he was,' agreed Ella. 'But as I was thinking about him doing his praying, I thought that if ever there was a time for me to pray, it was now. I longed so much for him to be found. And I was sitting on this bench in the sun with my eyes closed and... Well, trying to pray really, and I felt this thing.'

'What thing were that?'

Ella looked up to the tall rafters for a moment, then ahead of her to the altar shining in sunlight at the east end of the church. 'I felt I was connecting with something very deep inside of myself. The only word I could really find for it was *faith*. Not any old faith. Not someone else's faith.' She turned to Jenny and said, 'I felt I had grasped *my* faith in God. The bit of me - the true me - that was able to know God. It was so real, Jen. So real.'

'I get yer,' said Jenny. 'I got just that in my cathedral, I did. It was special, it was. To be honest with yer, it was the first time I really felt loved. You wouldn't think that in a big barn of a place like that, you'd get to feel such a thing. But I did. It was like me and Him were together in a private place. And - well, it felt like He was pleased to be with me. Shan't ever forget that, I won't. Course, I wasn't a prozzie then, so not sure what He'd make of me now.' Ella was looking hard at her new friend, admiring her capacity to find love and hope in a world that had so wounded her.

'Well, we'll check that one out with Sister Maria, shall we?' said Ella, and squeezed Jenny's hand.

The girls were quiet for a while, then Ella said, 'Soon after that moment, Rahab came along and we chatted. And she asked me about my name.'

'Oh yeah?'

'Yeah. She asked me what my name meant, and I didn't know.'

325

'Oh, I've no idea what mine means. Did you find out about yours?'

'I looked it up this morning,' replied Ella. 'It means... Don't laugh... It means *beautiful goddess*.' Both girls did laugh.

'Well, you were named right,' said Jenny. 'You are beautiful.'

'Hm,' said Ella. 'I'm not so sure. How about goddess?' She laughed again.

'Well, sorry to disappoint you,' said Jenny. 'But I shan't be starting to worship yer, even though you have been kind to me. But listen. It doesn't mean you're some starry goddess, does it? It means you got something of god in you. That can't be bad. Maybe when you did that digging inside of yourself, that's what you found. Like your old uncle digging in your back garden for the treasure. You got digging in your own soul and found some treasure. That's the bit of you that God made, I reckon. That's the bit to hold on to. That's whar I think, any road.'

Ella smiled her warm smile at her new friend, and nudged her shoulder saying, 'There's lots of good wisdom in you, isn't there.'

'Course there is,' replied Jenny. 'I'm a Scouser.' She then said, 'Shall we come and hear your Uncle Sol in church here tomorrow?'

'Yeah, I was thinking of coming,' said Ella. 'And Rahab's coming too.'

'Whar about that nun of yours?'

'I'd love her to come, but I don't know how to contact her,' said Ella, standing up. 'But I know I'll see her again very soon, and I'll introduce her to you when I do.'

'God, I must be going religious,' said Jenny, as she also stood. 'I could be making friends with a priest and a nun! Not bad for a girl of my profession.' And with that, the two young women giggled their way out into the sunshine.

# 35

That Saturday evening proved to be a busy one for the Pilchard Inn. Ethel Cairnes had not been slow to air her theories about the strange events at Altarnun House. The news of the Rector's return was welcomed, but there was still the mystery of exactly how he disappeared (or *thinned,* if Daniel Moody was to be believed), and where he had been hiding during his weekend of absence. But what provoked the first gust of speculation in the pub that evening was the arrival of the three elderly choir members. They were seldom seen in the pub, so their sudden presence there was a sure sign that the village was truly troubled. Margaret was the first to arrive. Though she had lived in the village for many of her seventy-five years, she liked to convey that she had come from an altogether superior culture, expressed through her expensive clothes and her distinctive accent. Nothing pleased her more than when people remarked on the similarity of her voice with that of the Queen Consort.

As she was ordering her wine at the bar counter, the other two choir members arrived. These were Dolly and May, the two sisters, who boasted their combined age of a hundred and fifty-eight. They had seen off five husbands between them, and now lived together in a cottage by the harbour in blissful, male-free harmony.

'Thank you for coming' said Margaret, as they joined her at the bar.

'Never known such a thing,' said May. 'He's always had the choir. Every Sunday. Just like clockwork. Why has he suddenly banned us from singing?'

'Did he give you any reason, Margaret?' said Dolly, pushing in front of her sister to order her pint of *Doom Bar.*

'No, he didn't,' replied Margaret, sipping from her full glass of chilled Chardonnay. 'He simply said we wouldn't be required for the morning service. As blunt as that.'

'You saying he's sacked you, then?' asked Jan, as she pulled two pints of beer for the sisters.

'I believe that is how we are meant to understand it,' said Margaret.

'It's been a very strange week, it surely has,' called Daniel from the fireplace. 'Lots of strange goings ons.'

'We heard you'd seen a ghost,' said Dolly. 'The Rector was taken by a ghost, we heard.'

'Oh, give me strength,' sighed Daniel. 'I never said that. I seen ghosts in my time, but what I saw wasn't one of them. At any rate, the Rector's back now, so all's well.'

'It's far from well,' said Ethel, who was sitting with Daniel by the fire, cupping her pint of cider. 'There's trouble at that house where the Rector lives. I don't know what's going on there, but it's not regular. It's not right. Ours is a decent village.'

'With respect,' said Leo, who was sitting with Charles at a nearby table. 'You have had to revise your theories several times this week, Ethel. Not so long ago you were garnishing us with the theory that Matt had bumped off the old man, and buried him in the back garden, and then was selling up so he could go and enjoy a new life of carefree fun with a fresh bit of skirt.'

Ethel shuffled awkwardly. 'Well, that's not quite what I said. But there is still some digging going on at that house. And that young lady that we not seen before. She's hanging around the house still. I saw her yesterday. Looks to me like she's not been up to much good in her time. It's not proper, that's for sure.'

'But what about the old priest?' asked Jan, as she dried some glasses at the bar. 'Does anyone know how he is after that blow on the head? And does anyone know yet where he disappeared off to over the weekend?'

'Well, the blow on the head has clearly done him no good,' replied Margaret. 'He has always been most dependable. But to cancel the choir like he has done at such short notice is deplorable. Especially as we had put a lot of work into the Rutter.'

'Is that gutter leaking again?' said Daniel. 'I'll get my ladder up there tomorrow.'

'No, Daniel,' barked Margaret. 'Rutter! Not gutter. He writes music.'

'Oh, does he now?' said Daniel, scratching his beard. 'Don't know much about music, I don't. But I shouldn't worry yourselves about our Rector. We could put that strange behaviour down to his being taken

328

off like he was, couldn't we? I mean, it's not everyone who gets taken off like that. It's bound to have its effect.'

'That's no excuse for cancelling the choir,' said Margaret, who had settled herself with the sisters at a nearby table.

'Forgive me for repeating myself,' said Jan. 'But does anyone know where the poor old bloke went last weekend?'

'It's as clear as day to me,' said Daniel, and took a generous gulp from his glass.

'You back to your "thinning" theory again, Dan?' asked Charles, chuckling.

'Thinning?' said Margaret. 'Who's thinning?'

'Oh, don't listen to him, Margaret,' said Daniel. 'All I said was that I saw the Rector coming out of the church last Friday evening with another person, and they sort of disappeared. Disappeared into thin air, if you get my meaning.'

'The Rector is not the kind of man who just disappears into thin air,' said Margaret. 'No, there will be a natural explanation. But whatever did happen to him last weekend, it's affected him very badly.' She emptied her glass, and returned to the counter requesting a refill from Jan.

'When I say thin air,' said Daniel, 'That's my way of saying that there's a wonder going on. Something that's beyond our knowing. Probably the old man himself didn't know much of what was going on. But if I had a bet, I'd be saying he slipped past this world into something else for a time. And maybe it was no bad place.'

'Well, he's got no business slipping off to other worlds,' said Ethel. 'He's a priest. A man of God. They are not supposed to get up to things like that. And I don't know what effect it's had on him, but it's obviously had a very bad effect on the whole household at Altarnun House. As I say, it's not proper.'

'It certainly isn't,' said Margaret, returning to the table with her refilled glass. 'Now listen,' she added, looking at the two other choir members. 'We need things to return to normal in our village as soon as possible. We can't have this kind of disturbance. With respect Daniel, I can't go with your theory. No, let's keep our feet firmly fixed on the ground. I'm afraid what we are witnessing is the onset of dementia.

Clearly the Rector injured his head in the church, and this precipitated the beginnings of the dementia. I'm not alone in this view. I spoke to Lord Ternbury this week...'

'Who's Lord Turdbury when he's at home?' enquired Daniel.

Margaret fired a fierce stare at Daniel, and articulated 'Ternbury. Ternbury, Daniel. You know very well who he is. He is the patron of the church.'

'Oh, 'im,' said Daniel, and rose from the table to head to the bar for a refill.

'And he is very concerned,' continued Margaret, now addressing Leo, whom she regarded as the most intelligent of the present occupants of the pub. 'He agrees with my diagnosis. He says it came on his mother very suddenly like this. Hers was also after a fall. It's very sad, and I'm sorry for the Father. It must be troubling for him. But we can't let his ill health disturb our village in this way. So, my suggestion is that as many of us as possible go to church tomorrow morning, and we observe and note his behaviour. If, as it sadly seems likely, our Rector is sinking into that sorry state, then we simply gather the evidence, and pass it on to our patron and the bishop. It will be sad. But we can't have erratic behaviour in our church. The poor man must be moved on into proper retirement, and we will need a traditional priest back in our village post haste.'

'Quite right,' said a somewhat slurred Dolly, raising her glass. May also raised hers.

'Seems a sensible plan,' said Leo, sounding not entirely convinced.

'The Rector will get the shock of his life seeing all of us turning up on Sunday,' said Charles chuckling.

It was only Ethel Cairnes, who expressed some doubt about the plan. Her old anxiety of getting too close to the Almighty threatened to get the better of her. However, by the time she was finishing her second pint of Rattler, she was as determined as any of them to attend the Sunday mass, and witness for herself the sad decline of the faithful old priest.

*

Thus it was that on Sunday 22 April, the turnout to the Sunday morning church service in Tregovenek was larger than anyone could ever remember. Even seats in the side aisles were being filled. Matt, Lisa, Ella and Jenny had all arrived at church early and were in the front pew. Ella was delighted when Rahab also arrived to join them. Lisa was taken by surprise when she saw her parents making their way through the church entrance, and settle in the pew behind them.

'Good morning,' she said to them with raised eyebrows.

'Thought we'd come just to encourage the old chap,' said Ted, as he leaned forward to give his daughter a kiss.

'Didn't think you approved of this kind of church, Gran,' said Ella.

'Well, everyone should keep an open mind,' said Jean, whose mind, by common consensus, had never previously shown any inclination to openness. Her eyes were darting here and there across the growing congregation, betraying her awkwardness at being in a very unfamiliar context.

Ella was about to say more to her grandparents, when she spotted another friend entering the church. 'Oh!' she cried, and stood up, waving to the back of the church, which caused several people to turn and look at the door. They were surprised to see the round, hot and somewhat unkempt figure of a nun making her way down the aisle, adjusting her head veil as she travelled.

'Don't you want to be at the Porthann church?' asked Ella, as the flustered Sister Maria arrived at the family pew.

'What do you think?' replied the nun, frowning and smiling. She reached out her hand to the others in the pew, and said, 'Sister Maria. From the local convent. Sorry, I'm out of breath. It's a long way up the hill. I'll get myself fit one day.' She shook hands with each one, then turned to Ella, and said, 'You must have told Father Solomon about me. He contacted the convent yesterday and asked if I could come. So here I am.'

Ella smiled. 'Ah yes. He was interested to hear of my meeting with you. It's cool that you're here,' she said. She then leaned towards her, and said quietly, 'But no tut-tutting like you usually do in church!'

'Oh, now, there's a pity,' said Sister Maria. 'But already it seems better than that other place, don't you think?' Before Ella could answer, Rahab engaged Maria in conversation. She was thrilled to meet this sister from the local convent.

'I never met a nun before,' said Jenny quietly to Matt, as she watched the nun chatting to Rahab.

'Neither have I,' confessed Matt.

'But if she's a friend of El's, then she'll be all right,' said Jenny.

'Definitely,' said Matt.

'Oh, look!' said Lisa, who was staring at the church door.

'I don't believe it!' said Ella. All the family turned, and spied the distinctive and towering figure of Inspector Littlegown entering the church. She removed her cap, as she searched for a pew, and when she saw the row of faces from the front of the church all staring at her, she acknowledged them with a nod of her head, then sat down.

Ethel Cairnes was only a couple of pews away from the front, and was frowning disapprovingly at the conversation between Matt and the dubious young lady sitting next to him. The arrival of a nun did nothing to allay her suspicions. She reckoned that nuns could be very naive. The three decommissioned choir members were in the row behind her, and were also frowning. But no-one else was frowning. As many in the church that morning were unfamiliar with the normal customs of church behaviour, there was not the usual respectful silence in the building, but rather a hubbub of chatter with occasional bursts of laughter. This caused the few frowns that were present to be even more conspicuous.

In the vestry, Father Solomon Ogilvy was not frowning. He was standing very still, with his arms folded and his eyes closed. His feet were planted on the patch of carpet that revealed the signs of recently spilled wine. But Solomon could not care less about spilled Communion wine. He was listening to the unfamiliar sound of contented chatter coming from the nave. In fact, the sound of conversation was so loud, he could hardly hear the organ. Terry the faithful, yet hard-of-hearing, organist had been playing his standard round of pre-service tunes, oblivious of the congregational chatter. Today Solomon much preferred the buzz of human conversation to the

332

sound of the organ pipes. With his eyes closed, his mind was focussing on the service he attended a week ago: a service fifteen hundred years away, and yet at which he was most certainly present. He remembered the wooden barn, the simple rough-hewn benches, the children playing at the front, the loaf of freshly baked bread and the flagon of wine. He was remembering the female singer, her soul so alive as she offered her song to heaven.

'It's gone eleven, Father' said the voice of Marcus, the churchwarden, disturbing Solomon from his thoughts. 'Would you like me to help you robe?'

'Ah, no thank you,' said Solomon. 'I'll be through in a moment.'

'Very well,' said the bemused warden, and left. Solomon looked at the ornately decorated chasuble and stole that were neatly spread out, ready for donning. The ghostly white cassock alb was hanging on its peg. No, he was wearing none of these today. He brushed the front of the woollen smock that he had scarce been out of these past few days. Once he was sure it was free of toast crumbs from breakfast, he glanced briefly at the crucifix over the door, crossed himself, and then entered the church.

The sight of the normally dignified priest appearing from the vestry in his smock and casual trousers brought all the conversations in the church to an immediate halt. Even Terry stuttered to a sudden standstill, rather than his usual custom of bringing the organ music to a dignified halt. Instead of making his way to the clergy stall, Solomon stood at a microphone at the front of the church, and said, 'My friends, it is so good to welcome so many of you here today. And before I begin, may I thank you all for your kind words of concern, following my fall in this church last weekend. I am pleased to report that I am now quite recovered.' The three members of the choir, sitting in their unaccustomed position in the congregation, all glanced at each other with questioning looks. Solomon announced the first hymn, which the congregation sang with much gusto. The few regulars of the church were in a state of bewilderment. But for those who seldom darkened the heavy oak door of the church, there was something in the unexpected informality and warmth of the priest, that calmed their instinctive nerves at entering such unfamiliar terrain, and they celebrated by singing heartily.

At the ending of the hymn, Solomon stepped forward again, and said, 'I'd like to pray a prayer now that we usually say at the beginning of the Communion Service. But before I do, I want to say that this prayer has taken on a special meaning for me. Oh, we clergy can rattle out these set prayers, can't we? And we hardly give any thought to their meaning.' Several in the church nodded and smiled. But not the regulars who once again glanced at each other with anxious looks of disapproval. 'You see,' continued Solomon, 'The prayer starts with addressing God as Almighty. And so He is. But He is not up there in the rafters. Oh no. Listen to the next line of the prayer. It talks about God being so close to us, that He can even see the secrets of our hearts. Not so that he can point a finger at them. No, no. He does so, because He loves the very tender parts of us. The parts of us that we never dared share with each other. I have been so guilty of living my life with a closed heart, and I do apologise to you all. But never mind all that, let me get on with the prayer.'

Matt nudged Lisa, and whispered, 'I just can't get used to the change in him.'

'I can't,' said Lisa. 'But, do you know, I like it.' And then she heard the sound of a large sniff from behind her. Jean had pulled out a hanky from her sleeve and was mopping her nose.

Solomon looked up to the rafters and said the prayer he had known since he was a child, but it felt to him as if he was praying it for the first time. In a bold and surprisingly unquavering voice, he prayed, 'Almighty God, unto whom all hearts be open, all desires known, and from whom no secrets are hid: cleanse the thoughts of our hearts by the inspiration of thy Holy Spirit, that we may perfectly love thee, and worthily magnify thy holy name.'

He brought his eyes down from the rafters, and beamed at the congregation as everyone said 'Amen.' Nobody was in any doubt now that the village was witnessing a highly unexpected disturbance, expressed in the life of the very person who was least likely to disturb anyone. For a few in the church, this provoked a high degree of anxiety. But for many others, they sensed they were in contact with something that could only be described as *holy.* Not a frightening holiness, but an evocative and liberating holiness that quickened their hearts to imagine, to wonder and to adventure.

# 36

Solomon had even surprised himself at the way he had come to accept that for a few days he had actually stepped back in time. He had more or less adjusted to living back in the here and now, but the experience had nonetheless had the effect of leaving him with a sense of living in a liminal space. He felt fully present in this time, and yet he now often felt himself to be on the threshold between worlds. He felt it would not be difficult to step back fifteen hundred years and meet his friends again. He felt no distance between his world and theirs.

So here he was, leading a Sunday service in this parish church in the twenty-first century, but at the same time he was acutely aware of Monnine, Corman, Jowan and the others celebrating their sabbath. It was therefore not so much the memory of his time away that was inspiring him this Sunday morning, but more the sense of his being also with them as they worshipped in their time. He felt he really could be in two places at one time. Furthermore, this sense of liminality had also opened his soul to a vivid awareness of the world beyond all ages, the hallowed place that some called Paradise.

These heightened senses meant that in his leading of this Sunday worship, he became almost giddy at times, and had to steady himself by holding tight to his stall. So, the service had started. They had sung the opening hymn and he had recited the prayer. But what came next? For a few moments he had no recollection of what should happen next in the service, and he simply stood in silence as all faces in the congregation were fixed on him. However, the silence was interrupted by the sound of the heavy iron door handle rattling at the porch, followed by the creaking sound of the old oak door opening. All eyes turned in unison to the back of the church. Solomon looked towards the porch and saw an unshaven man, dressed in dungarees and jumper, who pulled his woollen hat from his head as he entered. 'Pardon me, Father, for my lateness,' he called. 'It was a strong tide this morning that kept me. But I'm here now.'

'And we are much the richer for your company,' called Solomon, beckoning him to a spare place in one of the front pews.

Matt's eyes lit up when he saw the man. He raised himself off his seat a little and waved to him, joining Solomon in the beckoning gestures to the front pew. 'Who is it?' whispered Lisa. 'Do you know him?'

'I do,' said Matt. 'It's Theo. My fisherman friend from Porthann.'

As Theo shuffled into the pew across the aisle from the Micklefield family, Solomon spoke again. He had remembered what was coming next in the service. 'My friends, we are not going to sing a hymn now as we usually do, but instead I have asked someone to sing to us. Sister Maria, would you step forward please?'

Solomon returned to his clergy stall, and a somewhat flustered Sister Maria made her way to the front of the church, straightening her robe and trying to tuck a bit of unruly hair back behind her veil. 'Good morning, everyone,' she said in her distinctive South Wales accent. The congregation, for whom the surprising was now becoming normal, reciprocated the welcome through nods and 'Morning's'.

'Well, now,' she continued, her round cheeks blushing pink, 'I'm not really used to this kind of thing, and I have to confess to not being a great singer, but I'm very pleased to be here on such a special occasion.' She then looked at a beaming Ella, and said, 'Ella, love, I hope you don't mind me mentioning this.' She then looked out to the congregation again, and said, 'But you see, last Sunday, I met Ella for the first time, and I have to say, I immediately loved her, and we have become good friends.' She turned to Solomon and said, 'She was out looking for you, you see Father, and I bumped into her. Well, to cut a long story short - well actually, where I come from, that's difficult to do, but I will do my best.' Several of the congregation chuckled, and Maria became more relaxed. 'But you see, Ella here is one of our dear young people, who live in this part of our land. Sadly, we don't often see them in our churches. And to be frank, I don't blame them, do you?' This provoked chuckles from most, and frowns from those, who had seldom stopped frowning since the start of the service. Maria continued, 'But I'm not here to preach, you'll be pleased to hear. I'm just saying that Ella and I did go to church together last Sunday, and we didn't enjoy ourselves, to be perfectly honest with you. But after church, when we were out on the coastal path, under the blue sky and skidding bright clouds, with the sound of the gulls and larks calling to us, and the sea lapping to our shore, we both felt the presence of the

336

God, whose heart is so tender to all of us. Well, you see, when I get that feeling, that's when I want to worship God, don't you? I'm not so good at doing it when we are all being stuffy and formal and having to behave ourselves.'

'Hear, hear!' cried Theo from the front pew.

'Thank you,' said Maria. When she realised who it was, she added, 'Oh, hello, Theo,' Then, clutching her hands hard together, she looked up to the rafters for a few moments, and sang the same hymn that she had sung to Ella. She sang it in her own Welsh language, and though there were only a couple of people in church that morning who understood Welsh, the rest of the congregation were in no doubt they were hearing the sound of one who was singing a love song, and she sang it with such heart and beauty, that few were untouched by it. While Solomon watched her, he was also watching a young woman in Monnine's community, standing at the front of that simple chapel with some musicians beside her, singing and dancing her song of worship. He was in both worlds and felt the vitality of each. Such life was almost more than he could bear, and it was something of a relief when Maria finished.

At the end of the song, Ella, who had been sitting enraptured by it, started clapping, and within moments others applauded, while Sister Maria hurried back to her pew, rose-cheeked and head bowed. Margaret was not applauding, yet she had to concede that something about the nun's song had broken through her stubborn defences, and during the singing, her defiant criticism of the Rector considerably lessened. May and Dolly were desperately trying to wipe the tears from their eyes without Margaret noticing. They were keen not to break ranks, but they were aware that they were weakening.

Solomon returned to the front step of the chancel and thanked Maria. Then he said, 'I have asked my friend, Rahab, to bring this morning's reading to us. Rahab is a remarkable young lady whom I have only met recently. Her homeland is Eritrea, but by God's grace, she has made her way to our shores, and how blessed we are that she should have made her new home among us here. She has a love for Christ that has been forged through many fierce fires. The faith of my soul is a poor metal compared to what I find in hers, but meeting her this week has brightened my heart. So, come forward, please, dear Rahab.'

Rahab struck a stunning figure as she stepped forward. She was wearing a bright red and gold African dress. Her beaded hair was catching the beams of coloured light filtering through the windows, and her bright white smile gleamed from her dark, handsome features. 'Thank you, Father,' she said, as she arrived at the sanctuary step. 'It is my privilege to bring you the scripture reading today. In my land, we did not often have the printed book, so we had to learn the parts of the bible we loved by heart. My parents loved the bible so much. Its words were ringing in our home, and we all loved them. So, please forgive me if I have remembered any of this wrong, but here is the story that Father Solomon has asked me to bring to you today, as I recall it.' She cast her gaze across the congregation for a few moments, and then drew her hands together, clutching them at her chest as she said, 'At daybreak, Jesus stood on the beach, but the disciples did not know it was Him...'

Solomon listened with his eyes closed. Again, he was in two worlds. As Rahab's beautiful African voice filled the English church, Solomon also heard the croaky, humble voice of his hermit friend Corman telling the same story. Once again, fifteen hundred years meant very little. He opened his eyes, and now saw not the old figure of Corman, but the young figure of Rahab, who had taken several paces down the church. She was enacting throwing out a fishing net, as she recited Christ's question to the disciples, 'Children, have you no fish?'

When she related Jesus' words to his disciples, to cast the net on the other side of the boat, Theo called out, 'That's good advice, that is. I've often known a shoal to hide on the other side of the boat. They're cheeky things, they are!' Rahab laughed, and walked back to the front of the church, and carried on with the story, her bright eyes shining, and her long arms expressing the various actions of the story. Even for those who knew the story well, Rahab's telling meant they felt they were hearing it for the first time. When she said the words uttered by Jesus, 'Come and have breakfast,' there were some who would have gladly left their seats, and come forward to a meal of bread and fish on the seashore that Rahab had so beautifully depicted for them. When she finished her story, she returned to her seat, but not before several in the church applauded, in response to which, she stood and gave a shy bow.

Solomon was one of those who was clapping as he moved to the front step again. He crossed himself, and said, 'In the name of the Father, the Son and the Holy Spirit.' The few regular members of the congregation also crossed themselves, as did Sister Maria, Rahab and Jenny. Jean shuffled awkwardly in her seat. She was in a mild state of shock. This elderly, gaunt priest standing at the front of church was her brother. This was the man, who lived in the shadows, who seldom spoke, whose faith was a mystery, who represented the kind of church against which she had long been determined to stand. And yet this same man was now conveying something extraordinary. He was allowing all this informal, warm activity to happen in his normally formal, frigid church. He had changed beyond all recognition. But she could see that he had not changed into a different person. No, this was most clearly her brother. This was him as the open flower, whereas before, all she ever saw was the tight bud. And now, radiating from this flower was a fragrance that she had to confess was utterly charming. And it was all she could do to prevent herself from doing something to which she was most definitely opposed: making the sign of the cross. 'My, my, my...' she muttered, to which Ted reached out a hand dampened by tears, to clutch hers.

'A week last Friday,' said Solomon, who had for the first time this morning become aware of his nerves. ' A week last Friday,' he repeated. 'I fell there - just there.' He pointed to the aisle in front of him. 'I gave myself a nasty bash on the head. When I came round, I had completely lost my memory. I didn't even know my own name. All I could remember were a few things from my early childhood. I remembered my father who, until I was five years old, was the Rector of this church. I remembered him very clearly. But there was little else I could recall. It was, as you can imagine, most distressing.' His eyes started to twinkle behind his steel-rimmed glasses, and the tuft of eyebrows danced for a moment above the rims. 'But I had to, you see. I had to lose my memory. I had to go back to square one.'

All in the church were now alert and listening. For those who knew the old priest before, they were still in some state of bewilderment at this new, strong, articulate Rector, who was standing before them. 'And so I went back in time' he continued. 'I had to become a child again. People had to take me by the hand and care for me. I met dear people who did take care of me. And I began to heal, and the healing came as

I dared inspect a very secret part of my soul. The place where I kept things like my fears, my regrets, my grief and my longings. I had kept these hidden even from myself. But the friends I discovered last weekend helped me see that our tender Christ can journey with us to these places. He and I carefully opened up the lid, and together we explored what I had kept in my secret place. Hm...'

Solomon looked down at his hands for a moment, and rubbed his palm with his thumb as he thought. He looked over to Rahab, and said, 'Thank you, dear Rahab, for that reading from John's gospel.' She smiled back at the priest, as he continued. 'These past days, like those disciples, I have also heard Him calling from the shore, you see, and I followed. But like Peter, I also felt so ashamed. I felt naked, and wanted to cover myself up. But there was Christ on the shore, cooking breakfast for me. I couldn't stay away. And, like Peter, I discovered that I could tell Him about my life and all the things that I have got wrong. And, my friends, I have got so much wrong, and for that I do ask your forgiveness.'

For a moment, he was distracted by some nose-blowing from the family row, and he noticed it was his sister making the noise. He smiled at her, and nodded his head briefly. 'Everyone is asking where I went last weekend.' Several heads looked up at this. 'I can only say that I went somewhere that was very special. Have any of you ever had the experience of having a dream at night that was so vivid, that when you woke up, you felt your waking world was less real than your dream world? Well, if that has been your experience, then you might understand me a little better. I caught sight of something last weekend which was very special. And what I realised was that it was not just me that lost my memory. In all kinds of ways, our church has lost its memory. We have forgotten who we are.' He looked over to Matt, as he said, 'Our church is like a lumpy old rock, but underneath it are treasures that would fill you with wonder.' Matt smiled in response. 'Our job now is to dig down and find that treasure.'

Solomon was about to continue, but was interrupted by Theo in the front pew, who called out, 'Beg your pardon, Father, but what does that mean, then? How do you dig in the church and find your treasure? I'm a simple man I am, and I like to have it straight.'

'Of course,' said Solomon. 'I've never been very good at giving it straight. Can anyone help me out?'

340

'If I may?' called Sister Maria, half standing in her pew.

'Yes, Sister?' said Solomon.

'Well, it's like the church is all wrapped up...'

There was a call from the back of the church, 'Speak up, my lover. We can't hear you.'

Maria acknowledged with a wave, and stood up, turning to face the congregation. 'I know I'm dressed up like this, and I'm as guilty as anyone else at being all religious, but I think this is the point Father Solomon is making. Church is not about correct behaviour, singing the right hymns, speaking in a certain way, and priests being set apart from the people wearing fine robes and all that. Yes, we have this beautiful building, but as we see today, it is a building for everyone. I am so sorry that we have made it uncomfortable for so many of you to come in here. We have got so much wrong. I am so sorry. I think we need a bit of losing our memory, and going back to who we really are. I'll shut up now.' And with that she sat down.

Solomon was about to respond, when Matt stood up. 'May I say something, Solomon?' Lisa looked up briefly at her husband, then looked down to her lap, as she clutched her hands tight.

'Of course, Matthew,' said Solomon.

'I'm the first to admit I've never been one for God,' said Matt, turning around to face the congregation. 'But this last week I've been made to change my mind. For me, it's been a week like no other. Solomon here talks about the secret place. I'll be honest, I caught sight of mine this week, and it wasn't pretty. As most of you know, I've been developing property in the Porthann area for many years now. And looking at the way some of you are looking down now, I know you haven't liked it. I just... I just feel I need to tell you that I'm truly sorry about this. I think I've got a lot wrong over the past years. But I've been sitting here this morning watching you, Solomon; listening to that beautiful song from you, Sister; and watching Rahab do that stunning reading. And I realise this: this thing we call church - the way we are doing it today - well, it feels very much like church should be. I don't know anything about church, and I've done my best to avoid it most of my life.'

This provoked a ripple of laughter in the congregation, prompting Matt to look at Solomon and say, 'Sorry, Solomon. But if church is anything, isn't it supposed to be the place where we can just be ourselves? We should feel at home here. We shouldn't have to posh up and impress each other, should we? Or pretend to be better people than we are?'

'Definitely not, I say,' chimed up Theo, smiling broadly. He then added, 'Sorry, Matt. You carry on.'

'Thanks, Theo,' responded Matt. He then continued, 'Well, as far as I can see, this should be the place where we can tell it as it is. So, all I want to say really is that I'm sorry about the way I've been living all these years. I can see now it's done no-one any good, least of all me. And I'm hoping to change. *About time* I hear you say.' He grinned awkwardly, and there was another flutter of laughter. And among those who had indeed felt offended by Matthew's disregard of local sensibilities, there were some nodding heads and knowing looks.

'It was Theo over here who helped me,' continued Matt. He pointed over to the fisherman, who was staring hard at Matt with his glistening eyes. 'He took me out in his boat. He got me to see everything so differently. As some of you know, things look very different from the sea.' Matt pointed to the ceiling as he said, 'And he told me about the Great Friend up there, and I liked the sound of what he said about Him. So, thanks, Theo.' He then glanced at Solomon, and said, 'Sorry, I'm rattling on a bit, but I just thought I'd say all that. Thank you.' With that, Matt sat down abruptly, and both Lisa and Ella grasped his arms and held him tight.

Solomon was about to continue when, much to his surprise, Jean stood. 'If everyone is having their say, then I'd like to give my pennyworth,' she said, also turning to face everyone. She blinked hard for a few moments, and wrung her hands together. 'I'm Jean Hancock from Pedrogwen, and I'm Solomon's younger sister,' she said, briefly nodding in the direction of her brother. 'He and I followed different paths in life, we did. His father died young, sadly. But Mum married again, and they had me. And I followed their way of faith, and Solomon kept with his father's. Well, I realise now, that all these years, I've stood in judgement over my brother. I never liked his high church ways - you know, his robes and the incense and that, and all this crossing yourself and the like.' She turned and looked at Solomon. 'But today, brother, I seen you in a very different light, I have. I realise I got you so wrong, and I just want to say how sorry I am. I've said bad things about you, I

342

have, and I had no right to. I hope you'll forgive me, 'cos if the light of Christ is shining through anyone today, it's though you, brother. I think it's probably always been there, but all this while I've been too blooming blind to see it.' Ted reached up and took her hand. With her free hand, she wiped the tears that were now flowing freely. 'Sorry to make a scene like this, but somehow it needed saying. I'm done now.' And with that she sat down.

There was now a fair bit of murmuring around the church. Solomon raised his hand in order to speak, but yet again he was interrupted. This time it was Jenny, who had pushed her way out of her pew, and came and stood next to him. She was wearing a bright daffodil yellow dress, borrowed from Ella, with a blue cardigan draped over her shoulders. She was clutching her hands together, and stooped a little, betraying her nerves. Yet with a confident voice, she said, 'Good morning everyone. As you can hear, I'm from Liverpool. And before you ask, I've no interest in football. Sorry to disappoint.' There were a few comments and some laughter. 'And I know what some of you are thinking. You might have seen me around in Porthann. So, let me own up. I've worked for some years as a sex worker.' At this point, Ethel started to feel very faint and started fanning herself with her hymn book.

Solomon reached out and took Jenny's hand. 'Carry on,' he said to her, nodding his head and smiling his warm smile.

She took courage from the warmth and strength of his hand, and continued. 'Mine's not a life to be proud of. As you'd expect, mine wasn't a happy home.' She turned to Solomon and said, 'I get what you're saying about that secret bit of us, Father. My secret place was full of bitterness and anger and it led me into drugs and prostitution.' She looked out at the congregation, still feeling the strength of Solomon's hand. 'No girl grows up wanting to be a prozzie,' she said. 'If a girl's doing that to make ends meet, then you know how desperate life's become for her. But you know, years ago, I sat in a big church in my home city. It were a lantern church with beautiful big windows. So lovely it was. And I met one kind person there and she gave me hope, she did. But she was the only one. Until this week, when I met Matt - the man who spoke to us just now.' She nodded at Matt. 'He was out searching for Ella, who was out searching for you, Father.' She glanced at Solomon, then turned back to Matt, as she said, 'Well, that's when I

343

bumped into yer. And you showed me kindness, you did. God, you'll never know what that meant to me. Straight away, you saw me as a person, not as a prozzie. And then I get to meet your family. And I get to meet you, Father, and come to this bloody wonderful service this morning. Oh, God, I was determined not to swear in church.' She covered her mouth, but was reassured by Solomon's kind smile and the laughter of the congregation. She looked back out to the faces before her, and said, 'All I want to say is, that if this is church, then I want to be part of it.' She turned back to Solomon and said, 'Count me in, Father.' Then she stepped towards him, kissed him on the cheek, and returned to her seat.

Solomon was now in completely unfamiliar territory, and yet he felt that such territory was holy ground. He took a few steps towards the congregation and stood by the front pews. 'I agree with Jenny. I couldn't have said it any better than she has. This is the church that I now want to be part of. I'm truly sorry that this will disappoint those who preferred it as it was. But don't worry, I'm an old man, and soon the bishop will have to say I'm past it, and properly retire me. But for a little while yet, I suggest we do our best to love God together, and build the kind of church that our forebears tried to build all those years ago. It's a church where every one of you is welcome and has a part to play. Now I think that is the end of my sermon, and we have one more thing to do before this service is over. I would like us all to share in bread and wine together.'

With that, Solomon moved to the altar, and stood behind it. 'Come forward, will you? All of you, come and crowd around here. I want you close. I've been too far removed from people all my life. It's now time to be close.'

Solomon's family were the first to come forward, and Ella walked behind the altar and stood next to her great uncle. For the first time in her life, she felt at home in church, and she was enjoying it. Standing next to Uncle Sol, with her new friends near her, she was aware again of the same opening of her soul that she had experienced on the hillside, the day she met Rahab. She sensed again an exquisite connection with the divine, that was both transcendent yet intimate.

The congregation all gathered at the table. Even Ethel made her way forward. And Margaret, May and Dolly couldn't resist the draw of

344

this table, and joined the throng. As they did so, May whispered to Margaret, 'What about Lord Ternbury?'

'Oh, forget about that sour old fool,' said Margaret. 'Come and get your Communion.'

Solomon watched the people assemble themselves around the altar, some standing among the choir pews, with one or two of the children standing on the pews. The eyes of Solomon's heart saw so clearly his predecessor, Jowan, standing at his altar all those generations ago, yet so present now. 'With angels, archangels, and all the company of heaven, living and departed, we praise your name,' said Solomon, as he looked to the rafters. 'Holy, holy, holy Lord! Heaven and earth are full of your glory,' he continued, and all who were gathered around the table that day did indeed feel a touch of sacred glory.

Solomon told the story of the Last Supper and, just like Jowan had done before him, he raised the freshly-baked loaf of bread and the cup of ruby red wine, crying, 'Christ is our victor!' This prompted Sister Maria to launch into 'Guide me, O thou Great Redeemer,' and it seemed that most in the church that morning knew the words, for they all joined with her, and by the time they reached the final cry of 'Feed me now and evermore', this piece of hallowed Cornish land was reverberating with a song of heartfelt praise, the like of which it had not known since the days when it hosted the very first community of faith led by Monnine, the engaging visionary from Eire.

# 37

Over a year had passed since that extraordinary week that culminated in the memorable Communion Service. The fire that had flared up in Father Solomon, the elderly priest of Tregovenek parish, showed no signs of abating in the months that followed. He could be found at the church every Sunday morning, always dressed in his woollen smock, greeting worshippers at the door with a shake of his gaunt yet strong hand, before leading the new-style informal service that was proving remarkably popular. Such a radical diversion from the traditional mass was for a village like Tregovenek, nothing short of traumatic, and the lack of protest regarding such a major change from the norm was a tribute to the winsome nature of the much-changed priest.

The previous incumbent (the infamous 'Rev Bev') had been singularly unsuccessful in her attempts to bring about changes, none of which were as outrageous as those now introduced by the transformed Father Solomon. But all agreed that the changes to the traditional service wrought by this parish priest somehow felt to be entirely natural and heart-warming. As Margaret, the former choir member of forty-eight years, put it in an article in the local newspaper, 'It has none of the enforced chumminess nor maddening trendiness of those unfortunate services led by his predecessor. ' She was never fully supportive of the new style of service, but she did concede that the new sense of warmth in the congregation was welcome. And in time she confessed that she, Dolly and May were all highly relieved to be no longer burdened with their former choral duties, and much preferred their present role of standing in the general mix of the congregation, and providing considerable (if not always tuneful) momentum to the hymn-singing.

Among the new attenders at church were members of Solomon's own family. Matt had always talked openly about his religious scepticism, yet he was now often to be found in the front row of the church, contributing as much as anyone to the lively discussions that were now a normal part of the church service. He was known for his fondness of addressing God as his *Great Friend,* and telling of the

346

down-to-earth ways that this Friend had been helping him during the week.

Lisa was also often in church on Sundays, though she preferred a quieter, reflective role and took no active part in the services. To her surprise, she had been experiencing a springtime in her spirit. The profound changes in both her uncle and her mother had caused her to review her own spirituality, and she could not deny that yeast-like faith was at work in her soul, lifting and lightening her. But it felt unformed and private, and not something that she wanted to discuss with others, apart, that is, from her uncle. The changes that had taken place in both of them had created common ground in which both were able to share with each other some of their hitherto private thoughts and feelings. Solomon would speak both of the great shafts of light that had entered his life since his accident, and also of the shadows of dark that still fringed his soul. There were still nagging moments of regret and loss, and he was not able to quite shift a lingering dread of death. In turn, Lisa was able to entrust him with the various emotional aches and pains that troubled her for much of her life, as well as talking with him about her own new explorations of the spirit.

No-one was more surprised than Ted at the change that had taken place in his wife, Jean. She was not completely rid of the old strident ways that had so often put a quick end to any reasonable argument about God. But mixed in with the occasional vociferous outbursts was something much more affable. In this less capricious climate, Ted was growing more confident to share his own well-considered views, and there was no shortage of people in their village who now knocked on his door for a cup of tea and a piece of down-to-earth wisdom.

At Altarnun House, the archaeological dig was completed by midsummer, and the large rock was heaved back to its original position, sealing the location of the burial site of the hoard. All the artefacts found there were duly catalogued, with collections sold to two museums, and a handsome reward was granted to the owner of the house. After taking a little time off work, Lisa returned and, after a tense and difficult series of conversations with Troy, she succeeded in establishing a clear end to their relationship. The situation was eased when he moved to Devon to set up his own counselling practice. Matt continued with his estate agent business in Porthann, but ceased his development work. He did retain the old farmhouse, and completed the renovation work. However, he completely changed the plans, for he had decided to build, not a set of holiday apartments, but instead he recruited an architect who turned the farmhouse and outbuildings into a very attractive refuge and recovery centre for women who required sanctuary and therapy following domestic abuse. He had worked day and night on the plans, on gaining permissions, and on raising funds for the project. Within eighteen months of Matt's personal crisis at Gerhard Leap, he was proudly opening Ogilvy House, and his two key live-in members of staff were Ms Rahab Mehari (originally from the land of Eritrea) and Ms Jenny Thomas (originally from the city of Liverpool).

As expected, Ella did well in her A levels. She attributed her success to her great uncle. After dinner most evenings during the build-up to the exams, she would join him in his room, and pass him her laptop, which he would place carefully on his leather-topped desk. He would peer at the screen that provided information about her exam subjects, and then drill her with questions in preparation for the several papers that awaited her in the exam halls. She would pace up and down his room, occasionally tapping her forehead with the palm of her hand in her effort to trawl from her mind the correct answers. Usually after an hour, Solomon would plead tiredness, and Ella would then flop on his bed for some moments. Then the old man would carefully fold up the laptop, and reach for a novel, and settle in his familiar armchair. To soothe her brain after its day's labours, Solomon would read a chapter to Ella, who would lay back on his bed with her eyes closed. At Solomon's recommendation, they read novels by Dickens. Together they worked their way through *Great Expectations, The Old Curiosity Shop* and *Little Dorrit*. And during the week of the hardest exams, at Ella's request, he read her *The Voyage of the Dawn Treader* by CS Lewis. Ella was convinced that it wasn't so much the revision that prepared her well for her exams, but more the delightful sense of peace his reading gave to her mind, and the subsequent tranquil sleep that followed.

After the exams, Ella decided to do some travelling with a couple of her school friends and they ventured into Eastern Europe for a few months before she embarked on her degree course at Exeter University. She kept in close touch with her new friends, Jenny and Rahab, each of whom visited her at Exeter. She also always made a point of meeting up with Sister Maria when she came back for vacations. Nearly always they met at the same café and, no matter what day of the week it was, Maria insisted that it was 'love-a-nun' day. The café was always sure of much laughter when they visited, but in between the moments of hilarity, Ella took the opportunity to share with Maria all the questions about life, God and the universe that ferreted away in her busy and lively mind during this first year at University.

So, a new normal became established in Tregovenek, whose villagers still enjoyed the quiet and secluded life of the village, yet now had made room for the surprising and the unconventional. And a new normal was also established at Altarnun House. There were no longer the rows that all too often had characterised the life of the house. And during the term-time, there was none of the music that normally emanated from Ella's room, nor the happy buzz of activity from her friends who were frequent visitors. But whereas at one level it was a quieter house, on the other hand, the member of the household who had once been so very quiet, was now the most talkative. It was as if Solomon was making up for lost time, and there were occasions when Matt and Lisa had to work quite hard to extricate themselves from conversations with him. But it was a change they welcomed. He had become an embodiment of the story of the garden: A great rock of silence had been shifted from the surface of his soul, and now all kinds of treasures were being revealed, whether they be stories from the past or insights about the future. A conversation with Solomon was never dull, for his mind and spirit pulsed with extraordinary vitality.

Then, just as the village and the household were becoming accustomed to these new normals, they were disturbed by a major event that only Solomon was expecting, and it happened on a very normal Monday morning. Ella was at University, and Jenny had long moved out to her flat at Ogilvy House, so it was just Lisa, Matt and Solomon in the house. On a usual weekday morning, Matt and Lisa would breakfast together at just before eight o'clock before heading off to their offices. Towards the end of their breakfast, Solomon would make his way down in his striped pyjamas and chequered dressing gown, and they would leave him contentedly with his coffee, porridge and newspaper.

On this particular Monday, Matt was hurriedly finishing his slice of toast, and Lisa was sitting at the table texting Ella. 'Is the old boy not up, yet?' Matt asked, as he rose from the table and put on his jacket.

Lisa finished her text, then looked at the time and said, 'Oh, no. He must have overslept. I'll go and wake him.'

Matt gathered his phone from the table, and said, 'Well, he worked hard yesterday, didn't he? He gave us another great service. I expect the poor bloke's exhausted. I should let him rest a bit.' With that, he gave his wife a kiss, and said, 'Should be back at the usual.' He then left the home that he now treasured more than ever, and drove off to his office in Porthann.

Lisa glanced at the time again. She had to be away in the next half hour. She wondered whether to let her uncle lie in, but then decided to look in and say goodbye before she left. She knocked on the door and heard just a faint mumble in response. She tentatively opened the door. The curtain was still closed, but there was enough light for her to see that the old man was still in bed. She opened the curtain a little and said, 'It's nearly half past eight, Uncle Sol.' As the June sunlight filled the room, she looked again at her uncle, and she saw that he looked different. It was hard to explain how he was different, but something was not quite right. She came and sat on his bed, and said, 'Uncle Sol?'

'Lisa,' he said so quietly, that she hardly heard him.

'What is it, Uncle?'

He blinked slowly a couple of times, then fixed his niece with his grey eyes, and said, 'Lisa, my dear. I have been back.' His dry lips stretched to a smile.

'Back, Uncle? Back where?' Solomon reached his free hand out to his bedside table, and he grasped his glasses and put them on. Lisa could see that there was effort involved in this simple action. She was aware of a curious paradox. At one level, her uncle was looking disturbingly frail. His pyjama shirt was hanging loosely on his gaunt shoulders. His wisps of unbrushed hair, together with his unshaven face, gave him a rather wild appearance. And yet she had seldom seen such strength in the soul of a man. His eyes now peered at his niece through his glasses, and he said in a quiet and husky voice, 'Last night, Lisa. Last night Monnine came here.'

350

'Monnine?' said Lisa. She reached out and took hold of his hand, which felt cold. She could feel the metacarpals prominent against the delicate covering of sallow skin.

'Yes. Monnine. That is the name of the very fine lady who led the community that I visited when I had my knock on the head.'

'Oh, yes. I remember,' said Lisa. 'You mean, you had a dream of her and her community last night.'

'No, my dear. It wasn't a dream. She came here. Here, to my room. To our house. Just as she came to the church that time.' Lisa's brow furrowed. He observed her puzzled countenance. 'I know, I know,' he said. 'It's hard to understand. But let me just tell you this while I have time. Could you pass me the water, please.'

Lisa could see that her uncle was now very weak, and she helped him to sit up a little and pumped the pillow behind him. Then she offered him the glass of water, from which he took a few grateful sips. 'Tell me, Uncle Sol. I want to hear,' she said, as she returned the glass to the table. She was now aware of both a strong curiosity and a growing sense of foreboding. She was aware of the time. She should be on her way to work by now, but she knew she could not leave him.

'She took my hand,' he said. 'Do you know, as she did so, I felt young again. When you are as old as I am, that's a wonderful feeling. She passed me my smock and trousers and shoes. I put them on so easily. Not the usual palaver. And then we walked down the stairs. I'm surprised you didn't hear us. We were talking all the time. Did you not hear?'

'No,' said Lisa, shaking her head.

'Oh,' said Solomon, raising his eyebrows. 'Well, once we were downstairs, it all changed a bit, because very soon I realised that we were back in Monnine's world again.' His face creased briefly in another smile. Then he looked at Lisa, and said, 'It was so nice to be there again. It's such a dear place. And the sun was out, and the air was filled with the sounds of gulls and skylarks. I felt so strong and happy, Lisa. I can't tell you…'. His eyes moistened for a moment, and he reached a slender finger behind his glasses and wiped his eyelash. 'Corman was there as well.' He looked toward the window as he spoke, his mind now fixed on the apparitions of the night. 'It was so good to see my old friend again. As ever, he had one eye fixed on me, and the other raised to

351

heaven!' He chuckled briefly. 'Monnine was holding my hand - just like you are doing now.' He shook his head again. 'It was so nice to see her. Sorry, I'm repeating myself. No, what was I saying?'

'She took your hand.'

'Yes, yes, she did. She was holding it so warmly, and she said, "So Seanchara" - that's what they called me at first. I rather liked it. I preferred it to my own name actually when I was there. It was their name for me, you see. Anyway... Sorry, I keep rambling. I just want to tell you this, Lisa.' He eased himself up on his pillow a little, then, still gazing out of the window to the bright sky beyond, he said, 'Monnine said to me, "So, Seanchara, you found our treasure, did you?"' He looked back to Lisa and said, 'Well, I felt just a little guilty at that point, if I am honest. But I confessed, "Yes, Monnine. We did find it. Under that rock." And I pointed to the very rock. We were standing near it. Well, I needn't have felt guilty, for she said, "Well, we are sure pleased you found the treasure. We guessed that it might be for you and your family in your world." Then she asked me what we had done with it, and I told her all about Matt and Jenny and Rahab and the centre. Oh, they were so happy with that news.

'Then my friend Corman said, "So how's it been in your church, then?" He beckoned me over to a bench in the sun and we sat down - him, me and Monnine. Well, I told them all about that first service.' Solomon chuckled again. 'I told them how nothing went to plan that Sunday, and yet how wonderful it was. I told him about what Matt and Jean and everyone had said. I told them it was all because of what Monnine and the others had done for me.' His glistening eyes looked at his niece as he said, 'I was so happy to be back there, Lisa. I wish you could visit it.'

'What is it you love so much about that place, Uncle?' said Lisa, stroking the back of his hand. 'Why is it so special?'

Solomon struggled for a few moments to manage his emotions, then he said, 'I've never known such deep kindness. But it wasn't just that. It was a safe place, Lisa. Such a safe place. And yet so full of adventure. If I had lived there, I could have crossed the oceans in a little boat, as many of them did. I would have been up for any exploits. I felt courage when I was in their world, like I have never known here in this world. There was something about the place that helped me to become my brave self. In this world, my life has been a cowardly one. Does that sound strange to you?'

'No. It doesn't sound strange.'

'And it was their faith, Lisa. Not the insipid stuff that I have been peddling all my life. Nor the pushy sort like my dear sister once had. No, Lisa. Theirs was made of very different stuff. You felt Christ was there, right in the midst of that place. And not just Christ, but His angels as well. You felt them, Lisa. All over the place they were. I know, you'll just put it down to me being a crazy old man. But I honestly believe that if you were ever to visit that place, you would feel them too. Ella would certainly feel them, bless her. And Jenny and Rahab and Sister Maria. Oh, I wish I could take you all there. Maybe you'll be allowed to visit one day.'

There was a pause for a few moments as Solomon looked back through his window at the morning sky, his lower lip trembling a little. 'So, how long were you there when you visited them last night?' asked Lisa.

'Hm? Oh, I don't think it was very long,' said the old priest, as he shook his head slowly. 'But long enough.'

'So, did anything else happen while you were there?'

'Yes,' said Solomon. 'Yes, something very special did happen.' He paused for a long time and rubbed his thumb over the back of Lisa's warm hand. He continued his gaze to the window as he said, 'Oddly enough, I wasn't completely surprised.'

'Surprised by what?'

Solomon looked back to Lisa and said, 'Corman put his arm around my shoulder for a few moments, and he said, "Seanchara, he's here. He's come to see you. Are you ready to see him?" Strangely enough, I knew straight away who he was talking about.'

Here Solomon started to breathe heavily, and Lisa passed him the glass of water again. She was feeling concerned, as he was looking so pale and his breathing became laboured. 'Perhaps you need to rest, Uncle,' she said.

'Yes,' said Solomon, and looked at his niece with a look that she described later as a look of almost unbearable goodness. 'Yes, I will be resting very soon now. But let me just tell you this. It's important.

Corman looked towards the door of the little shack that I had stayed in while I was there. I looked towards it and watched it open, and, lo and behold, out he walked and he came towards me.'

'Who walked out, Uncle?'

'Oh, sorry,' said Solomon. 'My father walked out. My father was there! Surprising isn't it? Oh, Lisa, how pleased I was to see him! When I first visited there, I had a dream about him, which was a very important dream. But this time, he really was there. He looked just as I remember him, but somehow this time he looked *complete*. I can't find a better word for it. I jumped up from my bench, and we had such a long hug.' Solomon pursed his lips for a time as his eyes glazed once more. 'We had a wonderful conversation. Remarkable really. I discovered that he had also been allowed to visit Monnine's community. He was taken there the night before he left us for the Far East. He said it gave him the courage he needed to leave us and embark on that mission to the poor soldiers. But not just that: when he was in that terrible jail in Changi, well, he was allowed to visit again. He told me of all the strength it gave him during his time of suffering. And when his time came, they helped him over. It clearly helped him so much. Yes, it was wonderful. Quite wonderful.' Solomon's moistened eyes were looking right and left as he recalled the scene so vividly in his mind. 'It was so comforting to hear this. So comforting.'

'So, he had visited there before you?' said Lisa.

'Ah, no,' replied Solomon. 'Time, you see, Lisa. Time is not what we all thought it was.' He sighed deeply.

'So, you mean he actually visited after you.'

'After me,' said Solomon, his voice getting a little weaker. 'Yes, a year or so of their time, so Monnine said.' He turned his shining dove grey eyes to his niece and said, 'It was so good to see him there. To be there together. So good.'

'You missed him so much through your life, didn't you, Uncle,' said Lisa.

'Oh, yes, I did,' said Solomon, looking back to Lisa. He no longer tried to stall the flow of moisture from his eyes. 'But I realise now that all through my road of sorrows, I was not alone. That is what I learned last night.' He looked at Lisa, and said, 'We are never alone, my dear.

354

Never. But for most of my life, I just didn't have the eyes to see. Had I seen, I would have known that I have never been alone.' He reached up and stroked her face for a few moments. 'And you are not alone, my dearest Lisa.' She cupped his hand and pressed it to her cheek. As she held it there, he said, 'And do you know what, Lisa?'

'What? Tell me.'

'I am no longer afraid to embark on the Great Journey now.' Almost imperceptibly his trembling thumb stroked her cheek as he continued, 'That fear, Lisa. That old fear of mine that used to lie so heavy in my soul. I know now that I can step over, and there is nothing to fear. Isn't that kindness, Lisa? To be given such a precious thing?'

Lisa did not try to hide her tears, and they flowed on to his hand that was still pressed to her cheek. 'Thank you, dear, dear Lisa,' he said. 'I could never have wanted a better niece. And you have allowed me to live in your beautiful home with your dear family. I have no words...'

Lisa shrugged a smile, sniffed and said, 'Well, Uncle Sol. There have been many times in the past when I think you would have much preferred a more peaceful house.'

Solomon's eyes smiled, as he said, 'I know, my dear. There have been storms, but now they have calmed. You gave me a home, Lisa. You gave this poor, silent old man a home that he never deserved. Thank you.' His voice was becoming weaker, and his tear-dampened hand slipped from Lisa's face back to the eiderdown.

'And thank you, dear Uncle Solomon,' said Lisa. It was her turn now to stroke his face. 'Thank you more than I can say for what you have given us.'

'This last year or so,' said Solomon, his voice now a whisper. 'We have done well, haven't we? By God's grace, we have done well.'

'We have,' whispered Lisa. 'Yes, we have, Uncle.'

'All shall be well, and all manner of things shall be well,' sighed Solomon, as he closed his eyes. 'I think it is time for me to rest now, dear Lisa.'

'Yes, of course,' said Lisa, frowning from the strain of controlling her feelings.

She continued to stroke his face as his breathing became shallower. 'God bless you, dearest Uncle,' she said.

Very slowly he pulled his hand to his forehead and made the sign of the cross. 'Faith...' he said, so faintly, Lisa hardly heard it. 'Faith...' he repeated, then added, 'Hope... and love... But the greatest of these... is love... The greatest is always love.' Each breath was now very shallow, and for several moments neither of them spoke.

Beams of the morning sun had now reached the edge of the bed, and Lisa became aware of their gleaming brightness. But she knew that the sense of radiance that now permeated the room was due to more than the rays of the sun. There was another brightness in the room. A beckoning brightness. A brightness to do with a magnificent future. A brightness of unfathomable hope. For a moment it felt as if a vast secret was being unfolded before her, and she was able to catch a glimpse of something few others could behold. It was with that glimpse of eternity in her mind, that she leaned down and kissed the still face before her, and said, 'Goodbye, darling Uncle Sol.'

And with that, the soul of Solomon Ogilvy, also known by some as Seanchara, slipped its moorings from the joys and the sorrows of this world, and ventured with bright and full sails toward the havens that had been its eternal destiny since the first awakenings of time.

Printed in Great Britain
by Amazon